Osmosis

I Found My Heart in
San Francisco
Book Fifteen

Susan X Meagher

OSMOSIS

I FOUND MY HEART IN SAN FRANCISCO: BOOK FIFTEEN

THIS TRADE PAPERBACK ORIGINAL IS PUBLISHED BY BRISK PRESS, BRIELLE, NJ 08730.

FIRST PRINTING: OCTOBER 2013

THIS IS A WORK OF FICTION. NAMES, CHARACTERS, PLACES, AND INCIDENTS ARE THE PRODUCT OF THE AUTHOR'S IMAGINATION OR ARE USED FICTITIOUSLY. ANY RESEMBLANCE TO ACTUAL PERSONS, LIVING OR DEAD, BUSINESS ESTABLISHMENTS, EVENTS, OR LOCALES IS ENTIRELY COINCIDENTAL.

ISBN-10: 09899895-0-X
ISBN-13: 978-0-9899895-0-3

By Susan X Meagher

Novels

Arbor Vitae
All That Matters
Cherry Grove
Girl Meets Girl
The Lies That Bind
The Legacy
Doublecrossed
Smooth Sailing
How To Wrangle a Woman
Almost Heaven
The Crush
The Reunion

Serial Novel

I Found My Heart In San Francisco

Awakenings
Beginnings
Coalescence
Disclosures
Entwined
Fidelity
Getaway
Honesty
Intentions
Journeys
Karma
Lifeline
Monogamy
Nurture
Osmosis

Anthologies

Undercover Tales
Outsiders

Dedication

To all the Jamie and Ryan fans out there around the world. Thank you for your continued appreciation of this exploration of the lives and loves of this small group of characters.

Osmosis

A gradual, often unconscious process of absorption or learning

Chapter One

"Hmm hmm hmm hmm, hmm hmm hmm hmm hmm—"

"What are you humming?"

"Are you awake, baby?" Jamie Evans moved thick, dark hair aside and kissed the nape of her lover's neck. "I didn't wake you, did I?"

"I can feel when you start to wake up. It's automatic." Ryan O'Flaherty rolled onto her back and wrapped Jamie in a loose embrace. "We're on the same wavelength."

Jamie smiled at her and kissed the tip of her nose. "Sail Away."

"Okay. Can I take a shower first?"

"That's what I was humming."

"Ooo. Sing it for me. Sounds pretty."

"I don't know all the words. But I was singing the bit I do know all night long. Do you ever do that?"

"Uh-huh. Especially if I hear something right before I go to bed."

"I didn't hear this, but it's appropriate. I think it came to me because of our...whatever we had last night."

She could feel Ryan's body grow tense, and Jamie winced at the reaction.

"I had a nuclear meltdown," Ryan said flatly. "My best friend on the team thinks I beat you, and we have to pay for a new chair that we'll never sit in. And if you tell me how much the hotel's gonna charge you for the chair, I'll probably have another fit."

Jamie began to gently rub Ryan's belly, an act that usually served to relax her. But it didn't take long to see the technique wasn't working today. "You didn't have a fit or a meltdown. Well, maybe you had a meltdown, but it was a good one."

Ryan's voice was nearly a growl. "Meltdowns aren't good."

"If they melt down some of the barriers you've been putting up, they can be very good."

Her tone was filled with self-loathing. "Is that why you've got a song about sailing away from me in your head?"

Lifting up on one elbow, Jamie reached out and grasped Ryan's chin with her free hand, forcing their eyes to meet. "Don't go to that dark place again. I'm not thinking about getting away from you. I was thinking about how it feels after a storm. Stay with me. We were in a good place when we went to sleep. Don't let that go."

The nod was almost imperceptible, but it was better than nothing. "Sorry. My new baseline is self-hatred."

"I know that, and that's something you have to work through. But I'm not gonna participate in it any more. I don't hate one thing about you. Not one thing."

"That's hard to believe. I'm not the same person I was when we met. It only makes sense that you'd feel different about me."

She spent a few moments letting Ryan's words really sink in, then spent a few more thinking of her response. The delay let Ryan's body grow even more rigid with tension, but Jamie didn't rush to reassure her. She'd learned that her opinion about Ryan wasn't what mattered. It was Ryan's opinion of herself that was the crux of the problem. "Do you wanna hear the unvarnished truth?"

Eyes wide, Ryan stared at her, and Jamie could see child-like fright glowing in her eyes. "Yeah."

"I *don't* feel the same way I did when we met."

Ryan's eyes closed for a second, and Jamie was fairly sure she was holding back tears.

"I didn't know you well, so I only had your public image to work with. I thought you were pretty and cool and smart and amazingly self-confident. No, more than that…self-involved."

A derisive laugh echoed through the room. "Had you fooled."

"Yeah," Jamie said softly. "You did. You're not self-involved at all."

Ryan's head turned sharply and she searched Jamie's eyes. "What's that mean?"

"It's not a hard concept. You care much more about everyone else than you do yourself. That's part of the reason you're such a good partner. But it's also part of the reason you get so down on yourself."

"I only get down on myself when I deserve it," Ryan muttered.

Jamie lay back down, knowing this would take a while. "Fine. Tell me why you deserve to be treated so poorly. What terrible thing have you done?"

Ryan sighed heavily. "I haven't done anything terrible. I'm just not myself. I've lost my confidence and I'm not as self-sufficient as I used to be. I don't even feel…sexy any more. I'm…hollow."

"You're not always like that," Jamie reminded her. "You forget the good days when you have a bad one. And you forget the happy ending when you have a bad beginning. Yes, you threw a fit yesterday, but we had such a nice time after you cleared some of that muck out of your head. Why do you wake up today and only think about the beginning? You've got to learn to see the whole picture."

"I acted like an asshole!" Ryan's voice bounced off the walls, and Jamie feared the neighbors would hear her again. "How can you ignore the facts?"

Sitting up, Jamie rested her elbows on her knees, her repositioning giving her a few seconds to think of her reply. "I don't ignore the facts. You're the one who has a selective memory."

Ryan blinked at her in surprise. Jamie didn't normally speak so frankly, but things had to change—and they had to change now. "I want to be more vulnerable, more open with you. Being that way is going to take time. I made a mistake and jumped the gun. It was wrong of me to tell you that I'm worried about your ability to be faithful. I don't have a reason in the world for worrying about that, and last night wasn't the time to tell you about my baseless fears."

"It was on your mind. You should be able to tell me anything that's on your mind and not be worried about my breaking a chair into kindling."

"Fine. Let's agree to disagree on that. But after you vented we had a good talk and we resolved some things. But now you act like that last part didn't happen. That's your selective memory. You hold onto the bad things and let the good things fly right out of your mind."

"It's…" Ryan roughly rubbed her face with her hands. "It's like an earthquake. If something gets high enough on the Richter scale it sticks with me. That tantrum last night was about a seven point zero. You don't forget those very quickly."

"You *can* forget them. Especially if you don't feel like you created them. You've got to learn how to let *go* of things, baby. You just have to."

"Easier said than done."

"I know. But you can learn how. Therapy can help."

Ryan lay back and tossed her arm over her face, looking like she was trying to hide from the mere concept. "Ugh. Words can't express how much I hate therapy. It's like paying someone to hit you with a switch."

"That's a matter of perspective. I agree that it's hard sometimes, but it's also freeing. At least it can be—if you're honest and talk about things before they explode on you."

Ryan fidgeted a little, and her voice grew tense."I told you I'd go. See if your therapist can recommend someone. But if I go to see someone on my own, I'm quitting the group. I can't take two hours of being stretched on the rack."

Jamie laughed softly. "If someone convinced you that being stretched on a rack would make you faster or stronger you'd do it in a second!"

"Well, yeah. But nothing good happens in therapy."

Jamie blew out a breath, grumbling, "I'm gonna act like you're kidding. Then I won't have to slap you."

The smile that slowly grew was pretty natural looking. Not full-fledged Ryan O'Flaherty charm, but it was definitely in the neighborhood. "I was. Sorta."

'That's what I thought. It's the sorta that freaks me out. But I know you'll give it your best. You always do."

Ryan maneuvered her hand to take a peek at her watch. "I'd better get shakin'. Breakfast starts in ten minutes."

"Don't you wanna hear the lyrics I was singing?"

"Oh, sure. Sing it for me."

"I can't sing the whole thing. I just know snippets. But the lines I kept singing were, 'We'll glide over tears, the saltiest sea, beyond all our fears back to you and me. After the darkness, after the gray and into the sun we shall sail away. Yes, into the sun we shall sail away.'"

Ryan looked up at her, then slowly traced her features with a finger. "You have such a pretty voice. I could listen to you sing for hours."

Embarrassed, Jamie said, "Thanks. I don't sing as well as you do, so I'm always a little hesitant."

"Who's the idiot who says you don't sing well?"

"Uhm…me?"

"Ha! I'd say you had a tin ear, but if you did you couldn't sing well. So we'll have to chalk this up to a lack of self-confidence. You'd better talk about this in therapy. For hours and hours and hours."

"God, you're funny," Jamie said, not breaking a smile.

"You think you can hold out. But I can make you smile."

"Can not."

Ryan pushed her down and climbed on top of her, then set about making the most ridiculous faces Jamie had ever seen. She managed to contort her lovely face into some configurations that would have made Caitlin cry, and it didn't take many of them to make Jamie laugh. "Stop! I'm gonna have nightmares."

"Kiss me," Ryan said, her mouth at a strange angle and her nostrils flaring.

"No way! Get that ugly mug away from me!"

"Come on, kiss me!" Ryan burrowed underneath Jamie's hands, getting to her chin, where she delivered some wet, sloppy kisses.

"Ahh! Gross!"

"Come on." Ryan slid off Jamie to get to her feet. "I'll wash the slobber off you."

"You're worse than Duffy." Jamie wiped at her wet face with both hands.

"Gruuuuuf!"

Ryan bent over and started to snuffle at various spots on Jamie's naked body, sending the giggling woman towards the safety of the bathroom. "Get that wet muzzle off me!"

Grabbing her just before she reached the door, Ryan trapped one of Jamie's thighs between her own and started to hump her, looking just like Duffy did when he caught a weaker dog and wanted to show him he was dominant.

"Stop humping me!" Jamie shouted, trying to wriggle out of Ryan's grasp.

There was a quiet knock on the door and Jamie gave Ryan a murderous look. "If that's security…" She went into the bathroom and grabbed a towel, wrapping herself in it. Looking out the peephole, she saw Jackie standing there. For just a moment, Jamie's stomach clutched. Jackie had come to the room the night before, certain Ryan was on the verge of violence. There were two ways to get past this. Apologize again or make light of it. Jamie chose the latter. She opened the door and said theatrically, "Yessss?"

"Uhm…breakfast?"

"No time. We're just getting in the shower."

"Okay. Tell Ryan I'll see her downstairs. Coach wants us there in ten." She looked down for a second, then slowly met Jamie's gaze. "Is everything okay? I heard some noises."

Ryan's voice called out, "If you're gonna come investigate every time Jamie squeals, you'd better just stay in our room."

"No thanks!" Jackie could not have looked more relieved. "I don't know what you people do to each other, but I don't think my heart could take it."

"Don't rush to judgment. Jamie used to be on your team."

With a surprised expression, Jackie said, "Really?"

"Yeah. It's been just about a year since I went over to the dark side."

"Wow, you must've caught on quick."

"She's a natural," Ryan called out. "Now close the damned door so we can get a shower."

"See you downstairs, O. And hurry up!"

Jamie closed the door and went into the bathroom where Ryan was adjusting the shower. "You're being very playful today. I thought you'd be uncomfortable around Jackie."

"I am. But that's how you get over it…with jocks."

Ryan was in such a vulnerable position that Jamie couldn't resist giving her butt a slap. "You know, I'm on a varsity sport, too. Why don't you treat me like a jock?"

"I could, but I don't think you'd like it. Lots of towel snapping and wrapping you up in athletic tape and throwing you into a whirlpool filled with ice. It's nothing very romantic."

Jamie wasn't sure which of Ryan's tales were accurate or heavily embellished, but she decided she wouldn't care to be treated to an ice bath. "Okay. You can continue to think of me as a girl."

"Mmm," Ryan said, popping a hard nipple into her mouth. "I like girls."

Chapter Two

Mia Christopher sat at the table in her spacious, nearly empty kitchen, idly stirring her coffee while reading every page of the *San Francisco Chronicle*. She'd finished breakfast—a bowl of the same health-saturated, sugar-free granola that Jordan ate before she left for practice. Like her partner, she'd added dates and a sliced banana; unlike Jordan, the addition of a few tablespoons of brown sugar made her actually like the stuff.

She craved a latte, but had trained herself to settle for coffee. Even though it wasn't her favorite, now that she didn't have a charge card and a doting, bill-paying father, she was careful with her money. It was hard for her to justify a four dollar latte for breakfast, especially since she'd have one later in the day if she went to her local espresso shrine to read. The latte tax was high, but she refused to be one of those people who took up a table and didn't buy anything. So she nursed her coffee and tried not to feel a little ache of longing when she read that the Bay Area was shrouded with fog. A quick look out the window in the living room confirmed that the Colorado skies were crystal clear and saturated with blue.

Realizing that she was perversely longing for foul weather, she got up and washed the few dishes they'd dirtied, then went into their bedroom and neatened it. There wasn't much to do, since Jordan was preternaturally neat, and she'd almost unintentionally become so herself. Their room was so small that it looked chaotic with just a few things lying about, so she'd learned to put her clothing away when she took it off. This morning, all she had to do was smooth the duvet out and arrange their pillows. Once that task was finished, she went to shower and dress for the day. Looking at the clock on the sink, she blinked, having to confirm that it was, indeed, only six thirty in the morning.

It was fairly warm, so Mia dressed in a fleece top and jeans, adding her tall shearling boots. She'd found that their apartment was cool even when it was sixty degrees outside, so bundling up was her default.

Her favorite bookstore didn't open until ten, and Jordan was due home a little after noon, so it didn't seem worth it to venture out, even for that lusted-after latte. Besides, Jordan had taken the car, so she'd have to take a bus to the bookstore, and that seemed like far too much trouble. So she bunched up the pillows in the living room and made herself comfortable, then started to read a book that one of her professors had assigned as additional reading. It was the first time in her life that she'd done anything extra for any class, but she was determined to pull straight A's her last term—just to show her parents that moving to Colorado hadn't been a mistake.

At eleven the doorbell rang. Mildly annoyed, Mia glared at the door, then went right back to her book. It had taken a while to arrange the floor pillows into any semblance of comfort. Once she was in a good position she didn't like to move. The fact that the only visitors they ever received were Mormon missionaries and the odd election worker made the decision to ignore intruders easy. But the person at the door was determined, and after the bell had been rung three times she got up, cursing softly, ready to give whomever it was a lesson in manners.

Peering out the peephole, she let out a gasp, sure that the person on the other side of the door was her mother. But that realization didn't help her body, which was frozen in something akin to panic. It wasn't until Anna Lisa started to walk back down the stairs that Mia flung the door open. "Mom!" She ran down the few stairs and lunged for her, grabbing her recklessly and pinning her against the wrought-iron railing.

Anna Lisa kissed her cheeks, murmuring, "My sweet girl." They were both crying while they hugged and kissed each other repeatedly. Once the first flush of emotion had quelled, Mia pulled back and led her mother into the apartment. But instead of continuing their tearful reunion, Anna Lisa stopped abruptly. "Oh, my dear God, don't tell me this is where you live."

Stung, Mia stepped away and glared. "Did you come here to bitch at me? You could do the same thing from Hillsborough…if you cared enough to call!" She started to turn and go to her room, but realized how silly that would be. This was *her* apartment, and if anyone were to leave, it would be her mother. Standing as tall as she could, Mia folded her arms over her chest. "You can stay if you treat me like a human. But if you're gonna yell at me…*go*." She emphasized her last word with as much cold disregard as she could manage, even though part of her wanted to lose herself in a warm maternal embrace.

"I wish I didn't *have* to yell at you! I wish you'd *act* like an adult!" Anna Lisa looked around the bare room, her eyes roving over the drab pillows on the floor. "An adult wouldn't live in some kind of…flop house!"

Mia marched to the door and yanked it open. "Leave."

"What? You wouldn't dare!"

Mia steeled her nerves against the impulses that urged her to hold onto her mother and feel the love that she knew was hidden under the hurtful words. But she held firm. "Leave my house. You can't come in here and insult me."

The rock-hard certainty to her voice clearly stunned Anna Lisa. She closed her mouth and didn't even attempt to speak. There was a moment or two of electric silence, then a quiet "I'm sorry" came out.

Mia gaped at her, not able to remember her mother ever apologizing for anything. "Are you really?"

Anna Lisa nodded. "Yes. I didn't come this far to argue with you." Her chin quivered, then her body began to shake. "I miss you so much," she whimpered as tears began to flow again.

Instantly, Mia was holding her, and they cried again, sniffling and wiping their eyes while they clung to each other. "Why do we fight like this? I hate it. I hate it!"

"I do too." Anna Lisa fumbled in her purse and found a packet of tissues. She wiped her eyes while Mia fished out a tissue for herself and did the same. "I can't explain it, but I love you so much…that sometimes I can't control myself. I see you do something stupid and I have to make you come to your senses."

Reaching out to grasp her mother's shoulders, Mia held her at arm's length. "You can't do that. No matter what I do…you can't make me think or act in a certain way. I'm an adult now. Even when you don't agree with me…I'm an adult. You've got to let me make my own choices or we can't have a relationship."

Blinking, Anna Lisa started to cry again. "You'd turn your back on me? Knowing how much I love you?"

Her heart was thudding in her chest, and she thought she might be sick, but Mia nodded slowly. "I'd have to. I wouldn't ever want to…but I'd have to."

"How can you say that to me? I'm your mother!"

Mia released her, but kept her gaze fixed on her mother's dark eyes. "I love you and Dad more than you'll ever know, but I have to live my own life. That means making my own decisions. If I let you make them…I'll blame you if they don't go well, and that's not how I want to live." She wiped at her eyes with her sleeve. "I miss you so much, Mom, but I can't go on like we have been."

Anna Lisa looked as stunned as Mia had ever seen her. She also looked so deeply wounded that Mia's heart hurt from seeing her expression. "What have I done that's so wrong?"

"It's not you," Mia said, trying to remove every bit of blame or judgment from her voice. "It's us. We're too much alike. Our emotions take over and we start yelling."

Anna Lisa made a dismissive gesture. "That's nothing. It all blows over in a few minutes."

"Not for me it doesn't. When I told you about Jordan, you hurt me more than I've ever been hurt. I replay what you said constantly. And if things had blown over for you, you would've called me before now."

Dropping her shoulders, Anna Lisa scanned the apartment again. "Is there anywhere to sit? I'm exhausted."

"In the kitchen."

They walked into the kitchen and both sat down. "Do you want something?" Mia asked. "I could make a fresh pot of coffee."

"No, no, don't get up. I've had too much coffee already." Anna Lisa sat still for a few moments, then gazed at her daughter. "Are you here because you want to be, or are you doing this just to punish me?"

Unable to stop a derisive laugh, Mia shook her head. "I know I've done a lot of stupid things, but I wouldn't fake being in love with someone just to piss you off."

"That's not what I meant and you know it." The snappish quality was back in Anna Lisa's voice. "I meant coming here…dropping out of school…cutting yourself off from us."

Holding up her hand, Mia ticked off her answers. "One, I didn't drop out of school. I'm going to finish on time. Two, I didn't cut myself off from you. You cut yourselves off from me. And three, I came here because I love Jordan and want to support her during a tough time." She blew out a weary breath. "But a part of me did come here when I did to get back at you. I was being dramatic."

Cocking her head, Anna Lisa asked, "Dramatic?"

"Yeah. When you told me that you weren't going to pay for my living expenses any more I got crazy. It was overly dramatic of me to pack up and leave."

"Thank God!" Her head dropped back and a smile bloomed. "It's so nice to hear you admit that."

"Don't jump to conclusions. I shouldn't have been so rash, but I'm glad I came. I'm doing really well with my course work and I'm being a good partner for Jordan. She works so hard that she really needs someone to make sure she eats a good meal and gets her rest."

With a puzzled look, Anna Lisa asked, "Who makes sure she eats well?"

"You don't have to look so shocked." A little snappishness came back to her voice. "Jamie's walked me through a bunch of things I can make. I suck at doing anything interesting, but you've got to admit you never let me do a thing in the kitchen."

"You never asked!"

"I most certainly did!" The volume was rising, but Mia felt powerless to stop. "When I was little I always wanted to help, but you always said that I was too little and cooking was too hard for a child."

"It is! It was! A five-year-old can't make a decent ragu!"

Mia slapped her hands onto the table. "This is nuts. We're arguing about things that happened fifteen years ago."

"Then don't blame me because you can't cook. Do you think I enjoy doing all of the work? I would have loved some help. You don't need much instruction to clean the table or load the dishwasher."

"I refuse to argue about this. The facts are that Nonna won't let you do a thing when you visit her and you won't let me do a thing at our house. That's just how you are."

"Nonna taught me how to cook when I got married. That's how we do things."

"Fine. You can teach me now. Jordan and I would marry in an instant if we could. She's your daughter-in-law."

Dismissively, Anna Lisa waved her hand. "She's no such thing. You can't get married, and even if you could, you're not mature enough. You're still a child, Mia, and you prove that again and again by doing childish things."

She looked around the room. "This apartment is the best indication of that. What came over you to pick such an awful place?"

Her inclination was to snap off a smart remark, but Mia didn't give in. "I know this is a dump. But Jordan's trying to pay as little as possible for rent. We share this with four other women."

"Four!" Anna Lisa stood up and started to walk down the hall. Every door was open, and she looked into each mostly-bare room, shaking her head and mumbling. When she reached the end of the hall, she stopped on the threshold of Jordan's room. Eyes wide, Anna Lisa seemed at a loss for words. She stood in the tiny, cramped space; her eyes scanning over the plastic bins that held clothes and books and personal items. "They lock people in a house on TV to turn them into psychopaths. They live better than this. Much better."

"This is how you live when you don't have money. Jordan gets a small stipend, and, as you know, I get nothing."

"You have a lovely home in Berkeley. And you'll never convince me that Jamie would have thrown you out for being behind in rent."

"No, she wouldn't. But it's a moot point because I wouldn't take advantage of her that way. I wouldn't sponge off my best friend just because my parents were being unreasonable."

Anna Lisa brushed by her on the way back to the kitchen. "It's not unreasonable to expect your daughter to act like herself. I wouldn't support your living in a cult or joining the French Foreign Legion either."

When they'd both sat down, Mia stared at her mother for a little while, her eyes narrowed in thought. "I don't know how to prove to you that I love Jordan. I guess it's not possible." Reaching out, she grasped her hand firmly. "This is where our love for each other should take over. This should be when you trust me, not because you think I'm doing the right thing, but because you acknowledge I'm old enough to make my own decisions. It's that simple, Mom. Either you support my being an adult or you don't."

"And by support…you mean paying for you to do something we disapprove of."

"Nope. I don't want your money." Mia leaned back in her chair and met her mother's eyes. "I think we'll be better off if I support myself. Besides, if you're not really behind me, I'd rather you didn't fake it. All I want is to have a relationship with you and Dad again. That's it."

"And you'll stay here…in this boarding house?"

"Uh-huh. Until we decide we can afford something better. Obviously, we're paying next to nothing to live here. But if I get a job, we'll be able to move someplace nicer. Once we decide what our travel schedule is, I'll be able to look for work."

"Traveling? Why are you traveling?"

Mia paused for a second before she answered. She was fairly certain she'd explained this all before, but it obviously hadn't sunken in. "To get ready for the Olympics, the team travels to tournaments around the world. Russia is our first stop. That's in two weeks."

"Russia!"

"Yes, Russia."

"Who's paying for that?"

"Jordan's paying for my part. She gets to travel for free, of course."

"That must be a lot of money. Why not use that money to get a nicer apartment? And some furniture."

"Because Jordan wants me to go with her. She plays better when we're together."

Anna Lisa put her head in her hands and groaned. "Is this some sort of hero-worship thing you have going on? Do you wish you were *on* this team?"

Mia grasped her mother's arm and pulled it from her face. "I'm...in... love. That's all there is to it. I love Jordan, and I'm doing what's best for her at this point in her life. When her career is over, we'll decide where to live and what to do."

A long minute passed while Anna Lisa stared hard, her feelings masked behind her puzzled expression. "There are a lot of things I don't understand about young women, and this...experimenting with homosexuality is one of them. I've been doing some reading, and it seems like it's a nationwide fad. I've thought about this every way I can, but I can't imagine why this appeals to you girls. When I was your age..." She shook her head, looking totally confused as well as frustrated. "I can't even imagine what would have become of a girl who not only played around with other girls...but wasn't even ashamed of it!"

"Would that make you happy?" Mia jumped to her feet, on the verge of throwing something...possibly a punch. "Would you like it better if I was ready to hang myself because of my disgusting urges?"

"Calm down!" Anna Lisa shouted. "I didn't say it was disgusting. Especially not if that's the only thing you know. If you'd been a little tom-boy who never looked at a boy I'd understand better. But you're not like that." She growled with frustration, then slapped her hands on the table. "I've spent hours pulling you off boys. You were always trying to go too far…right under my roof! You can't tell me you were acting when you had some boy on his back on my good sofa, looking like you were going to mount him at any second."

"I wasn't acting!" She kicked the nearest cabinet and whirled around in a tight circle, about to explode. "I like having sex with men! But I also like having sex with women. I like them both…a lot. And I've had enough experience to know what really satisfies me. And I know…" She leaned over and put her hands flat on the table, resting her weight on them while she glared at her mother. "That no one has ever pleased me like Jordan does. And that's not because of her sex. It's because she loves me and I love her."

Acting as though she hadn't heard a word, Anna Lisa shook her head and looked away. "Is Jordan going to make all of your decisions?"

Feeling like her head was going to spin right off her body, Mia said, "What in the hell are you talking about?"

"Your story about delaying law school was just that, wasn't it? A story? Something you told us to placate us? Something you came up with so you could follow *Jordan's* dream?"

"No, it wasn't. And we don't have the kind of relationship where one of us makes the decisions. We'll each have time to do what we want, and her time is now."

"You swear to me that you didn't just make that up to please us? To get us off your back?"

"No, I didn't. But I also didn't know all of the facts when I told you I was delaying law school for a year. I didn't know that Jordan might want to stay with the team for the next quadrennial."

"A what?"

"Quadrennial. That's what they call the four years leading up to the next Olympics. She might want to play in 2004. She's pretty excited about being able to play in Athens."

"And you'd…what?"

"We're not sure. There's nothing very concrete about being a world-class athlete. A thousand things could happen to make her stick with this or leave."

"For *four* more years?"

"Yep. One of her teammates is playing in her fourth Olympics. That's sixteen years, and she'll come back for a fifth if she has a ghost of a chance."

"Oh, my God! Don't tell me Jordan wants to do that."

Mia shrugged. "She might. And if she does, I want to be there for her. This isn't just a whim. She's worked for this since she was a little girl."

"And her dream has to be yours?"

Nodding, Mia said, "Yep. When you fall in love with someone who has a dream, you have to do your best to help her realize it. It's not really love if you don't."

Anna Lisa sighed and closed her eyes. After a moment, she reached out and stroked Mia's cheek, her expression full of tenderness. "This isn't what I want for you, sweetheart. Nothing about this is what I've dreamed for you."

Mia covered her mother's hand with her own. "I know that. But it's what *I* want. Jordan's *who* I want. I'd love her if she were a demolitions expert or a stunt woman or a helicopter pilot. When you love a woman you have to love all of her...even the things that worry you or make life unpredictable."

Picking up Mia's other hand, Anna Lisa kissed it tenderly, then clutched it to her heart for a moment, clearly struggling with her emotions. "Where is this woman?"

Mia glanced at the clock on the stove. "She should be home soon. Everyone else stays at the facility after practice for the free food. But we need to be together as much as possible, so she comes straight home."

"What do you have for her to eat?"

"Nothing. I was going to go to the grocery store when she got here."

Anna Lisa stood. "I have a rental car. Let's go now."

Mia looked up at her. "Now?"

"This is your job, right? Feeding her and making this...place into a home for her. How are you going to do that if you don't have food in the house?"

Stunned, Mia stood and gamely followed her mother out of the apartment, then dashed back in and left a note for Jordan.

Hi, babe.

Big surprise. My mom's here. We went to the store. Be back soon.

Love you!

Me

When Mia opened the door to the apartment, she heard the blow dryer in the bathroom. "She just took a shower. Doing that here gets her home sooner."

"I'll put the groceries away. You go tell her that I'm not carrying a weapon."

"I don't know that you're not!" Mia wrinkled her nose and took off down the hall.

Without knocking, she flung the door open, making Jordan squeal. "Ahh!"

"It's just me." Mia wrapped her arms around Jordan's warm body and kissed her gently. "Miss me?"

"Is your mother here?"

"Yeah. She's in the kitchen."

"Then why are you so…normal?"

Pulling away, Mia sat on the edge of the tub. "I'm not sure. Things have flared a few times, but she seems like she wants to make peace. It was her idea to go to the store so we could get something ready for your lunch."

Jordan tilted her head. "Really?"

"Yeah. It feels weird, but…also kinda normal. I'm…I'm not sure how I feel yet, but it's going okay so far. She really wants to meet you."

"I wanna meet her, too, but I'm worried about doing it in the kitchen."

Mia stood and patted Jordan's bare butt. "We don't have any knives sharp enough to kill. Don't sweat it."

It took a very, very long time for Jordan to emerge from their room, but Mia thought it was well worth the wait. Jordan walked into the kitchen wearing a sky-blue cashmere turtleneck and off-white corduroy jeans—both of which fit her like they'd been custom-made. Her hair was just like Mia liked it—parted on the side so that a few strands tumbled across her forehead. Mia noted that she'd put on makeup…just enough to make her look fantastically casual. You could say what you liked about modeling, but it had taught Jordan how to pull off any look she wanted with just mascara, eye liner, blush and lip gloss. "Hi," she said, making Anna Lisa turn from the sink and stare at her. "I'm Jordan."

Wiping her hands on a towel, Anna Lisa shook Jordan's proffered hand. "Anna Lisa. It's good to finally meet you."

"It is." Jordan stood there, looking like she didn't have another word to offer. But she was smiling as if she were waiting for a camera shutter to snap. Not some anxious "please like me" smile, either. A cool, "go ahead and take a look" smile that gave nothing away.

This was Jordan at her wariest. Once she knew you, she was open and vulnerable and could jabber away like a magpie. But when she didn't trust someone she was like a billboard. Her trick seemed to be to make herself as lovely as possible and let people react. It had been hard for Mia to get used to her ways, but now that she understood them they seemed perfectly reasonable. Jordan never gave a stranger enough information about herself to regret it later. You had to earn your way into her real personality.

"We're making you lunch," Anna Lisa said. "I've never had tofu. Do you really like it?"

Still smiling, Jordan shook her head. "No, not really. It's not bad if you can flavor it with something good, but I'm not eating fat now. That makes it tough. It's a good way to add protein to my salad, though, so I just gobble it down. I'm usually so hungry that I barely register what goes into my mouth."

Scoffing, Anna Lisa said, "That's no way to go through life. Food is one of the most wonderful things we have."

"I agree, and I love to eat good food. My nutritionist just has some firm rules and I'm doing my best to stick with them."

"I don't know if what I'm trying will be edible, but when Mia told me how you were limited I decided to see if I could think of something a little bit different. You must be going mad."

Jordan shrugged, looking adorable to Mia, who was studying her with affection. "I don't mind. I'm used to making sacrifices."

"Sit down," Anna Lisa insisted. "You must be tired."

Jordan did, then asked, "Did you fly in…Mrs. Christopher?"

"Call me Anna Lisa. And, yes, I did. Early this morning."

"Uhm…staying long?"

Anna Lisa looked over her shoulder and smiled at Jordan. "Don't worry. I'm not moving in."

"Oh! I didn't mean anything by that. I just don't know…uhm… anything."

"I didn't plan on coming, but I was moping around the house yesterday and decided this has gone on long enough."

"What has?" Jordan asked, her eyes going round in what looked like terror. Mia was quite sure her Jordy had never had to deal with a personality like Anna Lisa's. It would probably take years for her to stop flinching.

Anna Lisa turned and put her arm around Mia, who was standing next to her. "I'm not here to drag my little girl home…although I wish I could."

"Mom!" Mia scowled at her.

"I'm being honest. I wish I could take your hand and bring you home. But I can't. Since I can't bear to have this distance between us…you win. I'm going to try to keep my mouth shut and let you make your own decisions."

Jordan beamed at her. "That's gonna make Mia so happy. She's really been down."

"I've been fine," Mia said, scowling. "But it's been hard knowing I couldn't call home."

"You can call any time," Anna Lisa said. "And I'll call you every week. I hate the fact that I can't put you over my knee and spank you to get you to do what I want, but I suppose those days are over."

Mia laughed. "You didn't spank me very often, and I'm absolutely sure it never did any good."

"Maybe not. But it made me feel like I was doing something! Sometimes you had me at the end of my rope."

"I think the last time you spanked me was when you caught me trying to cross El Camino Real."

Anna Lisa looked at Jordan. "That road is basically a highway. And this little one was trying to dash across it. I spanked her so hard my hand hurt for days."

Jordan's eyes were wide, but Mia was laughing. "I'd gotten off the school bus and was supposed to walk down our nice, safe street and head straight home. But there was candy on the other side of the road and I had a dollar burning a hole in my pocket. Nobody was there to stop me, so I raced across. Mom unexpectedly drove down to get me, seeing the whole thing. Wow! The fur flew! I'm surprised she didn't whack me right then and there."

"I would have if I could have, but I might have killed you if I hadn't had a moment to calm down."

There was nothing funny about the incident at the time, but now it made for a great story. "You didn't just hit me with your hand," Mia said.

"When your hand got sore you hit me with a metal spatula. I thought you were gonna kill me. I should never have let you catch me in the kitchen."

Anna Lisa laughed along with her daughter. "I'm surprised the neighbors didn't call the police. I was yelling, you were screaming at the top of your lungs, we were both crying…it was mayhem!"

"It was," Mia agreed. "Dad was mad at you for hitting me so hard."

"I never should have done that while I was so scared and angry. I think that's why I never did it again." She patted Mia's butt. "But I think it made an impression."

"It did. It didn't stop me, though. A couple of weeks later, when I knew you weren't home, I did it again. I almost got hit by a truck, though, so that was my last attempt." Mia started to laugh at the befuddled look on her mother's face. "You should have known by then that the best way to get me to do something was to forbid it."

Chuckling, Anna Lisa said, "It's amazing I have one dark hair on my head. This child made me old before my time."

"But…she's so…easy-going," Jordan said, looking bewildered.

Anna Lisa threw her head back and laughed. "She doesn't know you very well yet. Poor thing."

The trio ate together, both Mia and Jordan complimenting Anna Lisa on her experimentation. "It's just a Waldorf salad. Simple as pie."

Jordan poked at a bite of apple. "Everything in here is on my approved list?"

"Uh-huh. I put the tofu in the blender with lemon juice and a speck of olive oil to make the dressing. It isn't as good as mayonnaise, but it's not half bad if I do say so myself."

"It's so much better than a plain green salad," Jordan said. "But I shouldn't have the olive oil."

"You're a young woman. And you look like you stopped growing about ten minutes ago. You need some fat in your diet. Don't let people tell you what to do when it doesn't make sense. You have to judge things for yourself. Be your own boss."

Jordan smiled at her, then snuck a glance at her lover, who grinned back. "I didn't get my independent streak from the wind," Mia said, chuckling.

After lunch, Mia suggested going for a drive. "I've wanted to do that Gold Belt tour I read about. I think the roads are all open now that the snow has had a little time to melt. Anyone up for it?"

"Sure," Jordan said. "It's about time we got out of this apartment. Anna Lisa?"

"Anything you two want is fine with me. I've never been here before."

"Neither have we," Jordan said, chuckling.

They took Mia's car after Anna Lisa found out that much of the drive was on gravel roads. "I know how your mind works, Mia. But the rental car companies check for damage, and I'm not paying for a new…whatever the bottom of the car is called."

"Oh, they'd have to get down on the ground to check that. Let's take the rental and have some fun!"

"Mia!" Jordan looked at her like she was a stranger. "We can't do that."

"I'm kidding, honey." *Since I know you wouldn't have fun.* She put her arm around her waist to give her a squeeze, and was only slightly upset to see her mother turn her head to avoid witnessing that small intimacy.

The scenic drive gobbled up the entire afternoon. Since none of them had yet experienced much of the inherent beauty of Colorado Springs, they pulled off at every opportunity to get out and smell the crisp, clean air and marvel at the stark but alluring grandeur of the scenery. It was getting dark when they drew near the city. Anna Lisa said, "Let me treat you to dinner. Where's your favorite restaurant?"

"Uhm…" Mia looked at Jordan. "Have we been anywhere besides the place at the end of the street?"

"No, I don't think we have. I guess we're not very good resources."

"You two have honestly not been out for a good dinner?"

"We don't want to throw money away so we eat at home," Mia said.

"Have you even heard of any nice places?"

"No. None of the other women go out, either. We're all poor." Mia's face lit up in a bright smile. "I know someone who's not, though." She pulled her cell phone out of her jacket and handed it to Jordan. "Call Jamie and ask her where to eat. She'll know."

Dialing, Jordan asked, "Has she been here before?"

"Doesn't matter. She'll know."

As expected, Jamie made a few recommendations. She had to resort to the Internet to pull it off, but Mia knew her friend would never disappoint when it came to finding a restaurant. They decided on a place that specialized in seafood, since that was Jordan's usual protein. The place was nice...much nicer than Mia would have ever chosen to spend their money on. "We could go someplace less expensive," she whispered to her mother while the man at the reservations desk discretely assessed them.

"Don't be silly. Since when do you even notice how much things cost?"

"Since I have to pay for them. We try to live on two hundred a week."

The maitre d'hotel began to lead them to a table, and when they were seated, Anna Lisa stared at them, looking stunned. "You live on two hundred dollars a week?"

"We try to," Jordan said. "But it usually ends up closer to two-fifty."

Anna Lisa gaped. "Only two hundred and fifty dollars for *all* of your food and entertainment?"

"No," Mia said. "For everything. Rent, utilities, cell phone, gas, car insurance, food...everything."

"How is that possible? You spent more than that on clothes in Berkeley, Mia. It was a rare month that you didn't fly through three thousand dollars, and that was just for you!"

Mia shrugged. "I'm not going to run through Jordan's savings. We do all right."

"But you're not doing anything fun! You don't go out and enjoy this beautiful town."

"We'll go out more now that it's warm. We can go hiking and do things like that. And we've heard there are things at the university that are really cheap."

"I don't want you to live like a pauper." Anna Lisa reached into her purse and took out her wallet. "I'm giving you back your charge cards."

Mia didn't reach for them when they were waved right in front of her. "No, I don't think that's a good idea. I...don't want to feel like you're..." She looked away and shook her head. "It's not a good idea."

The waiter came and delivered water and menus, and before he had taken two steps, Anna Lisa said, "You don't want to feel like I'm what?"

"Nothing." She felt Jordan's hand grasp her knee and give it a gentle squeeze.

"You have something to say. Say it."

"I don't want to argue," Mia said quietly. "And I don't want everyone in this place to hear us."

"Fine," Anna Lisa whispered. "Then quietly tell me what's on your mind."

Mia shot a look at Jordan, then met her mother's gaze. "I know you don't approve of…us. You don't want me to live here, and you think I'm making a big mistake. I don't want to take your money and come to rely on it again. It's better if we keep it clean between us."

"Clean? What does that mean?"

"It means," Mia said, scooting her chair closer to her mother's, "that we have to learn how to be more like…friends. If you give me money that gives you a right to say how I spend it, and I don't want it to be like that again."

"You'd rather live in that terrible apartment?"

Mia saw Jordan start to slump in her chair. She knew her partner hated to be involved in any kind of argument, and she was going to stop this one before it began. "New topic," she said. "We can talk about anything but money."

"But…!"

"Later, Mom. We can talk later. You're being very generous in treating us, and I don't want to ruin the best meal I've had since I've been here. Arguments about money and fine dining don't go together."

Despite or perhaps because of Mia's edict, the mood at the table was fairly upbeat. Both she and Jordan raved so exuberantly over the well-prepared meal that Anna Lisa got over her pique. Jordan ate very slowly, even though Mia teased her about her pace. "You normally eat so fast that sparks fly."

"This is just soooo good. I don't know how they kept this salmon so moist without any butter or oil."

"You don't need anything on a good piece of fish," Anna Lisa said. "As long as it's very fresh, just a little lemon is perfect. Do you have a good fish store?"

"There might be one, but we don't go there," Mia said. "We just go to the local grocery. I only buy fish when it's on sale."

"It's on sale because it's old! Don't ever buy fish on sale, honey."

"It's the only way we can afford it, Mom. You don't have to worry that we'll be killed by botulism. They put the frozen stuff on sale. Like whitefish or turbot."

Anna Lisa opened her mouth to speak, then shut it. Obviously deciding against another tiff, she turned to Jordan. "Tell me about this traveling you two are going to be doing."

"Oh! Well, we're going to Moscow in two weeks."

"That sounds exciting. How long will you be there?"

"Almost a week…including two travel days."

Frowning, Anna Lisa said, "Only five days then. Well, you can still see a lot in five days. Moscow is a big city, but if you plan well you can get a good feel for it."

"I don't think we'll be able to see much, Mom. At least Jordan won't."

"But…" Anna Lisa turned her puzzled gaze from her daughter to Jordan. "Why?"

"I won't have any time. We'll play every day, and we won't know what time we'll be playing until the day before the match. If we play late, we go early to watch the other match, and if we play early, we stay to watch the other match."

"But that won't give you any time at all! You're going all that way just to be in a gym?"

Giving her a half-smile, Jordan nodded. "I've traveled a lot during my career, and just about all I can describe are airports and gyms. They have some very nice ones in Italy."

"You honestly don't get to do any sight-seeing?"

"Not really. And if we do, it's something arranged for us. You know… for publicity. Volleyball is a big sport in Russia, so they'll probably troop us around for photo-ops. It's a little like being on a school trip."

"What will *you* do, honey?" Anna Lisa asked.

"I'll look around a little, but I want to go to Jordan's matches. So I'll try to go to a museum or something before or after she plays."

"You'll be able to go to some interesting restaurants won't you? After your games?"

Jordan shook her head. "I'll have to eat with the team. They keep us on a short leash when we tour. They're always afraid we'll eat something that disagrees with us. A bout of food poisoning would ruin the whole trip."

"But…that's the point of travel! Doing something different… experiencing how the local people live…eating their food…" She looked at each woman in turn, as if they were missing something elemental and needed a little instruction.

"This isn't really travel," Jordan said. "We're just playing volleyball in a different place. It's all about the game. But Mia can do whatever she wants. I'd love for her to really get out and see the city. It's fine with me if she doesn't come to any of the matches."

Mia glared at her. "Why would I travel half-way around the world and not come to your games?"

"I want you to do what makes you happy," Jordan said, staring into her eyes. "Whatever that is. If you want to go on some all-day tours…that's what I want you to do."

Mia smiled, shaking her head. "You're not getting rid of me. Even in Moscow, I'll be sitting there watching your every move."

"You…" Anna Lisa make a dismissive gesture with her hand when both women looked at her. "Never mind. I just hope you both have a good time. Your father and I went to Russia for a few days when we went to an international law conference a couple of years ago. I'll let you know the names of a few places I really enjoyed."

"Thanks, Mom. I'll figure out a way to get a little tourist action in. But Jordan's what I'm most interested in seeing."

On the way back to their apartment, Anna Lisa said, "Can I talk you into going to church with me in the morning, honey?"

Mia started to cough, then it became apparent that she was choking. She pulled over and Jordan slapped her on the back. "Whew!" She leaned her head back and said, "You almost killed me."

"I'll go if you don't want to," Jordan said, her expression a mixture of bafflement and concern.

Laughing, Mia said, "My mother hasn't been to church since I was born!" She turned and stared at Anna Lisa, who was sitting placidly in the back seat. "What's going on?"

Her mother shrugged her shoulders. "I was moping around the house a few weeks ago and had the urge to go. It'd been a while…"

"A while? You stopped going before you got married!"

"Like I said," Anna Lisa continued, looking at Jordan, "It had been a while, but I remembered how much I used to enjoy going to church. I decided it was silly to let a little argument keep me from doing something I liked."

Jordan cast a nervous glance at her partner. "Uhm…sounds good to me."

"You went to Mass?" Mia asked again.

Anna Lisa laughed. "Of course not. The Catholic Church could hand out gold bouillon instead of communion and I wouldn't step foot into one of those dumps. I went to a nice Unitarian Universalist church. I don't know much about it, but it doesn't even seem Christian. They don't mention God."

"Oh. Well, I guess I don't have to call in an exorcist," Mia chuckled. "I'll go with you if you're sure I don't have to confess my sins or anything."

"I'll go, too," Jordan repeated.

"No way," Mia said. "That's the last thing you want to do on Sunday morning. That's your only day to sleep in."

"I don't mind. Really."

"I'll go, Mom, but Jordan has no religious drive. She's gonna stay home and sleep."

"How about breakfast?" Anna Lisa said to Jordan. "We can come get you after church."

"Great. That'll be great."

Anna Lisa chuckled. "Now Mia just has to get out the phone book and figure out where the nearest least Catholic church is."

Mia spent a little time on the Internet, searching for a church and easy-to-follow directions. She and Jordan were lying in bed, and she scooted closer when Jordan started stroking her back, languidly letting her hand drift across her skin. "About done?" Jordan asked.

Turning to look at her, Mia saw utter fatigue in the clear blue eyes. She nodded and saved the page of directions so she could take another look at it in the morning. Quickly shutting down her computer, she set it on the floor and shifted so she and Jordan were face to face. When she extended her arms, Jordan slid into them, resting her head on Mia's breast. "Very tired," Jordan said, her voice soft and slow.

"Go to sleep, baby. You've had a long day." Mia started to massage her back—a surefire knockout recipe. "Close those pretty eyes and listen to my heart beat."

Jordan started to breathe heavily, but her body jerked roughly just a minute later. "Are you okay?" she asked, her voice sounding anxious to Mia's trained ears.

"Sure. Sure I am. There's nothing to worry about, Jordy. Just close your eyes and sleep."

"But..." Jordan extricated herself from the embrace and looked into Mia's eyes. "Are you sure? I know today was hard for you. Don't feel like you have to keep things to yourself. If you're upset, we can talk about it."

Mia gazed at her, finding her stomach doing a flip when she looked into her lover's eyes. Jordan was so sincere, so concerned for her that it nearly made her light-headed. "Today was tough," she admitted, "but it was good too. Seeing my mom made me feel her love again." She pulled Jordan down and kissed her. "I've missed her and my dad so much that it's too much for me to…I don't know…I guess…take it all in. You know?"

"Yeah." Jordan kissed her, moving her lips slowly and softly all across Mia's face. "I know, honey."

"It's gonna take me a while to think about everything she said and how we interacted. But that isn't bad. It's gonna be good in the long run." Mia looked into Jordan's eyes and was touched to see so much empathy in them. She knew that Jordan didn't really have any idea how it felt to have such a loving/contentious relationship with anyone, but Jordan knew her well enough to be able to experience it second-hand. Pressing her lips to her partner's, she whispered. "Sleep now. We'll talk tomorrow."

"Sure?" In seconds, Jordan was snuggling against Mia again, getting into her favorite sleep position.

Mia kissed her golden hair. "Positive. I want you to sleep for at least ten hours. You've got to let this beautiful body repair itself." She rubbed her hand along Jordan's flank, feeling her ribs and hip bone right under the skin. "You don't have much fuel in this pretty tank."

"Mmm." Jordan sighed and snuggled closer, a contented smile on her face. "I love you."

"I love you too, Jordy." Mia kissed her forehead, smiling when she could feel Jordan's body twitch in various places. Her hand was resting on Mia's belly, and her fingers flicked involuntarily before settling down. "I love you," Mia whispered, feeling her heart swell in her chest.

Chapter Three

When a quiet but determined knock roused Ryan from a deep sleep, it took her a few moments to get her bearings. The room was so dark she assumed it was the middle of the night, but something wasn't right. They'd fallen asleep after making love, but no one should be in their house knocking on their bedroom door. And she couldn't figure out how someone was knocking loudly enough on their front door for her to hear it so clearly. Her heart was pounding when she pulled away from Jamie and got to her feet, walking directly into a wall that shouldn't have been there. "Fuck!" More from shock than pain, she grabbed her head and fell back onto the bed.

"What's wrong?" Jamie's arms were around her, hands moving over her body, probably trying to see if anything was broken.

"I ran into the wall." Ryan sat there for a second, then asked, "Where in the hell are we?"

"Los Angeles. Who's knocking on our door?"

"Damned if I know. It's the middle of the night." Naked, Ryan felt along the wall, finally finding the door. She opened it a crack and saw Jackie standing there, fully dressed and looking concerned. "What…?" Ryan blinked, and shook her head. "What time is it?"

"Ten o'clock. Time to go. I wanted to come by earlier, but you kinda gave me the impression you wanted me to keep my nose outta your business."

"Fuck," she muttered. "We were asleep…" She shot a malignant glare at the heavy drapes that they had drawn to prevent the bright lights outside their window from keeping them awake. Which was also why neither of them had seen or sensed the sun rising. "I guess I *do* want you to wake me up, but only when I really need you to. Got that?"

"Clear as mud. We're leaving right now. Can you make it?"

"Hell no!" Ryan opened the door another few inches, letting Jackie see some of her. Her hair was sticking up and she was clearly not dressed.

"I'll tell Coach you're gonna get there on your own. Good luck," she added, chuckling as she turned and jogged away.

Jamie leaned against Ryan's body as the door closed. "Nice way to wake up," she murmured. "I think a fire drill would have been more fun."

"Well, at least we can stop for breakfast on the way. If I don't get something to eat, there's gonna be trouble."

They hugged briefly, then Ryan felt around for the bathroom door. "Is it a good idea to make rooms this dark? What if there *had* been a fire?"

"I suppose that's why they call them blackout drapes. You start to shower and I'll get some clothes out for you. We can be out of here in no time."

"Screw it," Ryan said, taking Jamie's hand and pulling her into the bathroom. "I'm just as fucked if I'm ten minutes or a half hour late. I'm sure we both need showers."

"Only if we plan on interacting with humans." Jamie giggled, looking at their images in the mirror. "Dogs would be chasing our cab if we didn't shower."

Her scowl fading, Ryan put her arms around her partner and hugged her. When they parted, she plucked at a hank of Jamie's hair that was sticking up in an odd direction. "I don't think I wanna know what's in your hair. It's stiff."

"Let's assume it's gel, okay? I don't think I'll ever be as comfortable being covered with bodily fluids as you are. They're pretty gross."

Ryan kissed Jamie's forehead. "Yours aren't, but you can't change what you like and dislike. Let's go wash 'em off."

"Are you sure we have time for breakfast?"

"We're taking time. I'm gonna have to clean the locker room after the game, so I'll need some energy."

"Punishment?"

"Yep." Ryan started the water, waiting for it to warm to the proper temperature before she stepped inside. "So we're gonna take a cab and have it stop at some kinda drive-through. I screwed up by not setting my watch, but I'm not gonna punish myself all day long." She gave her partner a small smile. "Life's too short."

"Ooo...that's my good girl. Lesson number one in how to treat yourself well."

After the remarkably un-churchlike service, Mia and Anna Lisa went to get a latte to give Jordan some time to get ready. They sat at a small table outside the coffeehouse, enjoying the crisp air and the warm sun. "There's one thing I have to know before I leave," Anna Lisa said.

"'Kay. Ask away."

"Are you really happy?"

Her mother's eyes were boring into her, making Mia feel not only exposed, but painfully vulnerable. She surprised herself when she started to cry quietly. "I'm happier with Jordan than I ever thought I could be," she said, sniffling. "But it's hard being here. I'm not busy enough, and I don't have much interest in getting out and doing things by myself."

"You've never been much of a solo explorer." Anna Lisa took her daughter's hand. "You need people."

"Yeah." Mia nodded. "I'm not a loner. And Jordan doesn't get home most nights until six. She needs to be asleep by nine, so we don't have much time together. It seems like we just eat dinner and go to sleep an hour later."

Anna Lisa's eyes sharpened. "Then why stay here? What's in this for you?"

Swallowing the urge to snap, Mia gathered her thoughts and asked, "Don't you remember what it was like to fall in love? Or didn't loving Dad make you feel like you'd do anything for him?"

Sighing heavily, Anna Lisa sat back and gazed at her daughter reflectively. "Oh, I did. I would have stood in front of a train if he'd asked me to." She leaned forward and said earnestly, "But at the same time, he wouldn't have asked me to do anything that made me unhappy. My happiness was as important to him as his was to me. Is that true with Jordan?"

"Of course it is!" Irritated and hurt, Mia said, "She never asked me to come here. Hell, she tried so hard to talk me out of it that she really hurt my feelings. I have to reassure her every day that I'm keeping busy and enjoying myself."

"Even when you're not."

"*Especially* when I'm not. She watches me with those big, blue eyes, just trying to find the smallest sign that I'm wavering."

"Damn it, Mia! Why don't you just admit this isn't working and come home?"

"Because," she said, taking a moment to breathe, "she needs me. That's all that matters. I watch over her and make sure she eats enough."

"She's skin and bones! Her veins are so prominent I could see her pulse beating. She's a gorgeous woman, but she's so pale and gaunt, the poor thing looks like she's starving."

"I know, damn it!" Mia started to cry again. "She won't budge from what her trainer tells her. She let you put oil in that dressing yesterday, but she'd never let me do that. I refuse to lie to her, so I do what she asks me to."

"So your biggest reason to be here isn't a valid one."

"That's not true. I *do* watch over her. I make sure she's in bed early, and I make her sleep late on Sunday. And I'm always there when she needs to talk."

"When would she go to bed if you weren't here? Would she stay up late and watch TV?"

Mia laughed. "Of course not. She'd probably go to bed even earlier. She forces herself to stay up to talk or…" She just barely stopped herself from revealing that they frequently missed Jordan's ideal bedtime because they were making love. Mia shook her head. "No. She wouldn't stay up late."

"Then why are you here?"

"Because I love her, God damn it! I *need* to be with her. I *need* to hold her and sleep with her. Feeling her body against mine is the highlight of every day. Damn it, don't you remember?"

Slowly, Anna Lisa nodded. "Of course I do." She held Mia's hand, looking at her with sympathy. "But is that enough?"

"Yes." Mia wiped at her chilled tears. "It has to be."

After brunch, the threesome went back to the apartment and Jordan tactfully said she had a few things to do in their room, leaving Mia and Anna Lisa to say their goodbyes.

Anna Lisa put her hands on her daughter's shoulders, holding her still while she gazed into her eyes. "Is there any way I can talk you into coming home with me?"

Mia shook her head. "I can't do that, Mom. I need to work things out here and find a way to be happy with all of this free time. I won't leave just because everything isn't perfect."

"There's a difference between perfect and…" Anna Lisa bit her lip, letting the rest of her thought die quietly. "I'd love it if you came home."

"I will. I don't know when, but I'll come home. I can't imagine living anywhere else."

Anna Lisa put her arms out and hugged Mia roughly. "I wish I could make you do what I want."

Gently, Mia ran her hand across her mother's back. "I wish you could be happy that I'm doing what I think is right. You raised me to decide what I need and make sure I get it."

Pulling away, Anna Lisa looked at Mia for a moment, a smile slowly growing. "Why did you only listen to the things that you could use to drive me crazy?"

"Only the good stuff stuck." She pressed her face against her mother's neck and held on to her until she was sure she wouldn't cry. "You'd better go. You don't wanna be late." Turning her head, she called, "Jordy!"

In seconds, Jordan was standing next to her with her arm around Mia's waist. "Getting ready to leave?"

"Yes. I've got to allow time to return my rental car." She extended her hand and when Jordan took it, she pulled her close. "Be good to my baby," she whispered fiercely, her hand digging into the skin on Jordan's neck. "She's not as strong as she seems."

When she released her hold, Jordan pulled away, nodding at Anna Lisa. "I will," she said, her gaze unblinking.

Mia rolled her eyes dramatically. "Don't threaten her!"

Anna Lisa wrapped her arms around her daughter. "I wouldn't threaten her. I save that for you." She swatted Mia sharply on the butt and kissed her cheek simultaneously. "Be good." Her voice was a little shaky, and she headed for the door without another word.

That evening, Mia watched a reality show about college students, keeping the sound down low so it didn't disturb Jordan. One of the women was struggling with her decision to stay at her college rather than move across the country to be with her boyfriend. She'd been admitted to the new school, but transferring would set her back just enough credits to preclude her graduating on time. Mia had been watching the woman's story unfold for several weeks, and had found herself rooting for her to make the move. Tonight, she wasn't so sure. She shifted just enough to be able to wrap her arms around Jordan, who lay heavily against her body. Jordan moved in her sleep, clutching Mia to herself like a teddy-bear.

Using the remote, Mia turned off the TV, then tried to relax enough to sleep. But Jordan's body had gotten so lean that various bones poked at her when they held each other tightly. She didn't want to move away, since nothing calmed her as much as holding her lover, so she did her best to ignore the discomfort and empty her mind. But her mother's words kept coming back to her, tormenting her. Were these few hours of sleep worth what she was giving up to be here? Was being here helping or hurting Jordan's chances? How could she ever judge that?

The alarm went off about fifteen minutes after Mia fell asleep. Or perhaps it just seemed that way because she couldn't force her eyes open. Jordan didn't try to wake her, she just went about her normal morning routine—moving like a cat, barely making a sound. Unclear as to how much time had passed since she'd heard the alarm, Mia felt a pair of soft lips brush across her cheek, waking her.

"What time is it?"

"Five thirty. I'm heading out now."

Eyes opening wider, Mia asked, "I missed breakfast?"

Jordan smiled at her, giving her such a love-filled look that Mia's heart melted a little. "There's plenty of granola left. It'll still be there when you get up. Only a lunatic gets up this early when she doesn't have to."

Mia put her hands behind Jordan's thighs and pulled her forward, giggling when Jordan had to grab the wall to avoid falling onto her body. "Come down here and give me some kisses."

"Uhm…that's not my mouth," Jordan deadpanned, laughing when Mia nuzzled between her thighs. "I'm getting a cramp, honey."

Mia let her go and Jordan straightened out. "You'd think all of the exercises we do would prepare me for almost anything." She squatted down next to the mattress and tenderly applied several kisses to Mia's lips. "Better?"

Her eyes were bright and clear and she looked like she'd been up for hours. "Always." Mia draped an arm around her neck and pulled her close, kissing her again. "Everything's better when you kiss me."

"Gotta go." Jordan ran her hand through Mia's hair, fluffing her curls. "Sleep in. You're obviously tired."

Yawning and stretching, Mia nodded. "Being with my mom was draining. I didn't sleep well, either. She wired me up."

"You're in a good spot to unwind. Have a good day." Smoothly, Jordan got to her feet and waved. "See you around six."

Mia waved back, then grabbed Jordan's pillow and cradled it to her chest. "Still smells like you," she said, then closed her eyes and was asleep before the athletes left the apartment.

A "thunk" woke Mia, and she blindly reached for the alarm clock, amazed to see that it was after nine. She lay still for a moment, decided that the noise hadn't been anything to worry about and went back to sleep. On and off all morning she woke briefly, considered what she'd planned for the day, then went back to sleep. It wasn't until noon that her body demanded she get up. Stomach rumbling from hunger, bladder full, she stopped in the bath, scowling at her pale, grumpy image.

Seeing that the only things in the house were granola and various forms of protein powders didn't help her mood, but she couldn't summon the energy to get dressed to go to the store. She sat at the kitchen table, stabbing innocent bits of granola with her spoon, her mouth curled into such a sour expression it was almost hard to get the spoon into it.

After breakfast, she settled on the floor and started reading a book for her humanities class. But her attention wandered constantly, returning again and again to her conversation with her mother. *Why was she living like this? Was she really helping Jordan?* She fought the heaviness of her eyelids for what seemed like hours, then slowly gave in, sleeping on the floor until a burst of bright light hit her. Her hand went to her eyes, shielding them.

"Are you all right?"

Jordan was kneeling next to her, and Mia couldn't resist her body's demand to wrap her arms around her lover and hold on as tightly as she could. "Fine," she mumbled.

Jordan's hand began to stroke her hair, slowly scratching her scalp. "What's wrong, honey?"

Mia released her hold and made her mouth curl into a weak smile. Sitting up, she said, "I guess I didn't know how tired I was." She got her feet under herself and stood, feeling a little woozy. "I've got to get to the store."

Jordan was looking at her with concern. "We can go out. You don't look like you're in the mood to cook."

Mia gave her a quick kiss. "I'm fine. Damn, I've been napping all day. I need to go out just to get my blood moving."

"Fine. Let me shower and we'll walk down to the restaurant at the end of the street."

"I'm fine. Really!" Mia was putting every watt of power she could generate into her smile, but it was clear Jordan wasn't buying it.

"That's great. No better time to go out to dinner. We can have a meal without our roommates salivating over our stuff."

Blowing out a breath, Mia nodded. "Can we shower together?"

Jordan's expression was between a smirk and a smile. "If we can fit."

They did fit, but maneuvering enough to get clean was a challenge. Mia finished first and got out to let Jordan wash her hair. She dashed across the hallway just as the front door opened and their roommates returned for the night. Mia closed the bedroom door, unreasonably angry at their arrival.

After getting dressed she went back to the bathroom to offer to help Jordan blow-dry her hair. Mia paused at the door, thinking Jordan must have a radio on. But she realized they didn't have a radio in the bathroom and tentatively opened the door. Jill was leaning on the sink, arms crossed over her chest, chatting with Jordan, who was still in the shower drying off. The shower curtain was open, and a flicker of jealousy flared at the thought of Jill looking at Jordan's body so blatantly. It crossed her mind to throw the door open hard enough to send Jill headfirst into the shower, but she controlled her temper as best she could. "Hi," she said, trying not to look as angry as she was.

"Hey," Jill said. "We were just chatting about the team."

"Mmm. Jordan, do you want help drying your hair?"

"No, I can handle it. Besides," she said, grinning, "it's getting crowded in here."

"I can help," Jill said, looking at Jordan. "It's a bitch to dry long hair, isn't it? You've got it easy with your cute little curls, Mia. You probably don't even have to comb it, do you?"

"Never have." She backed out of the room and closed the door behind her.

As she went back to their room, she heard Jill ask, "Is she pissed off?" Prudently, Mia dove for the door, not wanting to hear Jordan say something that would make her even angrier.

Jordan was full of what seemed like false cheerfulness when she walked into the bedroom, her naked body glowing from her hot shower. "I'll be ready in five."

Mia was sitting on the unmade bed, watching the network news. "No rush. That place is never crowded."

Rushing around the room, Jordan was ready in world-class time. "Let's go," she said, extending a hand to pull Mia to her feet. They walked down the hall, with Jordan sticking her head into each of the other rooms, telling their roommates that they were going out. By the time they hit the outdoor stairwell, Mia's anger was beginning to rise, and she knew she wouldn't be able to control it if it managed to escape. She concentrated on swallowing her feelings, attempting to do so by responding to Jordan's comments with the fewest words possible.

By the time they'd been seated and had ordered, neither woman was speaking. Jordan looked intensely uncomfortable, but Mia couldn't focus on her. She was far too busy trying to keep a lid on the volcano she knew was building in her gut. Head down, she ate the chef's salad she'd ordered, automatically depositing the things she didn't like onto Jordan's salad, nodding when Jordan put a black olive on her plate. It took no more than twenty minutes for them to finish and pay the bill, then walk out into the dark evening.

The break had given Mia time to calm down, and she took Jordan's hand on the walk home. "I know this is…kinda out of the blue," she said, "but we've got to come up with a plan to get our own place."

Jordan came to an abrupt halt. "What? Since when?" Her face fell and she rushed to explain, "I'm naked around the other girls all of the time. It doesn't mean a thing. Really!"

Mia shook her head and started to walk, with Jordan's long gait allowing her to catch up quickly. "It's not because Jill was in the bathroom with you, even though I don't appreciate her barging in. It's the fact that we don't have any privacy."

"We have our own room…"

Mia turned to glare at her, and Jordan's mouth shut quickly. "We live out in the middle of nowhere, Jordy. We don't hang out with our roommates or even talk to them much."

"We could if you wanted to," Jordan jumped in. "I'm just sick of 'em after being with them all day."

"No!" Without warning, Mia stopped and Jordan barreled into her. Mia didn't react to the crash, even though she skidded on the macadam. She balled her hands into fists and spoke through gritted teeth. "I don't want to be friends with them. I…don't…like…them!"

Jordan's jaw dropped. "What? Why?"

"Makela and Ekaterina don't give me the time of day, and I'd have trouble understanding them if they did. Toni comes in the door and gets on the phone with her husband. And I don't like Jill because she wants to fuck you!"

"She…but…it's not…" Jordan stopped speaking and stared at the ground. "I'm only interested in you. Isn't that what matters?"

"*Fuck!*" Mia's voice was so loud that windows would have vibrated if any had been nearby. She bent at the waist, hands on her knees, panting softly. After a few moments, she stood and faced Jordan. Her voice was calm by the time she spoke. "Of course that's what matters. But she… irritates me. They all irritate me. And it's not because they're assholes. They're keeping me from being alone with you."

Jordan let out a heavy sigh and shoved her hands into the pockets of her jeans. Twitching her head to signal Mia, she began to walk. It took her a while to speak again, and when she did her voice was low and soft. "This pisses me off."

Mia's heart started to pound in her chest. She reached for Jordan's arm, and was immensely relieved when her lover didn't pull away. "Why? What did I do?"

Slowly, Jordan's head turned and her eyes were hooded when she gazed at her partner. "I've asked you ten times a day if you're happy. I don't like to be lied to."

Feeling sick, the words rushed out of Mia's mouth. She was nearly frantic, on the verge of tears. "I didn't want to make things hard for you. I wanted to just lay low and try to get comfortable before I started making demands."

"Demands? Is that what it's called when you tell me how you feel about something? What kind of relationship is that?" Jordan faced Mia again, her expression filled with hurt. "Who are you using as a model, my parents?"

Desperately, Mia grabbed her lover's arm and pulled her to a stop. She flung her arms around her and held her tightly. "No, no, I'm…I'm trying my best. I wanna support you, not make things harder. It's just getting to me."

"What's getting to you? Having roommates?"

Mia pulled away and looked into Jordan's eyes. "No. It's more than that. It's where we live, it's how we live, it's how little there is to do out here." Jordan's open expression seemed to slam closed. Her eyes took on a coldness Mia had rarely seen, and it frightened her to the core.

"That's everything except me. Are you sure I'm not on the list, too?"

"No! God, no! You're everything to me, Jordy. I've left my home, my friends, my family, my school to be with you."

"You've been telling me that everything's great. You like where we live, you don't mind our roommates, you don't mind my schedule. Why wouldn't I wonder if you're sick of me, too?"

Mia could feel the fear leaving her body, immediately replaced by anger. "Look, you either believe I love you or you don't. There isn't one more thing I can do to prove it to you." She closed her eyes and felt her hands ball into fists. Holding them next to her reddening face, she shouted, "God damn it, Jordan! I'd give you a kidney if you needed it. I'd probably give you both of 'em! How can you say something like that to me? How can you doubt my love?"

Jordan's nostrils flared and she stood a little straighter. "Because I'm not very good at figuring out which of your statements are lies. Before tonight, I thought you liked being here. Now I find out the only thing you like is me. It's...hard for me to face the fact that you've been lying. I thought I could trust you."

"You can! I've always told you the truth about everything important."

"It's important that you've been here for three weeks and have been unhappy the entire time. That's damned important to me. That's why I've asked you about how you feel a couple of hundred times." Her eyes narrowed and she spoke even more softly. "I could tell that you weren't happy, that's why I kept asking. It sucks. It sucks a lot that you continued to lie even when I begged you to tell me the truth."

"Damn it, Jordan! Give me a fucking break. I'm trying to fit into your life, a life that I'm on the very edge of. I didn't want to come here and start complaining about everything. My whole reason for being here is to help you...support you."

Clearly puzzled, Jordan asked, "Help me what?"

"Help you with anything you need. That's what partners do!"

Jordan shook her head, her jaw clenched tightly. "Not my partner. My partner's here because she wants to be here. She's not here to nurse me."

"I love being with you," Mia said, stunned at her lover's reaction. "I was so unhappy when you were gone."

"And now you're unhappy here."

"Not when you're home! That makes it all worth while."

"Only until you lose it and tell me how you really feel. Then you want to move, or kick the other girls out, or…I don't even know what you want."

Mia's lower lip quivered and her voice cracked. "That's because you haven't let me tell you."

Her voice was still cool when Jordan said, "I'm sorry. Tell me what you want."

"I want us to have our own apartment. I want it to be closer to the center of town so I can walk places when you're gone."

Jordan stared at her, her eyes cold and unblinking. "That'll make you happy?"

"I…I'm not sure, but I think it will. Having our own place'll let us be ourselves. That'll help."

"What if it doesn't?" Jordan asked, her expression stony.

"Then we'll figure out something else. Jesus! I can't be sure what'll work."

"And I can't be sure you'll tell me the truth."

"*Damn it*, will you get over that?"

"I can't. Trust means everything to me, and to have you selfishly keep secrets—"

"Selfishly?" Her voice rising, Mia demanded, "I moved to the middle of nowhere, spend all day alone, live with people I barely know in a piece of shit apartment…to spend three hours a day with you. And you have the nerve to tell me I'm being selfish?"

"Yeah." Jordan's face was a mask. "That's exactly what I'm saying. When you're unhappy and you lie to me about it…you're not helping our relationship. You might think you are, but you're not."

Defeated, Mia closed her eyes. "Fine. I did this all out of a hidden need to live in a dump and act like I love you. Now that you've found me out, I guess I'll go home."

Jordan turned and started to walk again. "Maybe that's something you should consider," she said quietly, the words barely reaching Mia's ears.

It took about fifteen minutes to finish the walk to the apartment, and Mia's head was spinning the entire time. She wasn't sure what she'd done to make Jordan so angry and cold, but it was bad. They'd never had a significant fight, and her lack of experience with Jordan's temper had her fumbling for a response. Another word was not uttered on their walk home. Mia couldn't make herself go into their room and endure more of the silent treatment, so when Jordan headed for the steps, she continued to walk.

"Where are you going?" Jordan asked coolly when she noticed Mia wasn't behind her.

"For a walk. If I'm gonna be ignored, I'd rather be alone."

Jordan's expression turned even chillier. She continued up the stairs and went into the apartment without sparing another look.

Stunned and heartsick, Mia started walking, her only goal to be away from Jordan. Loneliness and sorrow filled her head and her heart. Images of hopping into the car and driving to Berkeley flitted through her head, but she knew that was a very harsh payback for Jordan's snit, so she dismissed the idea before she could seriously consider it.

She froze in fear when she heard footsteps behind her, then realized the person was running, not creeping up on her. It took just a few moments for her to recognize the soft cadence of her lover's footfalls and that almost brought a smile to her face. She'd just started to turn when Jordan grasped her shoulder and turned her, enfolding her in a crushing embrace.

"I'm sorry," she whispered, her breath coming in quick gasps. "I'm so sorry."

Mia returned the hug, but with less fervor. "It's okay. I said some shitty things. I don't blame you for being mad."

"I'm not mad. I'm really not."

Pulling back, Mia looked up at her lover. "Then what are you?"

Jordan shook her head, her long, blonde hair sliding over her shoulders to rest on her red fleece jacket. "I…I don't know. But I can't stand to have things like this between us. Can we go home?"

Mia rested her cheek on Jordan's chest. "I'm home when I'm with you. It's you that matters to me…not where we are. I'm sorry. I'm sorry for hurting you."

"Doesn't matter." Jordan kissed the crown of her head, hugging her tightly. "You had a hard day. I think having your mom here was tough on you."

"A little," Mia admitted. She nuzzled against Jordan's soft jacket, the springy fibers and Jordan's soft hair giving her face a duet of sensations. "We can go home if you want, but I'd rather stay outside a while longer."

"Wanna walk some more?"

"Yeah." Mia took Jordan's hand and they continued walking away from the apartment. "I'm sorry I didn't tell you I was unhappy. That was stupid."

"You're never stupid. And you're never selfish. You were trying to be supportive. It was stupid of me not to be able to see that."

"It's okay. I hurt your feelings."

"Ehh…I'm not sure what happened. I just went off. I promise it doesn't happen very often."

"I know. That was the first time I've ever seen you get angry." She looked up at Jordan until their eyes met. "I don't wanna see it very often."

"You won't." Jordan kissed her head again. "You won't. I'm on edge this week, and it felt like you were pressing me to do something that isn't a good idea right now."

"What? Moving?"

"Yeah. They're gonna cut two more this week. There's a chance we'll be going home this weekend…so it seemed ridiculous to think of renting an apartment."

Mia stopped and twirled, putting her hand on Jordan's breastbone. "Why didn't you tell me that?"

"What?"

"That you're worried about getting cut."

Looking down at the ground, Jordan made a face like a child being scolded. "I dunno. Talking about it makes it too real, I guess."

"Are you really worried?"

They made eye contact and Mia could see the anxiety in her lover's eyes. "Yeah. We've got five outside hitters, and they'll take four at the most. So…one of us has to go before the final roster's set. Two of the girls are untouchable…so that leaves three of us to fight for one or two spots."

Mia took her hand and tugged on Jordan to start them walking again. "How do you think you compare to the other two?"

"We're…different," she said thoughtfully. "I'm better offensively than either of the others, but Rachel is a much better server and Lina is a little bit better at defense than Rachel or I are." She shrugged. "It depends on what the coaches are looking for."

"Aren't they looking for offense? Isn't that what wins games?"

"Sure. But the veterans are both excellent offensively and have a lot of experience in international play. They might want the subs to be better defensively in the event of a tight match. It's impossible to tell."

"So you and Rachel and Lina are all new?"

"Yeah. Rachel is only a freshman, so she'd be a great choice. She could get some experience this year and really know what she's doing in 2004."

Mia put her arm around Jordan's shoulder. "I can see why you're worried." Giving her a squeeze that made her gasp, she added, "But I can't see why you didn't tell me about this. You can't expect me to tell you everything that's bothering me when you won't tell me when you're afraid of getting cut! Being on the team is kind of an important detail, honey."

"I know," Jordan said, sounding contrite.

"I know they're gonna keep you. You're too fantastic to even consider cutting. So I'm gonna look for an apartment."

Jordan sighed. "Fine."

"Come on, honey. You're a total stud! They'd be idiots to cut you."

Barely smiling, Jordan looked at her watch. "It's just about time for bed. Let's head home." She draped her arm around Mia's shoulders and they walked back toward the apartment, each silently mulling over the weeks to come.

Chapter Four

Jamie got home a little late on Monday night, and was looking over some menus from their favorite take-out places when Ryan walked into the kitchen.

"Hi." Ryan bent and kissed her head. "Just get home from therapy, or not in the mood to cook?"

Jamie put her arm around Ryan's hips and hugged her. "The former. Right before my time was up, I asked Anna about making a referral for you. She spent a good fifteen minutes of her own time telling me why she wouldn't." She smiled up at Ryan. "She must love me since she gave me a little freebie."

"Why wouldn't she make a referral?" Ryan was frowning as she walked to the refrigerator and pulled out a container of yogurt. "It's not hard." She grabbed a spoon and pulled out a chair, straddling it backwards, as was her habit.

Jamie watched her meticulously arrange the fruit throughout the container. "She said she didn't think she was the best person to make a referral for you."

"Who is? The Yellow Pages?"

"Nooo. She reminded me that you have a therapist who knows you. She thinks Ellen's the right person. She's been seeing you for a while and she'd probably have some idea of the type of person you'd click with."

Jabbing at her yogurt, Ryan grumbled, "I was gonna call and quit. I don't wanna talk to her again."

Jamie reached across the table and brushed some dust off Ryan's arm, then gently stroked it. "Why not, honey?"

"'Cause I'm done. I told you I don't like going, so why go back?"

"Uhm…because you're in a group. I'd think you'd want to say goodbye to the other people. I mean…you've shared things with them, right?"

"Not much." Ryan's eyes were focused on her rapidly dwindling yogurt.

"Well, it's rude to call and cancel now. Go tomorrow and tell them that you're leaving."

Ryan spooned the last of the yogurt into her mouth and stood up. "I'm gonna call her now, then she can think of a referral for me for tomorrow." She started to leave but added, "Order something spicy, 'kay?"

"Okay." Jamie watched her leave, wondering what was going on in that adorably irritating mind.

The phone rang not long after they'd finished dinner and Jamie went into the living room to answer it. "Hello?'

"Jamie! Niall."

"Hi, Niall." She smiled at the way he spoke on the phone. It reminded her of roll call more than conversation, but she was used to the odd habits of the O'Flaherty cousins.

"Your ma hooked me up with her real estate guy. You know him?"

"No, I haven't met him. Have you?"

"No. But I talked to him. He doesn't do commercial or rental properties, so he turned me over to a guy he works with—Ray something or other. Anyway, I'm gonna go meet with this guy tomorrow and I thought one of you might wanna go with me."

"Uhm…Ryan's probably busy, but I can make it as long as it's in the afternoon."

"Yeah. Three o'clock. That good?"

"That's great. Where should I meet you?"

"At the guy's office. It's on Castro, just up from the theater."

"Okay. I'll be there and I might have Ryan with me."

"Great. See ya!" He hung up before she could add another word.

She walked upstairs and stood in the doorway, watching Ryan type. Waiting until her partner paused, she said, "Can I interrupt?"

Ryan looked up and smiled. "Never. I mean, you're never an interruption. What's up?"

"Niall's got a meeting with a real estate agent tomorrow at three. I said I'd go with him."

"Really?"

"Yeah. He knows what he wants in a building, but I'm…how can I say this?" She tapped her chin with her finger. "I'm a little more…"

"Polite…civilized…conversational…pretty?"

"Thank you. I was going to say patient."

"I'm glad you're going. Niall can be a real ass. He's so abrupt."

"Yeah, he is, but he's a good guy. I like him."

Ryan's eyes widened. "You'd better! He's family!"

Ryan showed up right on time for therapy on Tuesday morning, and nodded to all of her companions. Even though it had been quite a few weeks, she always stood alone on the street corner while they waited for Ellen to open the office. It had to be clear to the group that she wasn't really one of them, since she offered no more than a polite smile.

Ellen arrived on time and opened the door to the building. She handed Barb the key to the office and said, "Will you open up? I need a minute."

Barb took the key and the group started to follow, with Ryan trailing behind. Ellen tapped her on the shoulder. "I got your message."

"Right." Ryan looked down and moved a discarded piece of paper around with her shoe. "Uhm…can you help me?" Glancing up, she caught Ellen's gaze and held it, uncertainly, for a moment.

"I hope I can. I've got a little time after group. Can you stay?"

"Sure. But you could just call me. I hate to take up your time. You can even leave a message if I'm not there."

"I have time." Ellen smiled at Ryan. "Ready?"

Everyone but Ryan filed out at the end of the session, and she looked longingly after them. Ellen took out her appointment calendar and set it on her lap. "Tell me what you're thinking."

"About…?"

"Therapy. Are you serious about it?"

"Uhm…yes, I'm serious."

Ellen gazed at her for a moment. "You don't seem it. You might be the type of person who needs privacy, but from what I've gathered…that's not really who you are. My guess is that you're not committed to this."

"I…" Ryan put her hands on her knees and seemed to gather her thoughts. "I'm very serious about wanting to feel better."

"And you think you'll feel better if you find a new therapist?" Ellen's voice carried no animosity, just gentle concern.

"Maybe. I…I really don't know. I just know that I hate…this. I feel like I've been sentenced to come here."

"Why?"

Shrugging, Ryan said, "I don't feel like I have much in common with the other women. Well…maybe Barb. But I don't feel like I can really let go with the others. I'm always afraid of their reactions if I said what's really on my mind."

Ellen leaned forward and looked into Ryan's eyes. "What is on your mind?"

"It depends," Ryan said, fidgeting a little. "Sometimes I feel fine. But when something sets me off I can really feel out-of-control. I don't think the other women can get that."

"You might be right. Most of them haven't been through the same type of thing you have. But I still think you can benefit from a group. Sharing how you feel with someone who knows what you're going through can help you, if you'll let it."

Ryan nodded. "Yeah, I guess you're right. But this isn't the right group. It's just not."

"How about this?" Ellen looked down at her book. "Would you consider spending an hour with Barb and me? Her trauma's very close to yours. And having a smaller group would let each of you talk a little more."

"Uhm…I guess I could try it."

"No pressure. If you want to see someone else…I'm happy to give you some names. As a matter of fact, I've written down three. I called each of them and they have time available." She handed Ryan the paper.

"Why don't we try a few sessions?" Ryan said. "It can't hurt."

"You can think about it and leave me a message. I don't want you to feel pressured."

"No, no, I'm good. Let's do it."

"I'll talk to Barb and see if she's interested. I think she will be."

Ryan opened her book and wrote a few things. "Here's when I'm available. If Barb agrees, go ahead and set something up. You can leave me a message."

Ellen took the sheet and glanced at it. "I think we'll be able to figure something out. I'll give you a call."

Ryan stood up and shook Ellen's hand. "Thanks. I wasn't really looking forward to starting with someone new." She grinned. "I just couldn't take another day with the whole group."

"We'll try something new," Ellen said. "We both have the same goal, and that's making you feel more like yourself."

When Ryan got home from practice, Jamie was still out. She started to make some pasta, unable to wait to see when her partner would arrive. The water was just reaching a boil when Jamie came in the back door, carrying a big, greasy, brown paper bag, redolent with the smell of garlic.

"Combos?"

"Welcome home, Jamie," her partner said. "Gosh, I've missed you." She put the bag down and walked over to the stove, turning it off.

Ryan hugged and kissed her quickly. "Combos?"

"Yes, dear. I was in the neighborhood, so I bought you two combos. I'll never stop smelling like tomato sauce and garlic, but I did it for love."

Ryan tore into the bag, unwrapping her favorite treat and getting the food on plates in what seemed like seconds. "Kitchen?" she asked, already putting the plates on the kitchen table.

"Sure." Jamie washed her hands and grabbed a long strip of paper towels before she sat down.

"Drink?"

"Do we have any beer?"

Ryan looked in the refrigerator. "Yep." She took two out and set them on the table.

"You know," Jamie said after taking a sip, "you and Niall have the same speech patterns sometimes. You treat your words like they're pretty valuable, too."

"Huh." Ryan smiled coyly and took a drink of her beer.

"Stop it!" Jamie pinched her and asked, "Do you want to know about my day?"

Ryan just nodded and dug into her sandwich.

"Brat." She arranged a napkin in the placket of her blouse, then put another on her lap, hoping that a delay would make Ryan talk. But her partner could wait anyone out. Especially when she had one of her favorite foods in front of her. "We met Andrew, the guy who Mom worked with."

Another nod from Ryan.

"And I'm glad we're not going to work with him."

One raised eyebrow asked why.

"He's very, very gay. Very classy. I know the boys aren't anti-gay—"

"Sure they are," Ryan finally spoke. "They're just not anti-lesbian."

Jamie thought about that for a second and saw her partner's point. "Do you think they make gay jokes and things like that when we're not around?"

"Of course. You have to expect the worst from the boyos. I'm sure they make all kinds of racial and ethnic jokes too. They just don't do it in front of me. Or Brendan."

"Only you two dislike those kinds of jokes?"

"No, I don't think Rory does, and maybe Colm, but they aren't the types to complain or tell the others what to do."

"But you and Bren do?"

"Yeah. We lecture them, which they really hate."

"I'd hate it if they said negative things about gay people around me."

"They won't. They treat you like a girl. They know girls usually don't like that stuff."

"So it's what they can get away with, huh?"

"I suppose. But they're no worse than any other group of twenty-something guys."

"Well, then I'm really glad we're not working with Andrew. The guy we talked to looked like he could crack walnuts with his bare hands. He wasn't very tall, but he was built. He looked like a big fire plug."

"Straight?"

"Yep. Had the picture of the wife and kids on his desk."

"Good. The boys would work with a gay guy, but a cultured, well-dressed gay guy might be too much for them." She smiled wryly. "Did you see any places?"

"Just pictures. We spent most of the time telling him what we were looking for. That took over an hour."

"Who talked?"

"Me," Jamie said, smiling. "And Niall interrupted."

"That's my boy. I knew I could count on him to do the O'Flaherty name proud."

When Jordan came home that night, she was uncharacteristically quiet. They were halfway through dinner when she said, "I've been thinking about something I said last night."

Mia covered her hand with her own and asked, "What's that?"

"I said that you should probably think about whether or not you should leave."

Smiling, Mia said, "Hey…don't worry about that. I know you didn't mean it."

Jordan swallowed noticeably, then seemed to force herself to look into Mia's eyes. "I think I did mean it."

"Wha…are you serious? God damn it, Jordan, I said I was sorry!" Mia jumped to her feet. "What do I have to do?"

Jordan was beside her in a moment, trying to get her arms around Mia who was actively pushing her away. "Come on, let me explain."

"What? That you don't want me here?"

Jordan dropped her hands, giving up on the struggle. "Don't even think that. I've been thinking about everything you said last night, and I'm not sure it makes sense to go on like we've been doing." She reached out and touched Mia's cheek, leaving it there when it wasn't pushed away. "Come on. Sit down and let me tell you what I've been thinking."

Seething, Mia nonetheless sat back down and stared at her partner.

"You said a lot of things last night, and I know that some of them are true."

"Thanks," Mia snapped. "Good to hear that you don't assume everything I say is a lie."

Jordan cupped a hand over Mia's knee and said, "That's not what I meant and I think you know that."

Mia rolled her eyes, but didn't respond, waiting for Jordan to continue.

"You told me you're unhappy with our apartment, but I think there's more to it than that. I don't think you're gonna be happy traveling with me, either."

"I didn't say that!"

"I know." Jordan sat quietly, gazing into Mia's eyes. "It's…a feeling I have. I know you, and I know how you are. I don't think you'll be any happier sitting in a stadium in Moscow than you are sitting in our apartment. Hell, at least you can watch TV in our apartment. You won't even be able to do that in Moscow."

"I'm not going to watch TV. I'm going to be with you, and that's what counts."

Jordan nodded. "That *is* what counts at this point. I thought…I truly believed that you'd have a good time traveling with us. But that's just stupid. It's no fun to be in another country walking around by yourself... unless that's what you enjoy, and you're not like that."

"No, I'm not. It'd only be fun if you were with me."

"So...if you won't enjoy it and it'll cost us thousands of dollars...maybe you shouldn't come."

"But...don't you want me?"

"Of course I do. I always want you. That's never in question, Mia." She grasped her chin and held her head steady, looking into her eyes. "Never. I'd love for you to be there."

Mia felt like crying. "Then I'll go with you!"

Moving her chair back, Jordan patted her thighs, and Mia practically leapt for her. She sat on Jordan's lap, her face burrowed into her neck. "Shhh," Jordan murmured, stroking her back. "It's all right, baby. It's all right."

"I wanna be with you," Mia said, her voice catching. "I wanna take care of you."

"You take care of me by taking care of yourself. I'm happy when you're happy. And knowing that you're just going with me to sleep together isn't gonna do it."

Mia lifted her head and gazed into Jordan's eyes. "But I love sleeping with you. Don't you love it?"

"Ohh..." Jordan gently soothed the hurt frown Mia wore. "Of course I do. It's the highlight of my day. But it's not worth it if I'm worried about you the rest of the time. I need to...I *have* to concentrate when we're touring. Each game means a lot...a whole lot. If you're at home, I'll miss you. But only at night. That's the only time I have to reflect. The rest of the time I'll be in my playing zone. And since I fall asleep in minutes... it won't be that bad."

"So you *don't* want me to go?"

"I want you to go if you want to go. If you'll enjoy being in Russia, touring the museums, going to some interesting restaurants with...I don't know who...I'd love to have you. But I don't want you to go if you're only going to sleep with me. It just isn't worth it."

Mia's chin was still quivering, and her voice was unsteady when she asked, "But don't you need me to take care of you?"

Jordan hugged her hard and long. "I love to have you take care of me. But you won't get much chance. The team has to eat together, so you can't cook for me. We have to do all sorts of dumb things like go to visit the Russian team's practice facility…all of that kind of promotional stuff. You can't go to any of that. All we'll be able to do is sleep together." She smiled as her eyes hooded with embarrassment, making Mia's heart melt. "And I'll probably actually want to sleep."

Mia leaned forward and rested her forehead against Jordan's. "Can we let this go for tonight? I don't know what's best. All I know is that I want to be with you…no matter where you are or what you're doing. *You're* what matters."

"I want that too," Jordan said. "That's all I've ever wanted. I just didn't know it until I met you."

"Damn, you know how to make me smile." She tilted her chin and pulled Jordan's lower lip into her mouth. Mia began to suck it gently, then put her arms around her and pulled her close.

The front door opened, and all of the roommates entered, with Jill saying, "Hey! No making out in the living room."

Jordan tightened her hold, making Mia feel like a treasured doll. "We're not making out. We just like to be as close as possible."

Jill gestured at the table. "You haven't even finished eating. Are you gonna feed her?"

"Yep." Jordan patted Mia on the butt, and when they were both standing she took her hand. "Thanks for the suggestion." The pair walked down the hall to their room to the titters of their roommates.

When Jordan closed the door she whispered, "That didn't upset you, did it? I didn't want to be around them for another minute."

Jordan was standing right in front of the door, and Mia put her hands against her shoulders, pinning her against it. "No, it didn't upset me. I thought it was a good idea. I'm tired of talking. I wanna use my mouth for something more fun."

Smiling sexily, Jordan bent and picked Mia up, making her squeak in surprise. "Let's go." She turned and carefully knelt on the bed, lowering Mia to the mattress. "Since I chose when, you can choose how."

Mia lay on her back, gazing up at her partner with a thoughtful expression. "I think I'd like…hmm…let's see…" She put her hand on Jordan's ass, grasping a handful of muscle that barely moved under her probing. "I like to look down and see your cheeks flexing when you're…" She grabbed Jordan and pulled her on top of her body, whispering her request into her ear.

Jordan's eyebrows popped up and down. "We're never very quiet when we do that. Sure you don't mind if the roomies hear us?"

"If I get too noisy, just stick something into my mouth. Like your tongue," she murmured, batting her eyes.

"Be right back." Jordan got to her feet and moved quickly. to one of their plastic bins to get what she needed. "I've gotta put on my supergirl outfit."

"It's so cute that you call that your supergirl outfit."

"Well, most girls don't have one of these," Jordan said, rooting through the toys Mia had brought with her. "Thank God."

"I'm glad you don't have one very often, but every once in a while..." She grinned lasciviously.

"I'm glad I can have one when you want one and toss it aside when we're done. Besides," she said, finding what she wanted, "I don't think I'd have any stamina if I had a real one. You're too hot for words."

The next morning, Jordan woke to soft kisses being tenderly placed along her chest. She opened one eye and sucked in a sharp breath when Mia gently pulled a nipple into her mouth. "Morning," she said, her hips instinctively moving against her lover. "That's a nice way to wake up."

"Does this make it nicer?" Mia moved up and captured Jordan's lips while slowly slipping her hand between her legs.

"Unh...yeah. Much nicer." Jordan lifted her knees to give Mia better access. Then she pulled Mia's earlobe into her mouth and nipped at it. "Feels good...very, very good. Ahh!" She gasped when Mia filled her, slipping in and out of her wetness. Their mouths met, and Jordan began to suckle Mia's tongue. Moving against each other, stroking and caressing as things began to heat up, Jordan managed to get an arm around Mia and held her tenderly while her fingers found their mark.

Now Mia gasped and smiled through their kiss. "Delicious," she murmured. "Touch me just like that. All day."

"I promise," Jordan said softly, even though she knew they only had a few minutes before she had to get ready for another day on the practice court.

Even though her legs were wobbly, Mia got up and made Jordan's breakfast while her lover was in the shower. She was humming to herself when Jill walked into the kitchen, and they both mumbled hellos. Jill looked like the cat that ate the canary, but Mia wasn't about to ask her about the smirk she wasn't hiding well. Jill started to concoct her normal breakfast drink and Mia had to look away. She knew that athletes had odd appetites, but she'd never figured out what made her drink something the color of a leaf, and she didn't want to learn the secret today.

Jordan came into the room, a bright smile affixed to her face. "I love having you get up to have breakfast with me," she said, giving Mia a kiss on the cheek.

Jill leaned against the counter, her smirk now bordering on ostentatious. She leaned forward and patted the top of Jordan's head, saying, "Not you. Must be Mia."

Jordan reached up and felt her own head. "What?"

"I was trying to figure out which one of you was banging your head into the wall last night. You don't have a knot up there so it must be Mia." She laughed at her joke, and slapped Jordan hard on the ass. "You don't look like a wild woman, Ericsson, but you sure must be. It takes two to make that kinda noise."

Jordan looked mildly embarrassed, but she shrugged off the comment. "Must've been next door. I think they're remodeling."

Mia's expression was a complete blank. "Be right back," she said, patting Jordan on the hip as she passed. "Don't eat all the granola."

Jordan watched her go, her brow slightly furrowed.

"Did I piss her off?" Jill asked.

"I don't think so. She doesn't mind being teased."

"Maybe she didn't get enough sleep…with the neighbors remodeling."

"Yeah. That's probably it," Jordan said. She sat down and dug into her granola, patiently waiting for Mia to return.

Chapter Five

Catherine picked up the phone on Wednesday morning, mildly surprised to hear her former husband's voice.

"Hi, Cat."

When he sounded so chipper, he always wanted something. "Good morning, Senator. How are things?"

"Good. I'm thinking about going to my San Francisco office on Friday. How about getting together while I'm in town?"

She almost pulled the phone away from her ear to inspect it. "Get together?"

There was a pause, then he said, "I...thought we were going to stay friends. We're still parents together."

"I...of course I want to be friendly. But I haven't given much thought to how that would play out."

"Friends see each other and talk, don't they?" His good humor sounded like it was ebbing.

"Of course. It's not that I'm averse to seeing you. You just caught me by surprise."

He made a gruff little noise that she'd heard thousands of times. She knew it meant he was puzzled as to why he wasn't getting his way. The fact that she didn't have to give in to his wishes any longer gave her a slight thrill.

"Maybe another time then."

"I'd be happy to see you *this* time, but I'm not going to be in town."

"Oh." A pause. "Really?"

"Mmm-hmm. I'm going to New York for the weekend."

"New York? Huh. What are you doing there?"

She started to tell him that was a little personal, but realized she'd tell a woman friend. They should be at least that open with one another. "I'm going to a few galleries and to the spring art show at The Armory."

"Oh…right. We did that together a few times."

"Yes, we did," she said, thinking that they'd always had a good time in New York.

"Well, I don't have anything booked in San Francisco for this weekend. I could come up and meet you in New York. We could take in a play."

Now the warning bells went off. She didn't know what he wanted, but he definitely wanted something. "That's very thoughtful, but I'm meeting a friend."

"A…friend?"

"Mmm-hmm." She didn't add another word.

"So…you're busy all weekend?"

"Yes. I'm going for the art, but also to see my friend."

"Oh. Uhm…that's great. I hope you and…your friend have a good time."

"I'm sure we will. Now make sure you tell me the next time you're coming to town. I'd like to show you my new house."

"Right…right. That'd be nice. Have a good time and…well, just have a good time. Bye."

"Bye, Jim. Take care." She hung up and sat for a minute, trying to figure out what he wanted, but she couldn't come up with a thing.

Ryan walked into the waiting area of Ellen's office and smiled tensely at Barb. They'd been unable to use the space when they were in group, since the building was locked prior to their early-morning session. But now that they were going to meet after the usual group, they could relax in the waiting room. But Ryan wasn't able to relax, and she quickly wished they were outside again, since the silence was much more pronounced in the small, quiet room. She was going to pick up a magazine, but that seemed odd, so she laced her fingers around a knee and rocked a little bit, knowing she looked nervous and uncomfortable.

"Do you wanna do this?" Barb asked.

"No. You?"

"No. I hate therapy."

"Me too," Ryan said, feeling a little better at hearing Barb's revelation. "I thought you were into it. You always talk in group."

Shrugging, Barb said, "I wanna feel better. Sometimes talking helped, but not enough."

"Yeah," Ryan said thoughtfully. "Same for me. It helped a little, but it didn't help enough to make me wanna keep coming."

"So…why do this?"

"Mmm…I didn't want to find a new therapist, and I promised my girlfriend I'd keep trying."

"That's not a very good reason."

Even though her words were frank, she didn't sound like she was scolding Ryan. "You're probably right. But I hate this therapy stuff. It works great for some people, but I don't like to talk about things that upset me."

"That's kinda the entrance requirement." Barb smirked at her.

"I know. And I *do* try."

"Do you really? It doesn't seem like it."

Ryan thought for a moment, then said, "You must be right. Ellen says the same thing. Maybe I'm an underachiever."

"You don't look like that, either. And the stuff I read about you in the papers made you sound like a super hero."

Ryan laughed. "They create an image for you. Whatever they think will make people buy the paper becomes who you are."

Ellen opened the door and beckoned them in. They made a few awkward moves to choose a place to sit, and finally wound up next to each other on the sofa. Ellen took her usual chair and said, "I heard you laughing in the waiting room. That's a good sign."

Barb smiled and said, "We were talking about how neither of us really likes therapy, but we're still gonna do our best."

"I didn't say that," Ryan corrected, giving her a grin.

"I have confidence in you both," Ellen said. "I was thinking about how to start, and it doesn't make sense to have you tell your stories again. If you're willing, I'd like to try something a little different. I think we all agree we want to get a little deeper than we did in the group."

"I don't wanna, but I know I have to," Ryan said.

Barb nodded and Ellen continued, "Why don't you each tell me what you know about the other. Tell me why she's here, and what's really stopping her from living life to the fullest?"

"You want me to tell you about Barb?" Ryan asked, looking puzzled.

"Yes. I don't want you to analyze her. Just say what you've learned about her. I think it's a way to let you each see what you're projecting."

"I'm willing," Barb said. "I was kinda doing that in the waiting room."

Ryan smiled at her. "Go ahead."

"Okay." Barb pursed her lips, her eyes narrowed. "I think Ryan's very, very angry. Mostly at herself. I think she's got really high personal standards, and when she doesn't meet 'em, she beats herself up."

"True," Ryan said, nodding.

"I think she's also scared. She's probably afraid that she's not able to take care of the people she loves. This whole thing probably made her realize how powerless she is, and nobody likes to face that."

Ryan didn't nod this time. She folded her arms over her chest and leaned against the arm of the sofa.

"She's said that she regrets that she didn't act earlier and kill the guy who was driving the car. But I don't think that's true," Barb said, glancing at Ryan. "I think she feels guilty about having anything to do with a guy dying. Even though he deserved to. Twice."

It didn't take long for Ryan's reserve to shatter. Tears were rolling down her cheeks by the time Barb finished talking. Ellen held out a box of tissues and Ryan took the first of many she would use in the next forty minutes.

A full hour hadn't passed, but Ryan felt like she'd been on the sofa for a week. Her body was so heavy and lethargic that she wasn't sure she'd be able to stand up. Ellen escorted them out and they stood outside the door for a second before Ryan impulsively put her arms around Barb and hugged her. "You get it," she whispered. "You're the only person I've talked to who gets it."

"Yeah, I do. It's awful, isn't it?"

"The fucking worst." Ryan laughed ruefully. "I used to feel like I'd been hit with a stick after a session. Now I feel like I've been beaten with a belt. I guess that's progress."

Ryan had a long list of things she needed to accomplish, but she couldn't bear to even look at her day-planner. Instead of going to campus, she headed for home, enormously pleased to find Jamie gone. She didn't want to say one word to another human, not even her lover. There was only one thing she wanted to do, and she couldn't wait to get to it. Kicking off her shoes, she lay down on the bed fully clothed, and fell asleep in minutes.

Jamie was walking across campus, headed for the library when her cell phone rang. "Hello?" she said after wrestling it out of her pocket.

"Hi, Jamie?"

"Yeah?"

"It's Ray Wisnewski. A couple of new properties came on the market this week and Niall said you might be able to come look at them."

"Oh, he did, did he?" She laughed, shaking her head.

"Is…that okay? I don't really know who I should be dealing with here."

"Oh, it's fine that you call me. We've got a whole crew and everyone acts like the boss until it's time to actually make a decision. But don't let that put you off. We usually argue amongst ourselves and not in public."

"To be honest, I don't recall ever working with a group as large as yours where there wasn't one or two decision makers."

"Hmm…maybe you should just call me. I'm not particularly knowledgeable about any of the rehab issues, but I think I know enough about the neighborhood to know if something is worth looking at. And, to be honest, my schedule is the most flexible."

"Great. That's one hurdle down. Do you have time to come today?"

"Sure. I was going to study, but that's never any fun. I can be there in an hour."

After a two-hour nap, Ryan woke up feeling better—lighter—than she had in days. The emotional bruises were still fresh, but talking to someone who really, truly understood how she felt—and how guilt was consuming her—might eventually help. If it didn't kill her first.

That evening Jamie struggled down the stairs with her traveling bag, scowling at Ryan who was sitting placidly on the couch, reading a book. "Thanks for the help!"

"I'm sorry," Ryan said, looking anything but. "Did you ask for help? I must not have heard you."

"A really good girlfriend would have jumped to her feet the minute she heard me hit the first stair."

"See? I've been telling you I'm not a good girlfriend. I always know best." She got up and took the bag from Jamie, helpfully relieving her of her burden for one step.

Jamie stayed on the first step and grabbed Ryan's collar, holding her still. "I've never criticized your kissing, so get busy."

Dutifully, Ryan put her hands on Jamie's hips and spent a moment looking into her eyes. "Sometimes I wish you were taller. It's nice being able to look at you without bending."

"Hey, you could be shorter. I'm not crazy about having to stretch to get a kiss."

A silly look settled on Ryan's face. "We could work with what we have." She stood next to Jamie on the step and started to kiss the top of her head, making ridiculously enthusiastic sounds while she rubbed against her. Jamie followed suit, smacking noisily against the point where Ryan's clavicles met. They were both giggling when Ryan pulled away. "I'd rather bend."

"And I'd rather stretch. Your mouth is much more responsive than your sternum."

Grasping her hips again, Ryan once more studied Jamie's eyes. "It's weird to be going to the same state, isn't it?"

"Yeah. Is this a first?"

"I think so. I'm glad we'll only be apart one night this time. I don't even know how far Tucson is from Tempe, but it's too far for me."

"It must not be too far if you're taking a bus after your game."

"Don't be so sure. The athletic department doesn't throw money away. For all I know it's a twelve hour ride."

"You hate buses, don't you?"

"Yeah. It's impossible for me to get comfortable. Buses were made for people your size."

Jamie put her arms around Ryan's neck and clasped her hands. "This step was made for people my size to get a kiss. What's with the holdout?"

"Nothin'. I just like looking at you. I never have enough time to just look at you." She brushed her fingers across Jamie's forehead, fluffing her hair. "You're such a beautiful woman."

Jamie smiled and looked into Ryan's eyes, searching them for a few moments. "How're you feeling about going? Okay?"

"I'm fine. Really fine. See?" She smiled so brightly and artificially that Jamie had to laugh.

"That's a beauty." She kissed Ryan's smiling face. "When's your flight?"

"Not sure. I just know I have to be on the bus in two hours."

"You've gotten very laid-back about your travel plans, buddy. That's not like you."

"Yeah, it is. When I'm on a team I just do what I'm told. It's like the military. Don't ask, 'cause they don't tell you much."

"Well, I've got to go now. Give me enough kisses to last until tomorrow."

Ryan gave her a dramatically lovesick look. "Not possible. No matter how many I give you, I'll still want more."

"Then stop talking and start kissing."

Jordan came home on Thursday singing a little song. "I'm not going home. I'm not going home. I get to stay and pla-ay."

Mia came barreling out of their room and threw her arms around Jordan before she'd stopped running. "I knew it! I knew it! You rule!"

"I shouldn't feel so good. I had to watch Rachel cleaning out her locker, and she looked like someone just died."

"Ooo...that's because you're my sweet, generous girl. You don't like to see someone else suffer."

"No, I really don't. But at this point it's her or me. And I don't want it to be me."

Bright and early the next morning, Mia set out to start looking for apartments. She'd used the Internet and the local free paper, and had a list of ten buildings to check out. Her list of "musts" was short, since her main goal was to be away from their roommates. But if they were going to move, it only made sense to live close to the Olympic Training Center. She focused her search to a three mile circle around the complex.

The first three buildings didn't merit getting out of the car. But the fourth one was decent enough. Mia parked and went looking for the building manager. It took her a few minutes, since the place was fairly large, but she eventually found the office and buzzed. An apartment had been turned into an office and when she entered she smiled at the woman behind a desk. "Hi. I'm looking for an apartment."

The woman didn't smile back. In fact, she didn't look up. "Student?"

"Uhm...no," Mia said, figuring that was the correct answer given the tone in the woman's voice.

"How many bedrooms?"

"Ahh...a one bedroom, I guess."

The woman idly looked through a large book, and said, "Interior, first floor, $450, and View, third floor, $650." She finally lifted her head and met Mia's eyes. "Interested?"

"Uhm…sure. Can I see the cheaper one?"

The woman chortled to herself. "Everybody wants the cheaper one." But she hauled herself to her feet and grabbed a huge key ring before leading Mia to the apartment. It was, as advertised, on the interior. But the way the building was designed meant there wasn't a hint of sun in the unit.

"Does it get sun in the afternoon?" Mia asked.

The woman pointed at the window. "That's East."

Mia waited patiently until it became clear that was going to be the entire statement. Luckily, she knew the sun set in the West, so an East facing apartment would be bright in the morning—which it now was. She went to the window in the living room and saw that the sun was hitting the upper floors, but couldn't reach far enough to get to the first floor.

"The unit on the third floor gets sun all day. It's on a corner, so it gets a cross-breeze, too."

Mia was tempted, but she couldn't ask Jordan to spend that kind of money on rent, and she couldn't bear to be in a place that was dark all day. "No thanks. That's a little too much for me to spend. I guess I'll keep looking."

"You're not gonna find a nicer place for $650," the woman said. "Two hundred bucks isn't that big of a deal. Cut back on something else."

"I'm living on $800 a month." The number seemed even smaller when she heard it come out of her mouth. "I'd have to cut out eating."

"Can't have everything," the woman said, laughing at her own joke.

The next place looked promising. Too promising to Mia's view. It was very close to a nice business district, there were small restaurants and bookstores all around, and a one dollar movie theatre just a block away. And the building looked better maintained than the last place. So she was sure she wouldn't be able to afford a decent place, but she rang the bell anyway.

A gruff-looking man answered. "Help ya?"

"Yeah. I'm looking for an apartment. An inexpensive apartment," she added.

He smiled. "That's what everyone's looking for. We just have different ideas of what inexpensive means."

Mia smiled back. "I'm looking for a one bedroom, and I'd love to have some light."

He nodded his head in the direction of the elevator. "I've got just what ya want. Just learned about it yesterday." She followed him to the elevator, and they went to the third floor. He opened the door, and she was struck with the smell of...she twitched her nose and decided it was either incense or a strange variety of pot. "These guys will be out in two weeks. It's not due for painting, but I think we're gonna have to re-carpet."

She looked down at the floor and saw stains that she couldn't begin to identify. "Yeah. I think that's a must."

"Young guys tear a place up faster than a pack of wild dogs," he said, with a surprising bit of amusement in his voice.

The unit was flooded with light, and it was big, much bigger than she would have guessed. The bedroom was jammed, but when she realized there were two futons and a full-sized bed she realized just how big it was. The kitchen was much bigger than their current one, although she wasn't sure it would ever be usable again, given the cans, bottles, take-out containers and pizza boxes that covered every surface, including the floor. "It could use a little cleaning," she said, unable to stop herself from making a face.

"And people wonder why they get roaches. One bunch like this and I've got the whole line complaining about roaches and mice." He shrugged. "What can I do? Clean everybody's apartment?"

"No, I guess not. You didn't tell me how much this was."

"These guys are paying $450," he said, smiling when Mia's eyes opened wide. "If I clean it up right and re-carpet I could easily get $550. But..." He paused, looking at her carefully. "You seem like a nice kid. How many people?" His eyes narrowed. "Be honest."

"Two." She held up a pair of fingers. "Two women. Clean women."

"Which means two boyfriends."

"No, no boyfriends. We're...partners. Life partners."

He looked a little surprised, but nodded agreeably. "You two party much?"

She laughed. "Not at all. We're in bed by nine almost every night."

"Okay. I assume you're bullshitting me, but you look clean. I'll let you have it for $450 for six months, then $500 for the rest of the lease."

"That seems like a good deal. Too good if you know what I mean. What's the catch?"

"No catch. I don't like to screw with people, so I'll tell you the truth. We've got a lot of Section 8 housing here."

"Section 8?"

"Welfare. A lot of single mothers with kids. So it can be noisy. We also have a lot of students. Our tenants turn over pretty quick. And we have to keep the security deposit on most of 'em to repair the damage. So this isn't the place for a person who's lookin' for quiet and considerate neighbors."

"But the apartment is nice," she said, looking around again. "And big."

"Yeah, it is. It's a good deal for the money."

"Can I bring my girlfriend over tomorrow to see it?"

He made a face and started to say no, but he hesitated for just a moment then said, "Early?"

"We're up by five thirty. How early do you want us here?"

Chapter Six

Jamie stood on the eighteenth green and tried to look interested, but Juliet was having the worst game Jamie had ever seen her have, and her mind had started to wander at about the sixth hole. They were going to lose the match because of Juliet's play, and Jamie just couldn't force herself to stay interested.

Juliet looked like she'd been eating sour grapes; clearly furious with herself. Normally Jamie would have had empathy for a teammate who was struggling. But once she'd realized that Juliet was really a jerk, she'd let her drop off her radar screen. Completely. They didn't speak or even acknowledge each other's presence.

After what seemed like twenty minutes, Juliet finally putted out, ending the match. Jamie shook hands with their opponents and started to walk toward the trailer where the tournament officials were collecting the scorecards. It took just a few moments to read off her scores and sign her card, and she was heading for the clubhouse when a young man caught her attention.

"Hey! Excuse me." He pointed toward a woman loaded down with cameras and lenses. "We're with the ASU newspaper. Could we get a picture of you?"

Jamie looked over her shoulder, then back at the duo. "Me?"

"Yeah. We wanted a photo of your foursome. Melissa Walker shot the lowest round today."

Melissa was a student at ASU, so it made sense they'd want her, but Jamie was puzzled. "Why the foursome? Why not just her?"

He frowned. "It won't take long. My editor likes to have a lot of shots to choose from."

"I don't mind," Jamie said. "Just wondering." Juliet walked out of the scorer's trailer and Jamie smirked at the thought of what the reporter would have to do to get her to stop.

The persistent staffer jogged in front of Juliet and gave her the same pitch he'd given Jamie. Juliet obviously thought he wanted a picture of just her, because she smiled and said, "Sure. Any time."

Oh. She's in her "I'm gonna be a big star on the LPGA tour" mode. No wonder she didn't kick him in the crotch.

The reporter led her over toward Jamie, and Juliet's smile faded instantly. The photographer rounded up the other two women and they stood there awkwardly for a moment as the photographer set up the shot.

"Was this your idea?" Juliet muttered just loud enough for Jamie to hear.

"Yeah. I'm so crazy about you that I'd do anything to get a picture of us together."

Melissa heard Jamie and she might have tried not to look shocked, but she didn't succeed.

The photographer said, "Can you all look like you just finished your round? Shake hands or something."

Jamie played along, reaching out to shake the hand of the golfer from Texas A&M. Much to Jamie's surprise, Juliet also did as she was asked.

A series of pictures was snapped, but the photographer wasn't finished with them. She said, "This time I want the Cal women to pose. Your baseball team's here this weekend and I want a couple of shots to show you were all here, too. Will you two…I don't know…kinda put an arm around each other's shoulder?"

Jamie saw the color drain from Juliet's face and knew she was gone. Without a word, Juliet walked away, not pausing when both the photographer and the reporter called out to her. Still smiling, albeit falsely, Jamie stood there, waiting to see if they wanted to take a different picture.

The photographer looked a little puzzled. "I guess I'll just take a couple of shots of Melissa. Thanks."

The reporter walked over to them and asked for their names. The woman from Texas identified herself and took off, leaving Jamie. "Uhm… did I do something wrong?" he asked.

"Why? Because of Juliet?"

"Is that your teammate's name? She really looked pissed."

"Oh, don't worry about it. She's…like that."

He looked completely befuddled. "Like what?"

Jamie wasn't sure why things had gotten to her, but her patience was shot. She looked at the man and asked, "Off the record?"

"Uhm...sure."

"She's an ass...hole."

His eyes grew wide, then he nodded. "She seemed like one."

"One of the biggest."

"That sucks. Can I have your names if they use that picture?"

"Just say 'unidentified Cal golfers.' That'll drive her nuts."

Jamie's cell phone rang on the way to dinner, showing it was Ryan. "Hey, good lookin'. What's the good news?"

"Got our asses handed to us again," Ryan said, sounding disgusted. "We can't buy a run. We're in such a slump, Jamers. Nothing Coach does seems to help."

"That's 'cause he hasn't put you in."

"Ha ha. Takes more than one person. The whole team's not able to hit the broad side of a barn. Pisses me off."

"Well, we came in thirteenth place today."

"In the PAC-10? How'd you do that?"

"You're too funny. There were fifteen teams. And two of them sucked more than we did."

"I'm sorry, babe. Are you upset?"

"No, not really. I did pretty well."

"Cool! How'd you play?"

"Got a seventy-three. I came in twenty-eighth."

"Wow. Twenty-eighth. Good for you."

"Led the team...not that that's much to crow about. We're in a slump, too. Juliet had an eighty-one. I thought she was gonna break her clubs."

"She's an asshole," Ryan said, having never changed her mind about Juliet's worth.

"Yeah. But only on her best day."

"You oughta hit her with a nine-iron."

"I'd get some satisfaction from that, but it's not really my style. But again, not a bad idea. When will you be here? Soon?"

"Nope. We just finished. The bus isn't gonna leave for an hour, and then we're gonna stop for dinner. We'll probably get to Tempe at ten or eleven. If you're tired, don't wait up for me."

"You know I will, but thanks for the offer. I hope your bus ride isn't too bad."

"It's only about two hours, so I'll be fine. Have a good evening, babe."

"Love you. See you later."

After walking into the dining room, Jamie saw her usual place waiting for her. Lauren and Samantha, the two shy freshmen, waved at her and she joined them. As always, she talked while the two younger women smiled at everything she said. Juliet was eating by herself, and one of the assistant coaches sat with her. Jamie figured he was trying to cheer her up, but she could have told him not to bother. When Juliet played badly, she was unmerciful with herself.

Juliet finished gulping down her food, and walked right by Jamie's table, not making eye contact with anyone. Lauren shot her a look, then cocked her head toward Jamie. "Does Juliet dislike us?"

"Dislike you? No, of course not."

"But she doesn't talk to us. She hardly says hello when we're paired with her. It doesn't seem like she's part of the team."

Lauren looked so earnest that Jamie's anger toward Juliet flared. It was tough, but she managed to say, "She's very self-involved. Golf means an awful lot to her, and she doesn't really think about anything else when she's playing." *Like being polite!*

It wasn't usually easy to get to Jamie. But once someone did, she was well-gotten. As soon as dinner was over, she got onto the elevator and went directly to Juliet's room. After knocking briskly, she heard an, "I'm busy."

That didn't help her mood. More determined than ever, Jamie knocked louder. Juliet didn't bother to answer, so Jamie kicked the door loud enough to have someone down the hall open his door and glare at her. "Forgot my key," she said, trying to smile. "Heavy sleeper." The man shook his head and went back inside, and Jamie said loudly, "I'm not leaving. So you can open it, or I can stand out here and scream at you."

The door flew open. "Fuck you," Juliet said lethargically, turning her back on Jamie and walking over to one of the beds to lie down.

Jamie walked in, sat down on the other bed, and stared at Juliet who gazed blankly at the television. "Why'd you act like such a jerk today?"

"I didn't do anything wrong. I just didn't want to stand there and have some idiot take my picture."

Letting her comment hang in the air for a moment, Jamie said, "Bullshit. You didn't leave until she asked you to pose with me."

"Don't flatter yourself. They didn't want our pictures, they were just trying to show some of the chumps Melissa beat."

"Mmm...Then why'd you let them take the first picture?"

Juliet turned toward the window, letting her eyes wander idly. "Why not? It only took a second."

Jamie sat there for a moment wondering what sequence of events helped turn Juliet into such a mess, but her anger was greater than her sympathy. "The reporter and the photographer were really shocked when you walked away. But I told 'em a little bit about you and they understood."

Whirling, Juliet's feet hit the ground. She was inches from Jamie's face. "What did you say?"

Jamie could see the veins in her throat pulsing, and she got a little thrill from being evil. "Not much. I told them you were an asshole to everyone and that it wasn't personal."

"*You what?*"

"I told them the truth. You're an asshole, and you only care about yourself."

Juliet stormed over to the window and kicked the wall. "God damn it! My image is critical!"

"Oh, please. You only care about your image if you think someone can help you. You are one messed-up chick. I don't know how you got so screwed up, but someone's convinced you of some strange shit."

"What in the fuck are you talking about?"

"Your so called 'image' means so much to you that you make yourself look like an idiot to keep people from guessing your deep, dark, awful secret."

Juliet's eyes were nearly ablaze with anger. It seemed that the angrier she got, the quieter her voice became. "What are you hinting at?"

"I'm not *hinting* at anything. I'm stating it. You're a l-e-s-b-i-a-n. A dyed-in-the-wool dyke."

Juliet looked like Jamie had accused her of being into bestiality. "I am not!"

"You admitted to it after you tried to kiss me. Don't tell me you forgot."

"I'm not a real lesbian," she said, grinding her teeth. "I just...I said I had...that I wouldn't ever..."

Jamie tried to inject some concern into her voice. "No one cares. No one's *interested* enough to care. If you'd just live your life, you could have a girlfriend and no one would give a fuck. But you're so homophobic that you're making yourself miserable and paranoid."

"Oh, right. Look who's talking! People in Antarctica know you're a lesbian!"

"My situation was a little unique, but I wouldn't change things even if I could. I'd rather have everyone in the world know than try to hide who I am. I *did* that before, and it nearly drove me crazy."

"I...am...not...a...lesbian!"

Jamie had to laugh. She couldn't keep the mocking tone from her voice; she wouldn't have chosen to, even if she'd been able. "Okay. You're not a lesbian. You're a nice, normal, straight girl who tried to get me into bed. That's what *all* the straight girls do." She stood up and got right in Juliet's face. "I've been there. I've done that. You can't bullshit me."

"I told you about some...feelings I had, and now you try to use what I said against me." Her cheeks flushed and it looked like she was going to cry, but she held it in. "Get out of my way."

Her voice was so cold it was startling. Jamie stepped back and watched Juliet nearly run out the door. Before the furious woman passed her, Jamie started to feel guilty. Juliet deserved to have her butt kicked, but it still sucked to be in such a total state of denial. Both room keys were lying on the dresser, so she picked one up and went downstairs, assuming she'd find Juliet somewhere on the first floor.

There were still a few players lingering over dinner, but none of them had seen Juliet. Jamie was just leaving when Samantha walked in.

"Hi," she said when she saw Jamie. "What's wrong with Juliet?"

"Uhm...why?"

"I saw her leave the hotel a couple of minutes ago. She looked really, really mad."

"Did you see where she went?"

"No, she just started walking, but I don't know where she could have gone. There's nothing around here except gas stations."

Jamie patted her shoulder. "Thanks. I'll go take a look. Maybe she just went out for some snacks."

"Maybe. But she looked like she was gonna punch somebody."

Jamie didn't mention that she was the intended target. She went outside and scanned the parking lot, but didn't see anyone. There were a couple of gas stations across the four lane highway, but she didn't think Juliet could get across the road without being run over. And there was nothing on their side of the highway for as far as Jamie could see. So she sat down on a bench at the corner of the building to wait her out. Checking her watch, she decided to give her an hour. If she wasn't back by then, Jamie would tell Scott and let him worry about her. She only cared so much.

Just under the hour limit, Juliet walked across the parking lot, heading for the front door. "Hey!" Jamie called out.

Juliet gave her a brief glance and kept going.

"I've got your room key. You left both of them." Jamie could see the heavy sigh leave Juliet's lungs. She approached rather tentatively and held out her hand. Jamie pulled the key from her pocket, but didn't offer it up. "I'm sorry for the things I said."

"Sure you are."

"I believe them," Jamie clarified, "but I know you don't wanna hear them. And it's none of my business how you live your life. If you wanna build a nuclear bomb-proof closet—go right ahead. I just know how lonely it is."

Surprising Jamie, Juliet flopped down next to her on the bench. "You don't know anything," she said, sounding tired.

"I really do. I know what it's like to have feelings that you're afraid of. I know what it's like to be terrified of disappointing people. I get that," she said earnestly.

"I have..." Juliet's mouth tightened. "I have a problem with alcohol. When I drink, I do crazy things. That's why I...did whatever I did to you. I don't remember it, so I can't really know what I was thinking, but I'm sure I was just out of my mind."

"Alcohol lowers inhibitions. It doesn't make you into a different person."

"What are you, a psychiatrist? You don't know me, and you don't know what was going on in my head. For all I know, you were hitting on me. Maybe you just came up with this story to...convince your girlfriend you didn't start it."

Jamie's anger had faded and she didn't have the desire to continue the argument. She laughed softly. "Yeah. That's probably it. I'm always trying to think of ways to cheat on Ryan."

"I don't know how you people behave. You might fool around with anyone who'll let you."

"Yeah, we do," Jamie said, smiling agreeably. "All of the stories you've heard are true. We're like wild dogs. My favorite trick is to go to someone's house and get so drunk she has to take me home. Then, when I get her into my room, I try to hump her. Oh, wait! That's what you did!"

"I didn't do that," she snarled "You must have been drunk if that's what you thought."

"Nope. I wasn't drunk. But even if I had been, I wouldn't have hit on you."

Stung, Juliet drew back, looking like Jamie had hit her.

"I didn't mean it that way. I just mean that I'm happy and fulfilled in my relationship. Even though you probably find it hard to believe, lesbians can be happy."

"Whatever," Juliet said, trying to look like she didn't care. "I only want to make sure that people don't associate me with you. I've got to make sure sponsors don't think I'm gay, because even though you don't have much contact with the real world, people still want to sign straight women to endorsement contracts."

Once again, Jamie couldn't stop herself from laughing. "And what kind of endorsement contracts do you think you're gonna get?"

"What's that supposed to mean?" Juliet snapped.

"You heard me. Who do you think's gonna sign you?"

"The usual—a resort, a ball company, a shoe company. Maybe a watch or a car manufacturer."

"And why would they do that?"

"Are you stupid? They sign people who they think present a good image and make people want to buy their products."

"I'm not stupid," Jamie said, feeling her temper flare again. "And you're no Anna Kournikova. You're a decent looking woman, but no one's gonna sign you to make you an X-rated screensaver."

"You're such a bitch!"

"And you're delusional. The only way for you to get endorsement contracts is to play well. Really, really well. You're not going to get signed because you're sizzling hot, so the only thing…truly the only thing that matters…is how well you play. So stop your ridiculous paranoia and focus on your game. My guess is that you screwed up today partly because you were paired with me."

"Don't flatter yourself."

"While I was sitting out here, I was thinking about your play and it dawned on me that you have a shitty round every time we're paired. I think you've got half of your brain on your game and half on making sure no one thinks of me when they see you."

"Do you blame me?" Juliet jumped to her feet. "You've been on the cover of every tabloid in the country! Everywhere we go, people follow you just to see the woman from TV. I don't wanna be associated with that!" She was so upset she was panting, and she stepped back just enough to lose her balance on the sidewalk. Her arms waved wildly while she tried to right herself.

Jamie jumped up and grabbed her flailing hand. But Juliet was too far gone and she started to fall. Jamie should have let go, but she tried to pull her back—only to have the heavier, taller woman pull her down on top of her. Seeing that she was going to fall, Jamie pushed off the sidewalk, trying not to land on Juliet. It seemed like everything was in slow motion. Jamie knew she was going to hit the ground, but her feet still tried to come down first. They didn't. She felt her right arm hit the ground, then her chin hit her chest. Her legs were on something soft, and she assumed that softness was Juliet, but she couldn't make herself move. Everything seemed very quiet, and her brain didn't accept that she'd fallen. It was very much like a movie that she wanted to rewind, but she didn't quite know how.

"Oh, shit!"

Juliet's voice sounded far away, and isolated—like it was the only sound besides the pounding of blood that was throbbing in Jamie's ears. Struggling to move, Juliet got hold of Jamie's hips and tried to push her, but as soon as her body moved, Jamie felt a jolt of pain in her arm that made her scream. "Don't! Don't touch me!"

"You're lying on me! Get off, God damn it."

"Don't push me!" Jamie cried. "I'm hurt!"

"I'm hurt too and you're making it worse." Ignoring Jamie's protests, Juliet again tried to slide out from under her hips.

"Stop!" Jamie cried. "God damn it. Stop!"

A security guard saw them and ran across the parking lot. "What's going on?"

"We fell," Juliet said. "And she can't get off me."

"Are you two drunk?"

"No! Help get her off me!"

"Don't you dare!" Jamie said just as firmly. "Just let me make sure I'm okay."

"You're okay? I think I broke my tailbone."

"Will you shut up for a second? I'm trying to make sure I can move my legs."

When the guard heard that, he ran for the lobby. In moments, both the manager and the guard ran back outside to where Jamie was assessing her injuries.

"Don't move!" the manager said. "I called an ambulance and they'll be here in just a minute. They'll know what to do."

"It's okay," Jamie said. "I think I'm all right." She tried to roll off Juliet, but the pain hit her again and she gasped. "Fuck."

A cab pulled up in front of the hotel and Ryan got out, spending a moment to pay the driver. She saw men standing over a couple of people on the ground and assumed it was a liquor-driven fight, but she took a quick look before going inside. In an instant she recognized Jamie, lying atop another woman. Dropping her bag, she ran over to the scene and fell to her knees. "Baby! What happened?"

"God, I'm glad to see you." Jamie met her eyes and started to cry.

Ryan was desperate for information, but a quick look at the men showed her that either they didn't know or weren't going to say what had happened. She looked down again and saw Juliet. Her stomach flipped at the thought of Jamie lying atop Juliet, but swallowed her anxiety and asked again, "What happened?"

Juliet answered. "I started to fall and Jamie tried to catch me. I went down and she fell on top of me. Now she won't get off."

"I can't," Jamie sobbed. "It hurts."

Ryan's deep background with injuries came to the fore. "Okay. Let's take this one step at a time. Tell me where the pain is."

"My right…everything. My arm and my chest. And my knee."

"How about your head? Any pain there?"

Juliet interrupted. "I'm in pain too, and it doesn't help to have her on me."

Ryan looked her right in the eye. "I don't care about you. Shut up and wait." She shifted her gaze to Jamie and her expression softened. "How's your head?"

"Okay, but it hurts. I feel like I hit my chin."

Jamie's head was on the sidewalk, resting on her right cheek, and Ryan reached down and touched her face. "You're not bleeding. Is your neck stiff?"

"No, I don't think so. I think I'm fine, honey, except for my arm. Can you help me up?"

"I'm not sure I should. I'm worried you might have injured your head or your neck." She looked up and asked, "Is an ambulance coming?"

The manager pointed in the distance, and Ryan looked up to see the vehicle screaming up the highway. "We'll let the paramedics do this, baby. They'll make sure you're fine."

"Damn it," Juliet cried. "Get her off me!'

Ryan leaned down once again and got so close their noses nearly touched. "I'd be happy to knock you out so you don't notice her. Wanna give it a try?"

"Oh, you're tough, real tough. Just try it."

"You're obviously fine," Ryan said, standing up and brushing off her knees as the ambulance pulled up. "If you were really hurt, you wouldn't have the strength to be such a jerk."

The ambulance squealed to a stop and the driver walked over to the women while the passenger opened the back door of their vehicle. "What happened?" the driver asked.

Juliet volunteered, "I started to fall backwards and she grabbed me. But I fell and she fell on top of me. Can you get her off?"

"In a moment, ma'am. Can you tell me how you're feeling?"

"My butt hurts and she's crushing me, but other than that I think I'm okay."

He got down on his knees beside Jamie. "Did you lose consciousness?"

"I'm not sure. Things felt really funny. I think I hit my chin. Maybe...I don't know."

He looked at the other paramedic and twitched his head towards the ambulance. "Backboard." The woman pulled out a stretcher with a backboard on top of it, then rolled it over to the pair and they began attaching Jamie to it.

It took them quite a while, but Ryan was thankful that they worked carefully, making sure to secure Jamie's head and neck before they allowed her to move. The driver checked everything one last time, then looked at his partner. "Ready?"

"Yeah." They both crouched and lifted the backboard, then set it on the edge of the stretcher and slowly turned it so Jamie lay on her back. Ryan was right there, holding her hand and smiling encouragingly.

Juliet started to get up but the hotel manager said, "Wait! They didn't tell you to get up."

"Oh, quit worrying about your insurance." She sat up before the paramedics could say a word. "Damn, my butt hurts!" She rolled over and got to her knees, then stood. Just as she got steady on her feet, Scott Godfrey, the golf coach, ran out.

"What happened? Ryan?" he said, looking at her quickly. "What are you doing here?"

"Softball. Jamie and Juliet got tangled up somehow and they fell. Juliet seems fine, but she's a pain in the ass. I mean, she *has* a pain in the ass. Jamie's banged up, but it doesn't look too serious."

"Says you," Jamie said, wincing.

"I just meant it doesn't seem life threatening or anything," Ryan rushed to explain.

"Where I'm from, this is serious." Jamie managed a half smile, but looked startled when they started to move her into the ambulance. "Don't leave!' she said, grabbing Ryan's hand.

"I won't." Ryan looked at the ambulance driver and he shrugged.

"You can ride up front in the passenger seat."

"I'll take Juliet to the hospital," Scott said.

"I don't need to go.'

"Yeah, you do. If there's any possibility that you're hurt, we can't take any chances," Scott said.

"I'm fine!"

"No arguments. We'll get a cab." He turned to the ambulance driver. "Where are you going?"

"St. Luke's."

"We'll see you there as soon as I can get a cab."

Ryan got in and buckled up, then turned around to check on Jamie while the driver pulled into traffic. "Are you all right?"

"Yeah, but I wish you were back here."

"Stop!" Ryan ordered, making the driver do a double-take.

"What?"

"Stop the ambulance. My partner wants me in the back with her."

"Honey, it's all right," Jamie said. "Really."

"You're sure?" Ryan's tone indicated that she'd figure out a way to get back there, even if she had to take hostages.

"Yeah, I'm sure."

The woman sitting beside Jamie started to take her blood pressure. "We'll be at the hospital in less than five minutes. Let's all calm down."

"I started it," Jamie said. "I know Ryan does whatever I ask of her. I shouldn't have said anything."

"Being injured is hard," the woman said. "Nobody really likes being back here." She checked the readout. "Your pressure's low. Do you know what your normal reading is?"

"I forget, but it's usually a little low."

The woman nodded and made a note, then carefully put pressure on various parts of Jamie's body and asked if she could feel them. Ryan was practically turned around in her seat, watching the woman like a hawk. They pulled up at the emergency room entrance before the paramedic could finish her cursory evaluation, and in just a few moments they were inside.

A nurse approached and spoke to the paramedics, their voices too quiet for Ryan to hear—even though she tried. They moved Jamie into a large room filled with other patients on gurneys, then they pulled some blue drapes around her spot and took their leave.

It took a few minutes for anyone to appear; Ryan was just about to go collar someone when a young woman came in.

"Hi. I'm Doctor Singh. I'm going to examine you."

"Hi," Jamie said. Too intent on watching the doctor, Ryan didn't speak.

"So, tell me what happened."

"I was talking with someone and she started to fall backwards. She was kinda on the edge of a sidewalk. I grabbed at her hand but she fell anyway. I remember trying to jump so I didn't land right on her. Then…I remember falling…and that's about it."

"Did you black out?"

"I'm not sure. But things got…fuzzy."

"Did you hit your head?"

"I don't think so, but I hit my chin…somewhere."

"Hmm…" The doctor looked at her face. "No marks."

"It's her arm that hurts," Ryan said, unable to stay quiet.

"Yeah, my arm." Jamie held it up slightly.

"Okay." The doctor looked into Jamie's eyes with a small penlight, and had her follow the pinpoint. After spending a few minutes making sure Jamie could focus, she asked her some simple questions which Jamie answered without problem. "Any stiffness in your neck?"

"Hard to tell," Jamie said, "but I don't think so."

The doctor reached out to test her grip. When Jamie explained that her left arm hurt too much to move it, the doctor positioned herself so Jamie could keep it where it was, then asked her to grip. Then she removed Jamie's shoes and had her press against her hands with her feet. She continued doing all sorts of small tests for a few minutes, then said, "Okay. You seem fine, but I'll order a CAT scan just to make sure." She smiled and was gone before Ryan could grab her by the lapels of her starched white coat.

"She didn't look at your arm!"

"I noticed," Jamie said, scowling. "It's throbbing like a bitch."

"I'll get somebody to come in and look at it," Ryan said, starting to take off.

"No, no, baby, stay here. They know what they're doing."

"Says you!"

A nurse came in and said, "Do you need help getting undressed?"

Jamie blinked. "Uhm…no, why?"

"I'd like you to put on a gown."

"We can do it," Ryan said, taking it from her. "When is somebody gonna look at what hurts her?"

The nurse looked puzzled. "What do you mean?"

"That doctor just looked at her head."

"This is the neurology E.R. The doctor said we could take your friend off the backboard. She just wants a CAT scan to be sure."

Ryan's look could have melted ice. "It's her arm that hurts."

"Oh, right. Well, after the CAT scan, we'll move her to orthopedics."

"How long will that take?"

"I'm not sure. We're busy tonight." She took out a scissors and cut the tape that was holding Jamie's head still. She gently pulled the remnants away from her face and loosened the straps that held her. "Are you sure you can undress without help?"

"Yeah, I'm certain," Ryan said.

The nurse left and Ryan spent some time organizing the straps and pieces of tape that were far too haphazard for her tastes. "You just lie still and I'll get you undressed."

"Kinda like home."

"Yeah. I think my motor's really gonna be runnin' when I get you into this lovely puke-green gown."

Jamie lay still and let Ryan work.

She started at her feet and had no problem until she got to the long-sleeved shirt. That took some maneuvering, but she finally got it off. Ryan carefully examined the arm, wincing at the three-inch long scrape on Jamie's elbow. "This looks really raw."

"Hurts."

"Can you sit up so I can get your bra off?"

"If you help me."

Ryan did, bracing Jamie's body so she didn't have to hold herself up. Quickly, she got her bra off and her gown on with remarkable economy. "Okay. If you want me to take the board away, you're gonna have to stand up."

"I'd better. It's like lying on a board," she said, giving Ryan a glimmer of a smile.

They worked together and soon Jamie was lying on the fairly comfortable gurney. Ryan adjusted it so she was reclining, but not supine. Then she started to examine her arm. Jamie smiled at the level of concentration and care that Ryan exhibited. Ryan had her grip her hand, and nodded when Jamie was able to make a pretty good fist. She was also able to move her arm, even though she said it was very stiff.

"Mmm...I think it's broken," Ryan said.

"Broken!"

"Yeah." She looked truly sorry for delivering the bad news.

"But...I can move it. Isn't that the test?"

"I could be wrong, but I've broken mine...a couple of times...and it looks broken to me. It's really starting to swell. That's a bad sign." She looked thoughtful for a moment. "I'll see if I can get you an ice bag."

She went out to the nurses' station and asked for one, but the new nurse on duty said a doctor would have to approve it. Ryan was going to point out the inherent safety of frozen water, but she knew it wouldn't do any good. She'd spent far too many hours in Emergency Rooms to think that a lecture would get them to change their policies.

So she went back to the little room and left the curtain open so they could see what the competition was. It didn't take long to realize that nearly every other patient had suffered a stroke or some other form of brain injury. The women looked at each other and Ryan went in search of a chair, knowing it wouldn't be their turn very soon.

After an hour Jamie said, "I should call my mom."

"Wanna wait until we know what's wrong?"

"Mmm…if our daughter was in the hospital, when would you want to know?"

Without comment, Ryan pulled Jamie's cell phone from the pile of her belongings and handed it to her. Jamie smiled and dialed. "Hi, Marta. It's Jamie. Is my mom home?" She blinked. "In New York? When did she leave?" Jamie looked less than happy. "Was this planned?" She paused to let Marta reply, then said, "No, it's nothing. I can call her on her cell phone. Thanks. G'night, Marta."

She snapped her phone closed. "She left for New York on Thursday night and is coming back on Sunday, just like us."

Ryan raised her eyebrows. "Maybe she just decided to see a play or something."

"Nope. Marta said she told her about the trip over a week ago. She intentionally didn't tell me."

"Uhm…maybe she forgot," Ryan said, knowing that wasn't the case.

"She didn't want me to know." Jamie's scowl grew deeper. "She must be with Giacomo."

"Really? Why New York?"

"Well, he's an art dealer. I'm sure he goes to New York fairly often."

"Huh. I wonder why she didn't say anything."

"Either she doesn't want me to know or she doesn't want me to give her a hard time or she's embarrassed."

Ryan nodded. "Those sound like the most logical reasons. I hope she's not embarrassed."

"I hope she is," Jamie grumbled. "Then she might stop this nonsense."

"Aren't you gonna call her?"

Obviously pouting, Jamie said, "No. If she can have secrets, so can I."

They took Jamie for the CAT scan at one o'clock in the morning, and shortly after she left, Scott found Ryan sitting in the empty cubicle. "Hi," he said. "How's Jamie?"

"I think her elbow's broken, but I'm the only one who's looked at it.

She's having a CAT scan now—for no good reason. How's Juliet?"

"Just a bruised tailbone, thankfully. I'll send her back to the hotel in a cab and stay with you."

"Nah. Don't do that, Scott. We'll probably be here all night. You should get some rest. I can take care of Jamie."

He gave her a rueful grin. "How can I sleep when one of my best players is in the hospital?"

"She'll be fine. I might be wrong, she might just have a bad bruise. Think happy thoughts and go to sleep."

He looked reluctant, but said, "I normally wouldn't leave, but you two are clearly capable of taking care of yourselves. I can't say that about the rest of the team."

"This is kinda like having a bunch of college-aged daughters, isn't it?"

"A little bit. Jamie's the best of the bunch," he said, smiling.

"You don't have to convince me." Ryan's eyes shifted and she stood up. "Here's my girl now."

Jamie looked remarkably pale and small in the large, green gown, but she was smiling and looked good, all things considered. "Hi," she said to Scott. "They just took a picture of my head. They're working their way down to my arm."

Scott took a look at the elbow and made a face. It was already turning blue and was at least twice its normal size. Jamie had her hand resting on her belly, and Ryan had rolled a sheet up to support the arm. "That looks like it hurts," he said.

"Actually, it doesn't hurt much if I don't move it."

"Well, keep a good thought. Maybe it's just a bruise."

"That's what I think," Jamie said. "I think it'd hurt more if it was broken."

Ryan smiled, knowing that had never been the case with her broken bones. But she didn't want to dash Jamie's hopes for a quick recovery.

"Ryan told me to head back to the hotel," Scott said. "Is that okay with you?"

"Yeah. You don't need to stay. At this rate, today's match'll be over before I get anyone to look at me."

"I'll have my cell phone on," Scott said. "Call me if you need anything. Do you need me to call your parents, Jamie?"

"No, I'm good. Thanks, Scott. Good luck today."

"I'll count it lucky if you're not badly hurt."

As he left, Ryan said, "You didn't ask how Juliet was."

"Huh. Guess I don't care."

"That's a good sign. Shows you're coming to your senses."

The neurologist came by at two and said there was no indication of a head injury. She ordered an ice pack for Jamie's arm, but by that time the swelling was about as bad as it was going to get. When the ice pack arrived, Ryan got it placed around Jamie's arm and held it in place. Her brow furrowed and she pulled the gown down from Jamie's neck.

"Big bruise on your chest. That must be where your chin hit." She touched it lightly and Jamie winced.

"That's the spot."

"Hey, if we're here long enough, we'll have you completely diagnosed."

"Super. Would you get me a soda? I need some caffeine if I'm gonna be up all night."

"You can sleep, honey. You're on a nice bed."

"If this is a nice bed, Juliet's a nice teammate."

They moved Jamie to the regular E.R. at three thirty, and a little before five she was finally taken for an x-ray. A very tired looking young man showed up at six, holding Jamie's x-ray in his hand. "Hi," he said, "Dr. Morgan. Looks like your elbow's broken."

"Damn," Jamie muttered. "Can I see the x-ray?"

"Yeah, sure. It's not too bad. It looks like a simple olecranon fracture."

"Displaced?" Ryan asked, looking over the doctor's shoulder.

He looked at Ryan quickly, clearly puzzled that she'd asked an intelligent question. "Not much." He pointed at a spot on the x-ray with his pen. "Maybe half an inch. It should heal fine." He examined Jamie for a few minutes, checking to make sure she didn't have any other injuries. "I'll splint you, and then you can make an appointment to see an orthopedist in a few days."

"Aren't *you* an orthopedist?" Ryan asked, narrowing her eyes.

"I'm a resident. But the orthopedist on duty looked at the x-ray with me. He agrees with the diagnosis."

Ryan didn't look happy, but she let him leave to get the material for the splint. "We'll get you to a good doctor when we get home."

"I'm sure we will," Jamie said, smiling at her partner. "What does displaced mean?"

"Oh. Just that the little piece that broke off isn't quite where it should be. That's not a big deal, though. I've had that one."

"You've had all of 'em."

The doctor came back and wet some long strips of gauze, then asked Jamie to straighten her arm. It took her a good minute to get it to comply.

"Would have been nice if I knew I should have had it straight," she grumbled. "It wasn't so swollen *yes*terday."

He didn't comment, just started to wrap her arm in something that looked almost like lamb's wool. Then he laid the gauze strips on Jamie's arm. They were fairly slimy, and she made a face when one of them touched her bare skin. "That high?" she asked, when he placed them from her shoulder to her wrist.

"We don't want your elbow or your wrist to move."

The gauze strips started to harden, and he fashioned it by making a few cuts with a sturdy scissors. Then he wrapped it in an elastic bandage, running it all the way up her arm.

"That looks lovely," she said grumpily.

"You'll be fine. Just keep it elevated whenever you can. The faster the swelling goes down, the faster you can have it casted."

"I have to get a cast?"

"Most likely. It depends on what the orthopedist thinks, of course. But he won't be able to do anything until the swelling goes down. You shouldn't even bother seeing someone for three days."

"Great. Just great."

He held her arm up and looked at it. "Looks good. Take care." Once again, he was gone before either woman could say a word.

"Do they learn that in medical school?"

"They must," Ryan said. "It's hard to imagine that all of these people figured out how to disappear on their own."

"It's time for us to disappear. I want some drugs and a bed."

"Damn! We didn't get a prescription."

"I'll call my doctor. She'll prescribe something over the phone."

"No, we should get something here. We won't be home until this afternoon. We need to make you comfortable until then."

"Don't be ridiculous. You've got games to play."

Clearly shocked, Ryan stared at her. "We're going home as soon as we can. We've got to get you to a real doctor and get you propped up in your own bed."

"Fine. I'll go home if you insist, but you're staying here." Jamie's eyes were slightly narrowed, a sure sign of her determination.

Ryan sat down, tired and frustrated. Rubbing her face with both hands she mumbled, "Why are you being so difficult?"

"I'm not. You have an obligation. You can't desert your team because I broke a bone. This isn't life and death."

Leaning forward, Ryan rested her forehead on the gurney. "Don't fight me, Jamie. I'm tired and sick of sitting here all night. My teammates will understand."

"You can talk all you want, but I'll be very disappointed in you if you leave. It's just not necessary."

Ryan sighed. "Fine." She got up, feeling like the weight of the world was on her shoulders. "I'll go see if someone will write you a prescription."

A few minutes later Ryan came back with the doctor who'd spoken to them when Jamie was moved to the regular E.R. "Everything looks good," she said. "Both the orthopedist and the neurologist have said you can leave."

"Can you write me a prescription for the pain?"

"Sure. What do you like?"

"Uhm…I don't know," Jamie said. "I've never been injured before."

The doctor gave her a funny look and Ryan said, "How about some Vicodin?"

"Okay. I'll give you enough to last until you see an orthopedist. Is that all right?"

"Uhm…sure. That's fine."

The doctor took her pad out and wrote a prescription for ten pills. Ryan thought that was a little miserly, but she knew that Jamie could get more if she needed it. After the doctor left, they had an interesting few minutes trying to get Jamie's shirt on. Luckily, Ryan wore a T-shirt under her warm-up jacket, so she took off the T-shirt and put it on Jamie, then zipped up her warm-up.

"Why don't you put my shirt on?" Jamie asked, eyes twinkling.

"I'd look like the Incredible Hulk."

"I know. I think it'd look cool."

"Maybe at home," Ryan said, smiling tiredly. She gently helped Jamie to her feet and they went outside to get into a waiting cab.

After a stop at a pharmacy, they walked into the hotel where they saw a few of the players gathering in the lobby to head off to the course. Jamie spent a few minutes telling her teammates what had happened while Ryan called Coach Roberts on her cell phone. She was just hanging up when Jamie took her hand.

"Take me to bed."

"Happy to. I called my coach and told him the whole story. He said I could be late if I had to."

"You don't need to be. You've got plenty of time to prop me up in bed and get there on time."

"Fine."

Ryan was a little miffed, but Jamie was clearly determined to take care of herself. As soon as they got in the room, she started to tear at the prescription bag with her teeth.

"Can I lend you a hand, sport?" Ryan chuckled at her partner's attempts to work with one hand. She opened the container and shook out a pill, then filled a glass with water. "Here you go."

Jamie downed the pill and sat on the bed. "I feel like I've been beaten."

"I'll bet," Ryan said, ruffling her hair. "This is a new thing for you, you're not used to the drill."

"I racked up a few skinned knees and a bloody nose or two. That's it."

Ryan sat down next to her. "How are you feeling? Pretty bad?"

"No, not too awful. It doesn't hurt as much as I thought a broken bone would."

"Sometimes they hurt more as the day goes on, but it'll feel better by tomorrow. And you can decide for yourself, but if it were me, I'd take ibuprofen and add a Vicodin only if you really need it."

"Really?"

"That's just what I do. Vicodin works on opioid receptors in your brain and spine and gut. It's the gut part I don't like."

"It works on my intestines?"

"Yeah. You have opioid receptors in your gastrointestinal tract. Every time I take codeine or hydrocodone, I have trouble."

"What kinda trouble?"

"It slows everything down, waaaaay down," Ryan said. "Your intestinal transit goes on strike." She made a face. "I really hate that."

"Eww! I can't imagine anyone likes it."

"Good point. So I take ibuprofen and only add a Vike if I'm really uncomfortable."

"A Vike, huh? Pretty familiar with these babies, aren't you, O'Flaherty?"

"Much more than I wish I was." She went over to the dresser, knowing that Jamie would have her clothing neatly arranged. "Ready for bed?" Out came a pair of pajamas, just where she knew they'd be. Her partner's consistency had its rewards.

"I'll just wear your shirt. I like it."

"Okay." Ryan put the pajamas away and helped Jamie out of the rest of her clothes. When she had her settled, with pillows elevating her arm, Ryan sat down on the other bed and called room service. "I can't believe I'm doing this, but I don't wanna leave you." When someone answered, she said, "Hi. I'd like some breakfast. Some kind of omelet…Yeah, that's fine. And a bagel and an order of toast. No, that's all." She hung up and smiled at Jamie.

"Carb loading?"

"I got the toast for you. The Vike can be hard on your tummy."

"You take good care of me, babe. I'm damned glad you were here."

"Me too." Ryan sat next to her and stroked her hair. "I really don't wanna leave you. Are you sure you won't reconsider?"

"Nope. I'll sleep the day away. If I feel horrible, I'll let you take me home tonight, but I don't think I will."

"Uhm…wanna call your mom now?"

"Yeah, I guess I should. I just don't want her to know I know where she is, since she obviously didn't want me to."

"It's up to you," Ryan said. "I'm gonna take a quick shower. Want the TV on?"

"Sure. See if there are any cartoons."

"It's Saturday morning, and this is America. Of course there are cartoons."

Chapter Seven

On Saturday morning at eight a.m., the potential landlord opened the door to his office and nodded to Mia. "Well, you don't lie."

"I do," Mia said, "but I wouldn't lie to you."

Jordan watched her lover interact with the man, smiling at Mia's effortless, probably unconscious flirting. Harvey was clearly charmed by her, but Jordan didn't mind. It was impossible to resist Mia's allure.

Harvey took them upstairs and banged on the door before he inserted his key. "I'm sure they're still asleep. Just ignore the bodies."

As predicted, a man was sleeping on the sofa, and his boxers didn't cover all of his equipment. The trio marched right past him, trying to look at the unit without commenting on the fact that a nearly naked man was either asleep or unconscious in the living room. The bedroom contained only two people, a man and a woman. Both were naked, but a rumpled sheet covered most of them. Mia and Jordan tried to visualize the bones of the apartment, but it was difficult to filter out the people and the mess.

"You don't wanna see the bathroom," Harvey said quietly. "We're gonna have to put new tile on the floor and probably a new toilet."

"That's fine," both women said quickly.

They looked briefly at the kitchen, but the grimy appliances were hard to see beneath the haphazard clutter of pizza boxes and take-out cartons. "I don't think they've ever turned the oven on, and they never buy food, so this room won't be too hard to clean."

"We don't have to clean it, do we?" Mia asked, chuckling.

"Not unless ya want to. Give you a month free if ya do."

Mia was seriously considering the offer when Jordan said, "Can we go outside? The smell's awful."

Harvey nodded and they went out into the hall.

"What *is* that smell?" Jordan asked.

"I think it's pot, isn't it?" Harvey looked to her for confirmation.

"Never smoked it."

"I have," Mia volunteered, making Harvey laugh. "But that didn't smell like anything I've ever smoked."

Jordan's nose wrinkled up in distaste. "Smells like a dirty locker room."

"It'll be fine once we replace the carpet," Harvey said. "I've had places that smelled a lot worse than that."

"Lucky you," Jordan said, her nose still twitching.

They went back to the office. "So? Ya want it?"

"Could we step outside for a minute?" Mia asked.

"Sure. Just so you know, I've got someone coming at nine, and whoever puts the application down first wins."

"No problem. We just need a few minutes." She took Jordan's hand and led her out of the building. "What do you think?"

"Uhm…well, it was big. And bright, but I don't know if it'll ever smell right."

"Oh, we could fix that. Do you think we can afford it?"

"Yeah, yeah, I guess so. It's a hundred and twenty more than we pay now, but we could cut back on—"

"Entertainment?" Mia supplied, smiling up at Jordan. "If I didn't go to Russia with you, that'd probably pay the difference for six months, wouldn't it?"

Jordan's stomach did a somersault. She looked down for just a moment, then met Mia's eyes. "Yeah, I suppose it would. I budgeted fifteen hundred for the trip."

"There are other ways to pay the difference. I was just…you know… thinking of ways to economize."

"You don't have to go to Russia with me. I'll be fine."

"It was about two minutes ago that you said you didn't think I *should* go. Damn it, Jordy, I don't know what you want!"

She couldn't look Mia in the eye, putting her energies into inspecting the outside of the building. "You shouldn't come. I can tell you don't want to."

"Argh! Please don't think for me. We need to decide this together. I swear I'm just thinking out loud while we work this through. We haven't decided anything."

"Okay, okay. We'll talk about it later."

"So?" Mia put her arms around Jordan's waist. "Do you wanna do it?"

Jordan looked down at her. "Yeah, but we should wait until we get home. I don't like an audience."

Mia bumped her with her hip. "Come on. What do you say?"

"If you wanna move, this looks like a good deal. I'd rather not pay more than we're paying now, but your happiness is worth a lot more to me than a hundred and twenty a month."

"A hundred and seventy after six months."

"Huh?"

"It's four fifty for six months, and five hundred for the next six." She put her hands on Jordan's hips and pushed her back and forth. "But it's still a good deal."

Jesus. How many more secrets did Mia have stored up? "A year's lease? We're only on a six-month now. I just assumed—"

"We're on a six-month lease? I didn't know that. I assumed every place would make you sign for a year."

"No, we didn't have to." She tried to work out the numbers in her head. "Uhm...I guess we can swing it, but it's gonna be empty most of the second half of the lease."

"Oh, fuck. I didn't think about that. I forgot you said that most people take time off after the Games."

"Yeah, but we can come back here to fulfill the lease."

"No, no, I don't want to. I wanna go home as soon as we can. Is it up to you where you go?"

"Who else?"

"I just thought that they might make some of you stay here. To keep the team going."

"Don't you get this? There *is* no team after the Games."

Mia blinked, then shook her head. "I'm always feeling like there's a big calendar somewhere, and you know what's on it. For some reason, you tell me only what I have to know." Her eyes narrowed and Jordan backed up a step.

"I'm sure I've told you this stuff. I'm sure of it."

"Well I'm sure you haven't."

"It doesn't matter now. We can move if you want to. This place is fine."

Mia slapped herself in the forehead. "But if we move, we'll have to pay rent here and in Berkeley?"

"Yeah. Unless…no, you wouldn't wanna do that."

"What? What don't I want now?"

"Well, we could stay with my mom. We wouldn't have to pay rent there."

"Good guess," Mia snapped. "We're not living with any of our parents." She closed her eyes tightly and let out a breath. "Stay here. I'm gonna go tell Harvey I've got my head up my ass and don't even know how long I can sign a lease for."

"Mia—" But Mia wasn't there to hear her speak. She was marching for Harvey's office, and Jordan was fairly sure that steam was coming out of her ears.

It was a lovely spring day, and Mia didn't want to spend it in their apartment. After she exited the office, she went to the car, with Jordan silently trailing along behind her. They got into the car and Jordan wisely kept her mouth shut while Mia drove. It soon became clear they were heading up into the hills, and after about forty-five minutes Mia pulled off the road and entered a state park.

They both got out and stretched, and Mia walked over to Jordan and took her hand. She didn't speak, just led her to a lovely vista where they could see for miles. Jordan was just the tiniest bit afraid that Mia might push her over the railing, and she breathed a sigh of relief when Mia wrapped an arm around her waist.

Mia was looking out at the view and staring at the scenery when she began to speak in a quiet voice. "We're not telling each other some important things. You freaked out when I didn't tell you how unhappy I was, but you're hiding stuff from me that affects all of our plans."

"I don't mean to—"

Mia spoke over her. "Maybe you don't like to think about the future. Hell, I don't know why you didn't tell me about making more cuts on the team, but you didn't. Now, you obviously don't want to talk about this, but we're going to. We're not leaving here until I know everything that you know about this team, and your schedule, and your plans." She looked into Jordan's eyes. "I'll leave you here if I have to, but you're not getting into that car until you spill it."

Jordan leaned on the railing and shook her head. "I'm so sorry I screwed up. I thought you knew this stuff, I really did."

"How could I?" Mia tried to keep the rancor from her voice. "Am I at your team meetings?"

"No, no, you're not. I just get focused and assume everyone knows what I know. It's so important…and I think about it so much…" She shivered and a few tears rolled down her cheeks. "I'm worried *all* the time. I've never felt this kinda pressure, and I guess I don't talk about it just so I have some breathing room."

"Jordy!" Mia's arms were around her in moments. "I didn't know you felt so much pressure. What's going on?"

Jordan shook her head and swiped angrily at her tears. "I shouldn't be letting it get to me. It's hard to play well when I'm tense."

"But why are you worried?"

Giving her a look that questioned her sanity, Jordan said, "I'm being judged every day, every single day. Do you know what it's like to have your every move watched? Knowing that one bad day can kill something you've dreamed of for fifteen years?" Her voice was high, her cheeks flushed with emotion.

"No, I don't. I have no idea of how that feels. But…" She tried to make sure she was framing her statement properly. "Why would one bad day hurt you?"

"Because they're gonna make another cut next week, and then two more in July. I have to make sure that there are three people consistently worse than me for the next three months."

"Okay." Mia put her hands on Jordan's chest. "Tell me—in order—what's going on for the next few months."

Jordan blew out a breath and her eyebrows popped up as she considered the question. "Well…there's another cut next week. Then we'll have sixteen players in camp."

"How many do you take to Sydney?"

"Eleven," Jordan said, swallowing hard. "And we've got three people in Europe who'll probably make the team, so…we've really got nineteen. That's a lot of people to cut."

"You won't be one of them," Mia said, enunciating each word. "Now, stick to the topic. What happens next?"

"We go to Russia. They're gonna expect a lot out of us on that trip. They wanna make sure we don't get spooked playing two great teams in a place where we're uncomfortable and not used to the food and jet lagged. Then we're home for two weeks to get ready for a short trip to Dallas and a few spots in Colorado. It's like that the rest of the summer—a couple of weeks of travel and a couple of weeks at home."

"Until September?"

"No. August. We leave for Asia about three weeks before the Games start. To give us time to adjust for jet lag and stuff like that."

"And after the Games?"

"We're done." Jordan held up her hands. "As soon as the Games are over, the 2000 team is history."

"What do people do then?"

"Everybody takes a few months off, then some people go to Europe to play. One of our best players is in Europe now. She won't join the team for another month."

"Would you do that?" Mia was terrified of the answer.

"Mmm…if we weren't together, I would; it'd be good for me to play in Europe. But I couldn't ask you to do that. So I'll probably come back to Colorado in six months or so. I can play in NORCECA matches and work with the coaches. It's always a good idea to be here so they don't forget about you."

"Then the whole thing starts again?"

"Kinda. But if you're returning, they try to give you more feedback about how you're doing, at least that's what Jill tells me. She says they let you know if you're not gonna make it."

"So we'd be here for…three…three and a half years?"

"Yeah." Jordan nodded solemnly. "Seems like a long time, huh?"

"No, no," Mia put her arm around Jordan and gave her a quick hug. "I'd just have to get a job and make a home for us."

"But then you wouldn't travel with me."

Mia looked at her, meeting her eyes for a few seconds. "I couldn't, honey. I'd have to have a job and make some friends; put down some roots. Three years is a long time."

"You'd do that for me?"

Jordan was looking at her with such a tender, grateful expression that Mia pulled her down and kissed her. "Jordan, when am I gonna convince you that I'd do anything for you? Living in Colorado is no big deal. It's beautiful here! And if we had our own place and some money to spend and some friends—we'd be set. It's only hard now because we're so unsettled."

"But you were gonna go to law school."

"I still can. God knows I'm not in a rush to be back in school. When you're finished with volleyball I'll go to law school, and you can get your masters in architecture. We can be study buddies again."

"But how will we pay for all of that tuition? And living expenses? I can't imagine how—"

Mia placed her hand over her lover's mouth, grinning at her outraged expression. "My parents will pay my tuition. And you've got savings for yours, right?"

"Yeah, but we still have to live."

"Don't think about that now." She slipped her arms around Jordan's waist. "You worry too much. Some of that 'in the moment' stuff that Ryan's so good at has to rub off on you."

"I'm no Ryan," Jordan said, smiling.

"You're my perfect Jordan, and I couldn't be happier with you." She kissed her tenderly, letting her fingers slide through her hair.

"Not mad at me?"

"Nope. I feel better, and I think I get why you don't like talking about it too much. Now that I know what's going on you can forget about the schedule and focus on being your best every day."

"Thanks." Jordan nuzzled her face into Mia's hair. "I'm sorry I screwed up and didn't tell you a lot of stuff."

"It's okay." Mia scratched Jordan's back roughly, making her squirm. "I think we're both trying to make sure the other one's happy. We just have to keep talking rather than guessing."

"I'll try. Now...what are we gonna do about Russia? I've got the money, I've made the reservation, do you wanna go or not?"

"Let's go home." Mia had Jordan's hand in both of hers and she was tugging her toward the car.

Jordan laughed at the playful look on Mia's face. "What's up with you?"

"I wanna go home and play with you."

"Okay, I'll play. Got anything in mind?"

Mia scrunched her face up, seemingly in thought. "I wanna play...hide the tongue."

"Hide the tongue, huh?" Jordan slipped an arm around Mia's waist and guided her to the car. "Sounds like fun. How do we play?"

"We get all naked and then try to hide our tongues on, or...in each other."

"Hmm...and what's the point of this game?"

"Don't be so competitive! Isn't just playing enough?"

"In this case...yes." She reached for Mia and let out an "oof" when Mia jumped into her arms and wrapped her legs around her waist. "So I have to carry you, huh?"

"Yep. And I get to play the game first."

"Sounds like a deal." Jordan was panting by the time they reached the car. "Hey, you didn't answer my question. Are you gonna go with me?"

"I'm not sure. Ask me again when I can concentrate. All I can think about now is where to hide my tongue."

"Please don't let me distract you. You've set a good goal."

Ryan quietly entered their hotel room at five thirty that afternoon, pleased to see that Jamie was sound asleep. She needed a shower, but she didn't want to wake her partner so she slipped off her warm-ups and lay down on the spare bed. She was so tired that she'd barely gotten settled before she was sound asleep.

A few hours later a soft voice said, "Honey, can you help me get up?"

Immediately, Ryan was on her feet. "Yeah. Just hold on a sec."

Jamie smiled at her, taking in her wild hair and glassy eyes. "I just need to pee. No rush."

Ryan went to the right side of the bed so she could use Jamie's good arm to help her. "No problem. I inherited my father's fire-bell response time."

"You really did," Jamie reflected. "Especially if I'm not feeling well. It's like you don't sleep soundly if you're worried about me."

"That's the truth. I can't concentrate on softball when I'm worried about you, either. Luckily, I didn't play and we didn't score, so I didn't have much to worry about."

"Ooo...another bad day?"

"I think we've scored three runs in the last two weeks. I'd say that's a bad streak." She slid her arm under Jamie's back and helped her sit, then ran to the other side of the bed and supported her while she stood. "Okay?"

"Not bad. I'm a little light-headed."

"That could be from the Vike, or from being up all night."

"I think I should have something to eat. Are you hungry?"

"Always." She guided her into the bathroom and held her good hand while Jamie sat. "Call me when you're done."

"I will if I need you."

"Need me," Ryan ordered. "If you're light-headed, I don't want to take any chances. I'll order from room service. Anything sound good?"

"A club sandwich, grilled cheese, something simple."

"Okay. I'm right here when you're finished."

"Got it. Now go get us some food. And some ibuprofen."

Ryan smiled. "I've got some in my bag. I never leave home without it."

By eleven o'clock, Jamie began to nod off. Ryan was sitting in a chair, with her feet up on the bed, and she got up and perched on the edge of the bed. "Hey," she whispered.

Jamie's eyes blinked open foggily. "Yeah?"

"Time to sleep."

An adorable grin split her lips. "Beat ya to it."

Ryan kissed her cheek and ran her hand through Jamie's mussed hair. "Yeah, you did. Want to use the bathroom?"

"I'd better. Help me?"

"Any time, princess." Ryan helped her put toothpaste on her brush and left her alone. When Jamie emerged, Ryan had put all of their pillows on the bed, some at the head, some at the side.

"What's up with the pillows?"

"I'm trying to make you more comfortable. I think you'll sleep better on your side."

Jamie sat down, then scooted across the bed to lie down. She let Ryan move her heavy arm and place it on the stacked pillows. "Hmm…I think you're on to something."

"Feel good?"

"Yeah, it's much better. It keeps surprising me how heavy this splint is. Is the cast gonna be even heavier?"

"You probably won't have to wear one. I don't think that resident knew what he was talking about. It's important to keep your elbow straight, not keep your hand immobile."

"Mmm…I'm not sure that's my preference. This isn't very cool looking." She cast a look at the offending appendage. "I want one people can sign."

Ryan gently tickled Jamie's bare hip. "If you get one I'll put little hearts on it so everyone knows you're my girl."

"You know, I'm a little surprised by something."

"What?"

"I'm surprised that…you're not more…mmm…freaked out about this. I was worried that you'd…I don't know…"

Ryan bent over and kissed Jamie's cheek, then nuzzled against her for a moment. "You lucked out," she whispered.

"Hmm? What do you mean?"

"I feel bad for you, babe. I know it hurts, and I know it's a pain not to be able to do things for yourself and all that. But it's not like having… uhm…an illness or something unpredictable. I'm not worried about you getting worse, and that makes a big difference."

"Huh." Jamie smiled at her. "I'm kinda worried about me. This whole thing has freaked me out a little bit."

Ryan stroked her back, leaning close to look in her eyes. "Tell me why you're freaked."

"I've never…ever had a serious injury. No stitches, no breaks, no operations…nothing. It's weird to think of how easy it is to hurt yourself. I mean, I could have hit my head or broken more than just my elbow."

"I know," Ryan said, kissing her gently. "I know, baby." She stayed right where she was and looked into her lover's eyes. "We all walk around with this belief that we're fine and safe, and nothing bad will happen to us. Most of the time, that's absolutely true. But when something like this happens…that invincible feeling goes away for a while. Not very long, though." She tapped Jamie's nose. "In a few days, you'll feel just like normal."

"Kinda like earthquakes?"

Ryan spent a moment trying to figure out the analogy. Then she smiled and nodded. "Yeah. We could have one at any second, but you don't think about 'em until you have one. Then you jump every time a truck rolls by."

"I'm jumpy," Jamie admitted. "I keep waking up feeling like I'm falling."

"That makes perfect sense. This is traumatic, baby. I'm sure I was the same way the first few times I broke something. I was too young to remember, but I'm sure I was."

"You always were a prodigy." Jamie giggled and snuggled up against her pillows. "Now get into bed."

"I'm gonna sleep in the other one. I want you to have room to move around, and I don't want you too close to the edge."

"Aw, don't do that."

"This is just a full-sized bed. You'll sleep better if you're not crowded." She kissed Jamie gently, spending a few minutes basking in the softness of her lips. "We'll sleep together when we get home." She gave her partner one more kiss and a tickle to remove the pout that had formed. "Promise."

"If I don't break anything else. Or we don't have a bad earthquake. Or our plane doesn't crash. Or—"

Ryan put a hand over her mouth. "You're doing really well at this 'I'm not invincible' thing." She kissed her again. "Sleep now. I'm right here if you need anything."

"You're all I need," Jamie said, yawning.

"Close those sweet eyes and get some sleep."

"G'night, sweetheart. Don't break anything while I'm not watching."

"Good night, Jamie," Ryan said, rolling her eyes. "Put that active little mind on hold. You can worry about things tomorrow."

"Oh, I will. I've got a whole list."

Jamie and Ryan repeated Saturday's argument on Sunday, with Jamie insisting that Ryan play. "I feel like I'm abandoning you," Ryan said, standing with her hands on her hips while looking around the room for something to do to make her partner more comfortable.

"I'm throwing you out. That's a big difference." Jamie smiled and said, "Come give me a kiss."

Ryan did, then inspected her set-up again. "I've done all I can," she said, looking unhappy.

"I can get up by myself and I'm not light-headed anymore. Now go play!"

"I will…but I won't like it," Ryan said, scowling dramatically.

Jordan got up at her usual time on Sunday and went to work out in the weight room. She usually did that on Saturday, but since she and Mia had been looking at the apartment, she'd skipped the usual team session. Now Mia was stuck at home with the roommates, so she decided to stay in bed rather than have to interact with them.

Around nine she finally got up and took a shower. To avoid eating another bowl of granola, she took Jordan's bike and rode to the Barnes and Noble to treat herself to breakfast. She was savoring her latte when she decided to give Jamie a call. Jamie answered promptly, and Mia smiled so brightly at just hearing her voice that she nearly lit up her corner of Starbucks. "Girlfriend!"

"Oh! My best friend! How are you, sweetie?"

"I'm all right. Is this a good time to talk?"

"Yeah. I'm stuck in a hotel room in Tempe, Arizona."

"Do you have a late tee off?"

"No. I broke my elbow on Friday night."

"*What?*"

"I broke my elbow. I was outside talking to that idiot Juliet and she got upset about something I said. She stood up too fast and started to fall over. Instinctively…and I do mean instinctively…I tried to stop her and she pulled me over. I landed on my elbow and broke it. I should have let her fall. Check that. I should have pushed her."

"God damn! It must hurt like hell."

"It's not too bad. Luckily, Ryan was here for a softball game and she went to the hospital with me. I've got a splint from my shoulder to my wrist, and when we get home I'll probably have to get a real cast."

"That is a major, major drag. I guess you're done for the year, huh?"

"Yep. I hate to say it, but I don't mind. It's been so hard to leave Ryan. I never would have joined the team if I'd known she was gonna have such a tough time."

"How's she doing?"

"Have I talked to you since she had her meltdown?"

"Uhm…which one?" Mia asked, hating to phrase it that way.

"Good point. She has had a few. This particular meltdown was in LA when I went down to be with her for her UCLA and Washington games."

"I talked to you that night. Remember? You were going out to some fancy restaurant."

"Right, right. Well, this was after we talked. We decided to stay in the hotel and tear up the furniture instead."

"You're fucking kidding me!" Several patrons turned to look at Mia and she slumped down in her chair and spoke quietly. "You *are* kidding, aren't you?"

"'Fraid not. Ryan got angry at something I said and she took a chair and bashed it until it broke into sticks. It sucked, but the end result was good. I finally got her to admit to some stuff she's been bottling up, and she seems better since it happened. She's a long way from being herself, but at least I feel like she's making some progress."

"This has been awful for you both, hasn't it."

"Yeah. It's been really, really bad. And I think it pisses her off that I haven't had as hard a time getting over the whole carjack thing. I think it makes her feel like she's...I don't know...more broken, I guess."

"That must be hard for her. It's obvious she likes to be strong and in control."

"That's obvious?" Jamie laughed. "Yeah, that's my little lunatic. She has this self-image of being really strong, but the truth is that she's as fragile as a beautiful piece of china."

"Is that...a problem for you? I mean...you didn't know that about her, did you?"

"Yeah, I had a pretty good idea. None of this has been a surprise... except that I didn't realize how having something bad happen would bring up all of her other insecurities. And she's got a lot of them. She's had more bad shit happen to her than most people have in their whole lives. I'm just thankful that she really wants to work through this and get back to normal. A lot of people would spiral into a depression they'd never get out of, but my girl's a trooper."

"So's mine. That makes me wanna hit her with a brick sometimes." Mia laughed and Jamie joined in, both women acknowledging how their partners' determination could have its drawbacks.

"Why's she in trouble now?"

"Oh, the usual. She does the same stuff Ryan does. Athletes should come with a warning label."

"As tall as they are, there wouldn't be enough room for all of the cautions."

"Nailed it. She's worried about getting cut, so she doesn't talk. There's about a billion things I don't know...even though they affect me! I almost left her on a mountain on Saturday. I told her if she didn't tell me her whole schedule, she'd have to walk home. And I meant it."

"Damn, you're harsh."

"You'd have done the same thing if Ryan had held out on you like Jordy has been."

"Is everything okay now?"

"Umm…kinda. It's been a scene, James. My mom dropped in…without warning…last week, and I'm still getting over that little encounter."

"Your mom! How did that go?"

"You don't have time. I'll tell you all about it when you're at home. Your cell phone'll die by the time I finish whining."

"Oh, you don't whine. You're as tough as Jordan, you just look sweet and malleable."

"Can't argue with that. You know my evil truths. But I'm trying to decide how malleable to be. I'd been planning on going to Russia with the team next week, but I'm having major second thoughts."

"Really? Why? Russia's really cool."

"You went with your parents, right?"

"Uh-huh. And Elizabeth."

"Right. Old Betty the Hawk. I swear that woman knew you were gonna burp before you ate a bowl of chili."

"Oh, she wasn't that bad. And we had fun in Russia. We read a bunch of books before we went so we'd get something out of the trip. Elizabeth hated to *just* have fun; I had to learn something too."

"How much fun would you have had if your parents and Elizabeth had stayed at the hotel and sent you out on your own?"

"Not much, I guess. Why? Is that what Jordan's gonna do?"

"Basically. She can't sightsee with me, she can't eat meals with me, she can't stay up late or go to a club. All we'll get to do is sleep together."

"Hmm…you could go on some tours, maybe hire a guide?"

"I don't have the money for that. Jordy's budgeted fifteen hundred for me, and that includes airfare and hotel. I'll probably have about three hundred bucks to spend."

"Mia, don't be hard-headed about this. Going to Russia is too cool, even just to walk around Red Square. Let me hire a guide for you."

Mia let out a sigh. "You know, I'd take you up on that if I really wanted to go. But it dawned on me recently that I've been looking at this as travel, while Jordan looks at it as work. And it's really important. It's like her having to give a huge presentation, and I sit in the back and yell, 'Hey, let's go out to lunch. Hurry up!'"

"Well, maybe you should just stay home. You don't wanna make things harder for her."

"Right. That's the whole problem. I can't decide what's best for her. I know she wants me to go but that's because she's got this fantasy that I'm gonna go out and have fun while she's playing. I'll have had this great day while she's at work, then we'll sleep together. She really feels like she's giving me something, James. She's giving me a trip to Russia. But I don't wanna go to Russia alone! I'd rather take that fifteen hundred bucks and use it to rent us an apartment, but I just found out we're gonna be back in Berkeley for at least six months after the Games."

"That's fantastic!"

"Yeah, it is, but I was only vaguely aware we were gonna be able to go home. I just found us a nice apartment, but it's stupid to pay rent when we're in Berkeley. I tell you, she's about to drive me mad!"

"You can't make her tell you what she really wants, huh?"

"Yeah, I can. She claims that all she wants is for me to be happy. But I can't be happy if I don't know what would make *her* happy." She blew out a breath. "I've gotta tell you, men are easier."

Jamie didn't laugh and there was a tense silence that she finally broke. "You're not…changing your—"

"Fuck no! Jordy's it for me. She can drive me stark raving mad and I'd still wanna be with her. She's mine. Until I kill her."

"That's my buddy. You had me worried there for a second."

"No worries, James. I love her. I love her more than I thought I could love anyone. She's kind and thoughtful and sensitive and smart and funny and—"

"Good in bed."

"That goes without saying. A girl's gotta have some standards."

"God, I miss you. Life just isn't the same without you. Things would be so much easier if you were home."

"Really?"

"Yes, really. Ryan would be much happier if you were back. She does much better when there's someone home, and with you skipping class all the time I could rely on you to be there." She laughed briefly, then added, "She obsesses about things when she's alone."

"Damn, James, don't make me feel worse."

"I don't mean to, really. It wouldn't fix Ryan by any means. It's just that we both miss you and we both love it when you're here. You and Jordan are part of our family—and neither of us likes to have our family members too far away."

“I miss you too, honey. As much as I love Jordan, it’s really hard for me to be away. I’d come home in a minute if I thought she didn’t need me here.”

“I know you would. You’re a good partner.”

“Trying my best. It’s tougher than it looks.”

“Amen! Good thing we’ve both got women who more than make up for the difficulties.”

“Damn straight. Or gay. Or bisexual. Whatever.”

“I’ve gotta go to the bathroom, and it takes me ten minutes to get there. I never knew how much that second arm helped.”

“You poor lamb. I wish I could be there with you.”

“Ryan’ll be back in a couple of hours—watching me like a hawk.”

“Okay, James. I’ll call you later in the week. Tell Ryan I love her.”

“I will. And you do the same with Jordan.”

“Will do. Talk to you soon. Thanks for listening.”

“Part of the job. Best friends are always on call. Love you.”

“Love you too. Bye.”

Mia hung up and took a bite of the apple fritter that she’d purchased. The sweetness of the pastry didn’t come close to the feeling she had after talking to Jamie. Being loved was the sweetest feeling a body could experience.

Many hours later, Ryan returned, belying her oath not to enjoy her day. “We won!” she said, grinning from ear to ear. “We finally scored a few runs and threw a shutout. It was the best game we’ve had in weeks.”

Jamie knew her lover too well not to guess an added element. “You played, didn’t you, Buffy?”

“Yeah,” she said, smiling brightly.

“Some of those runs were because of you, weren’t they?”

“Mmm…kinda,” she admitted, looking smug.

“Home run?’

“Nope. But I drove in a run with a double, and I scored on a bloop single to left field.”

“From second base?”

“No. I stole third.”

She was grinning like a kid and Jamie wanted to smother her with kisses, but she wasn’t mobile enough to scramble around on the bed like she usually did. “Come sit by me so I can congratulate you.”

Ryan sat down gingerly and Jamie wrapped her arm around her neck pulling her down for a few dozen kisses. "You're such a stud," she whispered.

"I'm a dirty stud. I didn't take a shower yet. I had a good-looking girl waiting for me in my hotel room."

"Go on," Jamie said, waving. "Then you can help me get cleaned up. I wanna go downstairs and eat with the team."

"Oh, boy! Dinner in the motel with a dozen mute golfers. You sure do know how to show a girl a good time."

The dinner wasn't particularly exciting, but Jamie wanted to reassure her young teammates that she was fine. Both Lauren and Samantha were filled with concern, and all of the other women gathered around to check on Jamie's injury. Everyone except Juliet, who skipped dinner.

Ryan entertained Lauren and Samantha with stories from their night in the E.R., and Jamie sat quietly, loving to watch her partner charm people. Ryan cut all of Jamie's food and kept trying to feed her, much to the delight of the younger women. After dinner, Scott walked them back to their room, where he stated the obvious. "This is a heck of a way to end your season."

"Yeah. I'm not very happy about it."

"How's Juliet?" Ryan asked. "Can she play?"

"She seems fine. It hurts her to sit down, but it hasn't affected her play. She had the low round for the tournament today. Shot a sixty-eight."

"Fascinating," Jamie said. "What time does the bus leave?"

He looked at his watch. "About a half hour. Are you going with us?"

"Yeah. Ryan's team's on the same flight. We're one big happy Cal family tonight."

"Great. I'll see you two in a few."

As they watched him walk down the hall, Jamie said, "I wonder why Juliet's making herself scarce. Lauren said she didn't eat with the team yesterday either."

"I hope her ass is so sore she can't sit down to take a leak, much less eat."

Chapter Eight

It was late when they got home, so Jamie begged off calling her mother. Ryan was a little puzzled by her reticence, but she didn't want to press the issue.

Jamie was only taking a Vicodin to sleep, but Ryan was still making her drink a glass of Metamucil—just to be sure. Jamie swallowed the drink, making a face. Then she took Ryan by the hand and they went up to bed. "Can I finally sleep with you?"

"I promised you, didn't I? I just didn't want to squish you."

"I'll let you know if you're squishing me." Jamie looked at the bed. "We might have to switch sides."

"Oh, right. You need to sleep on your right. We'll figure out a way to keep you comfortable."

"I won't be comfortable without you. That's the important thing."

The next morning, Ryan gasped when she slid back the curtain after her shower and saw Jamie perched on the edge of the sink, staring at her balefully. Ryan grabbed a towel and wiped her face so she could see her partner. "What's wrong?"

"I want a shower."

"Ooo...I'll give you a shower tonight. I just don't have time now, babe. You kept me in bed too long."

"I didn't know you had to be at school so early."

Ryan was quickly drying herself, doing a rather haphazard job. "I'll give you a quick sponge-bath. Just give me a sec."

Jamie grumbled to herself, but she adjusted the temperature of the water in the sink taps and handed Ryan a washcloth. "Just wash my right armpit, I can do the rest."

"Poor punkin...can't wash her own armpit." Ryan did a thorough job, then asked, "Are you sure you don't want me to do the rest?"

"No," Jamie sniffed. "It's undignified. I'll do it myself."

Ryan took her cue and scampered out of the bathroom, figuring it was better to go to school with her hair wet than hang around and annoy her ill-tempered lover.

Since she didn't have to go to golf practice, Jamie got to observe her favorite morning ritual...drinking coffee and reading The *New York Times* while listening to National Public Radio. Getting to meet the day in a leisurely way improved her mood substantially, and she was feeling good when she finally called her mother.

"Hey, Mom," she said when Catherine answered.

"Hello, sweetheart. How did your weekend go?"

"Mostly bad. A teammate and I were talking outside the hotel and she fell backwards. I tried to stop her, but she pulled me over. I landed on my elbow and broke it."

"Oh, my God!"

Jamie knew it was childish, but it made her feel good to have her mother over-react to her injury. "It's not a bad break. Ryan's had the same one and she said it's not a big deal."

"Why aren't you in the hospital?" Catherine's voice was so high-pitched it almost squeaked.

"It's really not that bad. I just need to see a doctor in the next couple of days."

"We'll go today. I'll find the best doctor in the Bay Area and get you an appointment. I'll call you right back."

Jamie stared at the phone in her hand, amazed that her mother was taking such control. Amazed and very pleased.

It took almost an hour, but Catherine delivered on her promise. "It looks like the best orthopedist is in the city. The best I could do is five o'clock tonight."

"You found a doctor who has office hours at five o'clock?"

"I'm not sure if he has office hours," Catherine said, chuckling softly, "but he's seeing you then. I'll come pick you up at around three thirty."

"Oh, Mom, that's so far out of your way. I can drive myself." She paused and said, "If I drive Ryan's car. I'm not gonna be driving mine until my arm's better."

"You're not driving anything. Now don't argue with me. We'll leave early and have a little snack first if we have to kill time."

"All right. Mother knows best. See you then." She hung up, feeling much better than when she'd started out. Her good mood lasted until she tried to get dressed and realized she couldn't put on her bra or her running shoes.

Around noon, Mia was lying on the floor of the living room, beginning to do research for a paper for one of her humanities classes when the doorbell rang. She was hesitant to open the door ever since Jordan had told her about the rapist in the neighborhood, so she went to the door and looked out the peephole. The person was standing far too close for her to make out who it was. "Would you back up please?" she yelled.

"Fed Ex," the man said, backing up so she could see his uniform.

She opened the door and gave him a puzzled look. "For who?"

He looked at the envelope. "Mia Christopher. Is that you?"

"Yeah. What did I get?"

Smiling, he said, "I don't send 'em, I just deliver 'em." He handed her the electronic register for her signature and looked at her as she signed. "Maybe it's a big check."

"You never know. Thanks." She took the envelope and went back inside. After ripping it open she fished inside, pulling out a couple of pieces of paper. The larger one was a piece of stationery, and her heart skipped a beat when she saw the elegant JDSE engraved on the outside of the folded note.

> Mia,
>
> I'm taking advantage of the momentary weakness you showed when we talked on the phone. I know it's hard for you to accept money from me, but I offer it because I'm your friend, and it's important to me that you're able to take advantage of some of the opportunities that are presented by Jordan's being on the Olympic team.
>
> You'll be in your fifties by the time you can afford to travel to Russia again, so if you go, I really want you to see as much as possible. Russia might not even be on your list of places that you'd like to see, but it's a remarkably lovely country, and I know you'd love it if you saw it.

So—if you go, I've arranged for you to have a tour guide. She's the same woman we used when we went, and I know you'd like her. Send her an e-mail if you decide to go and she'll work up an itinerary for you. She'll bill me, and I'll tip her. If you do this, you'll make me happy, and I *know* you want me to be happy, right?

In case you don't go, I'm enclosing a plane ticket back home. I don't want you sitting in that apartment by yourself, and Ryan and I miss you too much to even think of you having time available and not visiting us. So, again, it's all about me. If you don't use the plane ticket now, you can use it later. It doesn't have any restrictions, and it's good for a year.

We love you sweetie, and we want you to make the most of this experience. If I had my choice, you'd come home while Jordan's gone, but I want you to do what makes you and Jordan happy. That's my goal.

Love and kisses,

Jamie

Mia reached back into the envelope and found the airline ticket. She pressed it to her mouth and gave it a kiss, wishing she could do the same to her best friend.

Catherine knocked on the door at three fifteen, and Jamie dashed down the stairs to greet her. To her surprise, her mother almost broke into tears when she took in her massive splint.

"Oh, honey, that looks so awful." She reached out and touched Jamie's arm with a most gentle caress, then looked at her face. "Are you in a lot of pain?"

"No, not anymore. This happened on Friday night. It hurt a lot on Saturday, but it's better now." She could see her mother swallow, then Catherine smiled and walked into the house.

After putting her purse down, she said, "May I get a drink of water?"

"Sure. I'll get it for you."

"Nonsense. I know my way around your house very well." She went into the kitchen and got out a glass, then spent a minute letting the water run. After she took a few sips she put the glass in the sink. Jamie could see her shoulders rise and fall, then her mother turned to her. "Why didn't you call me sooner?"

She looked so hurt; Jamie felt the guilt hit her like a blow. Not having a valid excuse, she said, "I didn't want to worry you. I was in Arizona and there was nothing you could do."

Catherine approached and cupped her daughter's cheek. "It's important to me to know that you'll call me when bad things happen to you. I don't need to be protected. I need to be involved."

Her lower lip quivered and Jamie started to cry. "I'm s…sorry."

Catherine wrapped her arms around her and ran a hand through her hair. "It's all right, Jamie. It's all right."

"It was stupid of me not to call you. I…really feel bad."

"It's all right. Just promise you'll call if something major happens to you…good or bad." She pulled back and kissed Jamie's wet cheek. "I hope it's all good."

"I'm just…I'm a little emotional," Jamie said. "I'm depressed about not being able to play anymore, and I keep finding things I can't do. It frustrates me."

In seconds, Catherine had a solution. "I'll send Marta to stay with you until you're better."

"No, no," Jamie said, laughing a little. "It's nothing big. Ryan can take care of me."

"Is there anything I can do?"

"Yeah. Would you mind tying my shoes? I could only put on these slip-ons, and they give me a blister when I don't wear stockings."

"Oh, my! I suppose you can't tie your shoes. We'll stop and get you some tennis shoes that you don't have to tie."

"I could use a nice bra that you don't have to hook. All I had were sports bras and there was no way I could shimmy into one of those with one arm."

"Are you sure you don't want Marta to come? She could dress you and make you a nice breakfast."

"Tempting, but I'm sure Ryan will be happy to dress me. It just didn't dawn on me this morning before she left."

"You keep a list, honey. If there's anything you need, I'll make sure you have it."

They were almost a half hour early for the appointment. Catherine guided her Mercedes into an underground parking lot and had started to walk away when the parking attendant handed her a receipt. "Oh! I left something in the trunk. Would you press the button on the dashboard by your knee?"

The young man did as she asked, and Jamie watched her mother struggle to remove a large basket from the car. "What in the heck is that?"

"Oh." Catherine cast a quick glance at the bundle. "I called a friend of mine whose husband is a well-known orthopedic surgeon. He recommended the fellow we're seeing this afternoon."

"Uh-huh." Jamie put her sunglasses back on when they reached the sidewalk. "Why the basket?"

"He told me that Doctor Maynard is a wine collector, so I brought him a few bottles for going out of his way for us." Jamie tried to look in the basket, but her mother moved it to her other hand. "No peeking. You know too much about wine."

Jamie made a face and laughed. "That bad, huh?"

"I hate to drop names and call in favors. When I do it, the least I can do is offer a little gift in return."

"I saw an Haut Brion in there," Jamie said, wiggling her eyebrows. "If that's over ten years old…that's not a little gift."

"None of your business," Catherine said, shaking her head and looking oddly adolescent. "This is my deal."

"Let's get some coffee," Jamie said, twitching her head towards a Starbucks. "I'll buy."

When they were settled with their drinks, Jamie said, "You seem very chipper today." Then she remembered what might have cheered her mother up over the weekend and she regretted having said anything.

"I'm just happy to be with you."

Now that she'd raised the issue, Jamie didn't want to let it go. "Did you have a good weekend?"

"Yes. It was…good." Catherine smiled, offering nothing more.

"Did you do anything special?"

Catherine took a sip of her coffee. "Hot," she said, frowning at the cup. She was clearly ready to let the question drop, but Jamie was gazing at her, waiting for an answer. "Special?" she asked, looking thoughtful. "No, not really. I went out to dinner, looked at some art."

"At a museum?"

"No. I did a gallery stroll. Oh!" she said, her eyes sparkling with excitement. "I bought a new piece! I've been watching a young artist named Vincent Ricchiardi for a few years, and I've wanted to acquire something of his. I saw this painting and knew it was the one."

"Cool. I want to see it."

"It'll take a little while. It has to be shipped…" Catherine looked like she wanted to pull her sentence right back into her mouth. "I mean… delivered."

"Right," Jamie said, smiling tightly. "Well, let me know when you've had it hung." She actually felt sorry for her mother, who looked a little ill. "Where will you put it?"

"In the city. My new library, I think."

"Cool. How's that going?"

"Oh, we haven't gotten very far. Building permits and all that sort of thing make a project take forever. But I'm not in a hurry. I'm not really looking forward to having my new house in disarray, so even though I want a library—I'm not excited about the process."

"You love to redecorate. Admit it."

"Yes, I do. But I'm enjoying my new home, and I think there will be too much mess to live there while the work is going on."

"Mmm…you could always stay at Dad's place in the city. The doorman would probably wave you right in. 'Good afternoon, Mrs. Evans.' He'd probably act like he'd just seen you yesterday."

Checking her watch, Catherine seemed to gather herself before she said, "I've made a decision about my name."

"Your name?"

"My surname. I've decided to go back to my maiden name."

"You're kidding!"

"No, I'm not kidding. I hadn't thought much about it, but I need a new start. And one way to reclaim my identity is to go back to the name I was born with."

"I'm…stunned." Jamie struggled not to cry. "I…never considered that you'd do that." She looked down for a moment, then asked, "Do you hate Daddy that much?"

Catherine covered her hand. "No, of course I don't. Your father and I are getting along very well, honey. Better than we did when we were married, to be honest. This has nothing to do with him."

"How can it not?"

"I'm doing this for me, Jamie. I've been thinking a lot about my great-grandmother."

"Dunlop?"

"No. Smith. I think I've told you that her maiden name was Smith. I'm getting a late start, but she's the person in my family I'd most like to emulate. I want to reclaim her name and remind myself that if she could make a difference in her world…I should have a very easy time making a difference in mine."

Jamie blinked and looked at her mother for a moment. "Is that…is that something you've been thinking about for a while?"

"Yes," Catherine said decisively. "Very much. It's time to stop licking my wounds and start living my life."

Jamie's face lit up. "That's so good to hear, Mom. Really."

"I've been down for months. It's time to get out of my funk."

"God, if both you and Ryan start feeling better, I won't know what to do."

"Just relax and enjoy it," Catherine said. "Live in the moment."

"My God, you're sounding more like Ryan every day."

"Now *that* would be a wonderful goal."

Ryan was already home when Jamie and Catherine arrived bearing dinner. "Ooo…what do we have?" She played like she was only interested in the food, trying to get the bag from Catherine's hand, but neither woman was fooled.

"Get your nose out of the food, O'Flaherty," Jamie said. "Act like a human in front of my mother."

"Oh! Your mother's here!" She reached out and hugged Catherine, then took a look at Jamie's arm. "Not much difference there, sport."

"There's a big difference." Jamie followed her mother into the house. "Dr. Maynard took off that wrapping under the splint. It's in two pieces and he said I can take it off to shower. I can't wait," she said dramatically.

"Can we have dinner first? I'm faint with the hunger."

"I suppose. Oh, before I forget, you have to dress me in the morning. I can't hook my bra."

"But we got her some nice tennis shoes that have Velcro on them," Catherine said.

"The shopping twins are at it again. You know, I'm a little surprised the doc left you with the splint. I thought you'd have something fancy."

"I will by tomorrow," Jamie said, grinning. "He had a guy take an impression of my arm and he's gonna make a custom, high-tech splint for me. I don't think I'll be able to get it autographed, though."

"That's the Evans women I know and love. A jury-rigged splint will never do."

Lying in bed, Ryan watched her lover brush her teeth. Jamie was clearly thinking about something that was troubling her, and Ryan was struggling not to giggle. The more Jamie concentrated, the younger she looked, and Ryan got great pleasure from watching her partner regress in age as she continued to ponder. She knew Jamie would feel a little self-conscious if she told her, and she didn't want to ruin her own pleasure, so she kept it to herself and hoped that Jamie never caught her grinning.

The electric toothbrush had cycled through its timer three times, and Ryan was about to remind Jamie that the enamel on her teeth wasn't very thick when slightly slitted green eyes shifted and settled on her.

"My mother basically lied to me today."

That brought Ryan up short. "Basically?"

"Yeah." Jamie went into the bath and finished up, then came out and sat on the edge of the bed. "She tried to make me think she was in town this weekend, just doing a gallery stroll and having dinner with friends. But I got on the internet and saw that the big spring art show was in New York this past weekend. So, she told me the truth…she did look at art…but she didn't go on a gallery stroll and she was with Giacomo. I just know it."

Ryan scooted over so she could scratch Jamie's back. "Maybe she's just…uhm…working things out. Give her some time, babe."

Jamie shot an annoyed look over her shoulder. "Working what out?"

"How she feels." Ryan tossed her leg over Jamie, who let out a sigh and leaned against her. "She's probably not sure how she wants things to go. Maybe she's unsure if she wants to keep seeing him."

"She was sure before," Jamie said acidly. "She made a big deal about how she deserved better." Turning to look at Ryan she demanded, "What happened? Why doesn't she deserve better now?"

"I don't know, honey." Ryan hugged her, holding on and resting her head on Jamie's shoulder. "But you're gonna have to be patient with her. You can't make her talk about it before she's ready."

"But she's lying to me."

Jamie sounded like a wounded child, and Ryan hugged her again, hoping to take away some of the pain. "I'm sure she didn't feel good about doing that. Why don't you give her a little space? Don't ask her specific questions about what she's doing and who she's seeing for a while."

"Great. All of the progress we've made…phfft!"

"That's not true. It's just not. She's working something out, baby. She's lying because she's uncomfortable. When she's ready, she'll talk to you about it."

"She's making changes, Ryan, and she doesn't want me to be part of them. She doesn't even want me to know about them."

"What else?"

Jamie turned again and regarded her lover with a stern look. "She's changing her name."

"Huh? To what?"

"Back to her maiden name…kinda."

"Kinda? How do you kinda change your name?"

"She's changing it to Smith, but not for her father's family. Her great-grandmother was a Smith, and that's who she'd like to…I don't know…imitate, or model her life after, or something."

"Weird. Do you know this woman?"

"I don't think *she* knew her."

"What's up with that? What was special about her?"

"I don't know a lot about her, but she was a doctor. She was in one of the first graduating classes at Stanford."

"Wow. It must have been hard to be a woman in college back then, much less medical school." Ryan thought for a minute. "I think you told me about her a while ago. Maybe when we rode our bikes around Stanford that time."

Jamie smiled brightly. "I might have. I remember giving you the grand tour."

"I kinda had the impression you knew a lot about your mom's family."

Shaking her head, Jamie said, "No, not a lot. I mean, this woman was my great-great-grandmother. Like I said, I don't think my mother ever met her. I just know a few things about her."

"Well, she must have been cool for your mom to want to take her name."

Jamie tilted her head and spent a moment chewing on her lip. "It doesn't feel like she's honoring her; it feels like she's trying to erase my father from her life. It feels really sucky to have her change her name. It's…distancing."

Ryan started to rub Jamie's back, keeping her touch light and gentle. "Makes you feel…?"

"We're not in the same family any more. She's a Smith and I'm an Evans."

"Ooo…does that feel really bad?"

Jamie looked at her again and Ryan recognized the look as one that meant "You'd better not only agree with me, you'd better know why I'm upset." "I understand," Ryan said, even though she didn't see why this was so upsetting. "Does it make you feel like she's giving up on your family?"

"Yes! Haven't you been listening?"

"Yes, of course I have." Since her verbal support wasn't going over very well, Ryan chose physical support, hugging her tight and rocking her a bit. "I'm really sorry this is hard for you, babe. Really sorry."

"I'll get over it. I know I'm being a baby about the whole thing. It's just that she sprang this on me when I was still steamed over her lying to me. It was too much."

"It would have been for me too," Ryan said, seeing how the incidents could build on one another. "But it's kinda cool that she wants to make a new start. That must mean she's feeling less down."

Jamie gazed at her for a moment, then smiled briefly. "Yeah, I think she is. Probably because of Giacomo," she added, making the name sound like a curse.

"Well, whatever it is, I know you want her to feel better. If this is a step in that direction, I know you'll support her."

"Of course I will." Jamie stood up and stretched. "That's not in question." She got into bed and pushed against Ryan to get her to move to her rightful space. "But I don't have to like it."

Chapter Nine

It took a day to make the decision, and a night to sleep on it, but once Mia had made up her mind, it was easy. Even though it was just five-thirty in the morning and Jordan was barely awake, she scooted over to her, closing the gap that had grown between them during the night. Mia swept a handful of Jordan's golden hair away from her shoulder and pressed her lips to it, then slowly moved to her lover's ear, where she kissed it tenderly.

"I'm not going to Russia." Her hand was resting on Jordan's waist, and she felt the quick intake of breath as Jordan woke and registered the import of her words.

Turning and swiping at the hair tickling her eyes, Jordan moved around, likely trying to see Mia's face, but she was facing the wall and didn't have enough room to turn over. Blindly, she reached out and patted Mia's hip, their signal for more space. Mia moved just enough for Jordan to be able to roll over and face her. "Are you sure?" Her expression gave nothing away. They could have been talking about what to have for breakfast.

"Yeah, I am."

Cool, blue eyes darted from Mia's eyes to her lips, searching. "Wanna tell me why?"

"Sure." Mia put her hand on the small of her lover's back and pulled her closer. "Jamie helped me think it through. Even though she might not know it." One blonde eyebrow lifted. "I talked to her on Sunday when you were working out and told her that I didn't really want to be alone when you were playing, and I didn't have the money to go on a good tour."

"We have enough—"

"Shh," Mia said, gently pressing her finger to Jordan's lips. "I know you would have paid for me to go anywhere I wanted to, honey, but I feel guilty about using our money just to keep myself entertained." Jordan started to speak again, but Mia stroked her cheek and said, "Let me finish, babe."

"Do *I* ever get to talk?"

"Yes." Mia smiled at her. "You can say anything you want."

"I wanna know how Jamie helped you."

Kissing her quickly, Mia said, "That's what I was getting to. I know what's on that little mind." She tapped Jordan's forehead, then kissed it. "Jamie arranged for me to use the tour guide she and her family used when they went to Russia when we were in high school. My generous buddy was going to pay for anything I wanted to do and even tip the woman."

"Damn!" Jordan blinked, then her smile faltered. "You were gonna let her pay for you?"

"Yeah, I was. I know that's not my usual reaction, but if I thought you needed me to go, I was going to let her pay for me to really experience Russia. She convinced me that it's a huge waste to go on a trip like that and not get something out of it."

Jordan's forehead was wrinkled in confusion. "But…that made you decide not to go."

"Yeah, it did. Once I didn't have the excuse of not having the money to see stuff, I had to look at what made the most sense, and I decided that we'd both be better off if I didn't go this time."

"Okay." Jordan still looked puzzled, but she was nodding thoughtfully.

"I also spent some time actually talking to our roommates on Saturday. Don't look so shocked."

"I am! Have you ever talked to any of 'em when I'm not around?"

"No, but that's partly because they're not here if you're not here. Anyway, I talked to Jill and Toni about what it's like to play in a tournament like that. Toni said that her husband went to a few international tournaments with her when she was on her first team, but she asked him to stop."

"How come?"

"She said that she was so focused that she completely ignored him and his feelings were hurt the whole time. That was the kicker. You're going to be anxious about playing in your first big tournament and being around the other players will be better for you than hanging out with me."

Scowling, Jordan said, "I'd always rather be with you."

"I know that, but I think they have a good point. You can bond with your teammates better if you're not rushing to get back to me. And I can go to Berkeley for a week and see my parents and check on my classes and hang with J and R. We can each fill ourselves up with the things that mean a lot to us."

Jordan wasn't smiling, but her face was relaxed and she appeared untroubled. "That sounds good. It's not what I really want, but I think you're right."

"We'll use this trip as an experiment. You'll see how you do traveling without me, and I'll see how I do being at home. Then we'll have some experience to build on for the next trip."

"All right. I'll gut it up and try to be a big girl." She smiled, but there was more than a touch of sadness showing in her eyes.

Mia reached up and slid her thumb across Jordan's forehead. "If you need me to go with you, I will. You don't have to ask twice."

"No, no, Jill and Toni know what they're talking about. I'm glad you asked them. I should have thought of that."

Squeezing Jordan's bicep, Mia said, "You're the brawn. I'm the brains in this operation."

Jordan wrapped Mia in a bear hug and rolled onto her back. Nose to nose, she said, "We're in big, big trouble."

Tuesday morning, Ryan nodded at Ellen when she opened the door to her office. Just as Ellen started to give her a questioning look, the outside door opened and Barb rushed in, breathing heavily. "Slow bus," she said.

"You're right on time," Ellen said. They went in and got settled, then Ellen said, "Since Barb has to catch her breath, why don't you start, Ryan? Anything to report?"

"Yeah." Ryan fidgeted a little. "This is gonna sound strange, but I had a good weekend, partially because my lover broke her arm." She glanced quickly at Barb and Ellen, but neither reacted very strongly.

"Go on," Ellen said. "I'm sure there's more."

Ryan laughed. "Yeah, there's more. I hated to see her get hurt, of course. She's never had a major injury before and it's really hard for her. I think she's having a hard time realizing her body's not as impervious as she thought it was."

Ellen nodded, looking interested but saying nothing.

"But even though I'm upset *for* her, I'm not upset *about* her." She looked at both women. "Know what I mean?"

"I think I do, but tell us how that's different for you," Ellen said.

"I'm not...worried or anxious about her. I was afraid that I'd be freaked out if she broke a nail, but this shows it's not that way at all." She was smiling brightly, her energy level so high that she was practically hovering above the sofa. "I'm not worried about everything, just the thought of someone hurting her."

"That must feel really good," Barb said. "But I bet you can't tell her," she added, chuckling.

Ryan laughed, feeling more relaxed than she ever had in the room. "No, I don't have the guts to tell her that I'm happy I'm not more upset about her breaking her elbow. I've learned a couple of things in the past year, and one of them is that you can get yourself in a raft of trouble for volunteering too much information."

"I'm happy for you, Ryan," Ellen said. "And I can see why it's a relief to feel that your anxiety is more limited than you'd thought."

"Yeah, yeah. I feel like it's not such an insurmountable battle now, like there's a chance I can get over this if it's limited to worrying about violence."

"I'm sure you can get over it," Barb said. "You don't seem like the type who gives up easily."

"Not so far," Ryan said, smiling.

After Jamie enjoyed her morning rituals, she went into the house and called her father's office. It took a few minutes, but his secretary managed to get him on the phone. "Hi, Cupcake," he said, slightly out of breath.

"Bad time, Dad?"

"No, not at all. I was in the hallway talking to one of my esteemed colleagues." He chuckled softly. "But since we were talking about golf, I think it can wait. How are you?"

"Pretty good. But I had an accident on Friday night and broke my elbow."

"You what?" His voice was so loud, Jamie was sure his secretary had heard him. "Were you driving?"

"No, I wasn't in a car. I fell...off a sidewalk."

There was a pause and he started to laugh, obviously trying not to. "How much had you had to drink?"

"I wasn't drinking," she said, starting to laugh as well. "That's what makes it worse. Falling off a sidewalk is bad enough, but to do it when you're stone cold sober just makes you sound like a klutz."

"I'm sorry for laughing, honey, the image just struck me. But there's nothing funny about your being in pain. How exactly did it happen?"

"We were at a tournament in Arizona and I was outside with one of my teammates, sitting on a bench. When she got up, we kinda collided and she started to fall. I tried to stop her, but she pulled me over with her, and I landed on top of her with my arm hurting like heck."

"Ow! That sounds awful. Was she hurt?"

Not as badly as I wish she'd been. "Not really. She has a bruised tailbone, but she can play."

He made a whistling sound, then said, "Your season…"

"Over," she confirmed. "The break isn't bad. I chipped off the end of the bone that sticks out when you flex your arm. Luckily it didn't affect the joint or anything, but it's in a splint and will be for at least six weeks."

"Have you seen a good specialist? I can help—"

"Mom already called in her chits," she said, laughing softly. "I saw the best orthopedist in the city yesterday. Later today I'm going to get a nifty splint that Mom insisted they custom make for me."

"It sounds like she's taking good care of you." He sounded a little wistful.

"She and Ryan both. The doctor said I could wear the splint they made for me in Arizona, but Mom didn't think it fit well enough, and she didn't like his suggestion to wrap it up tighter." She chuckled. "You know she won't take no for an answer when she has her mind made up."

"I…didn't really know that about her until this last year."

Jamie blinked, stunned that her father had revealed something so intimate…so embarrassing for a man who'd been married for over twenty years to admit. "Maybe she wasn't always so forthright, but she is now."

"I screwed up my marriage by not knowing your mother as well as I should have. I don't want to make that same mistake with you. Why don't I come home this weekend so we can spend a little time together?"

"Ooo…this isn't the best weekend. We have a three-day tournament at Stanford, and even though I'm not gonna play, I told my coach I'd ride around in the cart and help him keep track of things. How about… the week after that? Ryan's in a softball tournament at Stanford that weekend and we'll be staying with Mom."

"I…could…sure," he said, his indecision momentary. "I'll stay at my apartment in the city, and get some work done at my local office."

"Great. Just don't make plans for Saturday. I'd like you to go to the game with me."

"I'd like that too."

"Oh…uhm…Mom usually goes. Will that make you uncomfortable?"

"No, honey." His voice sounded so sad that Jamie's heart clenched in sympathy. "Your mother doesn't make me uncomfortable at all. But you'd better ask her the same thing. If she doesn't want me there, I'll just see you another time."

"Okay, I'll mention it to her, but I'm sure she won't mind. She didn't mind your bringing Kayla to my birthday party, so why would she mind now?"

"I won't bring Kayla this time. I want to spend time alone with you."

"That'll be nice. Would you like to me come get you at the airport? Oh, wait! I can't drive my car."

"Don't even think of it. It's nice of you to offer, but I can take a limo or have someone from my office come get me. It's a nice way to have a meeting while stuck in traffic."

"Okay. But you'll call me when you get in, right?"

"Absolutely. I'm looking forward to seeing you, honey."

"Me too, Dad. See you in…a week or so."

After Ryan had shared her news about Jamie the trio resumed talking about the same topic they'd started during the previous session. "We spent most of last time talking about Ryan," Ellen said, "and I think we did a pretty thorough job of giving her our impressions. Are you ready for your time in the hot seat, Barb?"

"No, but I never am. Hit me."

As Barb had done the previous week, Ryan composed her thoughts, faced Barb and said, "I've been thinking about what you told me one of the first weeks I was here. You said that you were going to quit the police force because you didn't think you could stand to do the job again."

"Yeah, that's what I said."

"Do you still feel that way?"

She nodded slowly. "I think so. I'll have two options. If the police psychologist clears me, I can go back on duty. If he doesn't, I can go on permanent disability. But I don't wanna go through all of the stuff I'd have to do to get disability. If I keep feeling like I do now, I'll probably just quit."

"How many years do you have in?"

"Seven. Lucky seven."

"And how long were you and…Phil?"

"Yeah, Phil," Barb said, her face taking on the mask of pain it always carried when she talked about her partner on the force.

"How long were you partners?"

"Two years. When you're a rookie they try to put you with a more seasoned partner. My first guy retired after about five years, then Phil and I paired up. He was just two years older than me."

"I think," Ryan said, her eyes narrowing a little, "that you hold yourself to a higher standard than the rest of the world does."

"Mmm…maybe. But the world's standards aren't very high in my book."

"No, but the police department's are. And if they determined you weren't negligent in your partner's death—I believe them. They go over things like that more carefully than anything they do. And if they thought you did anything…anything…wrong, they would have called you on it. True?"

"Yeah, that's mostly true. They have to be tough-assed about any incident that involves another cop. Nobody would want to partner with someone who they thought had been given a pass."

"Do you think anyone would want to partner with you?"

Barb squirmed in her seat. "Yeah. Everybody I've talked to said it wasn't my fault, and a couple of people have said they'd like to pair up with me if I go back."

"But you don't trust them?"

"Hell, yeah, I trust them," she growled, shifting around in her seat. "That's not it."

"You don't trust yourself," Ryan said, and Barb nodded. "I know what that's like, I really do. But I don't know what it's like to accidentally kill someone I care about."

"Nobody does. Well, most people don't. The lucky ones don't."

"No matter what you do, you're always gonna struggle with Phil's death. But other cops know what it's like to shoot someone. They know what it's like to make the kind of decision you made the day Phil died. If you go into some job where people don't understand the stress—you're gonna feel even more alone—more cut off."

"Not many people have shot their partners."

"That's true, but it could happen to anyone at any time. Other cops know that. They don't wanna think about it, but they all know it. They'll have more empathy for you than anybody else, Barb. They're your best support group. Going back to work and getting on with your career is the best thing you could do for yourself."

"I just don't think I can face anyone," Barb said, her jaw starting to tremble. "I haven't seen anyone from the force since the funeral."

"That'll be hard. But there's someone you have to face every minute… and that's yourself. You've said that I'm not a quitter…well, you're not either. No woman who goes through the police academy is a quitter. I worry about you because I think you're gonna hate yourself if you quit. If you give up now, you'll always feel like you ran away." She took a deep breath. Knowing she was going to say something that might help didn't make it any easier to get it out. "I hate to say it this way, but you *will* have run away, and that's something you'll always be ashamed of."

"That's what stops me from quitting. I hate quitters. I've wanted to put a slug through my head a dozen times, but that would be the easy way out." Her jaw stuck out in defiance, and she looked more self-confident than Ryan had ever seen her. "That's what a coward would do."

"You're no coward. The people who investigated the accident know that, your fellow cops know that, and I know you know that. You just have to make yourself believe it."

"Easier said…"

"I know," Ryan interrupted. "People have been telling me to forgive myself ever since the day of our carjacking, but I'm my toughest critic. I think that's true for you, too."

"Yeah, it is. Phil's girlfriend and his mother keep telling me that it wasn't my fault, but that makes me feel worse. It's hard for me to face either one of them, and seeing them upset about me just makes me… wanna scream. They shouldn't waste their time thinking about me."

"They care about you," Ryan said softly. "And if they held you responsible…even a little…they probably wouldn't be able to face *you*."

"Maybe." She shrugged and looked away. "I don't know."

There was a pause and Ellen said, "I think Barb has a pretty good idea of how you see her situation, Ryan. Do you have any questions for Ryan, Barb?"

"No, but I'm gonna think about what you said about the cops being a good support group. Maybe I'll be able to make up my mind about going back if I start to talk to one or two of the people I used to hang out with. Maybe I can get a feel for how they think it'd go for me if I went back."

"It couldn't hurt," Ryan said. "I know a lot of cops, and they're usually good at giving it to you straight."

Barb gave her a half smile. "Without a doubt."

Chapter Ten

Ryan was just getting on her bike to ride home when her cell phone rang. "Ryan?"

"Yeah."

"Robin Berkowitz."

"Hi, Professor. What's up?"

"Professor Skadden just got the results for the Putnam Competition. He's going to announce them at ten in the Common Room in Evans Hall. I thought you might like to be there."

"Mmm…I was gonna work on my project today. I hate to waste the time."

"Aw, come on. I'm calling all of the people I know who took it. Surely you're curious."

"Sure, I wanna know how I did, but I could have my girlfriend go by and check. She's on campus today."

The professor laughed. "You're the most incurious woman I know!"

"No, not really. But since I wasn't on the team…"

"No, but you know some of the people on the team, don't you? You should come and support them."

"Okay, okay," Ryan said, laughing. "You guilt-tripped me into it."

"Good. Now that that's settled, I'd like to postpone our meeting for this afternoon, if possible. My husband lucked into a pair of tickets for the Giants' opening day, and I can't pass that up."

"Now I know why you called. You had an ulterior motive."

"I always do. See you at ten."

Jamie was half-dozing through a lecture on supply-side economics when her phone buzzed. *Ryan.* "Hi," Jamie whispered. "Thanks for making my pants vibrate. That's the most excitement I've had in an hour."

"That bad, huh?"

"Macro economics is, quite possibly, the dullest course offered at this fine university. Luckily, a zillion people take it, so I can sit in the back row and pray for the clock to move. What's up?"

"Are you free at ten?"

"Yeah, but I have class at ten thirty."

"I know that," Ryan said, feigning offense. "I know your schedule, I just didn't know if you had anything else going on."

"No, no secret trysts today. I was just gonna go over my notes while they're still pooled in a lifeless mass in my head."

"Wanna meet me in your hall? They're announcing the results of the Putnam."

"It's not my hall," Jamie said, giggling at Ryan's insistence that Evans Hall, had been named for her. "God, it's been forever! Did they have one guy grading 'em?"

"No, but almost three thousand people took it, and they have to grade them by hand."

"They should do it the easy way and make it multiple choice."

"I'll put that in the suggestion box. See you a little bit before ten. It's in the common room on the tenth floor. Save me a seat if you get there first."

"Unless someone cuter comes in before you do."

"Honey, I hate to sound like I'm full of myself, but this is the math department. Get real!"

Ryan slid into a seat next to Jamie in the large room overlooking the Bay. "No one cuter got here first, huh?"

Jamie leaned over and kissed her. "No, but I'm sure I could give some of these guys their first contact with a woman." She surreptitiously looked around. "We might be the only non-virgins here."

Ryan giggled and poked her partner with her elbow. "You're very naughty today. I like it when you're naughty."

"I'm in a strangely good mood. It's such a nice day for April. The sun makes me wanna do something…silly."

"Hmm…silly, huh? Maybe we can think of something later." She turned her head and nodded at the man in the front of the room. "That's the esteemed Professor Skadden."

"He's the jerk who wouldn't put you on the team, right?"

"He's your man. Come to think of it, you might be able to give *him* his first contact with a woman."

"Ugh! He dissed my baby. No nookie for him."

Ryan turned and stared at her. "What's gotten into you today?"

Grinning, Jamie shrugged. "I don't know. I just feel playful."

Ryan put her arm around her and said, "Shh…the great man is about to speak."

The professor stood at the podium and adjusted his glasses, then he spoke in a flat, nasal voice. "I have the results from the 1999 Putnam Competition. The committee reports that twenty-nine hundred people sat for the test, and teams represented three hundred and forty-six schools."

"Cal obviously didn't win," Ryan whispered, "or he would have started with that."

"I don't know. He doesn't look like he knows how to build suspense."

"The top five teams are as follows. The University of Waterloo, Harvard University, Duke University, the University of Michigan, and the University of Chicago."

Everyone in the room let out a disappointed sigh. People shifted around in their seats, and a few people started to get up.

"Some people from our department performed very well," he said. People stopped moving and paid attention again. "We aren't given team results past than the top five, but Gabriel Dominguez placed third in the entire competition."

Ryan let out a whoop and everyone in the auditorium applauded. "That's Gabe," Ryan said, pointing to a man who stood up and waved. "We've been in a lot of classes together. He's *real* smart," she added, wrinkling up her nose.

Professor Skadden continued, "Hiroshi Matsuhita, also on our team, placed ninetieth.

Ryan pointed out Hiroshi when he stood. "I don't know him. I think he's a freshman."

"And lastly, Siobhán O'Flaherty…" Jamie grabbed Ryan's arm and squeezed it hard. "…placed twenty-fifth and has been awarded the Elizabeth Lowell Putnam prize for particularly meritorious performance by a woman."

Jamie kissed Ryan on the lips, squeezing her tight while the entire room looked on in stunned silence. Ryan broke away and stood, and, after a pause, the crowd applauded vigorously.

"Congratulations to all of you," Professor Skadden said. "You should all be proud of your efforts." He walked over to Gabe and shook his hand, and Hiroshi walked over to him to be congratulated, too.

"That's so cool!" Jamie squealed. She put her good arm around Ryan and patted her hard on the back. "And you're the best women! I could have told 'em that." Ryan looked happy, but not as happy as Jamie expected. "What's up? You're not jazzed."

Distracted, Ryan gave her a quick glance. "Oh, I am." Jamie followed her eyes and saw her staring at Professor Skadden. "He should have mentioned me after Gabe. I came in twenty-fifth and Hiroshi came in ninetieth."

"Oh…right," Jamie glared at the elderly man.

Professor Berkowitz walked over and threw her arms around Ryan. "Glad you came?"

Ryan smiled at her. "You knew, didn't you!"

"I knew that you won the ELP, but I didn't know how well you did. Damn, twenty-fifth place is awesome."

Sheepishly, Ryan nodded. "I'm happy, really happy. Especially because of how I had to take it."

"I'd hate to see how you'd do if you hadn't been on a bus all day after playing a basketball game!"

"Who knows? That might have relaxed me. I have an odd metabolism."

"I'm really happy for you," the professor said again. "I never cracked the magic one-fifty when I took it, and I took it four times."

"Just goes to show it doesn't mean much," Ryan said, grinning at her.

"I've gotta go, but I'm really glad you two could make it. Good job!" She smiled at both of them, then was immediately approached by a student as she turned to go.

"She's nice," Jamie said.

"Yep, she's nice and smart. My favorite combo."

"You gonna go talk to your friend?"

"Yeah, as soon as Skadden takes off. He probably thinks there was a mistake in the grading."

Jamie gazed at the back of Ryan's head as her partner leaned forward to watch the professor chat with a few students. It wasn't like Ryan to get upset about someone not noticing her or not giving her the respect she deserved, and it puzzled her. She put her hand on her back and said, "I think he's leaving. Let's go."

Ryan grabbed her backpack and reached Gabe and Hiroshi as they were about to leave. "Hey, guys, good job," she said, awkwardly hugging each man.

"You kicked some serious tail, O'Flaherty," Gabe said, laughing. "Twenty-fifth is righteous!"

Hiroshi, whose English skills didn't match his mathematical abilities, nodded politely and mumbled something like, "Good job. Nice."

"You guys did great," Ryan said. "But I didn't hear Serban's score."

Gabe shrugged. "I'll go check out the announcement when Skadden has his secretary post it. I think they list the top hundred and fifty."

"Yeah," Ryan said. "I think they do." She smiled and shook each man's hand, then took Jamie by the hand to lead her out.

"Who's this Serban…did I say that right?"

"Uh-huh. He's the third guy on Cal's team. He got the spot I should've gotten…if Skadden wasn't a sexist."

"Well, I hope he's learned his lesson. You did great. And you beat all of the other women!"

Ryan made a face. "That doesn't impress me. I think it sucks that they even give that award out. It's like the 'We know women can't beat the men, so we have a special little prize for them' award."

"Ooo…that's why you didn't look happy."

"Partly," Ryan said, checking her watch. "Time for you to leave for class, punkin."

"What are you gonna do?"

"I thought I'd go home and work on my project. Same as always."

"Let's do something silly," Jamie said. "Just you and me."

"You're gonna skip class?"

"Yep. I haven't missed this one except for one golf match. I'm due." She kissed Ryan again. "And you're due a little celebration!"

"You also gave a lot of the guys in the room a bonus," Ryan said, chuckling. "Seeing two girls kiss probably shorted out some circuits in those tidy little brains. They may not have to resort to animé porn tonight."

"Ack!" Jamie threw her hand over her mouth. "I kissed you! I mean, I *really* kissed you!"

"Sure did, and I *liked* it."

When they were standing in the bright, warm sunshine, Jamie took out her cell phone and called her mother. "Hi, Mom. Do you mind if we go get my splint tomorrow?"

"No, that's fine. I thought you'd be in a hurry to get it, since it will fit so much better than the one you have."

"I am. But my sweetheart just found out she placed twenty-fifth out of almost six thousand people who took that big math test last fall. I think she deserves a treat."

"Twenty-fifth! Goodness, that's wonderful! She really *is* gifted, isn't she?"

"Oh, she's the most gifted little pixie in the world." She stuck her tongue out at Ryan, reeling it back in just as it was nearly grabbed.

"She's with you, isn't she? I can always tell. Your voice takes on the happiest tone."

"That's because she makes me happy. Always." She blew Ryan a kiss.

"Can I speak with her?"

"Sure." Jamie extended the phone. "Mom wants to say hi."

Ryan accepted it. "Hi, there."

"Hello to you! Congratulations on doing so well in that test. That's quite an accomplishment."

"Thanks. I was pleased."

"So self-effacing," Catherine said, gently chiding her. "Would you like to go out for a nice dinner tonight? Or do you two have plans?"

"No, we don't have plans for tonight, do we, Jamie?" Jamie shook her head. "We're free. But I have softball practice until six."

"I'll make reservations for seven," Catherine said. "You don't have to get too dressed up."

"Thanks for that. You know I'd prefer not to wear shoes if I didn't have to."

"Any place I pick will probably require shoes, but I'll try to keep it casual."

"Thanks, Catherine. We'll see you later." She clicked off and smiled at Jamie. "Now what?"

"Hmm...what would you do if you could do anything this afternoon?"

"That's easy. I'd go to opening day at PacBell Park."

Jamie slapped at her gently. "Why don't you tell me things like this? You know I could have easily gotten us tickets."

"I know, I know. But *I* couldn't have, and I hate to take advantage of your contacts and your money for things like that." She shrugged, looking a little guilty. "I know you don't like it, but I still feel that way."

Jamie hugged her, then rubbed her back. "I don't like it, but I like you, so I guess I have to live with all of your awful habits."

"You bear it well." She bent slightly and kissed the top of Jamie's head.

Eyes lighting up, Jamie said, "I've got a brilliant idea. It won't cost much and I can guarantee some fast driving and a unique experience."

"Duh," Ryan said, making a face. "When have I ever refused that combo?"

When they got home, Jamie made a few phone calls without allowing Ryan to hear any of them. At eleven, she went into Ryan's room and said, "Dress warmly, but in layers. And bring a jacket." She paused, eyes narrowed in thought. "And an extra set of clothes."

Ryan leaned back in her desk chair and gazed contemplatively at her partner. "You know I love a mystery. Where could we be going that I might have to change? Hmm…" She scratched her head. "I hope it's because you're going to rip my clothes off me."

"Maybe, if you play your cards right. Now get ready. We'll barely make it as it is."

Even though she didn't know where they were going, Ryan drove Jamie's car. She assumed they were going across the Bay Bridge to San Francisco, but Jamie had her turn at the exit for the Berkeley Marina. "Cool! We're going sailing."

"We're not, but you're warm."

Ryan looked at her, puzzled. "Uhm…I like to guess, but I have a feeling I'm missing some of the variables. It's hard to solve an equation when you're missing too many."

"I barely passed Algebra I, so you're wasting your breath making math analogies. But you won't have to guess for long. Park anywhere in here."

Ryan did and got out, spending a few seconds stretching. "Now where?"

"Will you carry our bag?" Jamie held up her splint, trying to look pathetic. "I'm injured."

Ryan draped an arm around her and hefted the bag with her other hand. "I know you are," she said, speaking as she would to Caitlin. "And I think it's just awful and terrible."

"Thank you." Jamie smiled up at her and led her to the harbormaster's office.

"This looks like it's gonna cost—"

"Nope. It's not. Really." They went inside and Jamie smiled at the young man behind the desk. "Hi. I'd like the keys to slip number sixteen."

The clerk smiled back. "Name?"

"Evans. Jamie Evans."

"Could I see some I.D?" She showed him her driver's license and he nodded, looked through a registration book, and then turned it around. "Sign right on the X, next to the slip number."

She complied, then gave Ryan a foxy smile while the young man retrieved a set of keys. As he handed them over, he said, "She hasn't been out this year, but we've been starting her every week. If you have any trouble, just let me know and I'll come out and get her going for you, Jamie."

"Thanks. I'll do that."

As soon as they got outside, Ryan tucked her arm around her possessively. "That jag-off can look all he wants, but I get to take you home."

Jamie looked up at her. "Did I miss something?"

"Nah." Ryan shook her head. "You never seem to notice how guys look at you."

Pointing back towards the office, Jamie said, "That guy?"

"Yes, dear. That guy. He looked like he was about to ask you out."

"Really? He just seemed friendly."

"It was more than that. It bugs me sometimes."

"I bug you or the guys bug you?"

"The guys." Ryan grinned. "You can't help being gorgeous."

"Yeah, that's me. Since Jordan's been unavailable, Ralph Lauren keeps calling."

"Go ahead, make fun. But I, and most of the men in the Bay Area, think you're prime eye-candy."

Jamie reached out and squeezed Ryan's hand. "I love every delusional thought in that pretty head."

Her pique never lasted long, and soon Ryan was looking around the docks carefully. "Right now my head's wondering what's in slip sixteen."

"Go down this aisle and you'll find out."

They turned and walked past a few boats, then Ryan stopped in front of a power boat. "Do you own this?"

Jamie shrugged. "Kinda. One Saturday when we were tailgating at a Stanford football game, my dad and some of his friends from college decided to buy a boat. I think they'd all had too many Bloody Marys," she said, laughing. "They've had it for a long time…maybe ten years, but I don't think we've been on it more than ten times. Why my father wanted another boat when he spent almost every weekend down in Pebble Beach is a mystery."

Ryan walked down the dock, coolly appraising the boat. "It's beautiful, but it's…kinda small." Chuckling, she added, "It's huge for me, but I'd picture your father going in for something like…" she pointed at a bright red Cigarette boat berthed just a few slips away, "…that." The sleek boat looked fast and dangerous, even just sitting placidly in the water.

"He's not really into power-boating. They bought this one for skiing. And don't let the size fool you. It can *move*."

"You've been skiing?"

"Yeah. We took it up to Lake Tahoe a couple of times, 'cause I'm not dumb enough to ski in the Bay."

"I am! Or wake boarding. That's what I'd really like to do."

"We could go down to the South Bay and wake board. You'd have to have a death wish to do it up here." She gave Ryan a narrow-eyed look. "That's not a dare."

"Let's do it!"

"I'll drive for you anytime, baby, but I am *not* getting into the Bay, even the South Bay, without a full wetsuit, and I don't own one."

"I own something you don't?" Ryan clutched dramatically at her heart.

With a wry grin, Jamie said, "Yes, you do. Probably a lot of things judging from the stuff I've seen in your closet. I've never yearned to open my own sporting goods store."

Ryan looked appraisingly at the other craft already out on the water. "I'd love to ride a jet ski out here. You never see anyone doing it."

Jamie cocked her head and gazed at her partner for a long moment. "Does it ever occur to you that there's a reason other people don't do it?"

"Nope." Ryan gave her a happy smile. "I just figure I'm the first one who's thought of it."

"Jet skis are illegal within like a thousand feet of shore all over San Francisco County. But if you're really into it we can go to Lake Berryessa and rent one."

Ryan scrunched up her nose in distaste. "Nah. I wanna be on the ocean. Lakes are for wimps."

"You just let me know when you find a place that'll rent a jet ski on the Bay. I'll be waving at you safely from shore."

"Every hero wants an appreciative crowd. I'll speed by you and do donuts until I splash the hell out of you." She stood there on the dock, dreaming of how epic it would be to jet ski the Bay. Just thinking of it made her heart race.

Jamie watched her partner, clearly lost in a daydream. If she seriously thought she could jet ski the Bay she might be more delusional than Jamie had feared. She snapped her fingers right under Ryan's nose. "Help me take off the cockpit cover and we can rock."

"Not so fast, Sparky." Ryan jumped onto the swim platform and got to work, unsnapping the canvas before Jamie could begin to help. "Girls with broken elbows only get to watch." She stowed the cover as instructed and then held out a hand to help Jamie board safely. "I'll cast off," she said, jumping back out onto the dock.

"Okay. Let me turn on the blower for a couple of minutes."

"Blower?"

"Yeah. To make sure it doesn't combust if there are any fumes."

"I thought boating wasn't dangerous until you were out of the dock."

"Not to worry. It's just a precaution." After waiting for a couple of minutes she said, "Ready?"

"Yup."

When she turned the key, Ryan's eyes grew wide as saucers. "Crap! How big are those engines?"

Jamie cupped her hand over her ear. "What?"

Ryan made the hand signal for "Never mind." Jamie let the boat idle for a while, then signaled and Ryan released the docking lines and jumped aboard. "How big are the engines?" she asked, right into Jamie's ear.

"Just one engine. An eight point something liter V-8. Small boat, big engine. I know you can do the math."

"Physics," Ryan said, grinning toothily. "Water displacement, weight, force, thrust…that's physics."

"That's nice, honey. Now shut up, sit down, and hold on."

Ryan looked surprised, but she did as she was told, settling herself in the seat next to Jamie. After backing out very slowly they cruised down the length of the dock, barely creating a wake.

"Can you feel it purr?" Jamie asked.

"Damn straight." Ryan had the most adorable expression on her face. It was a little like the one she often wore when she was feeling frisky. It wouldn't be too hard to put the Bimini up and make the back seats into a bed…Jamie shook her head, making herself focus on her goal. Making love outdoors usually sounded better than the reality.

They left the calm, protected waters and she slowly eased the throttle forward. With every nudge, Ryan's smile grew in intensity. The woman had an insatiable appetite for danger. After a few minutes they were clear of the marina and the no wake zone. Soon they were moving pretty quickly, the mist hitting them in the face and whipping their hair around—even though Ryan had tied hers back. "We can't ski at this speed," Ryan said, projecting her voice to be heard over the engine.

"We're not going skiing!" Jamie smiled and shook her head. "You'd get hypothermia in two minutes!"

"Just riding around is fun, but you've gotta go faster to make me happy."

"Wanna drive?" Jamie asked, already knowing the answer.

"Yeah!"

"Have you ever driven a power boat?"

"Nope. But I'm sure I can. How hard can it be?"

Ryan was smiling so brightly, that Jamie ignored her lack of experience and cut the throttle to switch seats. "Now, don't go nuts," she warned. "I'm not sure whether this engine could flip the boat, and I don't wanna find out."

Ryan scowled at her. "I'm not reckless. Just…reck-deficient."

"It responds very quickly. It doesn't take much to change direction, so don't over steer. You *do* know that the stern turns when you steer, don't you?"

"I forget what the stern is," Ryan said with a grin. "Just let me play a little. I'll go slow and see how it moves."

She did as promised, keeping the boat at low speed while she eased it through a series of gentle, then sharp turns. Then she increased the speed, obviously testing it. "You could easily lose your tail-end at full throttle," she said decisively. "Easily."

"That's the stern, by the way," Jamie reminded her. "And it's very easy to get into trouble with a small, fast boat. Add a little alcohol and you've got an express ticket to the trauma unit."

"You've had enough trauma for one lifetime." Ryan made a sad face when she looked at Jamie's splint. "I'll be a good girl."

"You don't have to be too good. Just don't flip it."

"Can I go anywhere I want?"

"Sure. But you'll enjoy going south."

"Cool. We can go under the Bay Bridge." Ryan headed for the massive structure and gazed up in wonder as they passed underneath it. "Cool! Way cool!" Frowning, she said, "It could use a little maintenance, though. I'm gonna cross my fingers next time we drive over it."

They continued to head south, picking up speed as they went. She kept increasing the speed until she reached one she must have thought was past her capabilities, and then backed off a hair. She might have been a novice, but Jamie felt perfectly safe with her in control. Ryan loved to take it to the edge, but she seemed to have a very clear view of where that edge was—and always stayed on the safe side of it.

The thrill of the water flying over the windshield to hit their faces, the wind whipping their hair and clothes, and the thud of the boat hitting the small swells had them both giddy with excitement. "You sure do know how to give me a treat," Ryan yelled.

"That's my job."

They continued hugging the coast until they approached the new ball park. "It looks so cool from this perspective!" Ryan yelled.

"Slow down!"

Ryan did, slowing until they could hear each other. "What?"

"Pull into the cove."

"Really?"

"Yeah. If we hang out here and turn on the radio, we can listen to the game and catch home runs."

"Cool!" Ryan slowly motored around, steering clear of the dozens of other boats doing the same thing.

"In case you haven't noticed, there aren't any brakes, so go super slow. When you get to where you want to be, just put it in neutral. I'll set the anchor when you're ready."

Ryan looked at the stadium, then at the position of the other boats.

There were sailboats and powerboats, a kayak and a row boat. "How in the hell did he get out here?"

"Perseverance," Jamie called back.

"This is a good position. A home run will come over the right field fence." She made an arc with her hand, her eyes bright with excitement.

Jamie got up and moved carefully to the bow, where she opened a small hatch. A complex looking but lightweight anchor emerged and she tossed it overboard. "Just let the current move the boat. It'll catch the anchor and keep us still." When she got back to the cockpit, she said, "Good job."

"You shouldn't have been up there. I'm worried about your balance."

"I'm fine." Jamie sat and turned on the radio, tuning it to the station that carried the Giants. The announcer was talking about the park, noting that the visiting Dodgers were just about to take batting practice.

"They won't announce when a ball's gonna reach the wall," Ryan said, frowning. "Not like they will during the game."

"True. But why would you want to hear an announcer describing batting practice?"

"So I'd know where to look to see a ball fly out."

Jamie looked at her, a little puzzled. "I guess you'll just have to look up." With a little help from Ryan, she took off her jacket, then leaned her seat back. Looking up into the clear, blue sky, she sighed dramatically. "La dolce vita, eh?"

"Oui," Ryan said, grinning back. She lowered her seat as well, lacing her hands behind her head. "I guess I don't mind *some* of your connections and *some* of your money."

"My dad has to pay his quarter share every month, whether he uses the boat or not, so all we have to do is fill it up when we get back."

"I don't know how much that'll cost, but it's probably less than paying a scalper for tickets. I heard they were going for up to a thousand bucks."

"I probably could have had my dad get us a pair," Jamie said, shooting a glance at her partner, "but I know you don't like that."

"No, not so much. Although it was cool when he gave us the tickets his law firm had."

"I don't think he has ready access to those like he used to, but I'm sure they'd jump through hoops to give them to him if he asked."

"That's why I don't like to ask. He was powerful before, but now..." She shook her head, "He could get whatever he asked for."

"I hope he doesn't abuse his power," Jamie said idly. "I'm sure it's hard not to."

They heard the crowd start to murmur, then people started to cheer. "Somebody must have hit one out," Ryan said, craning her neck.

"Cool. The crowd will tell us what's happening. That's as good as having an announcer."

They bobbed in the water, basking in the warm, sunny day. The excitement from the capacity crowd bubbled over the walls, and Ryan pointed out that pedestrians could stand just outside the stadium and watch the action through a large gate.

The announcer's voice was soothing and calm, and the sun was making Jamie so sleepy that she wished she'd had an extra coffee before they'd left. The Giants were taking batting practice and she vaguely heard the crowd start to roar, just as Ryan tried to stand up. Jamie's quick reflexes, combined with Ryan's difficulty in getting out of the small cockpit allowed her to throw herself at Ryan and grab her jeans pocket an instant before she tried to jump into the water.

A ball made a splash about ten feet in front of their boat, and several nearby boats converged, trying to reach the ball before anyone else. Jamie yanked hard, pulling Ryan back down into her seat just a moment before another boat hit them just off the bow. Their boat lurched hard to the left, both women shifting hard to the right. Hitting the gunwale with her right arm, Jamie yelped in pain.

"Fuck!" Ryan cried. "Mother-fucker hit us!"

"God damn it! If I hurt my good arm, somebody's gonna pay!" Jamie cradled it close to her body.

Ryan reached for her and carefully inspected her arm from wrist to shoulder. "Does it hurt?" she asked, moving it gently.

Jamie rubbed the spot, testing it, then shook her head. "Not too much. I think it's just a bruise." She looked over and saw the passenger from the boat that hit them fighting over the ball with another man who'd jumped out of his boat, leaving it idling with no one in the pilot's seat. "What in the hell do these idiots think they're doing?" She turned and punched Ryan hard on the shoulder. "What in the hell were *you* doing?"

"Ow!" Ryan rubbed her shoulder. Her eyes were cast downward when she answered, "I was gonna jump in to get the ball." She met Jamie's eyes and said, "It was irresistible!"

"Change seats," Jamie growled.

Ryan got up and stood tall, waving down a police boat when one came into view. The officers acknowledged her, but first went to the two men who were still in the water. They helped the pilot of the large boat get back into his craft, then fished out the other man. The second man held the ball while the first tried to lean over and take it from him, reaching around the police officer to try and grab it.

The policemen separated them, then began writing citations. Amid loud accusations and complaints, they cited each man then moved back to Jamie and Ryan. "What happened?" one officer asked.

"When the ball landed, the guy in the navy blue bowrider zoomed in on it and hit us. He didn't even stop to see if we were all right." Jamie cast a look of disbelief at the offending pilot.

"Where'd he hit you, ma'am?"

"Just off the bow, on the starboard side. He was the give-way vessel," she fumed. "I was at anchorage, you dim-wit!" Jamie shouted to the other boat. "Have you ever heard of the stand-on vessel!"

"He can't hear you, ma'am," the officer said, flinching when Jamie shot him a withering look. The police boat moved up a little and an officer jumped onto their boat. "I don't see any damage," he called back to his partner.

"Great," Jamie snapped. "But he should be cited for being reckless."

"He was. And the other guy was too. Are either of you ladies hurt?"

"I bumped against the gunwale pretty hard, but I'm just bruised. How about you?" she asked, looking at Ryan.

"I'm fine. But I'd like to get one free swing at that idiot. Any chance of that?"

"'Fraid not, Ma'am," the officer said, trying not to laugh. "I can give you his registration number if you want to make an insurance claim."

"I'd like that," Jamie said. "If I get whiplash…"

The officers took their information for a police report, then motored away, leaving Jamie to glare at her partner. "And you're almost as bad. Do you have *any* brains?"

"No," Ryan mumbled contritely.

Jamie grasped her ponytail and pulled until Ryan had to look at her. "How do I convince you that you can't react like a dog when you see something you want?"

Shaking her head, Ryan said, "I don't think you can. My father's been trying since I was a baby."

"Damn it, Ryan!" Jamie was so angry she was shaking.

"I'm *so* sorry, really I am."

"You could've been hit by one of those propellers. Do you think those idiots would have cared?"

"No."

"Do you think they would've even noticed if they'd run over you?"

"No."

"I just don't understand what gets into your head."

"Nothing. Really. Nothing. I just…react."

"Well, you'd better learn to react less and think more." She pushed Ryan's forehead with the heel of her hand. "You've got a huge brain. Use it!"

"I know I should," Ryan said plaintively. "I just…don't."

"Don't talk to me, right now. Just…don't talk." Jamie turned her head and stared out at the dozens of boats surrounding them. After a few minutes, she said, "I don't wanna be in this crowd. I'm gonna pull the anchor. Start the boat and go forward just a little bit." Silently, Ryan switched seats and followed instructions, letting Jamie bring the anchor back up. "Now take us over there," she said, pointing. Ryan gave her a quick look, but did as she asked. When they were well away from any other boats, Jamie set the anchor again then had Ryan kill the engine.

By the time they were settled, Bobby McFerrin was singing the National Anthem and a squadron of jets flew by in formation. Jamie didn't speak again until the bottom of the first inning, when she said, "Will you sit in the back with me?"

Ryan nodded, then got up and helped Jamie to make sure she had her balance. There was a nicely padded bench that curved around the stern, and when Jamie sat down, she patted the bench next to her and Ryan joined her. Looking into Ryan's eyes, Jamie quietly said, "I'm sorry."

"You? What've you got to be sorry for?"

Sighing, Jamie said, "For trying to make you be who I want you to be."

Ryan smiled tentatively. "Aww, honey, you can't help that. You don't want me to be an idiot. That's not asking a lot."

"It's the same as asking you to be right-handed." She took Ryan's hand and kissed it gently. "You are who you are, and you react to things in your own way. I don't have to like it, but I can't change you. I've obviously got an impulsive nature, too. Yelling at you and hitting you are just as instinctive for me, but I'm going to do my best not to give in to those instincts. It's wrong of me to get that angry with you for something you can't control. And I'm very, very sorry for that." Still holding Ryan's hand, she placed it over her breast. "Will you forgive me?"

"Jamie," Ryan soothed, stroking her hair, "you don't owe me an apology. I could've gotten myself killed. What I did was incredibly stupid. If you weren't upset, you'd be as crazy as I am."

"Will you behave differently in the future?"

Ryan looked into her eyes for several moments. "No."

"Then what purpose does it serve for me to scream at you and hit you? That's like hitting a little kid for running after a toy. If you don't have the ability to control yourself…it's just not fair of me to be so punitive."

Ryan took her hand and chafed it between her own. "You lashed out because you were worried and scared, right?"

"Of course. I can't bear the thought of losing you. Especially to something so pointless."

"So…how will you stop? I know I've told you that Da never hit us, but he's grabbed me so hard he pulled me off my feet. Heck, he pulled out a handful of my hair when I was little. He cried when he saw what he'd done, but he couldn't help himself."

"My God!" Jamie could feel the color drain from her face. "What had you done?"

"I don't remember. I did so many dumb things, there's no way to remember half of 'em. I think he grabbed me, like you caught the back of my pants, only I didn't stop. He wound up with a handful of my hair." She shrugged. "I didn't blame him. It hurt like hell, but I didn't blame him. I felt really bad when he cried. I knew it was all my fault, but I didn't…and still don't know how to stop."

Jamie leaned against her partner. "What are we gonna do? I hate myself for being rough with you. No one has ever raised a hand to me. Why do I react like that? Where did I learn that?"

"I don't know, babe. I guess it's just instinct. But I really, really don't blame you. The boys have done much worse when they were watching me." She smiled, but Jamie didn't. "Rory's as gentle as a lamb, and he once tackled me and knocked out my front teeth."

"Jesus!"

"I was about to run into traffic chasing a ball. They were just baby teeth," Ryan added, as though that made it better. When Jamie didn't lighten up, she said, "Come on…don't let what you did bother you. It's a perfectly normal reaction to being afraid."

"I don't think it's normal, and I don't want to do it again." Jamie's jaw was set and her eyes had gone steely.

"Let's both work to not get in that position again." Ryan kissed her head. "Okay?"

"All right." Jamie gave her a grudging smile. "I'm gonna talk to Anna about this and see if she has any advice. I refuse to act like this with our kids, and if I can't stop myself from doing it with you, I'm worried that I won't be able to control myself with them."

"Don't worry about that." Ryan put an arm around her and held her close. "Da grabbed me, and yanked on me, and picked me up roughly, and all sorts of things. He had to do something or he would have gone mad. I understood, I really did."

"I'm gonna find the two most calm, gentle, least-impulsive people on earth and pay them to have babies for us. It's clear that neither of us should pass on our genes."

Ryan looked at her for a long time before she said, "Please don't say things like that. Even if you're kidding—it hurts me."

Jamie rested her head against Ryan's shoulder. "I was kidding. But you're right—I shouldn't kid about something like that. You know I want all of your sweet genes in our babies."

"And I want yours. You're the woman I love, and I'd love nothing more than to have a little girl just like you."

"Not a little boy?"

"Ahh…no. A little boy just like you would get the snot kicked out of him," Ryan said, laughing. "The boys have to be more like me."

"It's a deal. Boys like you, girls like me. But without the impulse-control or anger-control issues."

"Tall order, but we'll work on it."

That night at dinner, Ryan regaled Catherine with stories of their afternoon, including her attempt to dive in and swim for a home run. It was fun to watch her mother's face morph from surprise to shock. Then she seemed to consider the whole picture and began to laugh. "Jamie, you must have been beside yourself!"

"Don't remind me. I *hit* her, Mom. I slugged her on the shoulder. She has a bruise."

"I'm not a fan of violence, but I think you were justified, honey." She and Ryan laughed, but Jamie couldn't join in. There was nothing funny about it. "You don't mind getting a punch for doing something so foolish, do you, Ryan?"

"I prefer it. If she didn't hit me, she'd cry, and that's much worse. I'd rather make her angry than sad."

"See?" Catherine said. "Ryan's able to look at this logically."

Jamie shook her head. "If the two of you think punching is logical, you've both lost your minds."

When they got home from dinner, Ryan took the phone into the living room, flopped down on the sofa, and called Conor. Jamie smiled when she heard her telling him about their afternoon, but when Ryan started to complain about the lack of hitting with men on base, she went up to their room. She had no idea who'd won the game or under what circumstances, but she knew that Ryan's capacious mind hadn't missed a trick.

Chapter Eleven

On Wednesday morning, Conor's cell phone rang. He had to step outside to avoid the whine of the chop saw. "Hello?"

"Mr. O'Flaherty? Catherine Smith."

"Well, hello, Ms. Smith. It's nice to hear from you."

"My, that sounded odd to my ears. I haven't called myself Catherine Smith since I was in college."

"Still testing it out?"

"I suppose I am. But I'm going through with it. When my divorce is finalized it'll be official. Now I'm just slowly telling people."

"I think it sounds great. Catherine Smith," he said, testing it out. "Yep. It's great."

"Thank you." Her voice tinkled with laugher. "Surprisingly, that's not why I called."

"That would've been enough. I'm always glad to hear from you."

"You might not be when I ask my question."

"Oh, sure I will. Ask me anything."

"Okay." Catherine took in an audible breath. "Are you busy on Saturday night?"

"This Saturday?"

"I know it's very short notice, but I wasn't going to go to this benefit for the symphony until a friend of mine called and practically begged me. I hate to let her down, and I don't want to go alone..."

Conor didn't hesitate. "I've got a tuxedo and I'm ready to use it. What time should I pick you up?"

"Oh, Conor, you're a doll."

"Nah, I just like to party."

"The symphony crowd is about the same age as the one for the opera benefit. I'm fairly sure your normal set is a few decades younger."

"Maybe. But you'll be there and we're practically the same age."

"Ha! You must not have your sister's math abilities."

"I can add pretty darned well, and when you're added to a party, everyone has a good time."

After a trip to the orthopedist to pick up her new splint, Jamie and Catherine drove to the Castro to meet with Ray, the real estate agent.

It wasn't clear that Ray was the right guy for her tastes. He was a little too controlling, but Jamie had decided she'd give him a good chance before making a change. He insisted they take his car, something she wasn't crazy about. But with her bum arm, it made sense. They got into his Mercedes and drove to a modest home in Noe, but the footprint of the house was so small that they agreed it wouldn't work. Back in the car, Jamie said, "Are the other houses bigger than this one?"

"Not really. You can't get much in Noe or Castro for the kind of money you're talking about. I know you want to flip the property, and you'll be able to, but…"

"But we won't make much money," Jamie finished for him.

"Probably not. Houses are so overpriced that even the real dogs are selling quickly. A couple of years ago you could make serious money flipping, but with inventory low and prices high…"

Jamie stared out the window, looking at the very modest homes. "What about small apartment buildings or duplexes? Wouldn't they be a better bet?"

"Well, yeah," Ray said, chuckling. "But you're talking a lot more money."

"What if money wasn't a big issue?"

He gave her a quick look. "Money's always a big issue."

Sighing, she said, "Okay. The idea is to take Niall's money and use it for a down payment. That's $200,000. We figured we'd get a loan for the balance and materials. I know the boys don't want to carry a big mortgage, but we could arrange for private financing. Why don't you show us something that wouldn't take too many months to fix up, but that we could make a good profit on?"

"Like a three flat?"

"Yeah. Something like that. No more than…what do you think, Mom?

Three or four apartments?"

Catherine frowned and took a moment to respond. "Why not look at a bigger building? You could make a nice profit if you were landlords, given how high rents are."

"That's what I'd do," Ray agreed.

"The bigger the building, the bigger the profit if you're going to be landlords, right?" Catherine asked.

"Usually," he said. "But if you're going to do all of the work yourselves, I'd limit it to five or six units. Do you think your...partners will go for being landlords?"

"They might not like it, but they're pretty malleable," Jamie said, sharing a smile with her mother.

Ryan stepped out of the shower that afternoon, having delayed her normal morning clean-up until her mind was completely boggled by the myriad of ideas she was trying to get to jell for her independent study. She'd been in her room, laboring over her computer with every spare moment for weeks, not bothering to comb her hair or put on decent clothes until she had to leave the house.

She and Maria Los had engaged in a few frustrating conversations about her room and its very messy state. But she had her papers where she wanted them, and didn't want any interference. She knew she was being unreasonable. But having a woman clean the house was a luxury she truly didn't appreciate. Maria Los did a great job, and kept her and Jamie from having to spend time they really didn't have on upkeep. But she was still a stranger, and Ryan would never be comfortable having a stranger in her home—especially one who moved her stuff.

Hearing the phone, Ryan dried off hurriedly and sprinted for it, catching it just before it went to the answering machine. "H'lo?"

"Hey, good-lookin'," the familiar tones of Ally's voice said.

"Hey, yourself. Give me a sec, will you? I'm just getting out of the shower."

"Sure. Want me to call back?"

"Give me five."

"You got 'em."

Ryan finished drying off and put her towel back in the bathroom, then put on her softball clothes. Then she jogged down the stairs and grabbed a bottle of water, before going into the living room to wait for Ally's call.

Maria Los poked her head out of the kitchen and gave Ryan an inquisitive look. "I clean room?" she asked, pointing to the second floor.

It was time to give up. "Si," Ryan said, smiling at her persistence. "I'm leaving."

"Good." Maria Los gave her a big smile as she took her bucket of cleaning supplies and headed upstairs.

I wonder if she knows that was an insult? The phone rang and Ryan picked it up. "Talk to me."

"That's why I called. Sara said she read that Jamie's out for the rest of the season. What happened?"

"Ooo...Right. I forgot that she reads the Bears newsletters. I should have called."

"Right. You should have," Ally said, her tone light but her message clear.

"I'm just so busy..." Ryan started to say, but she stopped herself. "Ahh, that's bull. I need to make time to keep up with our friends. I'm sorry."

"It's all right, Rock, you're not in the confessional. Just tell me what happened."

Ryan told the story, leaving out the long-simmering animosity between Jamie and Juliet. "So, she's done for the season and walking around with a splint from her shoulder to her wrist."

"Hoo! I bet she's madder'n a hornet. To work for all those months and get shut down at the end of the season really bites."

"You know," Ryan said, giving the thought some consideration, "she's not as mad as she should be. I think she was kinda tired of the whole thing. She didn't have any good friends and...Huh." She paused at the realization that struck her. "I bet she's glad that she's not gonna have to be away from home and from me."

"Well, who could blame her?" Ally said, laughing. "As modest as ever."

"No, no!" Ryan laughed at the way her comment had come off. "She's worried about me. I'm still not back to normal speed, and she feels like she has to keep an eye on me. It's been wearing on her."

Ally was quiet for a moment, then, with concern coloring her voice, said, "Are you that bad off, sugar?"

"Nah," Ryan said, lying just a little. "I'll be fine. It's just taking me a while. Kinda like after I was gay-bashed."

"You were pretty down then, buddy. I was afraid I was never gonna see those blue eyes sparkle again."

"Well, they did. I've just had a run of back luck in the last couple of years. Thankfully, there've been more great things than bad things, so I can't complain."

"You never do. But you might feel better if you did."

"Ugh…right…you're another therapy shill."

Ryan was clearly teasing and Ally seemed to take it as such. "Not lately. I think I might have seen the man behind the curtain or something. It's lost its magic."

"Wanna talk about it?"

"Nah. It just gets old after a while." She chuckled. "It's taken me a lot longer to get sick of it, but I'm starting to come around to your view."

"I should be a big fan. Without therapy, Jamie would probably be married and living down in the South Bay."

"You make a damn good point, Rock. It's helped me a lot too. It just doesn't work fast enough."

Ryan chuckled. "That's my biggest complaint. If they could speed it up, I'd be all in."

Ryan walked into the house that night, stopping short when she spied Jamie walking down the stairs. "Wow. You look fantastic."

"Really?" Jamie smiled and continued to descend. Standing on the bottom stair, she cocked her head. "More fantastic than usual?"

"Good point. You always look fantastic." She dropped her gym bag and put her arms around Jamie's waist. Standing perfectly still for a few moments, she gazed into her partner's eyes. "You look particularly fantastic in that shirt. You've been wearing a lot of Indian-style shirts, and they look really nice on you. This color is good, too," she said, fingering the brick-colored linen.

"They fit a little loose, so I can get away with not wearing a bra if I wear a snug camisole." She kissed Ryan, then brushed a little bit of softball field grit from her lips. "You're so involved with your work by the time I leave, I don't want to break your concentration enough to have you dress me."

"Ooo…don't feel like that. It's fine to interrupt me."

"You kissed my eye this morning," Jamie said, re-enacting the misplaced kiss. "And you didn't even realize it."

"Uhm…I meant to do that. Your eye looked very kissable this

morning."

"Don't bother kissing the Blarney Stone when we go to Ireland. You don't need any help." She patted Ryan's side and scooted past her. "Dinner's almost ready."

Ryan followed, nose twitching. "I smell…Mexican."

"Yep. With refrijoles made the way you like 'em."

"From scratch?"

"That's how you like 'em, isn't it?"

They passed into the kitchen. "I didn't know it until you made them for me, but now that's the only way I like them." Ryan grasped Jamie's left hand. "Hey, you got your new splint."

Jamie hiked up the loose-fitting sleeve. "Yep. Cool, huh?"

Ryan inspected the molded gray plastic and the black Velcro straps. "Totally. Can you put it on yourself?"

"Yeah. I think I might even be able to shower alone now."

"Don't rush, I like helping." She looked at the stove and calculated that dinner was imminent. "Speaking of which, I'd better go shower and change."

"Eh…don't bother. You can get clean enough to eat by washing your hands and face at the sink."

Looking down on her dusty, slightly damp clothes, Ryan said, "Are you sure?"

"Yeah. You can shower before bed." She went to the cabinet and took out plates and glasses.

Uncertainly, Ryan took a peek at Jamie. "Why don't you mind if I look like this?"

Jamie smiled at her and gave her a quick tap on her butt. "There's not much difference, honey. A T-shirt and sweats is a T-shirt and sweats. A little added dust won't hurt."

Ryan reached out and stopped Jamie's progress. "Hey, what did that mean?"

Blinking, Jamie said, "Nothing. It just seems like a senseless delay to go shower when I know you're hungry. You're not gonna get the food dirty." She laughed a little, but trailed off.

"Not that. What you said about the T-shirt and sweats."

"*Nothing.*" Jamie moved away and went into the dining room to put the plates on the table. Ryan stayed right on her heels. When Jamie was evasive, it was a good idea to stick to her until she said what was on her mind. "I didn't mean anything. It's just that since you've been playing sports, you don't vary your wardrobe much. It's no big deal."

"Really?" Ryan grasped her arm and held her still. "You don't mind?"

"No. It makes sense. When we first met, you weren't playing a sport. It's understandable that you spent more time on looking nice when you didn't have to change three times a day."

Ryan let her go and followed her into the kitchen, then went to the sink to wash her face and hands. Using the brush Jamie had bought specifically for that purpose, she scrubbed under her nails. She was still working diligently when Jamie scratched her back and said, "Dinner's on the table. Let's go."

Nodding, Ryan dried her hands and followed her. Suddenly, she felt ungainly when compared to Jamie. Standing behind her chair, she fussed with her hair, smoothing it back into a neater-looking ponytail.

Jamie stood by her and put an arm around her waist. "Before dinner kiss?"

Ryan complied, brushing her lips quickly. "Looks good," she said, nodding at the dinner.

"Thanks. Now sit down and tell me about your day."

Ryan didn't have much to report, so she listened to Jamie talk about a few things that had happened to her at school. "Oh, Anna said she could see me earlier in the day, since I don't have golf anymore."

Lifting an eyebrow, Ryan said, "I didn't know that was something you wanted to do."

"Yeah, I'd like to be home earlier so I can take a little more time with dinner. I hate to rush."

Spending a moment looking at her, Ryan said, "You made this fantastic dinner from scratch, you look like a million bucks, your hair's perfect, you've got just the right amount of perfume on and you brushed your teeth seconds before I got home. I could taste the mint on your lips."

Shrugging, Jamie said, "So?"

"You're always trying. You go out of your way to look nice and smell nice and make our home nice. And you do most of it for me."

"Yeah..." Looking puzzled, Jamie said, "Is that a surprise?"

"No, no, it's not a surprise, but I'm not keeping up my end of the deal. I'm not making any effort to be sure I look nice for you."

"Oh, don't be silly. You always look good to me. You're so beautiful you don't need to make an extra effort."

"That's not true," Ryan said earnestly. "I really noticed you today, and it made me feel good. It made me feel like I was important."

"Jeez, Ryan, of course you're important!"

She reached across the table and took Jamie's hand. "But you make the effort to show me that. That's important, and I appreciate it." She kissed Jamie's hand tenderly. "I *really* appreciate it."

"You're such a sweet girl." Jamie pushed aside her plate and got up, standing by Ryan's chair while she moved away from the table. "Let me sit on your lap."

Ryan smiled at her as Jamie squirmed around, getting comfortable. They kissed, slowly, for a few minutes, until Jamie put her forehead against Ryan's and took in a few slow breaths.

"You take my breath away…every time," Ryan murmured.

"I don't wanna take your dinner away. I know how hungry you are." She started to get up, but Ryan held onto her.

"I'm hungry for you too," she whispered and lavished several more heated kisses on her.

"Mmm," Jamie said, licking her lips. "You might not be dressed well, but you sure as heck can kiss."

Later that evening, Ryan was in her room working at her computer when Jamie came in to get ready for bed. Ryan dutifully helped Jamie take off her blouse. "Want a T-shirt?"

"Yeah, I'll go get one."

"I'll give you one. You like 'em big anyway."

"It's not that I like them that big, I just like to wear your clothes."

"Ally's the only woman I could do that with," Ryan said wistfully. She opened a drawer of shirts that Ally had given her over the years and chose a nice, bright yellow one. Tugging it over Jamie's head, she asked, "Mind if I take your splint off? I wanna see how it works."

"No, go ahead. Wanna try it on?"

"Nah. I've had enough casts, not much allure there." She gently undid the Velcro straps and slipped off the plastic pieces. "Cute little sleeve."

Jamie looked at the snug knit piece of material that covered her arm from wrist to shoulder. "That's so the plastic doesn't stick to me. Thoughtful, huh?"

"Yep." Ryan drew it off her arm, wincing and making a face at the Technicolor bruising. "How does it feel?"

"Not too bad. It aches a little, but not much."

"This is some bruise. I think I'll take a picture so you remember the only significant injury you're ever going to have." She leaned over and kissed several spots, touching blue, purple, and maroon skin. "My poor little chipmunk."

"Chipmunk?"

Sliding the sleeve back on, Ryan started to reassemble the splint. "You seemed chipmunkish just then. What did the doctor tell you about using your arm?"

"He said I should keep it elevated when I can, and that it's okay to use my hand. I haven't felt like it, though. It's still too stiff and swollen."

Ryan held her hand and inspected it. "Can you flex it?"

Jamie did, lips pursed as she slowly moved it. "It doesn't look or feel like my own hand. It's weird."

"It is an odd feeling, isn't it? A swollen hand always feels like I'm wearing a tight rubber glove."

"Hey, it does!" Jamie said, her nose wrinkling when she smiled.

"You're doing well, babe. When we're sitting around in the evening, you can still keep ice on it. That'll help the swelling."

"I forget to do that."

Ryan kissed her gently. "Then I'll remember for you. Need help in the bathroom?"

"I can manage. It's much easier when I'm not wearing pants."

"Most things are," Ryan said, giving her a wicked grin.

Jamie went into the bathroom and started to brush her teeth. She emerged a few seconds later, her mouth covered with white foam. "Nice shirt." She glanced down at the slogan, then back at her partner.

Grinning, Ryan looked up. "A girl can hope."

Jamie took the brush from her mouth and leaned over, wiping her mouth on Ryan's cheek. "Such a bad girl."

Ryan wiped the bubbles from her face, saying, "I don't think I've ever worn that one."

"If I see you walking around town with an 'I've saved you a seat' shirt on, you're not gonna be sitting anywhere for a while."

"It's not the words," Ryan decided, grinning, "it's the arrow pointing at your face that gives it meaning."

"That's the meaning that'll get your hide tanned, O'Flaherty. That seat is reserved for moi."

The next morning, Jamie was sitting in the backyard, drinking a cup of coffee and reading a textbook when the back door opened and Ryan started down the steps. Glancing up, Jamie's eyes opened wide and she let out a wolf whistle. "Whew! Did you have a date this morning?"

Grinning, Ryan stood on the grass and did a slow turn. "Just therapy. You like?"

Jamie let her eyes roam over her lover's body, her pulse quickening a little as she took in the crisply ironed denim shirt that was only partially buttoned. A very snug tank top was visible, but not visible enough for Jamie to see what were surely braless breasts. The fact that she knew Ryan never wore a bra with the spandex top piqued her interest, and made her strain to see if she could get a peek at what she hoped were erect nipples.

The shirt was tucked into wheat-colored jeans that Jamie'd recently had custom tailored for her long-legged partner. They fit even better than Jamie had hoped, and she was glad that she'd lowered the measurements an inch in the waist and hips. Ryan still hadn't gained back all of the weight she'd lost after the carjacking, but she finally looked healthy and fit. The fact that her breasts were almost back to their normal size didn't hurt her look one bit.

Shiny, dark brown, ankle-length boots and leather belt made Ryan look fully put together—for the first time in quite a while. Her hair hung loose around her shoulders, a big plus, in Jamie's opinion. It seemed like she'd had it in a ponytail or a braid ever since softball had started, and Jamie smiled when she saw the sun glinting off the raven strands, highlights leaping out at her.

"You look ravishing," she finally uttered, her voice husky. "And that's just what I'd like to do to you."

Feigning insult, Ryan put her hands on her hips. "I finally dressed up for you and now you want to ruin it?"

Standing, Jamie closed the small distance between her and her partner. "We can't get in sync. You're dressed and I'm in my jammies."

Ryan bent and kissed her tenderly, moving her lips slowly and gently over Jamie's. "Mmm…you may be in your jammies, but you still took the time to brush your teeth. I can taste…something clean through the coffee."

"Baking soda. I use the unflavored stuff when I'm gonna drink coffee.

I can't stand the taste of mint competing with my java."

"How did I not know that? All these months and you've still got secrets."

"Sure do." Jamie took her hand. "Let's go upstairs and I'll show you another couple."

Her expression filled with regret, Ryan stood her ground. "I can't, baby. I've got so much to do. I wouldn't be able to relax. Besides," she looked at her watch, "don't you have class in an hour?"

"Yeah, but I'd skip it to wrap my lips around you." She sidled up to Ryan and started to nuzzle at her neck, interspersing teasing licks with sharp little bites. Her uninjured arm circled the jean clad waist, and she rubbed her face against Ryan's breasts, feeling them move and shift with the pressure. "I'm a needy girl," she murmured, grasping Ryan's ass.

"How needy are you?" Ryan purred. Her hands were roaming over Jamie's back and sides, sliding over the swells and dips of her muscles, feeling Jamie's ribs expand and contract more quickly as her breathing sped up.

Sliding her foot between Ryan's to give her better access, she pressed her center against Ryan's leg, swirling her hips as she ground against her. "Very. It's been forever," she pouted dramatically.

"Show me how needy you are," Ryan said, her own voice now as deep and rough as Jamie's.

Jamie pulled her down for a dazzling, dizzying series of kisses. By the time she paused, Ryan seemed wobbly, but she was supported by Jamie's body—still astride and pressing against her leg. "Let's go."

When they reached the kitchen, Ryan turned and wrapped Jamie in her arms, kissing her with a nearly frantic passion. Jamie responded, holding on to Ryan as well as she could with one arm. Their bodies were pressed feverishly together, Ryan's hands running through her hair, along her body, and back to her face, where they held her as gently as a china doll.

Panting, Jamie backed away. "Bed. Now."

"Counter. Now." In a flash, Jamie's panties were on the floor, and her long T-shirt joined them a few seconds later. She was lifted and settled on the cold granite, letting out a gasp that was captured by Ryan's eager mouth. Again, Ryan was relentless in her assault upon Jamie's lips, the soft skin of her throat, her flushed ears. Slowly, she worked her way down, finally gathering Jamie's breasts in her hands and pressing them together firmly, where she worked at the rigid nipples with unflagging interest.

Jamie held on with her right arm, wishing desperately that she could grasp and hold her lover with her left as well. Ryan seemed to sense her need and released her breasts and held her tightly, not missing a beat with her warm, wet mouth.

"That's it," Jamie urged. "Hold me tight. Hold me…"

Ryan followed her command, holding her firmly while her mouth moved further down her body. She grasped her hips in a nearly bruising grip and nuzzled between her legs, breathing in deeply. Jamie's legs spread immediately, welcoming Ryan with alacrity. Blindly reaching behind herself for a chair, Ryan's foot found one and dragged it across the floor. She knelt on it, then sat back on her haunches to get the angle right.

As soon as Ryan's mouth covered her, Jamie slid closer to the edge of the counter and lifted her legs until they rested on Ryan's shoulders. She was braced on her good arm, her body contorted in a pose that would have been unimaginable if she weren't shaking with desire. But the only sensation she felt was Ryan's hot breath on her, and when that delectable tongue swiped along from bottom to top, she cried out with need. She would have fallen if she'd moved her good arm, so she had to lie there, passively letting Ryan work her magic. Though she couldn't move her arms, her hips were unrestrained, and Jamie swiveled and twitched them across the counter—trying to position herself to force Ryan to hit the magic spot.

It was so frustrating! Ryan knew exactly where her hot spots were; she just wasn't ready to probe them. She was totally in charge, and Jamie had to lie there and hope that Ryan gave her some relief before she combusted. Her body writhed under Ryan's gentle kisses, begging for more. Those beautiful lips lingered around her opening, delicately inserting the tip of her tongue again and again, then swirling it around in a tiny circle.

Jamie thumped the counter with her splint, her moans constant. "*Please*," she begged. "Please make me come."

Ryan growled like a big cat protecting her kill.

"Please," Jamie said again. "Come on, baby, do it."

Placing a wet kiss on her lips, Ryan tilted her head and met Jamie's eyes. "Tell me what you need. *Exactly* what you need."

"My clit," she begged. "Suck my clit. You know just how I like it."

"Is that all?" Ryan asked innocently, slowly lowering her head while keeping her eyes locked on Jamie's.

"No, no! Fingers! Put your fingers inside me. I need you inside me, baby. Come inside."

Grinning lustily, Ryan slid two fingers inside, pressing down, then spreading her fingers apart. That was perfect. Just perfect. A low moan escaped and as it did Ryan dipped her head and covered her clit, sucking gently but firmly. As soon as her tongue brushed across the tip, Jamie cried out and her body stiffened. She was completely still, save for the first spasm that rolled through her vulva. Another gentle swipe of the tongue sent her over the edge, and she thrust her hips hard, pushing against Ryan's hand to pull those talented fingers deep within herself.

Jamie's body was expressing itself clearly, but her mouth was unable to form a single syllable . She slid down to let her upper body fully rest on the counter, her torso winding up in a remarkably uncomfortable position.

Ryan stayed where she was, pressing tender kisses into the still-throbbing flesh. Then she got up and pushed the chair away, wrapped her arms around Jamie and pulled her limp body into a sitting position.

Her head resting on Ryan's shoulder, Jamie murmured, "The things you do to me..."

"The things you do to *me*," Ryan said, laughing softly. "Watching your body respond and hearing you beg for what you need makes me so hot... it's...unreal."

"Take me upstairs. I've got plans for you. Big, big plans."

Ryan turned her head and caught Jamie's lips—licking, sucking, teasing them with her mouth and tongue. Jamie was moaning again, rubbing her breasts against Ryan, who said, "I have plans for *you*, sweetheart. You're gonna get in the shower, get dressed, and go to class. Then I'm gonna clean up a little, change my undies, and get to work. I just have to."

Jamie sat back and stared at her, unblinking. "You're not serious."

"Yeah, I am. I told you I had to get moving."

"But...that was before we started to make love! Aren't you turned on?"

"Hell yes!" Ryan said, laughing. "But I'm happy. I had a lot of fun this morning, and I didn't even have to take off my new pants."

She looked very happy at her declaration, and Jamie, puzzled by her usually hair-trigger-response lover, could see that she was serious. "Did I pressure you too much?"

"No, not a bit. If I really wasn't into it, I would have told you. But I thought this would be a great way to start the day. I got to feel love and tenderness and passion—not a bad way to get the juices flowing."

Jamie put her good arm around Ryan, and was helped off the counter. "Come on, hot stuff, let's go rinse off some of these juices. I don't want my whole class to know how I spent my morning."

"They'd be jealous," Ryan smirked. "I bet every guy and half of the girls wish they were in my shoes."

"Yeah, that's probably true," Jamie said, humoring her partner. "But you're the only one I want. Although, next time, I'd like your shoes and your pants and your shirt on the floor, rather than on your body."

"That can be arranged. As a matter of fact," she said, leading Jamie up the stairs, "I don't have a thing on my agenda at about ten o'clock tonight."

"You're on. Pencil me in, babe."

Jordan was scheduled to leave for Russia late that night. At least ten times Mia had doubted her decision to go to San Francisco rather than make the trip, but in her heart she knew it was right for them. Still, that didn't make it any easier to leave. After a relatively somber lunch, Jordan drove Mia to the airport for her late afternoon flight. When they got there, Jordan started to head for short-term parking, but Mia said, "Just drop me off, Jordy. It's easier for me."

Giving her a quick glance, then grumbling quietly, she followed instructions, pulling up in front of the terminal a few minutes later. "I feel better when I go to the gate with you."

"Too risky." She leaned over and kissed Jordan, ramping up the emotion until she heard her lover groan. Mia felt a little light-headed, but she managed to say, "It's too tempting to grab you and drag you onto the plane with me. I know I'm not strong enough to carry you from here."

Her smile was sad, and Jordan's gaze didn't move from Mia's eyes. "I love you."

"I love you, too. And I'm gonna be thinking about you every minute." With great care she smoothed Jordan's hair into place, straightened her collar and the placket of her shirt. "But you, my Olympic beauty, have to concentrate on your game. I want you to be completely self-indulgent. Don't think about anything other than your body, your game and your team."

The corner of Jordan's mouth curled up in a half-smile. "You've gotta give me some time to think about you. I'm only human."

"Okay." Mia looked up, thinking. "You can think about me when you get into bed at night. You think about how nice it feels to be loved for being exactly who you are. Think about how we don't have to be together to be connected. And that whenever you think about me, I'm thinking about you." She slipped her arms around Jordan and kissed her again and again; their bodies pressed together, lips feverishly seeking the sweet softness of each other's mouth.

"I love you," Jordan finally said, her voice thin and soft. "And I love Jamie and Ryan for loving you."

"We're family."

"We are. And having you with them makes this so much easier. I know you'll be happy."

"I will be. But I'll be happier when we're back together. Now kiss me and get going before that cop over there has a stroke!"

Chapter Twelve

When Mia had spoken to Ryan the day before, Ryan said she wasn't sure who'd be at the airport to meet her—but someone would. Mia found the O'Flaherty rule about having someone pick you up a little odd—not to mention inconvenient for them, but she had to admit it did make her feel very welcome—and missed.

She was fairly sure that she didn't gasp aloud, but it was a near thing when she saw Conor standing by the gate. "Hi," she said, feeling uncharacteristically shy. She wasn't sure if she should hug him or not, but he resolved her dilemma by bending over and giving her a friendly, almost brotherly, hug.

"You look great!" he said, his big voice booming.

"Thanks. You look good too. I like your hair that way."

He reached up and ran his hand through his unusually long hair. "Jamie's got me going to the same place she and Ryan get their hair cut. The guy charges so much, I decided to wait as long as possible between haircuts. But I'm kinda getting used to it being longer. I think I'm gonna see how I like it as it grows."

Mia looked at him quickly, not wanting to let him see her checking him out. He was, she had to admit, even better looking with longer hair. It was so black and thick that she was nearly drawn to run her hands through it—probably exactly what his dates would do. "You might as well let it grow now. One day you'll get married and your wife will be in charge of it."

"Right," he said, laughing easily. "Jamie's in charge of Ryan's, Maggie's in charge of Brendan's. Heck, even Aunt Maeve changed the way Da cuts his." He snapped off a quick look at Mia. "Yours is getting long, too."

"Yeah. I don't have a stylist in Colorado, so I let it grow. Jordan likes it longer, so I'm gonna do what you're doing, and see what happens. If it drives me nuts, I'll cut it."

"Have you had it long before?"

They were walking now, and Mia was feeling more comfortable with him by the minute. "Oh, yeah. Until college. It straightens out a little bit when it's longer. But I had to braid it at night or it would have looked like a bird's nest in the morning."

"I think I'll stop before mine gets that long." He shot Mia a look and grinned, and she gave him a playful slap.

"You're in a good mood. What's going on with you?"

"Nothin' much. Ryan told me you were coming to town, and when she said your flight was after I finished work, I asked if I could pick you up."

Her stomach flipped and Mia prayed he wouldn't make a play for her. Deciding to get it over with if he was going to try and rekindle old feelings, she put it right out there. "Why?"

He shifted her big bag from one shoulder to the other. "Two reasons. One—I like you; two—I wanted to apologize."

"You do?"

"Yep. The last couple of times I saw you, I acted like a dick. I wanted you to know I was sorry. You were always up front with me, but I acted like we were engaged or something. That was just...dickish," he said, chuckling at the word.

They were crossing the street to the parking lot when she looked up at him. "What was up with that? I thought you were good with how things were between us."

"I was," he said, shrugging. "But that was when we both agreed we weren't ready to settle down. When you settled down about two minutes later..." He raised an eyebrow and looked at her. "I don't like to lose."

"I don't like to feel like a game," she said, scowling at him while he opened her door. She got in and waited for him to join her.

He settled in and buckled his seatbelt. "You're not a game. I just felt a little...played. If you'd said you were ready to get serious, I would've been down for it. It pissed me off when I realized you *were* ready to get serious, you just didn't want to get serious with me."

She reached over and grasped his forearm, blinking when she felt how large it was compared to Jordan's. "That's not how it was. I can't...I can't explain it, Conor, but I wasn't rejecting you. The timing was just bad for us. I think…no, I know…that pregnancy scare was kind of a deal breaker. It really freaked me out."

"Me too. But in a different way. It made me think I was ready to settle down; it made you wanna run away from anything that produced sperm." He gave her a half-smile, and she could see it was insincere. He was obviously still hurt.

"It wasn't sperm. The timing was just right with Jordan. I'm not into that 'there's only one person that can make you happy' stuff. But I do think you've gotta have some luck to have things click."

"And you and Jordan click."

"Totally," she said emphatically. "If I could, I'd marry her." He turned to her and she could see the muscles in his jaw loosen, then his mouth break into a smile.

"I'm happy for you…both of you."

Their eyes met and she could see the sincerity in them. "Thanks. Being in love is fantastic. I'd always tried to avoid getting too involved. But with Jordan—I don't have an option."

He put the key in the ignition and turned the engine over. "So, being a lesbian must be the right fit for you."

"Don't go nuts on me," she said, laughing. "I love Jordan, but I'm not a lesbian." She saw his eyebrow arch, and Mia was struck by the remarkable resemblance between him and Ryan. "I mean it. It's not an issue—since I plan on being with Jordan forever, but I don't feel gay, I never have."

Conor gave her a puzzled glance, then backed his truck out of the parking space. "Okay. I don't get it—but it's your life. You should know."

"I do. It's just hard to explain to people who think there are just two ways to be: gay and straight."

"There *are* only two in my book. The first time I check out a guy's ass—I'm gay."

"Not even in the locker room at the gym?" Mia taunted. "At the urinal?"

Conor shrugged. "I've looked, but just for comparison. I'm always worried about a guy who won't look any lower than my head. It's weird when a guy's really careful not to look. Always makes me think he wants to, but knows he won't be able to stop. It's funny," he said, clearly having given the matter some thought. "It's having a guy look at your ass that creeps you out. Every guy wants to know how big another guy's dick is. That's normal. But if a guy's looking at my ass—that's gay."

"Fascinating. Just fascinating. Do many guys look at your ass?"

"Yeeeeeeah," he said, blushing a little. "More than I like to admit. Ryan says I look just gay enough to make guys think I'm in the club."

"Huh." Mia sat sideways in her seat and looked him over. "You look straight to me. But you are a little…clean for a straight guy."

"Yeah." He nodded. "Ryan says I care too much about how I look to be straight."

Mia giggled. "It doesn't bother you to talk about this?"

He gave her a puzzled glance. "Why would it?"

"I don't know. Most guys wouldn't like to admit that they look a little gay."

"It'll bother me when more men than women check me out. Until then… the boys can look all they want. Just don't touch the merchandise."

"Has anyone ever tried?"

"To touch me?" he asked, his voice rising.

"Yeah."

"Hell no! I'd clock a guy who tried it!"

Mia sat up straighter in her seat. "Would you really? You'd bash a gay man?"

Looking over quickly, he said, "Bash? It's not bashing if he grabs you. What would you do if a guy grabbed your ass?"

"Probably try to knee him in the crotch."

"I rest my case. Men are dogs. It doesn't matter if they're gay or straight. Give 'em an inch—"

"And they'll grab your ass," Mia said, finishing his observation. "I guess I never thought of it like that. But you have a point."

"It doesn't bother me if a guy politely checks me out. I give him a 'not interested' look and that's the end of it. But if some jerk ever got aggressive with me—lights out. You gotta draw the line somewhere."

"What if a woman tried to grab your ass?"

He smiled at her, his sexy grin in place. "I have a double standard. I'd allow that. How about you?"

"Mmm…I probably would too. Or at least I would have before Jordan."

His grin remained. "Good thing you're not gay." He winced when she slapped his bare arm, and they teased each other all the way to Berkeley.

Jamie and Catherine sat in traffic on the 101 freeway, waiting to exit near The Mission. They were going to look at a building, and this time Jamie had laid down the law with Ray. No more chauffeuring. It was a small detail, but she liked to be in charge of her own agenda. If she wanted to take a quick peek and move on, she could.

"Do you think the cousins will consider a building outside their neighborhood?" Catherine asked.

"I don't think they much care where it is, so long as they don't have to drive too far to work on it."

"This one sounds promising. Did you bring your camera?"

"Yep." Jamie nodded to where it lay on the back seat. "You might have to take the pictures, though. I don't think I can do it with one hand."

"How's your arm feeling, honey?"

"Not too bad. I elevate it and that helps. I don't think about it much unless I try to use it and am reminded that it doesn't bend."

"I'm more than happy to take pictures." Catherine frowned. "Are we close?"

"Yeah." They'd exited the freeway and were slowly cruising down Dolores. "There it is. Chula Lane." She chuckled. "I hope the boyos don't know that's Mexican slang for a hot girl."

"If they do, we might as well leave right now. They'd all love a hot girl, but they probably wouldn't want to own a house on Hot Girl Street."

"I don't think any of them speak enough Spanish to know more than standard construction terms. We should be safe."

Catherine turned left and slowed down, looking for a place to park. "I'd better find something on Dolores; the smaller streets never have anything."

Jamie agreed, and a few minutes later they were blessed by the parking gods. Walking together down the street, Jamie stopped at Chula Lane and looked around. "Not bad. It goes through to Church, but it's not as busy as seventeenth or eighteenth."

Thoughtfully, Catherine said, "A year ago I wouldn't have believed we'd be walking around this neighborhood looking at apartment buildings."

"It would have been a stretch, wouldn't it? I remember the first time I drove to Ryan's. I was going through The Mission thinking, 'How am I gonna be polite if she lives over some little taco stand?'"

Catherine smiled fondly. "You wouldn't have noticed. Tacos would have become your favorite food."

Jamie nodded her head, a little embarrassed. "I guess I was a little dreamy-eyed."

Linking their arms together, Catherine said, "I wish I had known what you were going through then. It would have been nice to share that with you."

"Mmm...I wasn't much for sharing then, but I wish I could have been. I was as clueless as it's possible to be."

"You've done well for yourself in a year. I always knew you could master anything you put your mind to."

Jamie leaned over and kissed her mother on the cheek. "You helped me a lot. Without your support...I don't even wanna think of what I might have done if you'd let Daddy speak for both of you."

"You know," Catherine said thoughtfully, "even though it led to the breakup of my marriage, I'm very glad I'm learning to stand up for myself."

"And for me. That's what made me see how much you loved me."

Her smile was so wide her eyes nearly closed. "I do love you. I'm so happy that I'm your mother."

"We're both coming into our own, Mom. The Evans...uhm...we're doing well."

In a moment Catherine's smile was gone, replaced by a look of deep concern. "You don't like that I'm changing my name, do you."

Indecision slowed her down for a few moments, then Jamie told the truth. "No, I don't. But I'd probably do the same thing if I were in your shoes. I understand why you don't want Daddy's name any more."

Catherine stopped, grasping Jamie's arm to slow her down. "I told you before that's not why I've done this. Your father and his name had almost nothing to do with it."

"Then what did?" Jamie could feel her chin start to stick out.

"I truly wanted to honor my great-grandmother. Returning to my maiden name didn't have much allure, because I wasn't much of a person back then. But I also don't want to be known primarily as Senator Evans' ex-wife. I want to choose my identity, and I've chosen my great-grandmother to model myself after. It's your father's notoriety I want to escape, not him."

Jamie forced herself to smile. That was hard to take, but she was committed to try. "I'll try to think about it from that perspective."

It was clear from her expression that Catherine wasn't buying it, but she let it go. "Let's go see this apartment building."

As they approached, Jamie saw Ray waiting for them. She waved at him as they approached. Standing on the sidewalk, she looked up at the building and shook her head. "Why would anyone put those nasty shingles on a building?"

He shrugged. "That was the craze in the forties and fifties."

"Hmm…can they be taken off?"

"Sure. Anything can be taken off. But they're probably asbestos. That'll cost a bit."

Jamie handed Catherine her camera. "Take a picture of this lovely green building, will you?"

They spent about half an hour looking at the interior, and even though it took a lot of imagination, they all agreed that it belonged in the possible category.

Jamie took her phone out and made a call. "Hi, Niall. Mom and I just looked at the three flat on Chula Lane. It's a dump, but a reasonably priced dump."

"Now what?"

"Uhm…that's why I'm calling you. Would you like to take a look?"

"I could, but I'm not in charge."

Rolling her eyes, Jamie said, "I took pictures. I'll show them to all of you and see what you think. How's that?"

"Good. Good. See ya."

Jamie looked at her mother. "Being the real estate agent for the O'Flaherty cousins is a little tougher than I thought it would be." After thinking for a minute she said, "Do you have time to stop at Kinko's?"

"Of course. For what?"

"I'm gonna print these pictures and drop them off at each house. Then I'm gonna tell them to go look at the outside and let me know if they want to schedule a visit. I can't make the decision for them…at least not so they notice."

Chapter Thirteen

Conor carried Mia's bag to the front door and waited while she rang the bell six times in fifteen seconds. She had a key, but she wanted to make an entrance. She and Conor smiled at each other when they heard quick footsteps and a shouted, "Keep your shirt on!" booming from the house.

"Ryan's home," he said. "Such a dainty girl."

The door was flung open and Ryan reached out and grabbed Mia, lifting her off her feet. Instinctively, she wrapped her legs around Ryan's hips and kissed her. "I didn't know you cared," she giggled. "Don't let Jamie catch us."

"She'll never know. She called and said she'd be home soon, but we can have fun until she gets here." She nuzzled her face into Mia's neck and blew a loud raspberry against her skin. "Now that I've got you, I'm never letting you go. You're mine now."

Mia ran her hands over Ryan's shoulders, then leaned back a little and pinched her cheeks. "I might not argue. You're lots softer than Jordan is now. Would Jamie mind sharing?"

Conor reached in and slapped his sister on the shoulder. "I'm gonna take off before you even think about answering that."

"Hey, come in and hang out," Ryan said. "Stay for dinner. I promise I won't gross you out."

Conor laughed. "It wouldn't gross me out if *you* weren't involved. It'd be much better for me if Jamie and Mia and Jordan hooked up. Epic threesome."

"Not gonna happen," Ryan said. "Well, I can't speak for Mia and Jordan, but Jamie's not into sharing."

"There's not enough of Jordan to share," Mia interjected. "If she doesn't put on some weight, she's gonna blow away."

Ryan placed Mia onto the floor. "Come on in. You too, Conor. I'll make whatever you want for dinner."

"I want some of that pizza you and Jamie are always talking about."

"Done. I love to order out, especially when it's my day to cook. Pizza good for you, Mia?"

"Hell, yes. I haven't had pizza since I left. Jordan can't eat bread or cheese, so our version of pizza would be a small plate of tomato sauce, oregano and basil."

"You know you've lost a few pounds too," Ryan said, looking her over. "You look good, but you're almost too thin." She pulled on a few locks of Mia's hair, smiling when the curls sprang back into place. "Your hair looks cute. I've never seen it so long."

"Thanks. I was gonna get it cut, but now I think I might let it grow."

"What's with Jordan being so skinny?" Conor asked. "I didn't know you were supposed to be thin for volleyball."

"You're not." Ryan looked more than a little displeased. "Jordan has some trainer who wants her to be as skinny as a stick and then start putting muscle on. It sounds stupid to me, but he's calling the shots."

"What's up with that?" Conor asked. "She was thin before."

"Not like she is now," Mia said. "She's all bony and sharp. She's lost her…" she shot a look at Conor, "…some of her best parts. But she's down to the percentage of body fat that the trainer wants, so she's supposed to start eating more protein and working with heavier weights."

"I hope that guy knows what he's doing," Ryan said. "How's her energy level?"

"I don't think it's as good as it was, but she doesn't agree." Mia shrugged helplessly. "If they told her to eat rat poison, I think she might do it. She wants this sooooo bad."

"I assume the Olympic team has somebody competent," Ryan said. "But maybe she should go to the doctor and have some blood tests done. She might be hurting herself."

"Don't give me anything else to worry about. Being in a relationship is a full time job!"

Ryan gave her a big hug, holding onto her while kissing her head. "It is, but it's a great job, isn't it?"

"The best I've ever had. Of course, it's the first job I've ever had, so what the hell do I know?"

Dinner lasted until after ten o'clock, with Ryan having to run out to the store to buy another bottle of red wine when they ran out. She walked Conor out to his truck, and gave him an enthusiastic hug when they reached the door. "I don't know if you were being sincere, but you acted like everything was normal between you and Mia. Thanks for that."

"I had nowhere to go but up," he said, chuckling. "Besides, it's obvious Mia's hooked. If I keep acting like an ass, you guys won't want me around when she's here."

"This is true. But you're...okay? You're not just on good behavior?"

"No. I like her."

"I'm glad. It's fun having you here when Mia's home. I think you guys can be good friends."

"Yeah. Just what I need—more girl friends." He kissed Ryan's cheek. "You've gotta branch out and get some straight friends. *Really* straight friends. Ones who throw up a little at the thought of kissing a woman."

Ryan laughed. "I'll look around. Maybe there's a club at Cal."

"That's all I ask. My needs are simple."

"Thanks for picking Mia up, Con. I won't even charge you for the pizza."

"You're all heart. I might come see you play on Sunday. Any chance you'll get in the game?"

"The usual. I'm first off the bench, so you never know."

"Okay. See ya." He kissed her cheek and got into his truck and gunned the engine, the sound reverberating down the quiet street.

Jamie and Mia were still sitting at the table when Ryan got back inside. "One of you has to get up at seven," she said, looking pointedly at Jamie.

"I know, I know. But I wanna stay up all night and talk to my buddy!"

"Since I escaped having to cook, I'll clean up. You guys go get ready for bed. I assume you were up at dawn?" she asked Mia.

"Five thirty, as usual. I'm not sure what the time difference is between here and Russia, but Jordy's coach always wants them to stay on the same schedule. She might be getting up at four in the afternoon."

"Her coaches sound like...mmm..." Ryan considered her options, "...idiots."

"That's what I think. But I try not to say much to Jordan, she's like a cult member."

"Go get ready for bed," Ryan ordered. "Jamie needs her nine hours."

A blonde eyebrow rose. "Then why don't I ever get more than seven?"

"'Cause you're always up too late yapping." She ducked the spoon her lover threw at her, eyes going wide when it almost hit a vase filled with jonquils. "Ooo…that was close. I've gotta teach you better. You aim for the gut…then even if you're too high or too low, you still hit something. Being an only child really screwed you up."

"I'll get *you* later," Jamie said, squinting her eyes menacingly.

Ryan winked at her. "That's the other thing that keeps you up too late."

When Ryan went up to their bedroom, she wasn't surprised to find Jamie absent. As expected, she was sitting on Mia's bed, her back against the headboard, with Mia's head resting on her leg. Jamie was gently running her fingers through her friend's curls, while they chatted and giggled. Ryan put her hands on her hips. "I want in on this."

"Come on," Jamie said, patting her lap. "You can have my other thigh. But I'll have to alternate my hand from head to head."

Ryan poked her head into Mia's bathroom and grabbed some moisture lotion. "I want some Mia." She sat by the foot of the bed and plopped both of Mia's feet into her lap. "Can you tell we missed you?"

Mia purred when Ryan put some of the lotion on her hands and warmed it, then started to rub it into the sole of her foot. "I never would have left if you two would've done this every night."

"We couldn't get to you," Ryan complained. "Jordan was always wrapped around you."

"Mmm…right. Being with Jordan has definite advantages…but this is awfully nice."

Her eyes were closed, and Jamie smiled at Ryan when it became clear that Mia was going to be asleep in moments. "While you're home, we'll treat you like the princess you are," Ryan said. "We'll cook for you, massage you…anything your heart desires."

"Bring Jordy here to sleep with me," Mia mumbled, curling up against a pillow and hugging it.

"Almost anything your heart desires," Ryan amended, sharing a sympathetic look with Jamie.

Ryan was loping across campus when someone called out, "Hey! Ryan!"

She stopped and turned, seeing Gabe, the guy who'd been on the Cal math team, waving at her.

"Hey, what's up?"

He trotted over to her. "Did you look at the results from the Putnam?"

"No, why?"

"I looked at the team scores. If you'd been on the team instead of Serban, we would have come in second. Second! And we would've lost to Waterloo by just six points."

Ryan kicked the ground. "Damn!"

"Damn is right. If Skadden hadn't insisted on screwing things up, we would've rocked."

Ryan gave him a collegial slap on the back. "It's over now. Not much we can do about it."

"I'm gonna send an e-mail to the department head. Skadden shouldn't be in charge of the competition any more. He's a dinosaur."

"I agree. But I don't think that's a fight I wanna get involved in. It's too uphill a battle."

"Come on," he said, jumping up and down in front of her like a kid. "You're the one who was wronged."

"Yeah, yeah, I know. But I'm too busy to start a fight. Maybe after graduation."

Gabe shoved his hands into his pockets. "I was counting on you."

"I understand, but I can't do it. I've got other priorities right now."

"Okay." He turned, waving goodbye as he walked away.

Ryan watched him walk away. "Good luck, Gabe," she said quietly. "You'll need it."

When Ryan got home from her game, Jamie and Mia were sitting in the living room, drinking beer. "Hey!" Jamie said, lifting her bottle. "Welcome home!"

Ryan smiled and walked over to give her a kiss. "How was your tournament?"

"Good. Well, as good as a tournament can be when you watch from a golf cart. I just got home about fifteen minutes ago. I would have come over to see you, but I figured you'd be finished. Did you win?"

"Yep. We played well."

"Did you play?" Mia asked.

"Nope. I usually go in when we *don't* play well."

"And you're okay with that? Jordan goes nuts when she can't play."

"I'd rather play, but I'm enjoying this for what it is—my last time playing college sports. I chip in when the coach thinks he needs me, and if he doesn't—I'm cool."

"Wow, you've changed," Mia said, looking at Ryan curiously. "You weren't like that when you were playing volleyball."

Ryan sat next to Jamie and put her feet up on the coffee table. "You're right." She took Jamie's beer and took a long gulp. "Mmm…good," she said, waggling her eyebrows. "I'm trying to be a little more relaxed about things. I'm not always successful, but I'm trying."

Jamie put her arm around her partner and hugged her. "She's trying real hard."

Acknowledging that with a kiss, Ryan said casually, "I did something good today."

"What's that?"

"You know Gabe, who scored so high on the Putnam?"

"Oh!" Mia said. "Jamie told me how great you did. That's so cool."

"Thanks. Well, the guy who really kicked ass told me that if I'd been on the team instead of the guy Skadden put in my place…we would've come in second."

"No!" Jamie cried.

"Yep. And here's the good part. He wanted me to help him get Skadden fired as the team leader."

Jamie blinked at her. "And you said no?"

"Yep." Ryan smiled placidly. "Sure did."

"But why? You *and* Cal's team were screwed."

"I know. But Gabe didn't throw a fit until he saw that the team would have done better with me. If he was so concerned with equality, he would have fought for me back when Skadden decided not to put me on."

"Would that have done any good?"

"It might have. He's Skadden's golden boy, and he probably would have listened to him if he'd really taken a stand. It's too late now, and I'm too busy to bang my head against the wall. The department knows Skadden's a jerk. They know he's never had a woman on the team. They don't care, and I don't wanna whip myself into a frenzy trying to fight the bureaucracy."

"Damn," Mia said. "That's mature. When did you get to be mature?"

"Don't worry, it's not consistent," Ryan assured her. "Jamie can testify to that."

"I'm stunned," Jamie said, and her expression bore her out. "I can't imagine you letting this go."

"It does piss me off, and I don't want other women to get screwed. I might write a letter after graduation; I'm just not into it right now."

"I'm still stunned," Jamie said. "Proud of you, but stunned."

Ryan snagged the beer from her partner. "If you're gonna sit there with your mouth hanging open, I'm gonna finish this little baby."

"Go ahead. You know everything I have is yours. Oh, Niall called and said the boys want to look at that three-flat this weekend. I hope they can manage it without supervision."

"Is Brendan going?"

"Yeah, I think so."

"They'll be fine," Ryan said before draining the bottle.

On Saturday morning, Ryan was just getting ready to leave for the softball field when Mia came tottering out of her room. She walked right into Ryan and hugged her, holding on for a long time. "It didn't take me too long to get out of my five thirty wake-up call habit, did it?"

"When did you get home? I didn't hear you come in."

"When do the bars close?"

"Two."

"Then probably two fifteen," she said, giggling. "But I didn't get drunk. I just hung out and watched my friends guzzle. Man, I hang out with some drinkers!"

Ryan chuckled. "Yeah, you do, but that's part of the fun of college. If you can't get wasted every once in a while when you're in college, when can you?"

"I still like to drink, but I've cut way, way back since I've been with Jordan." Mia considered that for a moment. "In fact, we never have alcohol in the house."

Ryan reached down and tickled Mia's lower back. "Hear that, liver? There's still a chance you won't have to be replaced."

"Funny, O'Flaherty. Where are you off to?"

"Softball game. Wanna come?"

"Gosh, that sounds tempting," Mia said, rolling her eyes. "But I'm gonna go see my parents. I might stay down there and go to Jamie's match tomorrow. Her team's at Stanford, right?"

"Right. I'm not sure what her plans are, but she can tell you if you call her tonight."

"Okay. If my parents aren't behaving themselves, I'll come home."

"Call us," Ryan said. "And don't forget. I promised Jordan I'd take good care of you."

Mia hugged her tighter. "I wish I had someone to watch over her. All I've got is somebody who wants to get into her pants."

"Knowing how Jordan feels about you, someone would have to sedate her to get her clothes off. You've got nothing to worry about."

"I know. But it still makes me uncomfortable. Jill's just so obvious about it. When we were getting ready to leave on Thursday, she made a big deal about how she'd never let Jordan out of her sight. It was...gross," she said, making a face.

"Jordan's hooked on you, and that's all that matters. Now go get some coffee. I bought you a bagel and a muffin and some cereal."

"What kind?"

"Fruit Loops. Your favorite."

Mia stood on her tiptoes and pulled Ryan down for a kiss. "You spoil me." She rubbed the tip of her nose against Ryan's. "I love that. I might have chosen you if I'd met you before Jamie did."

"Lucky for me," Ryan said, laughing. "Neither one of us would have seen thirty."

Ryan had offered the use of her car, but Mia chose Jamie's, having driven it many times over the years. She pulled into her parents' drive around noon, pleased to see both cars in the garage. The stunned look on her father's face when he opened the door made the trip worthwhile.

"Mia!"

His hug engulfed her and she held onto him tightly, letting the hug soothe a part of her that had been seriously wounded.

"What a great surprise!"

"I should have called," she said when he released her. "But I like surprises."

"This one is wonderful!"

Her father looked so happy to see her that she was very glad she'd decided not to go to Russia. Being welcomed by her family was much more gratifying than sitting in an old gym for hours on end.

"I just got home from the course. You have great timing," he said

"Nah. I just slept late. We usually get up really early, so it was nice to be a sloth."

"Come on in, honey. Your mom's outside putting in some plants."

Mia walked through the living room, feeling comforted and safe among the familiar furniture and knick-knacks. The kitchen still smelled of bacon and pancakes, and her stomach grumbled, even though she'd had a huge bowl of Fruit Loops just an hour earlier. She opened the back door and her mother looked up—and her face brightened. "Mia!" She jumped to her feet and ripped off her gardening gloves, but didn't have time to take a step before Mia wrapped her in a hug.

"Hi, Mom. I thought I'd surprise you."

"Surprise me! I'm stunned! I was expecting a call telling me when you were leaving for Russia."

"Jordan left yesterday. I decided she'd play better if she didn't have to worry about me." She looked into her mother's eyes. "And I decided I needed to come home for a week. I miss you guys and I miss my friends. Colorado Spring's nice, but it's not my home."

"This is your home," Anna Lisa said, hugging her for a long time. "This will *always* be your home."

Mia didn't say what she was thinking because she didn't want her hurt her mother, but Hillsborough wasn't her home. Jordan would never be truly welcome as a member of the family. Her parents would come around and at least be cordial to her, but that wouldn't satisfy her. They needed not only acceptance, they needed to be embraced as a couple. Their home was in Berkeley—with Jamie and Ryan.

"Can I help you plant?" Mia asked. "It's so nice to be outside." She looked around the large, well-tended yard. "I miss having any outside space."

"Sure. I'll get you some gloves."

"No thanks. I like the dirt."

Anna Lisa bumped her with her shoulder. "You were always a little dirt-devil."

Mia was wearing jeans, and she knelt down next to her mother and started digging holes for the bedding plants. "I'll dig and you can plant. How deep do you want the holes?"

"About three inches. We'll be done in no time if we work together." They put a few plants in and Anna Lisa said, "Could I convince you to take a drive over to Nonna's?"

"Sure, I don't have any plans."

"Great. Adam, would you call my mom and see if she's home?"

"All right," he said, heading for the house with a resigned slump to his shoulders.

Anna Lisa giggled. "Twenty-five years and he still hates to call her. Men are such babies."

"He's not so bad. You've trained him pretty well."

"It's not easy." Anna Lisa worked quietly for a few minutes, then asked, "Everything's all right, isn't it?"

"Yeah. Why wouldn't it be?"

"I don't know. I was just worried that maybe you'd had a fight with Jordan. You seemed so sure that you were going with her…"

"I was. Now, I hate to have you think you have any influence over me," she said, laughing, "but you do. I thought about what you said and I started to really think about whether or not I wanted to go."

"Did Jordan want you to go?"

"Yeah, she kinda did. But she wanted me to go if I was gonna have a great time. And it just didn't seem like fun to sit around and wait for her to finish playing. It also seemed like an awful lot of money to spend only to have no time together. And, to be honest, I don't have much interest in that part of Europe. I like France and Italy."

"France is a dump," Anna Lisa sniffed. "But Italy's wonderful. And I agree—why waste time in Russia if you can be in Italy?"

"If Jordan decides to play professionally, she'd play in Italy."

"Oh, my God! Is she going to do that?"

"I doubt it, but it's an option. They have a good professional league there, and some of her teammates go there every winter."

"Are you sure you know what you've gotten yourself into, honey?"

"Nope." Mia sat back on her haunches. "Do you ever really know what's gonna happen when you love someone? You just kinda see what happens."

"But she seems to put this sports thing first in her life."

"She does. I've told you that. This is one of her life goals. She's not gonna do it her whole life, but being on the Olympic squad is the highest level of competition she'll ever have. This means the world to her."

"But what does it mean to you? Are you just along for the ride?"

Staring at her mother for a while, she finally said, "Yes. Jordan has a goal. My job is to help her do as well as she can. When she's finished, we'll figure out what we want to do with the rest of *our* lives. Things will be more equal then."

"How do you know? If you give in to everything she wants now, won't she expect that?"

Trying not to roll her eyes, Mia said, "She's not like that. Not at all. She's not bossy or pushy or anything like that. If I asked her to, she'd quit the team right now. But I wouldn't. I'd never ask her to stop doing something that really means everything to her."

"Honey, I'm not...I don't want you to set things up in a way that always puts her first. That's all."

It wasn't easy to keep her cool, but Mia was determined not to fight. "I don't think you understand, or maybe you don't believe me when I say we're partners. Right now, she has a goal. Later on, I'll have one, too. We share. Isn't that the point of being in love?"

Anna Lisa sat perfectly still for a minute, then she nodded. "Yes. That's the point of being in love. I...suppose I'm not really used to the whole thing yet."

"You'll get there, if you want to."

"Well, you know this isn't what I want for you, but you do seem happy, and that's very important to me." She leaned over and kissed Mia's cheek. "Even though you might not believe me, I really want you to be happy."

"I believe that. I just know that you'd rather I was happy the way you want me to be." She gave her mother a teasing smile.

"Oh, everyone's like that. So...what's *your* goal?"

"Mmm...I think I'll go to law school. Maybe not in a year, but as soon as I can. But my real goal is to have kids."

"Kids?"

"Yeah. You know—small humans."

"With Jordan?"

"Yep." Mia didn't say another word. She just watched the conflicting emotions whirl across her mother's face. She saw everything pass by in a matter of seconds, and didn't try to intervene. She knew this wouldn't be an easy sell, and she was prepared for a long fight.

"Well, I hope you're going to wait for a while to do that." Anna Lisa wasn't giving away much, but the look on her face was less than enthusiastic.

"Jordan and I haven't even talked about it seriously, but my life goal is to be a good mother. Everything else is just a job."

She looked like she was fighting with herself, but Anna Lisa couldn't help but smile. "You're always full of surprises, my sweet girl. I can never guess what's gonna pop out of your mouth next."

"Stay tuned. It's always something."

After they were finished in the garden, they went upstairs to clean up. Mia had some clothes in her closet that still fit her, and they were a little bit dressier than the jeans she was wearing—always a wise choice for a visit to her grandparents. Her mother was ready before her father, and she came downstairs looking edgy. She walked up behind Mia, who was sitting at the kitchen table, and started to play with her hair. "I like your hair this length. It's such a pretty color."

"Thanks. It's the same color as yours, you know."

"It's the same as mine *used* to be. I've had to start dying mine."

"Really?" Mia turned around and looked carefully. "You can't tell."

"For what those thieves charge me, you shouldn't be able to tell. I don't have a lot of gray, but I'm not giving in gracefully. I'm not going to be gray before Nonna is."

"She's got a twenty year head start on you."

"Thank God she started lightening it up. She looked like a vampire with that dark hair and pale skin."

"Who talked her into doing that?"

"God knows. I'd never have the nerve."

"It cracks me up that you're afraid to tell her something like that."

"It's not worth it, honey. There are some things you talk about, and some things you don't. Uhm…that…uhm…that's something I wanted to talk to you about."

"I won't talk about Jordan," Mia said, scowling. "That *is* what you were going to ask, right?"

"I hate to make you feel bad, but it's too soon. After you've been together for a while and know that you're stable…then it'll be easier."

"No, it won't. She'll still have a fit. But I'm not really in the mood to have her go nuclear on me, so I wasn't gonna talk about Jordan anyway."

Anna Lisa leaned down and kissed her cheek. "You're being so mature about all of this. You really are growing up."

"I am. And part of the reason I'm growing up is because of Jordan. She helps me think things through. That's something I haven't always been good at."

"I wish she were a man, but, for a woman, she seems like a good... What do you call her?"

"You can call her my partner. I call her my luscious lesbian lover."

Anna Lisa put her hands around Mia's throat and playfully choked her. "Forget what I said about being mature, you little devil!"

"Help! Dad! Mom's trying to kill me!"

Brendan rang Ryan that evening. "I think we need another pow-wow."

"How come?"

"Everybody saw the building, and we all agree that it's got potential. But it costs a lot more than we discussed, and it's not a house. Knowing Jamie, she's got something in mind, but we're stumped."

"Huh." Ryan looked at her partner, peacefully curled up on the sofa, reading a book. "You're right. She's always got a hidden agenda."

Jamie looked up and pointed at herself ostentatiously. Ryan wrinkled up her nose and nodded.

Chuckling, Brendan said, "Wanna ask her, or should we just do as she says?"

"It's easier if you just do as she says." Jamie nodded energetically. "But we should probably chat. How about Sunday night? We're planning on coming home for dinner."

"Okay. I'll set up a poker game. That'll attract a crowd."

"Sounds good. Will I see you and Maggie at dinner?"

"I don't think so. She's got a cocktail party for work that she's dragging me to. We'll probably have dinner with some of her co-workers."

"Sounds like fun," Ryan teased, knowing he hated to socialize with strangers.

"Yeah. Being in love stinks sometimes, but it's worth it in the long run." He laughed softly. "At least that's what I keep telling myself."

Chapter Fourteen

On Saturday evening, Conor pressed the bell at Catherine's Pacific Heights home. Marta answered the door and welcomed him. "Won't you have a seat?" she said, indicating the living room. "Catherine will be down in a few minutes. What can I get you to drink?"

"You don't need to go to any trouble for me, Marta. I'm fine."

"I'd enjoy making you a drink. I'm a good bartender." Her dark eyes were twinkling and Conor found himself unable to resist her offer. "Okay. Just a little whiskey and water."

She nodded and went to a bar hidden in an antique armoire. After naming six brands of whiskey and two kinds of bottled water, Conor made his choices, hoping he didn't have to specify a type of ice. Marta handed him the drink and put out a coaster, then left the room. Conor wished she would have stayed and chatted, but he assumed that wasn't done.

Catherine appeared relatively soon and he stood to greet her. "As usual...you look fantastic," he said. He studied her, looking at her hair, her jewelry, her clothing and her shoes. "Flawless. Just flawless."

Laughing softly, Catherine said, "Your sister does the same thing. She looks me over like she's my dresser. Did you two learn that from your father?"

"Ha! You've gotta be kidding. Da tells every woman she looks nice. He's completely untrustworthy."

"I'll have to remember that."

"Don't trust Rory or Brendan either. They don't have a clue."

"You're always a surprise. And may I sincerely tell you that you look fabulous in your suit. That's a very nice tie."

"Thanks. I wanted something to give the suit some pop. Polka dots won't be stylish for long, but they're in right now."

"You really do care about how you look, don't you?"

Conor smiled. "Sure. I get so dirty at work that I love to get cleaned up."

"You certainly don't look like your average carpenter."

"It's harder for me than for a guy who sits at a desk. I have to get a manicure to get the grime from my fingernails, and I need a facial every few weeks to get the dirt out of my pores."

Catherine blinked. "You go to a salon?"

"Yeah, unless I'm dating someone. I had a girlfriend for a long time and she used to love to give me facials and things like that. She said I was the only guy she'd ever gotten to play with like that."

"I...I'd guess so. I've certainly never done that for a man."

"I don't think I'd go to a salon if I lived in Moose Nose, Minnesota," he admitted. "But there are guy-only spas here. And not everybody who goes is gay." He paused and added, "Only ninety-five percent or so."

Catherine laughed. "You're full of as many contradictions as your sister. You two are most definitely interesting companions."

"I'm a lot more interesting." He dangled his keys in his hand. "Your car or mine?"

"Mine, if you don't mind. Will you drive?"

"Twist my arm."

The event was being held at Davies Symphony Hall, a place Conor had never entered. Being a good guest was more work than it looked, but he managed to be at Catherine's side when she looked for him and absent when she was having a serious conversation. He made a little small talk on his own, but primarily knocked himself out to act as a very proper, discreet companion.

Waiters carried hot and cold appetizers on trays, and he had a few of each, not wanting to appear too ravenous. Adding to his drive to fit in, he didn't want to risk dripping on his new tie, which had cost him a day's labor.

Waiters circulated with flutes of champagne, and he availed himself of two of those. A large table in the corner held various kinds of cheese and later in the evening a second table was revealed; this one filled with tiers of desserts.

Catherine had been mingling around the room, and when she appeared again, she asked, "Would you like something sweet?"

"No more real food?"

Her eyes widened. "Didn't you have enough canapés?"

"No, not if that's all we get."

"Oh, Conor, I'm sorry I didn't make it clear that this wasn't a formal dinner. The hall isn't big enough to seat all of these people, so they just serve heavy hors d'oeuvres."

"Those were heavy? A piece of mango stuck to a shrimp isn't heavy... it's light...it's ultra-light."

Catherine turned and peered at the various waiters still carrying trays. "Did you have some of that Kobe beef?"

"It was cut with a plane! Wood shavings are thicker than that. I'm gonna have to stand at that dessert table and make some sparks fly."

"You don't have much of a sweet tooth, do you?"

"No, not really. I like pie and a chocolate malt once in a while, but I'm an entrée kinda guy."

"Then we'll go get you an entrée." She started to walk away, but Conor touched her arm.

"We don't have to leave. I can stop and get a burger on my way home. You need to be here."

"I've spoken to everyone. I've done my duty and we can go...unless you're not ready."

"Oh, I could probably force myself to take off. Especially since there's no dance floor. I had my eye on that woman over there who's tapping her foot to the music."

Catherine looked over and saw a woman who was likely a nonagenarian, tapping her foot and shifting her shoulders while her ancient husband leaned against a wall to avoid falling over.

"Her husband doesn't look like he can lead her around the dance floor any more. I bet she misses it."

Surprisingly, Catherine took his arm and hugged it to herself. "You are possibly the sweetest man I've ever known. I can't think of another man I know who'd even notice that woman, much less think of asking her to dance."

He could feel his cheeks tint from embarrassment. "One day I'm gonna be old. I'd love it if some young woman thought about my feelings before she slapped me for hitting on her."

A short time later they were ensconced at a small table at an equally small bistro in Pacific Heights. Conor eyed the menu, finally deciding on a steak and fries. After their order was taken, they sipped at their cocktails, and Conor regarded Catherine for a moment. "You seem much happier than you were a month ago."

"Mmm..." She swallowed and considered his comment. "I am. I don't feel as lonely, and that's always a plus. And I..." She paused for a few seconds. "I feel desirable again."

"The guy who showed up at your house during the party?"

"Why...yes. Was it that obvious?"

"No, no." He shook his head decisively. "But he didn't look like an old family friend. Jamie didn't know him, so...I just guessed."

Her cheeks turned a very nice pink color. "I don't know why I'm embarrassed to have Giacomo in my life." Shifting in her seat, she waited another moment, then spoke again. "Yes, I do. He's married."

"Ooo...unhappily?"

"On the contrary. He's happily married, but both he and his wife have outside...interests."

"Now *that's* a marriage I could get into."

"I couldn't. At all. And that's one of my problems. I put myself in his wife's position and know how much I'd hate to have my husband be intimate with another woman."

"But she doesn't hate it? Do you know that for sure?"

"Do I know that?" She frowned. "I know that's what Giacomo has told me from the beginning. He says she has a lover...the same person for many years."

"Maybe you'd feel better if you talked to her. If she really doesn't care..."

"Giacomo has offered. They've always kept things an open secret, but he told her about me and asked if she'd talk to me."

"Then he must be telling the truth. That's a whopper to get out of if you're bluffing."

"I don't think he's the type to lie. I really don't."

"You're sure he's on...the up and up? He's trustworthy?" He winced as he asked the question, hoping it wasn't too obvious that he was checking to see if the guy was a gold-digger.

"I'm sure of that. He doesn't need anything from me. He has children, a wife who's younger than me, money, connections. There's not a reason in the world he cares for me—except me."

"Like that's not enough!"

She reached out and rubbed the back of his hand. "You're so good for my ego."

"Your ego isn't big enough. Neither is your appetite." Their server set his steak and her six oysters on the table. Conor eyed the heaping mound of ultra-thin, crispy fries on his plate and said, "I won't rest until you help me finish these off."

She grinned at him and snagged one, blowing on it to cool it. Taking a delicate bite, she closed her eyes for a moment then said, "Divine. The worse food is for you, the better it tastes."

He fixed her with an intense gaze. "That can be true for men too."

Once again she gripped his hand. "I think it can be. But it's not true for Giacomo."

They almost finished the fries, but Conor had to take care of two of Catherine's oysters. "How can you not have room for two oysters?" he asked, patting his mouth clean. "I could have two dozen as a *light* appetizer."

She laughed at his use of the term. "How many for a heavy one?"

"One of those numbers Ryan talks about. The ones so big they have to guess at how many zeroes there are."

"Your sister has been such a wonderful addition to our family, Conor. I hope you all know how much I love her."

"I do. She does too. Believe me, we wouldn't ask you over all the time if you weren't nice to her. You don't see Jim dropping by when he's in town, do you?"

"No, I suppose I don't. But he's coming around."

"I like him, but he could cure cancer and Da wouldn't...throw water on him if he were on fire." He'd barely caught himself before he'd said "piss." "He doesn't forgive or forget, especially where my little sister is concerned."

"But he's always been polite."

"Oh, sure, he's polite, but it's a very chilly polite." He chuckled, thinking of how his father would really like to treat Jim. A visit to the emergency room wouldn't be out of the question.

"How about you? Is there anyone special in your life?"

"No, but I wouldn't mind finding someone. I'm ready to settle down a little."

"It shouldn't be hard for you to find a nice woman. I'd guess you could have your pick."

"No, that's not true." He didn't feel comfortable talking about Mia, so he just smiled. "Uhm…are you…exclusive with Giacomo?"

"Hmm. Good question." She tilted her head and appeared to think for a moment. "I thought I wanted to get married or have another marriage-like relationship, but now I'm not so sure."

"Really? Why?"

"Oh, I think it's hard to find love. I certainly don't know anyone I'd like to date, and I probably know everyone in my economic class in San Francisco. At least people in my age range."

"That can't be your only reason to give up on marriage."

"No, I suppose not. The real reason is that I'm at the age where all of the men have been married once or twice or three times." She smiled wryly. "I don't really want to have step-children or vengeful ex-wives or all of the turmoil that entails. Having a…whatever Giacomo is to me…is easy. I know where I stand, I know what he wants, and I know neither of us expects anything to change. That makes things…tidy."

He gazed at her for a few moments, looking into her eyes. "Is that enough?"

"It is for now." She took a long sip of water, but Conor's eyes were still trained on her when she looked up. "I'd like more. Maybe not now, but one day I'd like to have someone I don't have to share."

"How often do you see each other?"

"Not very often, he lives in Milan."

"Full time?"

"Sadly, yes. It certainly increases the price of a date. Luckily, I can afford it."

Conor waited patiently while Catherine opened the door of her home. It was late, so he assumed he'd just walk her to the door. But she turned and said, "Come in, if you're not too tired."

He checked his watch. "It's almost midnight…"

"Oh, don't feel obligated. I just wanted to see how you felt about tonight."

"Felt?" No matter how well you knew a woman, it was still damned hard to understand them. "I had fun. Is that what you mean?"

"Yes. I…I'd love to ask you to some other events, but I want to make sure you'd really enjoy yourself."

"Catherine, if I hadn't gone with you tonight I'd either be at a pub with my cousins or playing cards, or lying on my bed watching TV. My life isn't very exciting. Hanging out with you shows me a whole new world. One I like, a lot."

She smiled warmly. "What do you like about it?"

"I like getting dressed up and going places I've never been. It's kinda like getting a day pass to a really cool club that you could never join."

"Are you certain? Because there are other people I could go with. You just seemed to enjoy going to the opera benefit…"

"I'm positive. Really. I'll go any time you need an escort. But I wish you would have let me pay for dinner. You really didn't have to buy."

"It's my fault you left the party hungry. Next time I'll warn you if we're not going to get a proper dinner."

"Cool. I hope next time is soon."

"How about next Friday? I'm going to a cocktail party at Stanford Law to raise funds for scholarships. It's just cocktails, so we can have dinner afterward—my treat."

"Only if I pay."

"We'll have dinner at my house." She playfully stuck her tongue out at him. "No charge."

He didn't think it appropriate to reply with his usual, "Don't stick that out if you're not gonna use it," so he just smiled. "Next Friday it is. When and where do you want me?"

Mia glumly walked downstairs that night. Noting her lethargic shuffle, Jamie asked, "What's up?"

"Jordy finally found an Internet café in Russia. She sends bad news. They're getting hammered."

"Ooo…is she bummed?"

Mia sat down and appeared to think for a moment. "Seemed so. She didn't have much to say, really. Just told me they were playing at about the level they usually do, but they couldn't keep up. Then she said she loved me and that I'd made a good decision not to come, but she didn't say why."

"Maybe the hotels aren't very good," Ryan suggested.

"Or maybe they don't have much free time," Jamie added.

"Kinda hard to tell when she writes about ten lines." She put her feet on the chair and rested her head on her knees. "She must be depressed and grouchy."

"Or tired," Ryan said. "It's draining to play at that level, and even though they've been practicing hard, playing real matches is very different. It's much more intense."

Mia nodded. "She does get quiet when she's tired."

"She's quiet when she's wide awake," Ryan teased. "Don't read too much into this." She stood and yawned. "Time for bed." Holding a hand out to Jamie, Ryan helped her to her feet. "Want anything rubbed, Mia?"

She smiled and narrowed her eyes. "Mini-backrub?"

"You got it. I'll even make it a maxi if the mini doesn't knock you out."

On Sunday afternoon, Mia walked up behind a beautifully attired blonde woman and whispered, "Rumor has it that the Evans kid faked the broken arm because she flunked a drug test."

Catherine whirled around and stared at Mia. "My God, I was about to slap you! Nobody talks about my baby like that." She gave Mia an enthusiastic hug. "It's so good to see you!"

Slightly stunned at the enthusiasm of the greeting, Mia gathered herself to say, "Thanks, Catherine. It's good to see you, too. Having fun?"

"I suppose. It's silly for me to come out to watch her team when she's not playing, but I've followed them all year and I hate to stop now."

"Where is she?"

"Oh, she rides around in a cart and takes drinks to the players. She seems to enjoy it."

As they started to walk to the next hole, Catherine said, "Jamie's just given me snippets about Jordan's big tournament. I'd love to hear the details."

"Well, they play the Russian national team tomorrow. The Russians are probably the best team in the world right now—well, either them or the Cubans. I'm afraid the U.S. is gonna get slaughtered, but I guess that's how they get better."

"Is Jordan happy? Does she enjoy being on the team?"

"Oh, yeah." Mia could feel how bright her smile was. "She loves it. The only bad thing is that she's worried she won't make the final cut. They have to get rid of seven or eight players before the Olympics, and she's afraid she might be one of 'em."

"Oh, dear, that would be awful, especially after all she's given up." She reached out and grasped Mia's arm. "Not to mention what you've sacrificed."

"Yeah, it would suck royally. I don't really wanna think about it, 'cause I know she won't be able to walk away. If she gets cut, she'll wanna play in Europe—to stay in shape and get better. And that's *not* what I want to do."

Catherine looked at Mia for a moment. "But you would, wouldn't you?"

"Yep. I'm hooked. I'd do just about anything to make her happy."

"Being in love can be hard, can't it?"

"It sure can be, but it's worth it. At least Jordan is." Catherine put her arm around Mia's waist, once again surprising the younger woman. She'd known Catherine for eight years, and they'd never been physically affectionate in the least.

"You look happy and healthy and very content. I think Jordan's lucky to have you."

"That's what I keep telling her." Mia laughed. "So far—she's bought it."

Jamie's team didn't improve their standing from the previous day, but her mood certainly wasn't affected by their play. Jamie hadn't seen her gallery once during the round, but when she spotted them she jogged over to Mia and gave her a very robust, one-armed hug. "I'm so excited you came," Jamie said, squeezing Mia until she was breathless.

"Then don't kill me!"

Jamie released her and gave Catherine a much more controlled hug. "Isn't it great to have Mia home?'

"I haven't had a better time at a tournament all year." Catherine smiled and patted Mia's shoulder. "It was so nice to walk around together. My sides hurt from laughing." She took a quick look at her watch. "Can I interest you two in dinner?"

Jamie looked at Mia, who amiably shrugged her shoulders. "I'd love to, but I need to call and see what Ryan's doing. Oh! I have to see if she won, too. They've lost the last two days."

"What are your plans, Mia?" Catherine asked.

"I told some friends I might go out with them later, but probably not 'til ten or eleven. I'm up for anything."

With a glance at Mia, Jamie asked, "How'd you get here?"

Smiling cherubically, Mia said, "Your car. Ryan gave me permission."

"You don't need permission. What's mine is yours."

Mia gave her a faux scowl. "You mean that too literally sometimes." She looked at Catherine. "She's always trying to give me money."

"She should. I don't want to say anything negative about your parents, but I don't think it's right to cut your child off financially just because you don't approve of her choices. If you need anything, Mia, absolutely anything, I hope you'll let Jamie or me help."

Squirming visibly, Mia said, "It's hard for me to take money. I know I shouldn't be so weird about it, but it makes me uncomfortable. Jamie sent me the ticket to come here and I'm determined to pay her back."

"Don't even think about it. If I could've traveled this month, I would've been to see you three times already. You're just saving me time." She slung an arm around Mia's shoulders. "It's fantastic to have you home for a few days. And every time Jordan has a trip that you don't want to go on, I'm sending you another ticket. So get used to it."

"We'll see about that. I might figure out a way to say 'no.'"

"Back to dinner," Jamie said. "I forgot we've got to go to the O'Flaherty's. Why don't you both come?"

"Mmm, I think I'll head back to Berkeley," Mia said. "On second thought, I'll stop and have dinner with my parents and then head back."

"You're a good daughter," Catherine said, giving Mia another quick hug. "And Jamie, you'd better call Martin and tell him you're bringing a guest."

"I will. Even though he always makes too much, you never know when Ryan's gonna be hungry enough to eat for three."

Frowning slightly, Catherine assessed Mia's thinness. "Maybe some of your mother's cooking will put a few pounds on you. You must be eating the same things Jordan is."

"Pretty much. I don't have the heart to eat normal food when she's got to eat like a rabbit."

Jamie kissed her cheek. "We'd better get going. Call us if you're not coming home."

Mia blinked in surprise. "Where would I go?"

"Oh!" Jamie laughed while sliding her arm around Mia for a rough hug. "I forgot you're living a clean life now. Sorry, bud."

"S'okay. It's hard to break old habits. You had three years of trying to keep track of me. Just convince yourself I'm on parole, it'll be easier."

When they reached the Mercedes, Catherine clicked a button on her key ring and the doors unlocked. Jamie started to open the passenger door, but paused for a moment before getting in. When they were both seated, she said, "When Ryan's with us, you always ask her if she wants to drive. You never do that with me."

Catherine took a quick look at her while she turned the key. "Really? I wonder why?"

"You don't know?"

"No, I don't. It hadn't occurred to me that I did that with Ryan. It must be because she loves to drive."

Jamie's voice was soft. She actually sounded a little hurt. "I love to drive too."

"You do?" Catherine spared a second to look at her. Something was up. "Ryan always drives your car when you're together, doesn't she?"

"Not always. We just got in the habit when she didn't have a car. I let her drive so she didn't drool."

Catherine turned again, but didn't see the expected smile on her daughter's face. Something clearly had her on edge. Maybe her injury? Not being able to play?

Jamie fussed with the radio for a few minutes, finally landing on a station. The Spanish language song had a lighthearted, rhythmic beat. "I think I hear an accordion," Catherine said.

"Yeah, that's common. This is a Norteña song."

"Norteña?"

"The people who live along the northern border of Mexico. This one's about running drugs across the border."

"Pardon?"

Jamie laughed a little. "It's kinda like gangsta rap, but only because of the topics they cover. It *is* weird, because it sounds like a big German band—but this song is about a guy who gets busted transporting drugs and has to go to prison in America."

"Do you listen to this kind of music…often?"

"Only when I want to listen to Spanish. Helps me stay sharp. This station plays mostly Norteña and Banda."

"I'm not sure what those are, but it's always nice to learn a little something new about you. I had no idea you listened to music to keep your Spanish in shape."

Jamie was quiet for a few moments, then she said, "It *is* nice to learn things about each other, isn't it? That's one of the things I missed during the time we weren't very close. I never felt that I really knew you."

Catherine nodded, keeping her eyes on the road. Something was definitely up. Jamie sounded nothing like her normal self. "I hope that's changed."

"It has…mostly."

"Mostly?" A blonde eyebrow rose. "Only mostly?"

"You haven't given me the whole story on Giacomo." Catherine heard her daughter let out a breath, as though she'd forced the sentence out in a rush.

"Whole story?" Catherine gave her a quick look. "What story is that?"

Sounding irritated for no reason Catherine could think of, Jamie said, "You told me you were going to break up with him. That was quite a while ago, Mother, and I've been trying to figure out why he showed up at your house if he wasn't welcome."

The "mother" reference caught Catherine by surprise. It had been almost a year since Jamie had used it rather than the much warmer "mom." Hurt at the tone, she thought for a minute, trying to decide what she was willing to share. "He surprised me that night. I thought I told you that at the time. I never would have invited him to come while I was having a party. It's…uncomfortable."

"But you would…you *do*…invite him when you're not having a party?"

Before she could censor herself, Catherine let her hurt show. "I don't like your tone. You sound as if I'm accountable to you."

Catherine caught Jamie's wide-eyed blink out of the corner of her eye. How had they gotten to this point? She couldn't recall the last time she'd had to treat Jamie like a child, and it was decidedly uncomfortable.

"You're not *accountable* to me." The way she stressed the word made it particularly offensive. "But you told me you were going to break it off because you deserved to be treated better. I didn't tell you I thought you should break up with him…although I would have if you'd asked."

Catherine worked to soften her voice, trying to blunt the edge of her words. "I didn't ask your opinion, Jamie, and I don't appreciate being scolded. It's quite disrespectful, and I can't understand what I've done to deserve your wrath."

"Damn it, Mother!" Catherine almost swerved off the road at the outburst. "Did you break up with him or not?"

A tense silence reigned while Catherine found a gas station and parked off to the side, out of the flow of customers. Turning off the engine, she shifted in her seat to be able to face her daughter. Jamie's face was bright pink and she looked like she was going to throw a tantrum. "Why are you so upset?"

"I'm *upset*," Jamie said, spitting out the word, "because you told me you felt bad about yourself for dating a married man. *You* said you deserved better. *You* said you knew what it was like to have your husband cheat. I didn't put those words into your mouth. And if you *do* feel that way, I'm angry at you for compromising your morals just to have sex!"

The car was deathly quiet for a few moments. Catherine couldn't decide whether she wanted to yell back or cry. Both seemed likely. But she'd do neither. Years of tamping down and ignoring her feelings had trained her to respond calmly. "My sex life and my moral code are no one's business but my own. I must have given you the impression that we're peers, but we're not. I can't demand that you respect me and my choices, but I will *not* have you dictating to me. The subject is now closed."

Without waiting for an answer, she started the car and began to back out of the parking space. A mumbled, "You're the one who wanted to be friends," caught her by surprise. She kept going, easing the car back onto the on-ramp for the freeway. She thought about Jamie's comment for a second, recalling the conversation they'd had in Rhode Island.

"Yes, I did," she said. "But you said you didn't need more friends." Jamie didn't respond, and Catherine took a moment to continue to think about their changing relationship. Finally, she said, "I've learned that good parents don't burden their children with their private issues, and this issue is most definitely private." She spared a look across the car, finding Jamie slumped down in her seat—jaw set, eyes facing forward, burning with anger. The thought briefly passed through her mind to apologize for causing that anger, but she quickly dismissed the idea. Jamie was going to have to come to terms with this—on her own.

When they reached the "children's house," as Martin called it, Jamie hopped out while Catherine was putting the car into park. Marching ahead, her erect, rigid posture showed her anger. In order to collect herself, Catherine took her time, freshening up her lipstick and making sure her hair was perfect. Jamie was waiting for her at the foot of the stairs, and she marched up without saying a word when Catherine arrived.

Surprisingly, once they entered, Jamie reverted to her usual cheerful self. Catherine knew her well enough to see that she was forcing it, but she was fairly sure that only she and Ryan knew anything was wrong. It made her smile to see the concerned look on Ryan's face after they'd been in the house a matter of moments. She went into the kitchen to chat with Martin and Maeve as Ryan led Jamie downstairs under the pretext of changing out of her golf clothes—which were as pressed and fresh as they'd been that morning.

Before they'd reached the room, Ryan asked, "What's wrong?"

Jamie shook her head, waiting until she closed the door to speak. She walked to the bed and flung herself on it face-first. "My mother's being a jerk."

Stunned, Ryan stood still. "She is?"

Jamie rolled over, gazing at Ryan with slitted eyes. "Yeah, she is. I asked her about Giacomo and she not only wouldn't tell me one thing, she told me it was none of my business. She's the mother and I'm the child. Period."

"Well...uhm..." Ryan approached and sat on the foot of the bed. "You are. Did you flat-out ask her what was going on, or were you more subtle?"

Blowing out a breath through pursed lips, Jamie said, "I was pretty direct." Their eyes met. "I'm pissed! She's doing the same thing that my father did. The thing that broke her heart. How can she do that to another woman?"

"I...thought that his wife didn't mind..."

"Oh, please!" Jamie sat up and glared at Ryan like she was slow. "Every cheating man says that. I'm sure my father told the women he was with that my mother didn't mind. And even if his wife *doesn't* mind, it's still wrong. There's no excuse, none whatsoever, for sleeping with a married man."

Ryan was silent for a few moments, then softly said, "I've slept with married women. Are you angry with me?"

Jamie's voice was sharp and stinging. "I would be if you didn't feel guilty!"

Scratching her head, Ryan half-closed one eye and looked at

Jamie quizzically. "I don't feel particularly guilty about it. And if we weren't together, I can't say I'd never do it again. It depends on the circumstances."

Jamie jumped to her feet. "Fine! So I'm the only one around here who values the vows…yes, the *vows*…of marriage."

Ryan didn't rise to the bait. She spoke more slowly and calmly than she had before. "That's hardly fair. I never cheated on anyone. I just had sex with a few women who chose not to honor their vows."

Hand on hip, Jamie gave her a withering glare. "There's no difference, and you know it. That's like driving the car while someone robs a bank. Those women wouldn't have been cheating without you."

It wasn't easy, but Ryan managed to put a smile on her face. "So…you've been holding in your contempt?"

"No, damn it, no! I don't feel contempt for you, but I hope you see that what you did was wrong."

Ryan got up and walked over to her, attempting to put her hands on Jamie's shoulders before they were shaken off. "Damn! What's gotten into you? You act like your mother killed someone and I helped bury the body."

"Do you…or do you not think that having sex with married women is wrong?"

Knowing she was making things worse by being honest, Ryan shrugged her shoulders. "I said it before and I'll say it again. It depends on the circumstances. I won't say that it's always wrong and I won't say I always felt guilty. I didn't."

"How many times did you do it?"

Jamie was yelling, and Ryan hoped that there was enough noise upstairs for the others not to hear. "A few…several…hell, I don't know! I didn't have a lot of info. Some of them could have been."

"How…many…do…you…know…were…married?"

Ryan truly hated to be spoken to like a child, but she tried to ignore it since she could see how upset Jamie was. "Four…no, five."

"Five? You fucked *five* married women? That's disgusting!"

"Yeah, I did," Ryan snapped. "And I'd do four of 'em again if I were single." She got closer and talked softly, but she wanted her words to sting. "I don't like having to justify my behavior to you or anyone else. I'm not gonna *fuck*…" She used the word with the same level of venom Jamie had, "…anyone, married or single, because I'm committed to you. That's all that matters. My past is mine alone." Sitting up, she added, "Don't go throwing that saintly pose around too much, because your past isn't lily-white, either."

"What? I was with one man. One!"

"Right. And you tried to cheat on him…with me! You put me in a bad position all the damn time! Kissing me on your birthday, dancing with me like you wanted to eat my clothes off, making me sleep under the covers with you when you were drunk. Not to mention the time you outright asked if you could fuck me to see if you liked lesbian sex. You might have only been with one man, but you put yourself in position to cheat on him…time and again. I just didn't wanna play that game…even though I'm obviously a common whore!" She kicked her desk chair on the way to the stairs, leaving the object spinning slowly.

It took a long time for Jamie to calm down enough to go upstairs, and when she entered the living room, she realized she hadn't changed her clothes—her ostensible reason for going downstairs in the first place. The guarded looks on Maeve, Martin, Conor and Kevin's faces, and the chilly ones on Catherine and Ryan's let her know that the ruse hadn't been necessary. The group had to have heard their raised voices. "Sorry," she said, grabbing a chair from the dining room to sit on.

Ever gracious, Maeve said, "Don't be silly, Jamie. We didn't mind waiting for you. Are you ready to eat?"

"Yes," she said, not looking up.

"Come on then," Maeve gave her a hand up. "You must be hungry after chasing around the golf course all day."

Putting on a faux smile, Jamie said, "It's a lot easier than playing, but I am hungry."

Ryan stepped behind her and put an arm around her waist. With a gentle kiss to her temple, she whispered, "I'm sorry." Jamie patted her hand and nodded, and they sat down to eat.

During dinner, Catherine said, "I've been doing my homework about your commitment ceremony, girls. Do you have time to go to the Ritz one day this week for tea?"

Ryan frowned. "Not this week, but I could schedule some time… maybe two weeks from now?"

Jamie shook her head. "I can't either," she said, not elaborating.

"Well, I suppose we'll just put it off." There was a tense few moments of silence, then Catherine looked at Maeve. "What about your schedule? Is it more flexible?"

Maeve smiled. "I don't have a thing stopping me from going to tea. I can go any day but Wednesday."

"Let's go tomorrow," Catherine said. "Come to think of it, you and I should do all of the preliminary scouting for locations. The girls are far too busy."

"I trust Aunt Maeve…I mean, Maeve to vote for me," Ryan said, grinning at her aunt. "I can't get the hang of the first name thing."

"Then drop it," Maeve said. "I only wanted to make you more comfortable, dear."

"I'm more comfortable with the old name. So if you don't mind…"

"I don't mind a bit. I'm proud to be your aunt."

"And I'm proud to have you as a step-mother. There just isn't a good name for that. And Maeve just seems too informal."

"Do I have to go back to 'Aunt Maeve'?" Conor asked. "I've only just gotten used to the new way."

"Of course not. You can call me whatever you like."

"Good. Then I'll call you a very good cook." He got up and headed for the kitchen. "If anyone wants seconds, you'd better ask now."

Conor announced it was time to walk over to Brendan's for the meeting, and Catherine got up to leave. They all said their goodbyes to the family, and Jamie and Ryan walked Catherine to her car. Ryan talked non-stop, just to avoid a long silence. When they got to the Mercedes, she kissed Catherine and waited while Jamie did the same. Pleased that the Smith-Evans women were being civil, Ryan led Jamie up the street. "Still mad at me?"

"I wasn't mad at you, but you have every reason to be mad at me."

"I'm not…now. You didn't seem like yourself so I thought I should cut you some slack."

Jamie nodded. "I'm sorry I was being such a jerk. This just has me confused. I thought my mother and I had the kind of relationship where we shared important things and it hurts to think she doesn't feel that way."

"Ahh, babe," Ryan put her arm around her, "don't feel that way. I'm sure that isn't it. She probably doesn't have this all worked out in her own head yet. Maybe she does feel a little guilty. Having you call her on it can't feel good."

Dropping her head, Jamie said, "I guess you're right. I should be more supportive."

"You don't have to give your approval, honey, especially if you think she's making a mistake. But she's her own woman and she's entitled to make her own mistakes. You wouldn't like it if she called you out on the things you do."

"Of course I wouldn't. But I'd hope I wouldn't do something as..." She trailed off, probably heading off another round of insults. Ryan tacitly accepted her retreat, and they walked for a while in silence. "I'm sorry," Jamie said quietly. "I don't have any right to harass you about your life before we met. I've told you that the past is past, and I'm not keeping my word."

"No, you're not, and it's not gonna be very cool if I have to worry about you going biblical on me every time someone else does something that I did before we met. That sucks."

"I know, I know." Jamie sighed. "It's just a gut reaction. Intellectually, I don't think about your past, and what you used to do doesn't even show up on my radar. But...when my parents get involved, I...lose it."

"Your parents are involved a lot, a whole lot. And I don't wanna get blasted every time they don't meet your standards."

Jamie looked up, staring at the side of Ryan's face for a moment. "You think I'm being moralistic, don't you."

"Yep." Ryan didn't turn her head, she just tightened her lips. "You don't have to approve of what they do, but it's not your place to lecture them. It's disrespectful."

Letting out a small sound, Jamie said, "Have you been talking to my mother? She said the same thing."

"She's right, in my opinion. If Da did something I thought was wrong I'd probably tell him it bothered me, but I wouldn't bust his chops about it. He's my father; we're not equals."

Silence settled upon them for a few minutes. Then Jamie said reflectively, "It hasn't been like that for me. My mother was more of a... mentor for me. Elizabeth was my mother in most of the ways that matter. God knows I'd never, ever tell *her* what to do."

Ryan's head turned slowly and she gazed at Jamie for a moment. Sometimes there was a gulf between them as wide as an ocean. "I don't know what that even means. Elizabeth was an employee. Your mom was always your mother and she still is." On the verge of tears, she added, "You ought to be damned glad you have her."

They were quiet until they were almost at Brendan's. Jamie put her hand around Ryan's arm and squeezed it. "Can we talk about this again in a few days? I think we're both too worked up about it."

Just hearing that Jamie was willing to think about it made Ryan's hurt ease. "Sure. I hate to fight."

"Me too. I know you don't understand the dynamic between my mother and me, but it's different than what you had with your mom. You and I don't do very well when we aren't viewing a situation from the same perspective."

"True, but I don't think I can ever view it from your perspective. To me, you're so lucky to have a mother who loves and supports you that I think you're nuts to complain about anything."

"Well, I'm sure people without a left arm would think I was a big baby to complain about having a broken elbow, too. They'd probably rather have every bone in the arm broken than not have an arm at all."

A genuine smile settled on Ryan's face. "Probably true. Losing something important makes you appreciate it more."

"I don't know if appreciation is the right word. Need might be more apt."

"I'll buy into that," Ryan said. "I need my mom. I haven't stopped needing her since the day I lost her."

Her voice cracked on the last word, and she mentally chided herself for being so thin-skinned.

"I'm so sorry your mom's gone, honey, I really am." Jamie put her arm around Ryan's waist and squeezed her tightly. "But it's not fair to expect me to treat my mom like you'd treat yours if she were here. It's a different situation, completely different."

"I know that, but it doesn't seem different in my gut."

"Let's let this sit for a while. I don't think we're gonna get anywhere with it tonight."

"Probably a good idea. But I'd really like it if you didn't bring up my past. We had an agreement."

"You're right," Jamie said. "I'll try harder."

Ryan took and kissed her hand. "That's all I can ask." She chuckled softly and added, "I can ask for more, but I'm probably not gonna get it."

Brendan had the foresight to buy beer and chips, and the gang spent a while chatting and drinking. When they finally got down to business, Ryan was thankful that Brendan acted like he'd called the meeting. He said all of the things he'd mentioned to Ryan on the phone, and asked Jamie what had led her to look for an apartment building rather than a house.

She mulled his question over for a minute. "There isn't a house for sale that would let us turn it over quickly and make a good profit. Niall bought right before this last big bubble, and houses like his…in bad shape…are selling for $700,000. The three-flat's expensive, but it's priced really well for the size. It needs a lot of work, but it seems like the kind of place we could use to have an income stream from the tenants."

"Three tenants isn't many," Ryan said.

"Well…" Jamie smiled at her, "I thought two tenants and one cousin would be about right."

"Which cousin?"

"The one who needs to move. Tommy and Annie are gonna be booted out as soon as their landlord finds someone dumb enough to pay $600,000 for that little shoebox. If they moved into the bottom floor of this apartment building, they'd get a nice backyard for Caitlin and Tommy could be the resident manager."

"Did you talk to Tommy about this?" Kevin asked. "He didn't mention anything about it."

Ryan answered for her partner. "Jamie doesn't like to tell the people involved what she's doing until she's got it all sorted out. Surprise is her modus operandi."

"Tommy'll be surprised," Kevin said. "And I think he'd love it, as long as he wasn't getting a sweet deal."

"Of course not," Jamie said, thinking this was the only family she'd ever met where they argued about how *not* to come out ahead in every situation.

The next day, Jamie came home from school to find Ryan lying on her back on the bed, staring at the ceiling. Jamie started to speak, but she could see that Ryan was transfixed, so she went into the bathroom to brush her teeth, thinking that would alert her. Several minutes later, she emerged to see that her lover hadn't moved. *When she's in one of these fugues, a burglar could clean us out. I don't think I'll be able to leave her alone with our kids!*

She wanted to sit at her desk and take some notes from her class, so she either had to break Ryan's trance or wait her out. Anxious to get to work, she called out, "Honey?" When there was no response, she said more loudly, "Ryan?" A quick headshake and the eyes fixed on her like a pair of blue LEDs.

"Hey. I didn't hear you come in. You're a quiet little thing."

Jamie sat on the edge of the bed and fussed with her lover's bangs while she looked into her eyes. "No, I'm not. You were concentrating."

"Oh, yeah. I'm trying to work something out, but not having much luck."

"I need to use my computer. Will I bother you?"

"Nope. Will I bother you if I stay here?"

"Nope." She bent and kissed Ryan's lips, then added another buss to her forehead. "Keep thinking, Tiger."

By the time Jamie had her books and notes in place Ryan already had the distant look in her eyes that overtook her when she was in a zone. She wasn't all the way there yet, but Jamie was always fascinated to watch her slip away from the conscious world. Frequent discreet glances kept her up to date as her computer powered up. Within a few minutes, Ryan was gone. Totally gone. For Jamie, it was almost like being alone in the room and she didn't really like the feeling. But this was one more of her endlessly quirky lover's quirks, and she knew it was one that was there to stay.

Chapter Fifteen

Feeling nearly royal, Maeve sat in an elegant room at the Ritz, drinking tea and eating delicate finger sandwiches with Catherine. "This is an afternoon ritual I could repeat ad infinitum," Maeve said.

"I'm glad you're enjoying yourself. It is nice, isn't it?"

"Very, but my Siobhán would be as uncomfortable as a dog wearing a top hat in this place. She can fit in anywhere and you'd never know she didn't feel like she belonged, but I know her. There's far too much... formality here. If she had her choice, the reception would be at your house. Or our house."

"I think you're right, but Jamie wants something unique. I know Ryan will give in...she always does. But I want her to be happy, too."

"We'll just keep looking. If we can have a good cup of tea, I'd do this every day."

"You're so easy to be with," Catherine said. "I can't express how nice it's been getting to know you this year."

Maeve grasped her arm, her affection always bubbling to the surface when they were together. "We're the lucky ones. Ryan's a different person since she met Jamie. She's so much happier, and so grounded."

"Grounded?"

"Yes, I think that's the right word. I was beginning to wonder if she'd ever settle down. I thought she might be like the boys...dating one girl after another for years and years." She blinked, then said, "You knew she...dated a lot, didn't you?"

"Yes, Maeve." Catherine laughed. "Jamie's told me she was quite popular."

"I don't know a lot about her adventures, just like I don't know what the boys are up to. But Jamie's the first girl she ever brought home. I knew she was special even before Jamie did." She laughed softly. "The poor girl didn't have a chance."

Catherine joined in her laughter. "That's about how Jamie describes it. She makes it sound like she was drawn into a force-field."

"All of the O'Flahertys have charm to burn. Sometimes things come too easily for them. I think Jamie keeps Ryan on her toes, and that's good for her."

"Jamie keeps us all on our toes. She's a little angry with me right now."

"She seemed…tense on Sunday. Do you want to talk about it?"

Catherine frowned and briskly shook her head. "I don't want to spend our time talking about my troubles. That'll put a damper on our afternoon."

They were at a turning point. They'd been getting closer, but hadn't shared many deeply personal things. Maybe they could change that—if Catherine was willing. "Rainy days as well as sunny ones. That's when you need a friend."

Catherine took a sip of her tea, gazing at the leaves in the bottom of her cup for a moment. It was clear she was on the verge of tearing up. "She's angry because I won't talk to her about the man I'm seeing."

Maeve tilted her head, saying nothing but giving a slight smile of encouragement.

"The man you met at my house last month, Giacomo Fontini, is who I'm seeing."

Maeve hadn't allowed herself to dwell on that event. Seeing a man carrying Catherine up to her bedroom had shocked her into muteness, but she'd never let on to that. Catherine was clearly much more worldly than she. "Jamie objects?"

"She does. I told her I was going to stop seeing him, but I changed my mind. I don't want to discuss the situation, and she's very annoyed with me because of that."

"Oh. Why…does she…how do you usually handle things like this? Do you usually tell her a lot about your personal life?"

Catherine nodded. "I've made the mistake of telling her too much. We weren't very close before she met Ryan."

"But that's clearly changed. I can see how much she values your place in her life."

"It has. Part of our distance was my fault, but I think part of it was also because Jamie was always hiding important things. I don't think I understand even a small part of what it's like to hide your sexuality, but it must be dreadful."

"And you think that to make up for the past, you started telling her too much?"

"Yes, that was part of it. It felt so nice to have her seem to enjoy being with me, it was like finding a very good friend again after years of separation."

Maeve thought of many of the mistakes she'd made with her boys. It was always hard to decide where to draw the line on privacy. "That doesn't work, does it?"

"No, it doesn't. She's not my friend, she's my child. Even though she's an adult now, I still need to treat her as a parent would."

Reaching across the small table, Maeve patted Catherine's hand. "It hasn't been that long. She'll figure out that you're changing the rules a small amount. I bet she'll appreciate it. I don't think it's comfortable for children to be too intimately involved in their parents' personal lives."

"I'm not too worried about Jamie. She gets angry and gets over it quickly. I suppose I'm more concerned about continuing my relationship with Giacomo. I would truly hate to have Jamie lose respect for me."

That made no sense at all. "Lose respect? Why would she lose respect for you?"

"You might lose respect for me as well." Catherine winced. "Giacomo's married."

"Oh."

"That doesn't bother you?"

Maeve's eyes shot open wide. "Me? Why would it bother me?"

"I'm sure you're not the type of person who'd date a married man, Maeve."

"Oh, Catherine, what I'd do has nothing to do with it. I was married to a man I stopped loving within five years of our marriage. When he drank, he was cruel. Brutal, really."

Now Catherine moved her hand, covering Maeve's. "I'm so sorry to hear that."

"It was awful." She let out a soft sound, almost a sigh. "Then my beautiful young son contracted AIDS when he was just a boy." It had been so many years…But the pain never went away. "He was so young, so trusting, so adventurous. He'd been having sex with men since he was very young and obviously thought he couldn't tell me about it." Trying to keep herself from crying, she took a breath. "I didn't judge either of them for their behavior—even though I went through more pain than I thought possible with both Charlie and Michael. I don't have the slightest interest in forming an opinion about your choices…unless you're hurting yourself. Then I'd get involved and try to reason with you."

"You're a good, good friend," Catherine said. She fumbled through her purse, finding a handkerchief and dabbing at her eyes. "Thank you for reassuring me."

Maeve patted her hand. "Now tell me about this man. He must be special."

"He is. He's the man I should have married." A wry chuckle floated from her. "But he was still in grade school when I married Jim."

"Oh!" Maeve laughed. "And what's wrong with that? Men have been dating girls since the beginning of time."

"True, but he's not a boy, he's definitely a man. He cares for me deeply, Maeve. But he's committed to his family, and I respect him for that."

"What about his wife?"

Catherine laughed, but it didn't sound very natural. "They have a unique relationship. His wife has a long-term lover and Giacomo has me. He and his wife are both aware of each other's outside interests, but they don't talk about it specifically. It's an open secret."

"Are there children?"

"Yes. Two. Giacomo has to travel for business, and he comes to the U.S. fairly frequently. And I used to go to Milan for a few weeks at a time several times a year. He'd take a long lunch or visit me after the children were in bed."

"Does he love his wife?"

Lifting her shoulders, Catherine said, "His actions show he does. Giacomo claims they're happy as a family, but that they're not happy being monogamous."

"Well," Maeve struggled to understand. That kind of arrangement was far, far from her own experience. But that wasn't important. Catherine's feelings about it were. "It's not a relationship that would work for me, but again, I'm not the one to judge what works for others. It's you I'm concerned about. How do you feel about continuing to see him?"

"I don't want to let him go," Catherine said, her voice soft but sure.

"I don't want to stop something that works for me on the chance that something better will come along."

"Then that's what you should do. That's all there is to it."

"But Jamie will not like that one bit, Maeve. Not one bit."

"Jamie's opinion isn't what's important. Yours is. Consider how *you* feel about this. If you think you're doing something wrong…I'd think twice. But if you feel right about it…if your conscience is clear…that's all that matters. *All* that matters.

At three thirty, Jamie stole another glance and saw that Ryan was still zoned out. She got up and went over to her, calling her name. As before, Ryan snapped out of it and looked at her.

"Huh?"

"You'd better get ready for practice. It's three thirty."

"Damn." Ryan rolled off the bed and grumbled to herself while going to her room to get her clothes ready. She came back a few minutes later, dressed and ready to go. "Sorry I'm grouchy. Vijay's coming over tonight and I really wanted to have this idea worked out in my head so he could help me with the programming."

Jamie smiled up at her. "Anything I can do to help?"

Ryan bent over and put her mouth on the top of her head, then made a loud sucking sound. "I could use another brain. My processor's working at full capacity."

"You'd better save that trick for Vijay. Mine wouldn't help a bit."

"You're a whiz, baby," Ryan said, grinning at her. "Your brain's just not fixated on the same things mine is."

Jamie ran a hand up Ryan's thigh. "Sometimes it is," she purred, giving her a sultry look.

"Thank God for that." Ryan kissed her soundly and turned for the door. "Don't lose that thought."

Jamie didn't lose the thought. In fact, she simmered with it all afternoon. Their sex life had been on the fritz ever since the carjacking, but things were starting to click again. Ryan was so spectacularly appealing now that her confidence was coming back that she could barely focus on her work. But Ryan was made of tougher stuff and she seemed perfectly able to balance her fixation on her project and a reawakening sex drive. Which was just the tiniest bit irritating.

Ryan got home a little after six o'clock, dropped her gym bag by the door, and strolled into the kitchen. "Hi," she said, giving Jamie a quick kiss and grabbing the first edible thing she could get her hands on.

Jamie smiled at her, watching her demolish a carrot in moments. "Salad okay?"

"Sure. I've gotta rush. Vijay's gonna be here in half an hour. Mind if I go take a shower before we eat?"

"No, go ahead. I'm still working on the veggies."

Ryan kissed her again, grabbed a big wedge of jicama and took off, leaving Jamie smiling at her partner's insatiable appetite.

Around ten o'clock, Jamie went to the study and found Ryan and Vijay hard at work. They had three laptops going, which seemed a little excessive, but she didn't comment. "Are you two anywhere near finished?"

Ryan glanced up and frowned. "Ooo…uhm…no, we're not. Should we…stop?"

"No, no, just take a little break and walk me upstairs, okay?"

Ryan looked more torn than Jamie was happy with, but she got up and said to Vijay, "Back in a sec."

"Goodnight, Jamie," he said. "Thanks for the snack."

"You're welcome. And feel free to stay as late at you need to. I know how Ryan is when she gets involved, and if you're anything like her…"

"I'm worse," he said, laughing.

"God help us." She took Ryan's hand and they walked upstairs.

Ryan put her hand on Jamie's neck and gave it a scratch. "Wanna be tucked in, little girl?"

"Not really." Jamie smiled at her. "I wanted some kisses. If you won't go to bed with me, the least you can do is warm up my lips."

"Always happy to."

They reached the bedroom and Jamie dropped her sweats and slid between the sheets. "Begin," she said, puckering up.

Sitting on the side of the bed, Ryan leaned over, placing her hand next to Jamie's pillow to support herself. She drew close and paused, gazing into Jamie's eyes. "I wish I could go to bed with you."

Jamie started to lift her left hand, then chuckled when she realized she'd hit Ryan on the head if she lifted it. Switching to her right, she brought it to Ryan's cheek and stroked it tenderly. "Me too. I always miss you when you don't."

"I'll be up as soon as we finish. Can't guarantee when that'll be, though."

"It's all right, really. I know how important this is to you. You've been working on this for two semesters. You can't drop the ball now."

"Thanks for understanding." Ryan dipped her head and placed a delicate, slow kiss on Jamie's lips. "Thanks for loving me."

Jamie threaded her fingers through Ryan's hair and held her still. "I do love you. I always will." They kissed, slowly and gently, for a few moments, then Jamie pressed Ryan a little more firmly against her mouth. "I always want you when I can't have you," she whispered. "I could eat you alive right now."

Ryan chuckled, then playfully nipped at her lover's nose. "You're getting as bad as me—forbidden fruit and all that."

"You're a good bad influence." Jamie kissed her again, harder this time, intentionally trying to make Ryan hot. She knew it was a little cruel, but she wanted to be missed. Her arm slipped down and she held on to Ryan's shoulder, holding her still. Then her tongue darted all around those soft lips, teasing her with a feather-light touch.

"No fair," Ryan growled. "You're taunting the wildlife."

"Mmm…I know you love math. I just want you to realize what you're giving up."

"I realize exactly what I'm giving up," Ryan murmured. "And I'm doubting my sanity. I'm just too polite to kick Vijay out right in the middle of draining his brain."

"Go," Jamie said, kissing her one last time. "I'll be here when you're finished."

Ryan smiled. "If I weren't sure of that, politeness would lose out."

It was after two when Ryan locked the door after seeing Vijay out. She was jazzed, higher than she'd been in months. If the bars had been open, she would have offered to take Vijay out for a celebratory drink for coming to what she was almost certain was the final solution to her project. But they weren't open and Vijay didn't drink, so she was left to celebrate on her own.

Nervous energy flowed from her body, and she had to do something to release it. Seriously considering the thought of going for a run, she remembered that she could play the drums in her room and not disturb Jamie. So she grabbed a beer and headed upstairs, nearly skipping with happiness.

Carefully closing both bathroom doors, she turned on her kit and put her headphones on. After picking up her sticks, she spent a moment twirling and tossing them, just to show off, then she started to play, venting her energy and her glee on the poor rubber pads that adequately substituted for skins.

After forty-five minutes, Ryan's tank top was soaked through. She let out a breath and wiped the perspiration from her forehead with the back of her arm, then gasped when she saw Mia lying on the bed on her belly, smiling at her. Ryan took off her headphones. "When did you get here?"

"A while ago. You're fun to watch."

"Gee, thanks." Ryan stood and stretched. "Good workout."

"It's a good thing we're both monogamous, 'cause I'd jump you right about now." Mia gave Ryan a cherubic smile. "You are sizzling hot, O'Flaherty."

Ducking her head in embarrassment, Ryan mumbled, "Thanks."

"Hey, that didn't upset you, did it?"

"Well, no, it didn't upset me…but it's kinda weird."

"Why? It's just a fact. There are thousands of hot women, but I wouldn't trade Jordy for any of 'em. I'm sure you feel the same about Jamie."

"I do."

"So? I think you're smart and funny and nice and red hot. It's just a part of who you are. But being hot doesn't make me like you better. I'd love you if you looked like a dog's butt."

Ryan grinned. "Glad to know I'm not on that end of your scale. Hey, if you're gonna be up for a few, can I use your shower? I don't wanna wake Jamie."

"Wake Jamie? You could jump on the bed and not wake her. But you're welcome to use mine if you want it."

"Eh…you're right. Jamie's impervious to noise."

"Use mine." She batted her eyes seductively and lowered her voice. "I'll wash your back."

Squealing, Ryan jumped up and ran for her own bathroom, giggling while she locked the door.

When she was clean, Ryan thought of the things she could do, but none of them appealed to her. She knew she wouldn't be able to concentrate enough to read, there was no television in any room but her and Jamie's, and the last thing she wanted was to answer e-mail or surf the web. So she decided to just lie in bed and feel good about what she'd accomplished.

It wasn't often that she took the time to review something she was very proud of, but tonight seemed like the perfect time. It was a remarkably warm night, and she looked forward to lying in bed and letting the soft sounds of the evening eventually lull her to sleep.

She opened the door to their room and was surprised to find Jamie sleeping on her right side, both of Ryan's pillows serving as props for her injured arm. Her mouth curled into a grin when the wan moonlight showed that her partner was completely naked, something of a rarity for her. The sheet was pushed down to her thighs, exposing a lovely expanse of skin for Ryan to admire.

Deciding she'd like a better look, Ryan walked around the bed and perched on the window sill, taking in her partner's bewitching body. There were few things she admired more than the gentle curve of a woman's hips, and Jamie's curve was perfection. Full and womanly, it never failed to capture her attention. She sat peacefully, gazing at both the curve and the small movement of Jamie's back each time she took in a breath.

Her eyes automatically slid lower and fixed themselves on the twin globes of her ass—also world-class in Ryan's learned opinion. A hint of moonlight provided just enough illumination to let Ryan feast on her lover's beauty, which she was content to do for long minutes. But she began to feel an urge to touch the loveliness she regarded and, since Jamie was such a sound sleeper, she knew she could engage in a little tactile appreciation with impunity.

There was barely enough room for her to sit just below Jamie's ass, and when she did, her lover didn't move a muscle. Ryan positioned herself so she could use both hands, and she started with her left—gently running it along Jamie's flank from her ribs to her thigh. A zing of excitement hit Ryan in a very nice place—the thrill of touching such a lovely body enough to generate the feeling. But the bigger charge was from doing something just a little bit wrong, even if she had to trick herself into believing it was wrong.

In fact, Jamie had given her explicit permission to touch her in her sleep, but Ryan had never done it. Given the profundity of the attraction she felt tonight, she was glad she'd saved the experience for a special occasion.

Taking her time, Ryan played with the supple skin, tracing patterns and following the subtle indentations of vertebrae. Moving down, she obviously hit a sensitive spot, because Jamie shivered and straightened out her bottom leg. That made things a little more interesting, and Ryan took advantage of the new position. Scooting back, she rested her face on the warm, soft skin that had just been revealed. Her mouth began to water as she breathed in Jamie's welcoming, distinctive scent, and she inched forward to tickle her just a tiny bit with her nose. The curly, sandy blonde hairs nearly made her sneeze, but Ryan furiously rubbed her nose, managing to stop the reflex.

Her hand was more tempted than her nose had been, and she reached between Jamie's legs and delicately caressed the skin. Only a few inches of the very desirable space was available to her, but she managed to build quite a buzz from stroking and probing those few inches. A shudder went through her and she shook her head, grinning from ear to ear. She felt like a child who'd snuck out of bed to wait for Santa Claus, but her clit had never throbbed like it did now for Santa. Only Jamie had that effect.

Suddenly overcome with emotion, Ryan leaned over and gently embraced her partner, kissing her pale skin again and again as she thanked whatever power had brought them together. She never would have believed that a woman could entrance her like this—while asleep—but she was overwhelmingly grateful that together they would stay.

Whether from the hug or the surfeit of kisses, Jamie stirred again, this time straightening both legs and stretching while a gentle sigh left her lips. Just the sigh set Ryan's heart beating, and she smirked at herself for falling so helplessly in love. She bent over again and placed one last kiss on Jamie's hip, then started to get up. But as she did, Jamie rolled over a little, almost lying flat on her back. Ryan managed to get out of her way and she went back to her side of the bed and got in. Leaning down to pull the sheet up, she stopped cold when Jamie slid her hand down her own belly and rested it between her slightly spread legs.

Sitting up like a dog who has heard a distant whistle, Ryan watched, transfixed, waiting to see what her partner would do. Nearly a minute passed, and Ryan decided that nothing would happen. But when she reached for the sheet again she saw that Jamie was slowly pressing her thighs together. A dangerous-looking grin split Ryan's face and she rested her head on her braced hand to see what would happen next.

As she'd hoped, the pressing continued—not in a rhythmic way—but in the foggy, haphazard way that a sleeping woman moves. Ryan watched her like a vulture watches a wounded animal. Every twitching muscle was noted, every sigh, every gentle purr that left Jamie's lips. After a long while, Jamie moved her hand and Ryan's momentary disappointment was replaced by a bigger grin when Jamie grasped and squeezed her own breast.

Ryan nearly leapt for her, but the dazzling sensation of watching her become aroused was too fascinating to halt prematurely. Blue eyes grew wide when Jamie began to press her ass into the mattress and gently thrust against the air. This was too much to take. Ryan popped a finger into her mouth and thoroughly wet it, then toyed with the crinkly hairs that guarded Jamie's most private spot.

On cue, Jamie's body reacted, her legs spreading apart just enough for Ryan to touch her lips. At first contact, a low, mumbled groan left her and Ryan's clit twitched like a live wire had brushed over it. Shivering, she kept probing, smiling when she realized that the last thing Jamie needed was extra lubrication. Her fingers were generously coated with the obvious expression of Jamie's somnolent desire, and Ryan continued to explore. Intently watching Jamie's face, her fingers slid forward, making progress in their journey until they were poised at her opening.

Spending just a moment debating, Ryan's fingers slid in, and she ground her teeth together when Jamie's hips thrust forward to meet her. Her own desire was reaching the boiling point, but she didn't have any idea how to touch herself while keeping her fingers inside her partner. And since being enveloped by Jamie's wet warmth was the engine driving her desire, she had no interest in withdrawing.

She scooted closer and started to kiss any part she could reach, while slowly and deliberately slipping her fingers in and out and in and out... just a few inches...the way Jamie liked it.

Jamie's breathing became more rapid and her nipples grew taut and firm. Ryan swirled her fingers around her opening, then turned her hand and massaged the roof of her vagina, tenderly but firmly pressing against the spongy tissue.

Without warning, Jamie's head turned and she slowly blinked her eyes open. Reaching between her legs she touched Ryan's hand, then jerked and sought her lover out in the dark. "Good God," she said, then began to laugh. "I was dreaming about being in the hospital after I fell, and the doctor started fucking me! I was so confused because I loved the way it felt, but I knew it was wrong to let him do it."

Ryan wrinkled her nose and grinned sheepishly. "Just me, baby. Do you like it?"

"Come here, you nut. Of course I like it. Now kiss me and keep doing what you're doing."

Ryan moved up and wrapped an arm around Jamie's shoulders, pulling her close to kiss her. As soon as her tongue entered her mouth she resumed the slow movement of her fingers and Jamie stayed right with her, picking up the rhythm immediately. "Ooo…this is good," she moaned. "So, so good."

Ryan kissed her again, exploring her mouth while her fingers probed her slick channel. "You're so fantastically hot," she murmured.

"I've been hot for you all day long. All…day." She raised her knees and started to thrust, meeting Ryan's hand hard enough to make a soft slapping sound. "Touch my clit, baby. Softly…softly."

Ryan rushed to meet her need, grazing over the engorged flesh with her thumb. Once…twice…and Jamie's flesh started to contract, squeezing Ryan's fingers in waves while her head roughly shook back and forth, not a sound coming from her parted lips.

Finally, she sighed heavily and her body began to relax. Seeking Ryan's lips, she kissed her again and again, while holding her hand in place. As soon as she could catch her breath she sucked Ryan's bottom lip between her teeth and gave it a gentle bite. "Again," she said, eyes gleaming in the moonlight. "Do it all again."

Chapter Sixteen

Jamie opened her eyes when the first light of dawn hit the bed. She reached out and found Ryan's warm body, then grasped her alarm clock and shut it off. Scooting across the bed, she cuddled up behind Ryan, kissed between her shoulder blades and fell back to sleep.

At eight thirty, Jamie opened one eye and looked at her clock. "Shit! Baby, you've gotta get up!"

Ryan sat up like she'd been pulled by the nose. "What? What?"

"It's eight thirty! You've gotta be at therapy in a half hour."

"What happened?" She jumped out of bed, dashed into the bathroom, and started running the water.

Jamie walked into the room and gave her a sheepish smile. "I was so tired when I woke up, that I turned off the alarm. I thought I'd just sleep for a little while."

"That'll teach me to sneak up on you in the middle of the night." Ryan frowned slightly while she started to brush her teeth.

Jamie approached her from the back and hugged her tightly. "Don't be grouchy. I'm very happy you snuck up on me. And you seemed pretty happy about it a couple of hours ago."

"I was." Ryan raised an eyebrow and asked drolly, "Didn't you hear me squealing with delight?"

"It's my fault you're late, so I'll drive you to therapy."

Whining slightly, Ryan said, "Then I've gotta take the bus back. I hate that."

"I'll go get coffee and then come back and pick you up. It's the least I can do." She kissed all across Ryan's bare shoulders. "I owe you for giving me such a nice, nice evening."

"It was really morning," Ryan said, finally smiling. "About three o'clock."

"Any time, any where. I'm your girl."

Ryan finished brushing and turned, holding Jamie in her arms. "I can drive myself. I'll park in one of the garages by the office. I know you don't like to drive my car."

"Don't be silly. I can drive it, I just prefer my own." Jamie went into their room and put the previous day's clothing back on. "Now don't argue with me. Paying for parking is pure punishment for you. I'll play chauffeur."

"It's a deal. And if you shake a leg, we might be able to get me a cup of coffee before my session. That'd be sweet."

"Anything for you." Jamie dashed across the room and hugged her again. "I *loved* the way you woke me up. Really loved it."

"I did too. Very much. And seeing the look on your face when you woke up and felt me inside you, nearly made me swoon." She tapped the tip of Jamie's nose. "I think we'll be doing that again."

"Don't promise if you don't mean it," Jamie said, patting Ryan's bare butt. "Now get dressed."

When they got home, Ryan went to her room to start working. She had an appointment to talk to Professor Berkowitz about her project, and she wanted to make sure she had everything in order.

Jamie had class in an hour, and she spent her available time working up the nerve to call her mother. She steeled her resolve and dialed the number. To her dismay, Catherine answered on the second ring.

"Hi, Mom."

"Hello, dear."

Jamie couldn't read anything from the brief greeting, so she dove right in. "I'm calling to apologize for the way I behaved on Sunday. I don't know what got into me, but I was out of line."

There was a definite lightness to her tone when Catherine said, "I assumed you weren't feeling up to par, honey. Don't give it another thought."

"I'm fine, Mom. I have no excuse. Your life is yours to live as you choose, and I shouldn't have tried to pry."

"Really, dear, it's fine. I'd forgotten about it."

Jamie was quite sure that wasn't true, but she forced herself to accept the statement at face value. "Okay. We'll just move on."

"Oh, honey, don't sound so dramatic. It was a minor tiff, and I told you how I felt at the time. Let's drop it."

"Okay. If you're sure you're not upset."

"Honey, it's good for you and for us when you to express your feelings. Even when they make both of us uncomfortable."

Jamie raked her lower lip against her teeth. She desperately wanted to say what she was thinking—that she wished her mother *had* been angry. That might have allowed them to have a real argument. And a real argument might have forced out the truth about Giacomo. But it was clear that wasn't going to happen. Just to make conversation she asked, "Uhm...did you have fun with Maeve yesterday?"

"Of course. I always enjoy being with Maeve. But we have our doubts about The Ritz for your reception."

Jamie didn't mention that Maeve had called Ryan as soon as she'd gotten home the previous day, and that the fact that Catherine hadn't done the same had been a good indication that she'd not forgotten their fight. "What was the problem?"

"Oh, no problem. But it felt too, "too," if you know what I mean. I can't imagine you two wanting a very formal reception, and the space doesn't lend itself to anything less."

"We don't...or at least I don't want it too casual, either. I mean, I want it to be a special place. This is a once-in-a-lifetime thing for me."

"I know that. I don't think there's a woman in the world who doesn't want a special way to commemorate the day she pledges to love someone for the rest of her life." Seemingly without thinking, she added, "Even though forever doesn't last nearly that long for many of us."

"Wow." Jamie was at a loss for more than that.

"Oh, honey, I'm so sorry! That was *so* insensitive of me. I'm just...I'm a little jaded about marriage right now, but I should never let my feelings about my own failure carry over to you."

"Uhm...are you sure you want to help with this, Mom? I don't want you to feel obligated."

Catherine sounded like she was on the verge of crying. "Yes, I definitely want to help. I'm not jaded about your and Ryan's commitment. I truly believe you're ready to take these vows."

"I've never heard you say anything so...negative about marriage. Are you feeling that down?"

"No, I'm fine. Really. I started talking, and thought about my own wedding, and my mouth started moving before my brain caught up."

"You're sure?"

"Positive. I've forgotten about our little spat, and I hope you can forget about my faux pas."

"I'm good at denial. That's why this is the second wedding I'm planning, and I'm only twenty-two."

That afternoon, Ryan sat on a chair in Professor Berkowitz' office, with Vijay sitting on the windowsill in the small room. The professor had been going over Ryan's notes, graphs, and spreadsheets for over an hour, asking the occasional question, but mostly concentrating, her dark eyes roaming from one stack of papers to another to check a number or a footnote. Ryan, full of nervous energy, was itching to move, but she didn't want to disturb her instructor. It was clear that Professor Berkowitz was devoting her full attention to thinking the theory through, and Ryan didn't want to take more of her time than she had already. So she silently tapped her feet in sets of ten while watching the professor's face for the smallest sign of a question.

After another thirty minutes, Ryan was chewing on the inside of her cheek. She jumped when Professor Berkowitz said, "This looks perfect. I can't find a flaw in your methods or your application. The theory should work." She looked at Ryan with narrowed eyes. "Why doesn't it?"

"Damned if I know." Ryan stood and started pacing. "If the theory's right, the stock market should have peaked over two months ago. My partner and I played a game where we had imaginary portfolios. I decided to sell our tech stocks weeks ago. And I missed another two percent increase in the portfolio." She stopped and frowned. "I'm stumped."

"If I had money in the stock market, I'd sell based on this paper. I suppose that means the market is affected by factors you can't account for using math alone. That will probably keep this from being published." She looked at Ryan and shook her head. "I guess every market analyst would be a billionaire if numbers alone could predict the market."

"I guess." Ryan looked down and said, "My father agrees with my theory and he didn't look at any numbers."

The professor looked at her, head cocked, so Ryan continued. "He said no one's making anything or building anything. The market's going crazy based on the belief that technology will revolutionize everything. But no Internet company has turned a profit. Not one!"

"I know. But the market doesn't behave rationally. If it did, a bunch of twenty-year-olds wouldn't be riding around in limos drinking champagne."

"And buying houses in my family's neighborhood, pricing normal people out," Ryan grumbled.

"Let me spend some more time looking at this. I don't imagine I'll find anything wrong, given how much time you and Vijay have spent, but I'll give it a try. Do you mind if I have a couple more grad students look at it?"

"Only if there's not a mistake," Vijay said, smiling despite his disappointment.

Later that day, Ryan spied her rooting section moments after she emerged from the locker room at the softball field. "Hey, Heather," she called to her teammate, "we've got extra groupies today."

Heather took a look and waved at Jamie, Mia, Jennie, and Ashley. "Not a bad turnout for a practice."

"Let's go say hi." The two women jogged across the field, reaching their fans in a few of their long strides. "Here to get dates, girls?"

"No thanks," Ashley said, wrinkling her nose. "Your coach isn't my type."

"I'll take one," Jamie said. "Give me a kiss so I can see if you're worth hanging out for."

Ryan climbed the bleachers and kissed her rather chastely. "Not my best effort," Ryan whispered. "Don't wanna scare the children."

"How did your meeting go?"

"Eh." Ryan shrugged. "Okay, I guess. My professor thinks the paper's solid, but it hasn't proven accurate. I guess I wasted my time."

"You'll get credit, won't you?" Jamie's eyes were comically wide.

"Sure. It's a theory. They don't have to work; you just have to show that you did the work properly. It wasn't my theory, anyway. I was just trying to apply it to this situation. I'd like to publish it just to stop other people from working as hard as I did to prove it."

"But you can't?"

"Nah. No one will publish a failed theory by an undergrad. When I get time, I'll post my work to all of the newsgroups I know of. Word might travel that way."

"Well, I'm proud of you. And I know you'll get an 'A.'"

Ryan chuckled. "I think that's a safe bet. I could have taken six classes in the time I spent on this project. Professor Berkowitz was impressed. She said she'd sell her stock if she had any."

"I'm gonna make some changes in my portfolio. I think we should talk to Mom about hers, too."

"Ryan!" Heather called. "Coach is making fun of you."

Ryan turned around and saw that Coach Roberts had turned his back to her and had wrapped his arms around himself—acting like he was being hugged passionately. "Gotta go," she said, kissing Jamie quickly.

"That guy's funny," Mia said, watching Ryan and Heather run away.

"Yeah. He's a good guy. Just the kind of coach Ryan likes. No nonsense, but he has a sense of humor."

"Sounds like her," Mia said.

"Hey, Jamie?" Jennie said.

"Yeah?"

"Are you gonna stay for a while? Ashley was gonna help drill me for a math test, but I don't wanna leave if you won't be here long."

"We're staying. Go sit someplace quiet and get your work done, then it won't be on your mind."

"It's not on my mind," she said, grinning. "Honest."

"Let's go," Ashley said, tugging on her shirt. "The sooner we start, the sooner we finish."

Mia watched them move over and down a few rows. "She acts like she's your kid."

"She kinda is. We're the only family she has that really cares about her. Ryan and I and my mom are in charge of her education, although Ashley and Heather have been doing most of the grunt work. They're both tutoring her—a lot."

"Does she really need it?"

"Yeah. She made it through eighth grade, but she didn't learn a heck of a lot. Her mom didn't supervise her and she skipped a lot of classes, but she's doing well now. She's really a bright kid."

"She's sweet, too," Mia said, looking over at Jennie. "Reminds me of myself at her age."

"Yours isn't the first name that comes to mind when I think of Jennie. She's had a tough life so far, but she's remarkably innocent about a lot of things."

Mia sniffed. "Oh. Well, then I change my mind."

Jamie put her arm around Mia and hugged her. "You seemed so worldly when I first met you. We were a year younger than Jen when we met, you know."

"Hard to believe." She shook her head. "It feels like it was three lifetimes ago."

Bumping her with her shoulder, Jamie said, "Are you down today?"

"Nah, I was just thinking about my Jordy. I hope she's taking care of herself."

"She's been on her own a lot longer than she's been with you. I'm sure she's out of practice, but it'll come back to her."

Mia smiled. "I guess you're right. I worry about her too much."

"It's...different when you're really in love, isn't it?"

Dropping her head into her hands, Mia groaned. "I had no idea! Now I know why my mother just smiled at me when I said I was desperately in love with one guy or another. I was way too selfish to love anyone when I was in high school. I didn't realize that love was more about giving than getting."

"Yeah, I know what you mean. I'm still amazed that my mom didn't try to talk me out of getting engaged to Jack. She had to see that it was a mistake. I gave him nothing. Nothing!"

Mia hugged her gently. "Did you ask her opinion?"

Laughing, Jamie said, "Good point. I'm sure she had the correct impression that I didn't want advice. That's one thing about my mom—she's always treated me like an adult...even when I wasn't one."

"Hey, do you think we could merge your mom and mine? We could get a relatively involved mother who only gave advice when it was really needed."

"That would be kinda cool. But I want the new creature to get your mom's cooking skills."

Mia extended her hand and Jamie shook it. "Deal. But she gets your mom's money."

"Deal," Jamie agreed, laughing.

They were idly watching the players go through their usual practice routine and Mia said, "What's up with Ryan not playing? I don't know much about softball, but she looks awfully good."

Jamie smiled and watched her lover fielding sharply-hit ground balls at first base. "She is. But her coach is a very loyal guy. Her friend Jackie plays first and has been a starter since she was a freshman. She hits as well as

Ryan does, but Ryan's a better fielder. And Ryan's arm is better, too. But I think the coach feels a real sense of loyalty to Jackie, and doesn't want to bench her for a newcomer." She shrugged. "I'm very proud of Ryan for not making an issue of it. She'd be much better in left field than the freshman who's out there now, but I think Coach Roberts wants to give the girl some confidence. Half of the team is graduating, and he's gotta get the newbies some playing time."

"I guess it's not easy to make everybody happy, but I'd put Ryan in just because of how cute she looks when she bats."

Jamie giggled and slapped Mia playfully on the leg. "She does have a cute ass, doesn't she?"

"Sure does. And the little wiggle she gives is sweet. The coach obviously doesn't let his testosterone influence his judgment—'cause Ryan's the best looking one on the team."

"I sure think so. But I'd think that at the Miss World competition."

Mia looked at Jamie for a second a puzzled frown on her face. "Do you think it bothers Ryan when I tell her she looks good?"

"Huh?"

"It kinda threw me the other night. I got home late and Ryan was in her room beating the hell out of her drums."

"She was? When was this?"

"Uhm…I forget. Maybe Monday or Tuesday."

"What time was it?"

"Late. After the bars closed."

"Huh." Jamie smiled, thinking of the fun they'd had that night. "The drums must have flipped her switch. I woke up with her fingers inside me."

"Ooo!" Mia's mouth formed a perfect circle and her eyes nearly did the same. "The little devil! Jordy's never done that to me. But it seems like every guy I've seriously dated has tried to slip it in first thing in the morning." She rolled her eyes. "Do they think I'm gonna like that? Guys are sooooo clueless."

"I would've hit Jack with whatever I could've gotten my hands on, but it was a very, very, very welcome visit from Ms. O'Flaherty."

"Have her tell Jordy to do it!" Mia said excitedly. "It'd ruin it if I had to ask for it."

Jamie looked at her, puzzled. "Why don't you do it to Jordan?"

"Damn!" Mia slapped herself on the forehead. "My brain's not working.

So…how'd she do it?"

Coloring slightly, Jamie said, "She started touching me in my sleep. Apparently, I was responsive enough to give her confidence. I kinda wish we had a videotape, to be honest. I'm not at all sure what she did—but I was ready."

"That's the problem with guys. It's so hard to convince them to preheat the oven. They wanna throw the door open and stick it in. But every woman knows you've gotta be hot to cook."

"I was *hot*," Jamie said. "And you can't imagine how good it felt to wake up from a sexy dream and have your partner watching your face while she touches you." She shivered roughly. "Makes me wanna take her home right now."

"You hit the jackpot, girlfriend—a woman who looks like Ryan and is into you, not just herself. Most chicks who look like her are *so* full of themselves."

"So what's the deal about the other night? What did you say to her?"

Mia frowned for a second, obviously giving the matter some thought. "I went into her room and she was wearing this little tank top. Like I said, she was banging the hell out of her drums, and she didn't see me. I didn't wanna startle her, so I sat on the bed until she stopped—just so I could say goodnight."

"Sounds harmless enough. But there's always more with you."

"Not much this time. Really!"

"Spill it," Jamie said, her voice dangerously low.

"Well, she didn't stop for the longest time. I finally lay down on my stomach and watched her. You can't…you absolutely can't fault me for that. It's not possible to turn away when she's playing the drums in a wet tank top. I mean, really!"

Jamie laughed and hugged her friend. "I'll give you that. You're only human."

"Thank you! So…when she stopped, she looked up and saw me. I told her that she was hot…super hot…and she looked embarrassed."

"Ryan? Looked embarrassed?"

"Yeah. I asked her if it bothered her when I said things like that and she said it felt weird."

"Huh. She didn't mention anything to me."

"I assumed she knew I was just teasing, like I always am about stuff like that. I mean, I wouldn't hit on Ryan if she was in my bed playing with herself."

Patting Mia on the arm, Jamie said, "If that ever happens, I'll give you a free pass."

Mia bumped her with her shoulder. "Thanks. But even if you didn't mind, I'd never cheat on Jordan. But the other night—Ryan didn't seem to understand that I was just making an observation. I mean...she *is* hot, right? It's like telling her she's tall or has big feet. Just a fact."

"I don't know why she would've minded your saying something to her," Jamie said, thoughtfully watching her partner who was now standing in right field, chasing down fly balls. "Maybe she felt too exposed."

"Well, she was! Those cute little nipples were popping out of that tank top like a pair of erasers."

Jamie laughed, amused by her friend's comfort in talking about Ryan's body. "They do look like erasers, don't they? Perfect little pencil erasers."

"Yep. But I don't wanna touch 'em. I just hope Ryan knows that."

"Maybe it's because you've been gone for a while. She might be out of practice."

"Well, if it comes up, make sure she knows I don't wanna sample the goods. I couldn't be happier with Jordy, and I'm never gonna do anything to screw that up."

"Not to mention that I'd cut you up with a chain saw if you tried."

"Huh." She gazed at Jamie for a few seconds. "I picture you as the type to hire someone to kill me."

"Nope. If Ryan's involved, it's personal." She narrowed her eyes and moved to rest her forehead against Mia's, trying to look menacing, until Mia burst out laughing at her attempt.

A few minutes later, Mia asked, "What's Ryan doing?"

"Licking her fingers," Jamie said with distaste.

Mia's nose wrinkled up. "Why? They have to be filthy."

"Oh, they are. She says it gives her better control on her throws. I think it's disgusting—but that's my girl. She's so...earthy."

"Jordy's not like that. She's very particular about cleanliness. She won't eat a thing before she washes her hands."

"Ryan would eat soup with her hands after playing in the mud if I'd let her. Almost nothing grosses her out." Jamie lowered her voice to make sure Jennie couldn't hear her. "She doesn't know I know it, but she pees in the shower."

Mia looked at her, then blinked. "*You* don't?"

"God, no!" Her voice was so loud Ryan looked up quizzically, and she was twenty-five yards away. "No," she said again, quieter this time. "I'm not a dog."

"Dogs don't take showers," Mia scoffed. "So...you get out of the shower if you have to go?"

"No! I hold it. Like I said, I don't have to give in to every impulse. That's what separates humans from other mammals."

"Any other mammal would tell you that's dumb. You're in the shower; everything's going down the drain anyway. Then you get nice and clean after you finish."

"And the tub's full of urine."

"No, it's not. That's just dumb."

Jennie and Ashley were either finished, or their interest had been piqued by the loudly whispered conversation going on behind them. Jennie sat next to Mia and asked, "What are you guys arguing about?"

Before Jamie could tell her to keep quiet, Mia said, "Peeing in the shower. Jamie thinks it's gross. How about you guys?"

Jennie looked a little nervous. "Uhm...is it bad to do it?"

"No," Mia said. "It's efficient and perfectly normal."

Jennie nodded her head. "I do it."

Ashley made a face. "Don't sit so close to me. That's beyond gross."

"You can come sit by me, Ashley," Jamie said. "I'd rather explode."

"Just because you two are prudes is no reason to label us," Mia said, putting her arm around Jennie, who giggled, still looking at Jamie for approval.

"It's not gross if you don't think it is," Jamie said, only to assure Jennie. "I just think it is."

"I *know* it is," Ashley said. "If somebody did that in the locker room showers, I'd never go in there again."

Jamie silently prayed her lover kept her habit to her home base.

"So how do you know Ryan does it, if she doesn't know you know?" Mia asked.

Internally shooting daggers at her indiscreet friend, Jamie said, "If we get up at the same time, I use the toilet while she gets into the shower. There's no way she could hold it that long."

"I knew Ryan would do it," Jennie said, smiling.

"Ryan isn't the best role model for some personal habits," Jamie said, unable to keep a straight face. "I think you should model yourself after

Ashley, who was obviously properly raised."

"You get into the shower after she does that, Jamie?" Ashley asked. "I'd make her clean it with bleach first."

"But then she'd know I know she does it, and I hate to take away all of her guilty pleasures."

"You're a better girlfriend than I'd be," Ashley said. "If a guy did that at my apartment, he'd never get in my shower again."

"Then you'd better not look," Mia giggled, "'Cause they *all* do it."

Jennie had to be home for dinner at six, so she took off a few minutes before practice was over. "Say bye to Ryan and Heather for me," she said before hopping on her bike.

As soon as she was gone, Jamie thunked Mia on the head with her fingers. "You shouldn't talk about stuff like that with Jennie. If you told her Ryan ate with her feet, she'd try it."

"Oh, she said she already does it. Besides, what's the problem? Everybody pees."

"But everybody doesn't talk about it," Jamie said, lifting her chin in a dignified manner. "Thank God."

"I bet you do things that you don't want Ryan to know about," Mia said, narrowing her eyes. "You probably pick your nose or something every time you think she's not looking."

Ashley giggled at Jamie's outraged look.

"I do *not* pick my nose."

"Come on, you perfect little Hillsborough debutante, you must do something bad."

Thinking for a minute, Jamie said, "It's not bad, but I do something Ryan doesn't know about."

"What?" Mia asked drolly, "Volunteer to help lepers?"

"No." Jamie ignored her jibe. "I have my legs waxed."

"That's not very bad," Ashley said. "Is Ryan opposed to wax or something?"

"No, but she doesn't know, and now I'm afraid to tell her."

"You've been together for quite some time," Mia said. "How does she not notice that you're stubbly one day and smooth the next?"

"Her schedule has worked in my favor. My legs aren't very stubbly, 'cause the hair is fine, and I always seem to need a touch-up when she's away."

"But why does it matter?" Ashley asked. "Just tell her the next time you go."

"Uhm…she thinks…" Jamie wrinkled her nose. "She thinks I'm perfectly groomed…naturally."

Ashley cocked her head, then the light obviously went on. "Bikini area?"

"Ahh…yeah. She marveled about how perfect…that area was when we were first together. I should have told her that I had some help, but I didn't. Now I feel stupid telling her that I kinda…"

"Lied to her," Mia supplied helpfully.

Slapping her leg, Jamie said, "It wasn't a lie, I just didn't correct her."

"That's a lie, that's a lie, that's a lie," Mia said, giggling.

"It's kind of a lie," Ashley agreed.

Jamie stuck out her lower lip. "It's not a lie. But…Ryan might think it is."

"It's no big deal," Mia said. "You'll tell lots bigger lies as time goes on."

"Gee, thanks."

Ashley said, "It's not a bad thing to lie about something to avoid hurting someone. I used to tell my high school boyfriend he was the best kisser in the world, and he wasn't even the best kisser on his street."

"But this isn't to avoid hurting Ryan. It's to keep her thinking I'm perfect in a follicular way."

"True. But Mia's right. You don't have to tell everything just because you're in a relationship. Just like she doesn't want you to know she has the vile, disgusting, stomach-turning habit of peeing in the shower."

"Don't you dare tell Heather," Jamie said.

"I won't. Besides, if Heather doesn't think it's disgusting, that might mean she does it. Then I'd have to find a new roommate."

"You're my kinda girl, Ash," Jamie said, patting her back.

"Looks like the jocks are about done." Ashley stood up. "It's Heather's turn to buy snacks for the room. I'm gonna go remind her." She waved. "See you guys, and have a nice time in Colorado if I don't see you again, Mia. Give Jordan a hug for me."

"I will. See ya."

Mia looked at Jamie. "How'd Ryan get here?"

"Motorcycle, I think. She parks it illegally on the grass." She scanned the area. "Yep, there it is."

"Do I have to walk home alone?"

"No, silly. We'll send Ryan to pick up dinner. We'll walk."

"Cool. I want something spicy and exotic. And full of fat, if possible."

They decided on fairly tame Chinese food, but Mia ordered the deep-fried chicken with honey-walnuts and mayonnaise sauce—pandering to her desire for fat.

Jamie assured her that Ryan always got something spicy and that they'd all share.

On the walk home, Mia wrapped her hand around Jamie's good arm and hugged it to herself. "I love being home with you guys. This has been so good for me."

"I love it, too. I just wish you didn't have to go back. But…I want Jordan to be happy, too, so I guess I have to give you up."

"Why don't you start an Olympic Training Center here? The climate's better."

Jamie laughed. "My mom probably has the money for that, but I think I'd be a little short. Besides, by the time it was ready, the Olympics would be over."

"I guess I'll just have to hang in there and try to do something to keep myself from going mad."

"Have you thought of getting a job?"

"I haven't tried, since I wanted to be available to travel with Jordy, especially in the U.S. But maybe I should get one and just stay home when she travels."

"Not a good option. You need to come here when you don't travel with her."

"Jamie, I can't keep taking money from you!"

Stopping, Jamie faced her. "Why?"

"Because it's not right. I don't wanna be one of those people who sponges off her friends."

"Honey, we've been friends for eight years. If you were after my money, don't you think I'd know that by now?"

"Maybe I'm patient," Mia said, making a face.

Resuming their walk, Jamie said, "That's not one of your signal characteristics, I'm afraid. I'm really being serious when I tell you I want you to let me pay your airfare to come home. I love you and Jordan, and so does Ryan. We both want you to let us help—just a little bit—when you need something."

"It's hard for me, James. It really is."

"I know. But when I have to buy you a ticket and send it to you it costs more than it would if you'd buy it in advance."

Mia gave her a puzzled look.

"I'm not gonna stop. If you don't travel with Jordan, I'm gonna Fed Ex you a ticket to come home. So why don't you use the Amex card I gave you and save me the trouble? It's really the least you can do," she added playfully.

Mia stopped and put her arms around Jamie's waist. "I love you," she whispered. "I'm so glad I don't have a sister, 'cause she'd be jealous that I loved you more."

"Aww...you're gonna make me cry."

"If you can't cry with your best friend, you're doing something wrong," Mia said, wiping at her own eyes.

Ryan wasn't home by the time Jamie and Mia arrived. "What's taking her so long?" Mia asked.

"Mmm...she hates to have her food sit, so she won't order until she gets there. One of her many little quirks," she said, smiling. "She might have wanted some beer, too, so she'd have to go get that first. It's best not to be too hungry when you send Ryan out."

"Well, I'd love a beer, so I won't complain."

"I think we have a couple left. I'll check." Mia plopped down on the sofa, and when Jamie returned with one beer, her shoes were off and her feet were resting on the coffee table.

"You don't want one?"

"We only have one. We're sharing." Jamie sat next to Mia and gave her the first sip.

"Ahh...that's good. Hey, what do you have planned for your anniversary? And which anniversary will you celebrate?"

"Uhm...what are my choices?"

"First kiss...first time you said you loved her...first time you got naked. You know, the usual."

Jamie's chin lifted and she gazed into space for a moment. "I think we should celebrate both our first kiss and the first time we made love. I'd better tell Ryan that, or she'll be upset if she's not prepared."

"You two are still on your honeymoon," Mia said, laughing. "You don't need a reason to celebrate."

A pair of green eyes shifted and lit on Mia, lingering for a few moments. "I don't think that's true."

"What? That you need a reason to celebrate?"

"No. The honeymoon thing. I think our honeymoon is over, and has been for a while."

"What?"

"I mean it, but I don't think it's a bad thing."

"Then why do they say 'The honeymoon's over' when they mean something's toast?"

"I guess it depends on your view. We learned something in our lesbian psychology class that's stuck with me. Falling in love is fun, no doubt about it, but it's what happens after that magic period's over that makes a relationship."

"Damn, James, I've always heard that you should be in that honeymoon thing for at least a year, maybe longer."

"That's probably true for most couples. But we've had so much junk go down this year that everything's sped up. We couldn't keep up that 'Gee, you're perfect' thing after seeing each other in the kinds of situations we've been in."

"I guess things have been a little…intense for you two."

"That's a remarkable understatement." Jamie took a long pull from their beer. "We've had a lifetime of stress this year. I've seen Ryan at what I hope is the lowest she'll ever be. It's just not possible to look at her and see her like I did when we were falling in love."

"But isn't that kinda…disappointing? I look at Jordy, and I'm still amazed that someone as wonderful as her is lying in bed with me. She gives me chills."

Quirking a grin, Jamie said, "I get my fair share of chills. But the woman I fell in love with was…this is hard to put into words…but I think that woman was more of an image than a real person."

"But it was a good image, wasn't it? Tall, dark, and gorgeous?"

"Yep. But she's a lot more than that. And I've started to learn how complex and simple, and fragile and strong, and bright and dumb she really is."

"Ryan? Dumb?"

Jamie laughed. "She can be as dumb—as she says—as a sack of potatoes. Mostly about herself."

"Point taken. She does do some pretty dumb things. But she's so smart that you try to convince yourself that what she did wasn't as dumb as it really was."

"Boy, I've been there! But we all do dumb things. She's not the rock I thought I could always rely on to do everything right. She doesn't always know the right answer. She's done some things that have really disappointed me. She's even done things that I think are morally wrong. But God, she tries hard. I admire her more now that I know how hard she works. Things aren't as easy for her as they appear."

"Hey, she's not my girlfriend; she's my fantasy! Don't destroy it."

Jamie put her arm around Mia's shoulders and hugged her hard. "She's close enough to perfect, buddy."

"The breasts are real, aren't they?" Mia asked, a hopeful look in her eyes.

"Definitely. And they feel better than they look."

"The fantasy lives!"

Chapter Seventeen

After dinner, Ryan went upstairs to study French, but Jamie couldn't make herself focus on school when Mia was home. They sat in the living room, making so much noise that Ryan finally appeared on the top stair and said, "Will you two go into the library? I'm trying to memorize these ridiculous verbs and it's hard enough without hearing you having fun."

Jamie gave Mia an "oo-oh, we're in trouble" look and said, "We'll behave."

"No we won't," Mia chimed in. "Do you mind if I drag James down to the bar on Telegraph? I wanna have an appletini."

"Appletini," Ryan scoffed. "Why does everything have to be a 'tini'? Gin or vodka and vermouth is a martini. Everything else is...something else."

"Somebody's grouchy," Mia said.

"Go," Ryan declared. "Both of you. Get out while the getting's good. If I don't memorize some of these verbs it's not gonna be pretty."

Jamie got up and went to the bottom stair. "Are you sure, baby? I'll help you study. We both could. Mia took four years of French in high school."

"I remember nothing," Mia yelled.

Jamie chided, "Shh! Be supportive."

Ryan smiled down at her. "Nah. You guys go have fun. I'll stay here and pout."

"Works for me." Mia got up and grasped Jamie's hand. "See ya later, grumpy."

"I won't be out late," Jamie said.

"Whatever. I know you lose track of time...and your name and address when you two go out, but that's cool."

Jamie dashed up the stairs and kissed her partner. "I always remember your name, and exactly where you are. And don't pout." She kissed her again, right on the downturned corner of her lips. "We won't be out late."

"I'll expect you at two fifteen, since the bar closes at two."

"I'll bring her home in one piece," Mia said.

"Whew." Ryan wiped her brow dramatically. "Now I can rest easy."

"I don't think Ryan considers me a good influence." Mia laughed demonically while jumping down the stone steps of the house.

"She can tease you all she wants, but it's the pot calling the kettle black. She was every bit as wild as you were. Just in different ways."

"How was she wild? She seems so...sedate in everything except sports. And sex...but that's just your opinion. I don't have any independent verification."

Jamie patted her friend's arm. "Thanks for the reassurance."

Mia turned and walked backwards to face Jamie. "Come on...what've you got on her?"

"I don't *have* anything on her." Jamie scowled briefly but couldn't maintain it.

"You can't be in a long-term relationship unless you have things to use against each other, James. You've gotta have something to pull out and hit 'em with when they get something on you."

Smirking, Jamie said, "So that's how it goes? I didn't realize that was the key to happiness."

"Yeah, yeah. If she says you shouldn't drink too much you hit her with 'well, I'm not the one who had to spend the night at the Hillsborough... or wherever...drunk tank.'"

"Sounds like the voice of personal experience. I remember when you got locked up. I bet your mom had to handcuff your dad to stop him from bailing you out."

"They don't have handcuffs," Mia tossed off. "I've searched every inch of that house. My mom has a vibrator, though!"

Jamie stuck her fingers in her ears. "Nah, nah, nah, I can't hear you."

"You've never poked around your parents' house?"

"No! I don't wanna know what goes on there. Actually, I don't think much was going on in the bedroom. My dad was too busy poking young associates."

Mia moved to walk alongside. She was quiet for a moment, then asked, "Does it bother you to talk about that?"

A light went on and Jamie stared at her. "Did you know? Before I did?"

"Uhm…kinda."

Pushing her shoulder roughly, Jamie demanded, "Why didn't you tell me?"

"No way! I heard my parents arguing a couple of times and my mom said she'd be damned if my dad was gonna uhm…be like Jim Evans. But knowing my mom she could've been talking out of her ass."

Jamie slapped her forehead and let her fingers slowly trail down her face. "The whole friggin' town must have known. My mom must have been a laughingstock."

"Nah. All the men cheated. Everybody in Hillsborough had a mistress. Your dad was just…a little more obvious than most of the guys. He didn't try very hard to hide it. At least that's what my mom said."

"Great. Just great."

"He had a powerful job and a lot of young women working for him. Not many men resist when you dangle toys right in front of 'em."

"But you think your dad did."

"I'm not sure he was faithful. But if he wasn't…he was damned careful about it. My mom would've neutered him. No doubt in my mind. And she wouldn't have let 'em reattach it either. She would have put it down the garbage disposal. She's vicious!"

"My mom should've threatened my dad early on. She might have had a fighting chance."

Slipping an arm around Jamie's waist, Mia hugged her and kissed her cheek. "You look sad. What's going on?"

"Eh…just some stuff with my mom…and Ryan." She looked at Mia and said, "Does Jordan ever give you a hard time about stuff you did before you met?"

"Oh, hell, no! She acts like I was born the day before we met. There's no way I'd put up with that."

"Really? You seem so…pliant around her. I'd think you'd let her do whatever she wanted."

"Nope. She must just have a sixth sense, 'cause she's never asked many questions about my past. When I talk about things I did she just smiles at me. No questions…no comments."

"Huh. I wish I could keep my mouth shut, but stuff keeps coming out."

"You're not like Jordy. She keeps her thoughts to herself most of the time."

"No, I'm not like that, but sometimes it'd be better for us if I was."

"You said something about Ryan doing things you thought were morally wrong. Is that what you're talking about?"

Nodding, Jamie pursed her lips. Then she turned and said, "She's done some things that I think are wrong. Wrong in any situation. And I thought she agreed with me. But now…now she's kinda backpedaling and it worries me."

Half-closing one eye, Mia twitched her head towards the bar. "Let me get a drink. Then I can try to figure out what in the hell you're talking about."

They entered the nearly-empty bar and flinched a little from the overly loud music. The bartender that Ryan always flirted with was there and she gave both women a long, appreciative look. Jamie led the way and they sat at the bar. "Hi," she said. "Can you make a good appletini?"

"I can make anything you want, honey," the bartender said, grinning wolfishly.

"Two appletinis then."

"Are you girls old enough to drink?"

"Sure are," Jamie said. "I was here on my twenty-first birthday with my partner. You know her. Ryan O'Flaherty."

"You're Ryan's girl? Still?"

Smiling was difficult, but Jamie managed. "Yes. Still."

"Oh, shit, I didn't mean that like it sounded."

"Yes you did," Jamie said wearily. "I know her history."

"I guess I'd better keep my mouth shut and start making some drinks, huh?"

"It's fine. Really. I knew what I was getting when I signed on." The bartender started to turn away when Jamie said, "Can you lower the volume until it gets more crowded?"

"Sure. I just keep it loud so it doesn't seem so lonely in here."

She walked over and turned down the volume, then started to make their drinks.

"Ooo…is that what you were talking about?" Mia asked. "About Ryan having a lot of…partners?"

"Ryan didn't have partners," Jamie said flatly. "She had sex."

"But is that what bothers you?"

"No, not really. Not usually." Jamie put her good arm on the bar and lay her head on it. "None of this usually bothers me. But when my parents do things that upset me I tend to start spouting off about their behavior and it always bleeds over into Ryan's."

Their drinks were delivered and Jamie put a twenty dollar bill down on the bar. "I'll buy the first round."

Mia touched the rim of her glass with Jamie's. "To good friends."

Smiling, Jamie leaned over and kissed her friend, briefly brushing her lips across Mia's. "To best friends."

"Even better." Mia took a sip. "Not bad."

Jamie drank a sip. "It's a mix. I had one not long ago that was made with apple schnapps and fresh lime juice. It wasn't this weird green color and it wasn't as sweet."

"I like 'em to taste like candy," Mia said, grinning. "Now tell me more about things bleeding onto Ryan."

Contemplatively taking another drink, Jamie said, "I promised her that I'd ignore her past, but I'm not doing a good job of it. Every time I flap my trap about something I wish I could bite my tongue. But…you know how I get."

"You get pissed and you spout off." Mia pinched Jamie's cheek playfully. "You can sound like a Baptist preacher."

"I wish I could argue, but that's about it. I did it the other night and I know I really hurt her."

"Does she hold a grudge?"

"Mmm…not one that I can see. But I think she stores her hurt feelings up. She rarely blows up and gets things off her chest because she really hates to fight, but I push her to the edge sometimes."

"So what's your question? How to forget about her past or how to keep your mouth shut?"

"I guess it's gonna have to be the mouth shut option. I honestly don't think I can forget her past."

Mia frowned. "What's bad enough to be unforgivable…" Her eyes popped open wide. "Damn, did she kill someone?"

"Of course not. She just…had sex with people she shouldn't have."

"Kids?" Mia's eyebrows were raised to their full height.

"No! Damn it, I shouldn't have started this whole conversation. Now you think she's a pedophile."

"Girls too drunk to consent?"

Frustrated, Jamie said, "She had sex with people who were in committed relationships."

Grunting, Mia said, "No she didn't."

"Yes she did! She admitted to it."

"I mean that the people weren't committed. If they were they wouldn't have had sex with Ryan."

Jamie gulped her drink and signaled for another round. "Now you sound like her."

"That's because she's right. I wouldn't go after a guy...or a girl who I knew was hooked up. But if he...or she came after me." She shrugged. "It's not my job to protect that relationship. It must suck or the person wouldn't be cheating."

"That's what she said the other night, but a few months ago she said she thought it was wrong and she wished she'd never done it."

Mia waved her off. "She was on good behavior. You'd only been together a short time, right?"

"Yeah, I guess so."

"You regret everything when you're first in love. You wish you were a virgin...you wish you'd never had a venereal disease...all that stuff."

"You've had VD?"

"I didn't say that," Mia sniffed. "But I've had sex with a guy who had herpes. Poor guy. I'd barely let him do anything to me. And I'd only give him a hand job when he was wearing a condom."

"Charming," Jamie said, wrinkling her nose. "So am I supposed to assume that everything Ryan told me when we were first together was a lie?"

"No, of course not. Only the 'I wish I'd never known I had a clitoris until I looked in your eyes' stuff. That's all a lie. You don't know it's a lie when you say it, but you come to your senses over time."

"I haven't," Jamie grumbled. "I wish I'd never met Jack, and I wish Ryan was the first person I'd ever kissed."

"That's 'cause you had a shitty sex life before you met her. Ryan didn't."

"Don't remind me. I'm sure other women rocked her world in ways I never will."

"Did she wanna marry them?" Mia asked dryly. She whipped out ten dollars and handed it to the bartender when their second round was delivered.

"It's fourteen," the woman said.

Jamie took her change and handed it to the bartender. "Thanks," she added.

"I've got more money," Mia said.

"I know, but mine was out. And no, Ryan didn't want to marry anyone before me. Besides Sara of course. I think she'd grab her in a minute if I wasn't around."

"She *is* cute. And she looks slyly sexy. Like she'd be unexpectedly dirty in bed. Ryan's got great taste. Sara's really tasty-looking."

"Thanks. You're building up my self-esteem every second."

"James! Will you knock it off? If Ryan wanted Sara she could have had her. Yes, she would have broken your heart—but if she really felt she loved her more, she would have done it. I don't think she's the kinda girl to settle for second best."

"No, she's not. And she swears she has no desire to be with Sara. I just know that she would have tried to make it work if we hadn't been involved."

"So what? I'd try to make it work with Ryan Phillippe or Ashton Kutcher if I could. But I'm not gonna."

Jamie blinked, staring blankly.

"What? Ryan Phillippe was really hot in "I Know What You Did Last Summer.""

"Aren't there any women on your 'to do' list?"

"Sure, I could go on all day. But I'm with a girl now, so if I was gonna branch out I'd go with a guy. I like to mix it up. You know."

"No, I don't know. Believe me, I don't know."

"Don't be such a tight-ass, James. Ryan loves you. It doesn't matter if she was a virgin or a prostitute. What matters is how she treats you now. What don't you get about that? Jesus, it's hard enough to find someone you love. It sounds like you wanna find someone who treats you like a princess and was kept in a locked room until you met her."

"I'm not that bad," Jamie said irritably.

"I think you are. I really do. And if you keep hurting Ryan's feelings she might start wishing she'd picked someone a little less..." She shut her mouth, her eyes shifting around the bar.

"What? Someone less what?"

Rolling her eyes, Mia uttered the word. "Judgmental. You can really get on your high horse about things. It's not good to feel like you're with someone who thinks she's morally superior."

Jamie's voice rose dramatically. "I don't think that!"

"What's it called when you think your partner's done morally wrong things that you'd never do? Easy-going? Open-minded? I don't think so, babe. All I'm saying is that you'd better chill."

Staring at the mirror behind the bar, Jamie took a drink. She stuck her tongue out at herself and finished her drink, signaling the bartender for another.

Ryan's prediction did not come true. Jamie and Mia stumbled into the house just after one, missing her guess by over an hour. Ryan had been sound asleep, but she woke as soon as Jamie's key missed the lock several times. Reminding herself not to lecture, she turned on the bedside lamp and smiled when the door opened. "Missed you," she said.

"I stayed out too late," Jamie said, slurring her words just a touch. "Drank too much too."

Ryan got up and helped her undress. "Did you have fun?" she asked, kissing her neck.

"Yeah. I drank too much though."

Patting her butt, Ryan sent her to the bath. "Brush your teeth and come cuddle."

"Okay," Jamie said, yawning. "I shouldn't have drunk so much."

"I'll be waiting for you. Hurry up." Jamie went into the bathroom and closed the door. Getting back into bed, Ryan mused, *I miss Mia, but if she were back Jamie might be in detox by now.*

"Hello, Conor," Catherine said when she reached him on Wednesday morning. "Are we still on for Friday?"

"My dance card is ready to be filled. I'm looking forward to it."

"I think you'll like this crowd a little better than the last group. It's a few decades younger than the symphony mavens."

"What's this for again?" he asked, not really caring, but wanting to be prepared.

"This is for a new scholarship fund at Stanford law. Jim usually handles these things, but I think it's important to continue my separate support."

"I'll spend a few minutes with Brendan, and ask for some legal terms I can drop."

"You don't need to do a thing," she chided him. "After sailing through that opera benefit, you can face any crowd."

"Well, that has been the toughest so far," he agreed with a chuckle. "But it was also my debut, so to speak. I think I've gotten better with each one, don't you?"

"I do indeed."

"So, I'll come down as soon as I can get away from work, okay?"

"That's fine. By any chance are you going to be home later today?"

"Yeah, I'll be home around five. Why?"

"I'd like to drop off a little something for you." Before he could ask what the gift was, she added, "See you later."

Jamie was reclining on a swath of grass, using the slight incline of the hill as a backrest, reading one of her textbooks. Her cell phone rang and she rolled onto her side to retrieve it from her pocket. "Hi, Dad," she said when she'd checked the caller ID.

"Hi, honey. I'm in town. How about dinner tonight?"

"Tonight?" She thought for a moment. "Yeah, I can make it. Ryan's got a double-header in Santa Clara, so she won't be able to join us."

"But I'll see her this weekend, right?"

Pleased, Jamie said, "You sound like you're looking forward to seeing her."

"I am." He was quiet for a second. "Does that surprise you?"

"Oh…I guess not. I've learned that you're as full of surprises as she is. The only consistent person in our family is Poppa."

"He sure is. Sometimes annoyingly so."

"Annoying? Poppa?"

"I'm teasing…mostly. You know how parents are. No matter how perfect they are, they can still get under your skin."

"I have no idea what you're talking about," Jamie said drolly.

"Sarcasm is best used sparingly, honey. What time is good for you?"

"Whatever you want. You're the one on Eastern time."

"Let's eat early then. How about six?"

"Great. Should I make reservations?"

"No. Someone in my office can do it."

"Okay. Shall I meet you?"

"No. I've got the Range Rover. I'll pick you up around five forty five."

"Great. And Dad, I won't be sarcastic tonight. I was just making a joke."

"Not a problem. I was, too. See you tonight, honey."

Conor was fresh from the shower when Catherine arrived. She carried so many bags that he had to back away from the door to allow her to squeeze through. "What in the heck?" He scratched at the back of his head, looking at her with a puzzled smile.

"Okay, I got carried away. I don't know why, but I like to shop for men's clothes more than I like to shop for my own. You don't mind indulging me a little, do you?"

He was unable to say no to those guileless brown eyes, and found himself shaking his head. "Uhm...let me help you with this stuff." He set the things on the dining room table and began to unwrap his bounty. Eventually, two pairs of shoes—one black and one brown, a black, chalk-striped suit and one of a warm brown light-weight wool, three shirts and four ties were laid out neatly against the worn wood. "My Lord, Catherine! This is...this is...fantastic!"

"Do you like it all? I know that you're perfectly capable of picking out your own clothes, but I also know you don't have much free time and I wanted you to have a few things to choose from for the event on Friday."

"It's all great. You have fantastic taste, and you sure don't skimp on quality. I just wish you hadn't gone to so much expense. God, this must have cost—"

"Please," she said, shaking her head, "you know that doesn't matter. I want you to feel comfortable going to these events with me, and having a selection of clothing to choose from will help."

"I do feel comfortable. I really do. But you're right. The same people were at both events we've been to, and I've just got two suits...plus a tux," he added, grinning. "This is...well, this is just great. Thanks." He beamed a grin at her, which she returned in kind.

"You're easier than your sister," she said, then blushed deeply. "I am *so* sorry. That did *not* come out like I meant it."

"No problem," he smiled, adding a wink. "Anyway, since Jamie's got her locked up, it's true."

She patted his arm, still laughing softly. "I'll let you go before I say anything even more embarrassing."

Gazing at her, he impulsively asked, "What are you doing the rest of the evening?"

"Nothing, to be honest. I thought I'd go home and read."

His eyes widened. "Read? What kinda fun is that? Let's at least go get dinner. What do you say?"

"I suppose I do have to eat. Where would you like to go?"

"I've seen how the upper crust lives. Wanna slum a little?"

"Conor, just having you enter would class up the slummiest place."

He dressed up a little, and since Catherine had dressed down, they were just about evenly attired. He brushed some lint from his navy blue Dockers, then checked to see that his multi-color stripe, button-down shirt was tucked in properly. After running a brush across his black loafers, he added a braided black leather belt. Satisfied with his look, he cast a glance back to his dresser, trying to decide if he should add some cologne. He rolled his eyes at his own indecision, then shook his head and went back into the living room, where Catherine was gazing raptly at the photographs that lined the bookcases.

"Your mother looks so very much like Moira," she said softly, as he entered.

"She does." He snuck a peek over her shoulder. "That's just how I remember her." The woman in the photo was sitting in a rocking chair, holding a very tiny Ryan. She was obviously cooing to her or perhaps singing, looking very peaceful and calm.

"I assume the demonically grinning boy standing on the rungs of the rocker is you?"

"It was. Mama was absolutely unflappable. And we could have flapped nearly any sane woman. Not her though," he added, fondly gazing at her image.

"That sounds a bit like Ryan," Catherine smiled at him as she placed the photo back on the shelf.

"Yeah, I guess it does. I've never thought of the similarities—probably because they look so different physically. Ryan's an O'Flaherty, through and through."

"That's not a bad thing to be."

Jamie dressed carefully, assuming that her father would be wearing at least a sports coat. She also acknowledged that her father's higher profile attracted attention that would fall upon her, too. He was right on time, and she checked her lipstick before opening the door. "Hi!"

His eyes sought out her left arm, and he felt up and down her splint, shaking his head. "Terrible," he said. "Just terrible."

"Oh, it's not so bad." She reached out and hugged him with her good arm, holding on for almost a minute.

"It's so good to see you," he murmured. "I've missed you."

Letting go, Jamie stood back and gave her father a long look. "I miss you too, Daddy. You look great, by the way."

"So do you. Maybe that's because you look more like your mother all the time."

"I do? Since when? I'm like a female Jim Evans—minus the height." She picked up her purse and coat and closed the door behind her.

He guided her by the elbow, leading her to the car in the driveway. "I have a driver tonight. Do you mind?"

"No…I guess not. Did you let your license lapse?"

"I still have a license. Karl and I were going over a few things when I had to leave, so we continued our meeting on the drive."

"Is Karl going to join us for dinner?"

Jim opened the back door of the car and kept his hand on Jamie's arm to make sure she didn't slip. "You're not going to have dinner with us, are you, Karl?"

"No, sir. I'm going to my mother's house for dinner. No matter what you order, I bet I'll have a better meal."

"Hi," Jamie said, extending her hand between the seats. "I'm Jamie."

"Hi, Jamie. Karl Thomas."

"Where does your mother live?"

"Oakland. Make sure you take your time over dinner. My mother makes a sweet-potato pie that I don't wanna miss."

"It's a deal." She sat back and asked, "Where are we going, Dad?"

"A new place Karl told me about. What's the name, Karl?"

"Bistro Jean? Something like that."

"Oh, that's the new place that's so popular," Jamie said. "I've been wanting to go there, but it's almost impossible to get Ryan to go out to dinner."

Jim's eyes twinkled. "Are you sure you're destined to be together? You'd eat out every night."

"Opposites attract. And I'm not sure destiny had anything to do with it; I just think I got lucky."

"All that matters is that you're happy together."

Jamie looked at her father while he made a comment to Karl. He took her by surprise nearly every time they spoke. And hearing him express his wishes solely for her happiness was the best kind of surprise.

Catherine sighed, pushing her plate far enough away as if to avoid temptation. "If I eat another bite I'll surely explode."

"You certainly seemed to enjoy it." Conor chuckled, surprised and pleased by the appetite she'd displayed. She'd only had a tamale and some chips and guacamole, but that was near gluttony for Catherine.

"I probably have Mexican food once a year, if that. I don't know why I have it so infrequently, since I truly love it."

"I have it around seven times a week." He laughed. "I'm the only Anglo on my crew, and I'm never in charge of ordering lunch. Luckily, I love Mexican food too."

"When we were dating, Jim used to take me to a place in Palo Alto that we both really liked. That was the last time I even had a favorite Mexican restaurant. I should investigate and find a place that I like."

"Why did you stop once you were married?"

"Oh…lots of reasons," she mused, as she picked up her water glass and drained it. "We had Marta then, and we ate most of our meals at home. She's Spanish, and even though she could manage to prepare Mexican dishes, they aren't her specialty." Looking up and meeting his eyes she said, "Things just changed after we married; I'm not even sure why."

"It was never great for you, was it?" he asked, seeing the sadness in her eyes.

Shaking her head briskly, she admitted, "No, it never was. We were too young, and too immature. We were married at the end of July, and after a short trip to Rhode Island, Jim started his job. In no time, he was working sixty and seventy hour weeks, and I was at home alone, struggling to get used to the idea of having a child."

She looked tired and defeated, and he reached across the table and grasped her hand.

"You deserve another chance, Catherine. I really hope you take it."

"Someone has to want to take a chance on *me*," she reminded him with a wry smile. "I haven't had much interest from people on this side of the

Atlantic."

"You're talking crazy again," he chided gently, giving her small hand a squeeze.

Jim and Jamie were led to a table immediately, gliding past a bar full of hungry-looking patrons. They ordered a cocktail and sat back in the comfy chairs to wait for them to be delivered. "Do you still want to know why I think you look like your mother?" Jim asked.

"Oh. Sure. I don't see it."

"It's not your features. Those are more like mine…but prettier, of course."

"Uh-huh." She smiled at him, waiting.

"It's the way you carry yourself. Your…style. As you mature, you remind me more and more of her at your age. She…and you have a real presence. You're much more mature and sophisticated than other girls your age."

"Thank you. That's nice to hear. It's always nice to be compared favorably to Mom."

"You have a lot more self-confidence than your mother had at your age." He looked up and nodded at their server when their drinks were set down. "Sometimes you have too much for my comfort." The beginnings of his smile were covered by his lifting his drink to his lips.

"It's too late to turn back now, Dad."

He shook his head quickly. "I don't want you to change. Well…that's not always true. But in my sane moments, I admire your spunk."

Brows knitting, she asked skeptically, "You do?"

"Only in my sane moments. Those aren't frequent."

She chuckled at his words and his self-effacing look. "I don't think that's true. Poppa says all parents and kids go through some tough times. I've made a lot of changes in the last year or two and I can't expect you to welcome all of them."

"There you go with that maturity again." He grinned at her, his eyes crinkling up just like hers did.

"I have some less-than-sane moments, too. Even though I know you have a lot of adjusting to do, I'm not always patient with you. I expect too much sometimes, and I'm sorry for that."

He waved her off. "There's no need to apologize. I've done so much I'm ashamed of. I'm dozens of points behind you in the maturity tally."

Jamie sipped at her drink and tilted her head. "Has Poppa been talking to you?"

"It's a good thing I'm not on the Intelligence Committee; I'm utterly transparent!"

"Not really. You just seem…reflective. And I know Poppa visited you a few weeks ago. He had a great time, by the way. He went on and on about how impressed he was with you and what you've accomplished."

"I hope he thinks that, but I know I've disappointed him a lot through the years. He reminded me of that when we were together."

"He called you out?"

Puzzled, Jim said, "He didn't lecture me, if that's what you mean. You know he's not like that. But he told me that he didn't think I'd done a very good job with the women in my life."

"I'm glad he didn't lecture you," she teased.

Jim shrugged. "It's not like I had a very good defense: a failed marriage, a tumultuous relationship with my only child, what will probably wind up being a meaningless relationship with Kayla. All in all…"

"Meaningless? Are you and Kayla not getting along?"

Their server returned and took their order, nodding politely when Jim told him they weren't in a hurry. "I want to make sure Karl gets some pie," he said. "It sounded good, didn't it?"

"Kayla?" Jamie reminded him.

He sighed. "I thought we were getting serious, but she doesn't seem to feel the same way. She thinks she'll stay in Washington when I come back to California."

"Does she…want you to stay with her?"

With a resigned smile, he shook his head. "I wish I could say she asked, but she didn't. She said she assumed I'd tire of her and move on, so she thought she'd do the same. She plans to find another job—with someone in Congress or a lobbying firm."

"Hmm…sounds like she'd thought this out from the beginning."

"I think she has. No, I'm *sure* she has. She was surprised that I wanted her to move in with me when I returned to California."

"Wow. Did you really want to make it permanent?"

Jim dipped his head, looking chagrined. "I hadn't thought it through, but it was stupid of me to think she'd want to stay with me. She's a young woman who wants a career. Being with me makes her look like a user."

Nodding, Jamie took another sip of her drink. "It does. That's what I assumed before I met her. But she seems like she's good for you. I think

I could grow to like her."

"She's been good for me, but I'm sure I'm not good for her. I may have already put a blot on her reputation that she can never erase."

A busboy delivered their salads and after a judicious grinding of fresh pepper, Jamie took a bite. "Delicious. Really well dressed."

"Mine's good, too. Karl was right."

"So, is Kayla ready to move on *now*?"

"She plans on staying until my term is over. But I assume she'll start looking for a job during the summer recess."

"You seem pretty down about it, Dad."

"Your grandfather thinks I'm getting some return on my bad investments."

"Investments?"

"I set things up this way. I dated young women in my firm and didn't mind that people found out. I treated them well—making sure they weren't harmed in terms of promotions and things like that—but I certainly never gave anyone the impression I was serious about having a relationship." He stared at his salad for a moment. "Except your mother."

"And you lied to her again and again, didn't you." It was tough, but she tried to keep the malice from her voice.

"Yes, I did. I lied again and again and again."

"You know...Ryan and I had a terrible fight a few weeks ago." His eyebrows popped up, as if she'd pinched him. "It's not that common for us to fight," she continued. "But I told her that I was worried about her cheating on me—"

His face started to redden. "Has she done anything—"

"No! Nothing. That's not the point. I'm still worried about it. Knowing that you cheated on Mom has made me doubt Ryan just enough to put a little kernel of suspicion in my mind. I don't worry that she's doing anything now. More that she'll eventually get tired of me, like you did with Mom."

"Why are you telling me this? You've never given me the slightest hint that you doubted Ryan. And I never tired of your mother. Never."

Jamie shrugged. "I'm just trying to explain why neither Mom nor Kayla nor any woman who knows your history will be able to trust you. I'm on the periphery and your cheating affects me; I can't imagine how Mom feels." She reached across the table and covered his cool hand with her own. "You *have* made some bad investments, Dad, and you're gonna have to do some work to convince a woman that you've changed—if you have."

He looked away and took a bite, chewing slowly. "It's probably useless. You're right, honey—no decent woman will ever trust me. I'll just have to keep going through women until each one tires of me or finds someone better."

"Oh, you sound like you're a big loser. I think you just want what you can't have. You were perfectly happy going from woman to woman before. It wasn't until Mom decided to divorce you that you wanted her back."

"That's not true," he said, staring into her eyes. "I've always loved your mother, and I never, ever wanted to hurt her. She's the brightest, funniest, warmest woman I've ever known. I was a complete idiot to betray her, but I swear I've never cared for anyone like I have for her."

"But you did things that would hurt any woman, Dad. Your actions are what counts."

"I know. Believe me, I know." He looked down at his salad and casually asked, "Is she seeing anyone?"

"Heh. No chance. If I did know Mom was dating someone, I wouldn't tell you. Just like I wouldn't tell her the things you tell me."

"Has she asked?"

He looked so hopeful that Jamie felt a stab of pity for him. Trying to sidestep the question she said, "She's not the type to ask. You know how private she is."

"True. She also has good manners. She wouldn't want to put you in an uncomfortable position, like I just did."

"Who *are* you?" Jamie laughed at her father's befuddled expression. "You're so…introspective."

He shrugged, looking embarrassed. "It won't last. Your grandfather's influence doesn't tend to stick."

"How about walking around the neighborhood to digest our dinner?" Conor asked as he and Catherine stepped out into the rather bracing evening. She was wearing warm clothes—a knee-length dark brown leather coat and a matching pair of gloves to fend off the chill, so she agreed. As they walked along, she slid her hand around his arm, finding that she couldn't even get it halfway around the muscled structure. The warmth just radiated from his body, and within a block she was as warm as toast.

They walked along Valencia, the main business district of the Mission, passing all manner of stores, all of them of a caliber substantially below those she normally frequented. Nonetheless, she was fascinated by the brightly decorated windows of many of the storefronts, and mused at the signs propped against the glass. "Many different Latin cultures live in this neighborhood, don't they?"

"Yeah. Quite a few. Do you speak Spanish?" he asked, sparing a glance at her intent perusal of the signs.

"Not well. I speak French and Italian, so I can guess at most words, but I'm far from fluent. Jamie is, you know."

"Yeah, I knew that. Ryan's actually a little jealous of the languages she speaks, now that she has to learn French."

"She's mentioned that," Catherine smiled. "She says her Gaelic doesn't help her a bit."

"In this country, speaking Gaelic is a nice trick to show off at parties. There's not much use for it." He chuckled. "You can barely use it in Ireland."

They'd passed the most populated parts of the street, so they crossed to return on the other side. As they walked in front of an all-night donut shop, one of the patrons caught sight of Conor. Martin was being waited on, so he couldn't step outside just then, but as soon as his order was paid for, he went outside to say hello to his son. *Ahh*, he thought to himself as he saw Conor escorting a stylishly dressed woman down the street. They were arm in arm, and occasionally stopped in front of a store to comment on something. *I didn't know he was dating anyone*, he mused as he turned to take his purchase back to the firehouse. *I suppose I'm always the last to know*, he reminded himself with a chuckle.

Chapter Eighteen

Ryan was already in bed when Jamie got home. She was half asleep, but she sat up the minute Jamie's feet hit the stairs. "Jamers?"

"Yeah, honey. I'm home."

"James?" Mia called out, giggling.

"Yes, dear?" She poked her head into Mia's room. "May I help you?"

Mia was lying on her bed, watching TV. "Miss me?"

"Always." Jamie went to the bed and kissed Mia's curly head. "But I have to go. As soon as Ryan's asleep, I'll come back." She ruffled Mia's hair and went into her own room, waggling her fingers at her lover. "I had to make sure the little one was tucked in properly."

"I tucked her in. After rubbing her feet and moisturizing them."

Jamie bent over and kissed her. "Good girl."

Ryan got up and started to undress her. "Did you have fun?"

"Ahh...yeah, I did. Things were very different between us. I have no idea what's gotten into him, but he was Mister Sensitive. He actually sounded like he was related to my grandfather for the first time that I can recall."

"Weird. Has he gotten religion?"

"That's highly doubtful."

"Do you need to take your splint off?"

"No, I'm fine. I'm gonna brush my teeth. Will you get me a T-shirt?"

Ryan turned and picked up the shirt that was lying on Jamie's pillow. "All ready for you."

"You...my little spouse...are very nice to come home to."

Ryan put her arms around Jamie and hugged her tightly. "Are you gonna sneak off to Mia's room when I'm asleep?"

"Damn, you've got good ears!"

Taking a playful nip from one of Jamie's, Ryan growled, "I'm keeping a close eye…and ear on you."

When Martin arrived home from work on Thursday morning, he asked Maeve if she wanted to go to the children's house, so they could all eat breakfast together. As usual, she was amenable, and they showed up just as the boys were getting up. When Conor appeared, bright-eyed and alert, Martin couldn't help but tease him. "I thought you might be a little bleary after your date last night."

Conor blinked at him. "I didn't have a date."

"It's all right, son." He chuckled. "You don't have to hide such things from me at this point in your life." When Conor still looked blank, he continued, "I saw you walking down Valencia last night with an attractive woman."

Conor nodded slowly in comprehension. "I wasn't on a date, Da, I was with Catherine."

"Catherine?" Martin gaped. "Really?"

"Yeah. She came by in the afternoon and neither of us had plans, so we just hung out. Why didn't you say something?"

"You know I don't see clearly in the darkness. I was fairly sure it was you, but I didn't want to run down the street carrying two dozen donuts only to find out I was wrong."

"No, it was me. I'm sorry we didn't get to chat. Catherine could have told you what a great meal we had. She's never been to The Mission so I took her to La Cabana. I think she really enjoyed herself."

Martin nodded, giving his son a concerned look before he went into the kitchen to pour himself a cup of coffee. "Anything wrong, Marty?" Maeve asked quietly.

"No, no, of course not," he said brightly. "Nothing at all." As he walked into the kitchen, he thought, *There had better not be.*

At six o'clock on Friday evening, Ryan pulled up to the three-flat in The Mission. She rolled down the window to wave to her cousins, uncles, and aunt. "We're the last ones," she said to Jamie. "Go on and start looking around. I'll find somewhere around here to park or go home and run back."

"Got your running shoes?"

"No. I tried to dress nice for my girlfriend. But if I have to run back, I've got plenty of single-girl clothes at home."

"Take your time, honey. With all of these people, we might be here until dawn."

Ryan did have to go to Noe to park, so she decided to take Duffy with her for the walk. It had been so long since she'd run with him that it took both of them a few blocks to get in synch, but they were both smiling when they arrived at the building. Her uncles Francis and Malachy were outside, looking at the foundation.

"I predicted you'd have the dog with you," Malachy said, giving her a kiss on the cheek.

"She likes to have Duffy around to remind her that she used to be the one in charge," Francis said, laughing. "Now she's the one on the leash."

"Not funny, but true." Ryan kissed her uncle. "Is everybody upstairs?"

"Yeah. We thought we'd better check out the important parts. A bad foundation is what costs big money."

"How does it look?"

"Remarkably good," Malachy said. "And I think we can take these shingles off. The wooden siding looks like it's in good shape. These ugly things might have protected it."

"Jamie said the real estate guy thought they were asbestos. Won't it cost a lot to have them removed?"

"Depends on who's watching," Francis said, adding a wink.

Ryan nodded, deciding not to discuss the issue with her pragmatic, cost-cutting uncle. She was determined to follow all of the city codes… especially where they involved hazardous waste, but her cousins would be much easier to manipulate than her uncle.

It had taken her so long to park, change and run back, that the crowd was almost finished touring when she and Duffy ran up the stairs, almost knocking down her Aunt Peggy in the dimly lit staircase. "Whoa! Sorry!"

Her aunt kissed her and patted Duffy. "This place reminds me of a building my family lived in when I was a girl. It could be nice if the boys do everything that needs to be done."

"I haven't seen it yet," Ryan said, "but Duffy likes it." The big dog hadn't stopped sniffing since they'd entered the building, his nose detecting scents from many, many years of use.

They decided to go to Francis' house for soup and salad while they discussed the pros and cons of the building. Ryan and Jamie stopped for the salad ingredients and what her uncles called "fancy bread." Despite the gentle derision, they always seemed to enjoy the baguettes and filoni Jamie and Ryan contributed. Francis still didn't understand why a salad had to contain more than a quartered head of iceberg lettuce with a half-cup of Thousand Island dressing, but he ate everything except the arugula, which he declared a weed.

Everyone agreed that the building was a good one—if they wanted to be landlords. That aspect of the discussion took quite a while, but Brendan had done some homework and explained that it would help them secure future loans if they already owned some property. And given that rents were always climbing, having two units to rent at market price could be very beneficial. The biggest sticking point was price. Niall's money would make a good down-payment, but they'd need a construction loan and money for supplies.

Jamie raised her hand. "I'd like to make the loan."

"You?" Frank said, his voice squeaking.

"Yeah, me. I'm ready to take my money out of the stock market and put it in something more secure. I think this is a good investment."

Never one to beat around the bush, Frank asked, "Do you have that kinda money?"

Kieran punched him gently on the shoulder. "Are you the only one who hasn't figure out that Jamie's rich?"

"You're rich?" Frank asked, clearly surprised.

"She's rich," Ryan said, sparing Jamie the need to reply.

Frank's eyes narrowed and he glared at his cousin. "Damn you, Ryan! It was bad enough that she was good-looking..."

"Behave," Francis said. "Don't embarrass the girl."

"Oh, who'd be embarrassed?" Jamie asked, blushing furiously.

Ryan put her arm around her. "She can't help that she was born rich and beautiful. If Jamie wants to invest some of her money, I think we should do it."

"I don't like it," Niall said. "What if we lose money on the deal?"

"That's the risk of investing," Jamie said. "I know you won't lose money because you do bad work or buy materials that are overpriced. The only reason we'd lose money is if the real estate market crashes. And if that happens, it happens. If I lost this money it wouldn't make me have to start working nights. This is just an investment to me—it's not any different from investing in stocks or bonds. I wouldn't do it if I couldn't afford to lose the money."

"Mortgage rates are about eight percent now, right?" Ryan asked. "Is that good?"

"I don't want that," Jamie said. "I want Treasury Bill rates. That's the safest investment, and that's where I was gonna park this chunk of money."

"Is that less than eight percent?"

"Yes, but it's fair. I shouldn't profit off the family, I should just stay even."

When she saw her cousins all looking at one another and nodding, Ryan smiled. Jamie was clearly one of the family.

Catherine was already sitting in the stands when Conor and Rory arrived at the Cal/Stanford game on Saturday afternoon. She saw them and waved, and they made their way through the crowd to join her. "Saving a lot of seats, aren't you, lady?" Conor asked. He bent and kissed her cheek, then Rory leaned around him and did the same.

"I've been getting some dirty looks," she admitted. "I hate to save seats, but I thought it was necessary today."

"We're the only two from the family. Everyone else had something going on." Conor looked around, nodding happily. Then he stretched his arms out and his deep voice proclaimed, "These are my people."

"You shouldn't take him to nice places, Catherine," Rory said. "He thinks he's a South Bay millionaire now."

"He fits in beautifully, Rory. You know…you would, too. I have more appointments than Conor could possibly help me with. How about giving it a whirl?"

The youngest O'Flaherty brother held up a hand. "No, thanks. I mean, I'd go anywhere you needed me to go, but Conor's your man. He's always been sure he was delivered to the wrong family."

"Someday, when my real parents find me, I won't forget you guys. I'll have you over every Christmas, when I have the party for my servants."

"I hate to add to his delusions," Catherine said, "but he honestly does seem like he was born to money."

"He was born to blarney," Rory said, chuckling.

"Hey, look who's here," Conor said. He pointed to Jim walking along the third base line, watching heads turn and people elbow each other to point him out. "See? I want people to do that when I walk into a place."

"They do," Rory teased. "They say, 'Isn't that the jerk who led my sister/daughter/cousin on?'"

"He's got your number," Catherine said, giggling.

"That was the old Conor. The new Conor is much more serious and mature. I'm looking for a relationship now."

"*That* I'll believe when I see," Rory said.

Conor jumped up. "I'll go tell Jim where we're sitting."

"You just want people to see that you know him!" Rory called out.

"He's impossible to offend, isn't he?" Catherine commented. "It's so nice that you can all take a good tease."

"You either learn to take it or end up in tears…or fights. Only one of the cousins doesn't take well to being made fun of."

"Donal?" Catherine asked.

"You know us well," Rory said, smiling.

"He seems like his skin is a little thin. I've heard him give some pretty sharp responses to some pretty benign comments."

"He'll burn your ears if you really get to him." He looked at Catherine for a second. "Is it okay that Jim's here? I can ask Conor to sit with him in another section—"

"It's fine, but thank you for asking. We're getting along well. We're united in being friendly, for Jamie's sake."

"That's what good parents do. Too bad there aren't more good parents." He stood and shook Jim's hand as Conor led the senator to their seats. "Rory," he said, obviously assuming Jim would have trouble remembering his name. "Welcome home."

"How are you, Rory? I'm surprised you're here. I thought you went to Ireland to play your music in the summer."

"I do. I'll leave right after graduation."

Jim put his hand on Rory's shoulder and squeezed it. "I'm glad to see you again. I may give you a call before you leave. I'm considering joining in the sponsorship of a bill to ease imports of certain Irish goods. Maybe you can do a little investigation for me while you're there."

"Sure. I have a lot of free time, and we travel all over the country."

"That's great!" He turned to Catherine, took her hand and kissed it. "The ever lovely Catherine Evans, I believe?"

She flinched, realizing she hadn't told him about changing her name.

Deciding that now wasn't the time, she smiled and inclined her head, silently inviting him to sit next to her. When he did, she leaned over and kissed his cheek. "How's the distinguished junior senator from California?"

"I'm good. Very good."

He'd barely settled in his seat when people began to approach him, wishing him well or reminding him they'd met fifteen years ago at a golf tournament or something similarly forgettable. Catherine watched him work, a little surprised at how comfortable he seemed to be in the unfamiliar spotlight. When they had a moment alone, she said, "Maybe you should have gone into politics. You're a natural."

He smiled. "Not really. Practicing law for all those years helped me get comfortable in uncomfortable situations. I truly prefer being a lawyer."

"I suppose you'll be back to that fairly soon. That *is* still your plan, isn't it?"

"Absolutely. I've enjoyed my time in Washington, but I much prefer San Francisco."

"You'll be able to walk to work from your apartment."

"Yes," he said, his brow furrowing. "That will be nice, but I've been putting aside some money to buy a small place in Carmel or somewhere else around Monterrey Bay. That's still my favorite place on earth." He gave her a smile that was heavy with memory and sadness.

She found herself almost reaching up to touch his cheek, but stopped herself an instant before her hand moved. The offer that came from her mouth surprised her as much as Jim, but as the words left her lips she didn't regret them. "Don't do that. I haven't been down to the house in so long I hardly recall what it looks like. And even though Jamie loves it, she doesn't want to spend her weekends down there. I want you to use it whenever you want. It was always your refuge, and there's no reason in the world that it can't continue to be." His eyes widened, then he tucked his lower lip into his mouth, a gesture she recognized as his guard against showing too much emotion.

"I…can't believe you're being so generous."

Laughing softly, she said, "Am I usually not?"

"Oh, no!" He touched her arm, looking almost panicked. "You know how much I admire you, and one of your best traits is your generosity. It's just that…I don't deserve a gift like that."

"That's for me to decide, isn't it? When you get back, treat the place as your own. If I'm ever planning on being there, I'll call you. You've kept up your golf membership, haven't you?"

He grinned, looking like a little boy. "They waived my fees during my term in office. It's just like you've always said, 'If you don't need the money, everyone is willing to give it to you.'"

Charmed that he'd recall her having said that, she smiled at him. "It's sad, but very true. The club would never do that for a man who'd lost his job."

"Not unless he lost his job as the head of a law firm to become a senator," Jim said, his eyes twinkling with mischief.

Jamie and Mia showed up just before the band played the National Anthem. "Hi!" Mia said to everyone, kissing each as she moved down the line. Jamie followed along behind her, doing the same. They ended up next to Catherine and Jim, and Jim moved aside so that Mia would sit between him and Catherine, leaving Jamie next to him.

"What took you so long, honey?" he asked Jamie.

"Oh, nothing important. I wanted to wear a long-sleeved shirt to cover up this stupid splint, but all of my nice ones were at the cleaners. We had to stop and buy something."

She smiled placidly, and her father chuckled at her expression. "You look very nice. But are you sure you didn't have even one long-sleeved shirt that could have worked?"

Catherine reached over and patted her daughter's leg. "He'll never understand, dear. Your father and I have had this discussion too many times to count."

Jim turned to Mia. "How's life treating you? Are you enjoying Colorado?"

She made a face. "I've seen about one one-hundredth of a percent of it, but what I've seen is nice. Jordan's so busy that we have almost no time to do anything fun. Thank god being with her makes it worthwhile."

"I'm going to see your father tomorrow. Are you and he…?"

"We're getting along pretty well. He knows I'm here, so you don't have to plead the fifth to protect me."

"I'd gladly stand up for you, Mia. Let me know if your father gives you any trouble. I might be able to arrange to have him named ambassador to…someplace very, very far away."

"Cool! Could you have me named ambassador for Colorado Springs?

I could use the dough."

"Really? Adam isn't taking good care of you?"

"Oh." She looked at Jamie, then back at Jim. "I thought you might know that my parents stopped supporting me."

Jim cocked his head, his brow narrowed. "They stopped? Why?"

"Because of Jordan. They don't think I'm a lesbian." That got Conor's attention, and he leaned over and raised an eyebrow. "Which I'm not," she added, sticking her tongue out at Conor. "But I'm in love with Jordan… no matter what you call me."

Scowling, Jim said, "I've got a lot of experience in being unreasonable. I'd be happy to try to knock some sense into him."

She laughed and leaned against him, pushing him a little, treating him just like one of her friends. "No need, but thanks for the offer. We've made some progress, but I think it's better if I don't take money from my parents. It's hard for my mom to keep her opinions to herself if she's footing the bills."

"I understand," Jim said. "Far too well. But by the time your child is ready to graduate from college, you don't have much control."

"You don't know my mom very well," she deadpanned. "I'll be fine. I just have to find a job that pays well, gives me unlimited vacation, and requires no experience."

"Sorry, but *I* got that job," Jim said, laughing as hard as Mia did.

The group spent the next hour and a half chatting more than watching the game. Since Ryan didn't play and the game lacked offense there wasn't much happening on the field to hold their attention. "Who wants to go out to dinner?" Jim asked. "I should treat since my team won."

"I'm not gonna tell Ryan you were openly rooting for Stanford," Jamie said, frowning.

"She'll understand. Years from now she'll be a Cal fan, no matter what."

"That's probably true. Well, we were planning on having dinner down here," Jamie said. "Mia?"

"Sure. I have plans, but not for hours."

"We should have a party," Jim said. "It's not often that I get home. What do you fellas say?"

"We can make it," Conor said, not even giving Rory a vote.

"Catherine?" Jim asked.

"I'd love to."

"Where should we go, Cat? Is there any place you know of that can seat a big group?"

"I know just the spot. It's in Hillsborough, and the chef is always ready to get to work."

Even though Catherine offered, Ryan didn't invite her teammates to the house. She knew Marta loved to cook, but she couldn't imagine anyone loved having twenty-five unexpected guests show up. Jamie called Marta and offered to stop at the grocery store to buy whatever she needed to feed the crowd. By the time she and Ryan arrived, Rory and Conor were sitting by the pool, sipping cool drinks and listening to Jim talk about something that obviously interested them.

Jamie looked out the door of the kitchen, then commented to her mother, "Dad's charming the boys, eh?"

"He seems to be." She leaned over and whispered, "He was doing his best with me this afternoon. That always makes me suspicious."

Turning, Jamie tried to put her arm around Catherine, then realized it was her left, which had no flexibility. She laughed and moved to her other side, giving her mother a hug. "He was very nice to me at dinner the other night. He seemed different somehow."

"Mmm...not to me. He was his same old charming self, the persona that was always able to talk me into nearly anything."

Jamie looked at her mother with a grimace. "That might be bordering on too much information."

"Oh! I didn't mean anything racy, dear. I'm not that insensitive."

"Aw, you're not insensitive at all." Jamie faced her and gave her a long, warm hug. "You're as sensitive a person as I've ever known. You and Ryan are very similar in that way. Maybe that's one of the reasons I was attracted to her."

Pulling back, Catherine stared at her daughter, obviously surprised. "If there's even a kernel of truth in that, I'm enormously pleased."

"There's much more than a kernel, Mom. I'm just sorry I've been so grouchy these last few weeks. You've been wonderful—taking care of me and getting me in to see a good doctor. I truly appreciate it."

Catherine kissed her gently. "You may be an adult, but you're still my sweet little baby in here." She tapped her chest over her heart. "I'll always try to be there for you."

Mia was hovering around Marta, sneaking a bite of food every time the cook turned her back. "Are you doing anything interesting tonight, Mia?" Catherine asked.

"I think we're going out clubbing. Probably somewhere in the city."

"Did you bring another outfit?" Jamie asked. "Or are you going to wear what you have on?"

"No, I didn't think to bring anything. I'll go home and change. I've gotta look good to get into the coolest places."

"Come up to my room. I've got some dresses here that might work."

"Let's go! I'd love not to have to go to Berkeley first."

They left the room, leaving Catherine smiling at Marta. "It seems like yesterday when they were riding their bikes to visit each other, doesn't it?"

"It does." Marta reached up and wiped away the tears that threatened to slip from her eyes. "The time has gone so fast. They seemed so young then…and now…" She shook her head and turned away, wiping at her eyes again.

Catherine moved to stand behind Marta and tentatively hugged her. "She's not our little girl any more."

"No," Marta sniffed. "She's a woman now with her own life. But I miss her." She turned and grasped Catherine, crying against her shoulder. "I don't know why I'm so emotional. The change of life makes me act like a different person." She pulled away and composed herself while letting out an embarrassed laugh. "I act like she's my daughter."

Catherine touched her cheek, looking into her eyes. "She's both of ours. She wouldn't be the woman she is without your influence."

"You're her mother," Marta said, her gaze intent. "I'm just lucky I was here to watch her grow up. You make me feel like I've done an important job and that means so very much to me."

"You *have* done an important job. Very important."

Marta turned Catherine around and gently pushed her towards the back door. "My job is cooking, so go visit your guests and let me do it."

Ryan sat by the edge of the pool, dangling her feet in the water.

"I'm disappointed I didn't get to see you play, Ryan," Jim said.

"I'm the secret weapon. So secret that even Coach Roberts forgets about me. But I love being outside and getting free sunflower seeds…

so I don't mind."

"Ryan would join any club that gave her free food," Rory teased.

"That depends on the food. Luckily, I really love sunflower seeds."

"Tell me about this math competition," Jim said. "I'd never heard of it."

"Nobody has. Nobody who's not into math, that is. It's the biggest collegiate math competition in the country. It's been going on for years."

"Jamie said it was an all-day thing. Is it like the SATs?"

"No, not really. There are only twelve questions."

"Twelve?" Conor asked. "I didn't know that!"

"Yep. Only twelve."

"How do they pick a winner? Don't most people get 'em right?"

"Ahh...no." She smiled. "You get up to ten points for each question. So even if you get the wrong answer, you can get points. But it's hard to get more than five or six points for a question."

"Oh, come on," Conor said. "You're a genius."

"Right. Well, your genius sister got a fifty-eight."

"Fifty-eight?" Both Conor and Rory looked surprised. Rory said, "But you got an award, right?"

"Right."

"'Cause you're the girl with the highest score?" Conor asked.

"I got a thousand bucks for that, but I don't think they should even have that award. It's not like we have to solve problems while carrying bags of cement on our shoulders. Women's brains are just as adept at math as men's."

"How did you do against the field?" Jim asked. "And how many people took it?"

"I came in twenty-fifth." Ryan smiled. "Out of about six thousand. *That* I'm proud of. Even though that only merits a measly two hundred and fifty bucks."

"People obviously don't take this test for the money," Jim said.

"No, it's all for bragging rights. They publish the top 150 scores and the solutions in American Mathematical Monthly, and it's an honor to have your name show up."

"How many guys got a hundred and twenty?" Conor asked.

"None," Ryan said. "I'm telling you, Conor, it's hard. The top score was seventy-four."

"That's a 'D'!"

"I know. But I got an 'F' and I came in twenty-fifth. I'm sure there were a lot of people who got zero."

Rory raised his hand. "I would have been one of them."

"I bet I could have gotten a five or a six," Conor said, grinning at his sister.

"I'll let you take the test. The solution's in the magazine. If you get more than a two, I'll give you the $1,000 I got for being the top woman."

Scowling, Conor said, "No thanks. You wouldn't make that kinda deal if there was a chance in hell I could do it. Prying a thou out of your hands is like trying to get Heidi Klum's phone number."

"I could have the INS look it up for you," Jim said. "She's a foreign national."

"Good lord," Ryan said, getting up and going into the house for a refill. "With Conor's mind and your connections—the federal pen isn't too far off for either of you."

Assembling in the living room when it got too chilly outside, the guests sipped cocktails and shared jokes and stories, the scene reminding Ryan of parties at her own home. The difference between this gathering and the first one she'd attended at the Evans house was playing in her mind when Jim asked, "How are your plans for the future shaping up, Ryan? The last time we talked about it, you were considering applying to every graduate program except astronomy, weren't you?"

She nodded, thinking of how he'd used her plans to make her feel insignificant and greedy.

"Tell Daddy what you're thinking of now, honey," Jamie prompted when it became clear Ryan wasn't going to elaborate.

"Oh." She tried to snap out of her reverie. "I'm a long way from making up my mind, but if I stick with biology, I'm thinking of sociogenomics."

"That's a new one for me," Catherine said. "It sounds like a cross between sociology and economics."

"It's not, but it does kinda sound like that. It's a term for a pretty new area of study. It's...complicated, but in short—it's the study of how genes affect the behavior of humans and how social forces can affect a gene."

"Sounds fascinating," Mia said, yawning dramatically.

Ryan scratched her cheek with her middle finger, making Jim laugh out loud. "I did that when I was in grade school!" he said.

"That's Ryan's emotional age," Jamie said fondly. "The math and science parts are overly developed—leaving precious little room for anything else. She's brain-bound."

"This clearly isn't my field, but I'm very interested," Catherine said. "I'm a little shaky on exactly what a gene is, but I know it's the main thing you study in biology, correct?"

"Absolutely correct," Ryan said, smiling. "I'm a biology major, but it's hard for me to find anything in biology alone that interests me enough to spend my life studying it. But it's difficult to branch out and not bang your head against a wall. I'd like to be a biophysicist if I work in research, but even that isn't everything I'm interested in."

Jamie put her hand about a foot away from her head. "Big, big, brain."

"Help your poor brother out," Rory said. "What's a biophysicist?"

"Uhm…let me see how to explain this without using too much jargon." She considered the topic for a few moments, then said, "It's the merger of biology, chemistry, and physics. That doesn't sound like a new thing, but it kinda is. Even though it's obvious to anyone who thinks about it that there aren't borders around the different systems of the body—biologists tend to study only genes and their infrastructure of cells and receptors and proteins and the complex systems they produce."

"Yeah, only an idiot wouldn't understand that," Mia said, batting her eyes.

"I'm interested," Rory said, staring at Ryan's mouth as if that would make her explanation more understandable.

"Well, chemists study the microscopic products those cellular systems put out. Those systems produce microscopic interaction…commerce really, between those molecular products. And physicists study the behavioral psychology of the forces and particles that are kinda the mechanics of that commerce." She looked puzzled. "I don't know why people think biophysics is a fad. It just seems obvious to me."

"Oh, me too," Mia said solemnly. "Plain as day."

"Did you understand that?" Jim asked, his mouth slightly open.

"Not a word. But she shuts up faster if you act like you agree with her."

"Hey!" Ryan said. "Rory asked!"

"I tracked a little bit," Catherine said. "But did you ever say what a gene was? I got a little lost."

"Oh, sorry. Maybe I didn't. A gene is the string of molecules," she spoke slowly, watching Catherine's face, "…which build cells, which then assemble into organs…"

Catherine nodded. "I'm with you."

Smiling, Ryan went on. "And the organs organize as systems…like the endocrine system or the alimentary track and so on…"

"Got it," Catherine said.

"And those systems make up the human body. So a gene is a small building block of the body, but it's not the smallest one by far."

"It sounds so simple when you describe it," Catherine said. "But I think I've had you explain this all to me many times. It just doesn't stick."

"It would if you took the basic classes. It's hard to jump in at the biophysics level and expect to get much out of it."

"Isn't the atom the smallest thing?" Jim asked, looking a little embarrassed at his lack of knowledge.

"In a way," Ryan said. "Unless you want to talk about sub-atomic particles and things like that."

"Do we have to?" Mia asked, folding her hands in prayer.

"No, we don't need to." Ryan turned to Jim. "Right now, both chemists and physicists study the atom, but chemists stick to the electrons and physicists stick to the nucleus. To me, that's like trying to understand a car by having one set of guys look at the transmission, another look only at the engine, and another look only at the cooling system."

"But that's what mechanics do," Conor said, suddenly interested. "They're all specialists now."

"Right, right," Ryan said, glad to see some spark of interest in the room. "But you need a generalist…someone who understands the whole system…to design the car. A designer has to be an engineer who can get all of those systems, and more, to work together. A biophysicist looks at the bigger picture…by looking at the small picture."

Conor threw up his hands. "You had me, but you lost me."

"That's because the analogy isn't perfect, but it's the only one that comes to mind. Biophysicists focus on particle science. They study atoms—both the nucleus and the electrons. They also study molecules and genes and cells and organs and systems—just the way an automotive engineer looks at everything from a drop of oil to an engine when designing a car."

"Okay, I think I understand that a biophysicist focuses on all of the three major branches of science," Catherine said, "but why isn't that enough for you?"

"Oh, right! That's where we started, isn't it?" Ryan chuckled. "I'd like to be a biophysicist who also made math and computer science part of my discipline. But math people are uncomfortable with hard science, and hard science people think math is too simple to bother with. They're really antagonistic to math, which I just don't get, since math is required in almost every scientific study at some level."

"Maybe they don't understand it," Mia said, her voice a monotone as she acted like she was fashioning a noose and hanging herself with it.

Ryan's face lit up. 'You know, you're probably right. Most scientists are pretty narrow and most mathematicians are, too. Maybe it's just a turf war."

Jamie got up, sat on the arm of Ryan's chair, and ran her hand along her partner's face, brushing some stray hair from her cheek. "I wish I understood more of what you love, but that was a really good explanation. Now let's see if I can repeat any of it tomorrow."

"Don't bother asking me," Mia said, blowing Ryan a kiss. "It's all gone already."

When Marta called them to dinner Jim pointedly sat in the chair Catherine had occupied during their marriage. She was taken aback, but didn't move to his old place at the head of the table. Instead, she sat opposite him, and everyone else sat on the sides of the table as well, leaving the head vacant. Jim gave her a sly smile as she sat and she returned it, adding a wink.

Helena started service by placing bowls of a rich, caramel-colored soup in front of each of them. "Mmm...chestnut puree," Jamie said, nearly squealing in delight.

"I think I have a better chance of understanding *your* career plans," Jim said, addressing his daughter. "Cooking school?"

"No. I don't think so. I don't want to work in a restaurant, so it would be kind of a waste."

"Do you have any plans yet, dear?" Catherine asked.

"Well..." Jamie pursed her lips in thought. "I wanna do something fun and pretty easy...I was considering a career making trivets out of Popsicle sticks." Ryan reached under the table and pinched her. "Ow!" She scowled at Ryan. "I really don't have any idea, Mom. I'm not like the big, giant brain here who can't find something hard enough."

"You can do anything you want, Jamie Evans," Ryan said. "You're as bright as a shiny, new dime."

"I know I have a lot of options. I just haven't settled on anything that speaks to me."

"Having time off will help," Ryan said. "I'm looking forward to this summer as much as I did when I was a kid. Graduation can't come soon enough for me."

At around ten, Mia looked at her watch and said, "I need to get going to meet my friends. Does anyone mind if I take off?"

"We'd love to have you stay over," Catherine said, "but we understand you have a busy social life while you're here."

"I do," she admitted, grinning happily. "Is it still okay if I drive your car, James?"

Jim looked up, then laughed. "I forgot you call Jamie that. But you can have my car if you want it, Mia."

"You guys are easy."

"Sure, you can drive my car. But will you be sober enough to drive home? That's the critical question." Jamie gazed intently at her friend, knowing Mia would be honest with her.

"Eww." Mia's sweet-looking mouth turned down in a grimace. "I guess I'll have to go to Berkeley anyway, so I can ride with Leighton. He's allergic to alcohol."

Conor's eyes had been darting back and forth between Mia and Jamie. He cleared his throat and said, "We're ready to leave. Want a ride?"

Jamie raised her hand. "Hey! Don't forget about me. You brought my car down here, and it's gotta get home. I can't drive it yet, and Ryan's is down here so she can't do it either."

Conor chuckled softly. "Be like Ryan. She drove her motorcycle with a broken wrist."

"Don't tell her that!" Ryan whispered menacingly.

"Sorry. I thought she knew all of your secrets."

"Not half of them," Jamie said, making a face at her partner.

"That estimate is a little high," Ryan teased.

Clearly puzzled, Jim said, "How do you drive a bike with one hand?"

"My throttle hand was fine, so I just drove slowly since I couldn't change gears."

"I could imagine myself doing something like that when I was in college," Jim said.

Catherine laughed. "Not after I got my hands on you."

"True," he said, smiling fondly at her. "I had to grow up. Finally."

"Ryan doesn't realize that yet," Jamie said. "But she's trying."

"I'm gonna go change into my clubbing clothes," Mia said. "I'll take the car back to Berkeley." She headed for the doorway, but stopped when she reached it and turned back to the group. "Why don't you guys go with me?"

"I don't wanna go back to the city tonight," Jamie said.

"I was talking to Conor and Rory, James. I don't wanna take a good-looking woman clubbing. Too much competition."

"Where are you going?" Conor asked, frowning slightly.

"I'm not sure. But it'll be fun."

"Will there be girls there? Besides you, that is."

"Yeah. The guys I'm going with are gay, but there are always a lot of straight chicks at the clubs. I'm not sure why they go, but they're always there. The odds are fantastic," Mia added, smiling wickedly.

"I'm in," Conor said.

"Ehh…I don't know." Rory looked very hesitant.

"Come on," Conor said. "I don't wanna be the only straight guy."

"Okay. But I'll only promise to stay for an hour. If there aren't girls there—I'm out."

Conor looked at him blankly for a few seconds. "If there aren't girls there, I'm out in ten minutes. I don't mind hanging out with gay guys, but I don't wanna dance with 'em."

"Argue amongst yourselves," Mia said. "I'll be back in a sec."

"You ride with Mia and meet me at home," Conor suggested to Rory. "Then we can all go in my truck. Mia can get a ride home from one of her sober friends."

"The world has changed," Jim mused. "When I was in college no one considered whether he was sober enough to drive. It's amazing all of my fraternity brothers reached adulthood."

"Thank God it's changed," Jamie said. "But that's one of the best things about living within walking distance of bars."

Mia got ready in a flash and she returned to appreciative murmurs from all of the men and Ryan. "Thank you," she said, bowing. "Jamie lent me this dress."

"Give it back in a hurry," Ryan said huskily, her eyes roaming over Mia's body.

Jamie elbowed her, whispering, "Don't ogle girls in front of my parents."

"Oh! Sorry," Ryan whispered back. "I just saw the dress and imagined how fantastic you'd look in it. I was really ogling you."

Slipping her hand under the table, Jamie squeezed her partner's upper thigh. "Good save."

Ryan's cheeks were rapidly coloring and she whispered intently, "I'm being serious. You'd look much better in that dress than Mia does. I took her out of it and put you in it. Really."

Turning, Jamie saw that Ryan was agitated as well as embarrassed. She started to stand up, whispering, "It's okay, honey. No big deal. Forget it. Everybody's leaving now. We've got to say goodbye."

The rest of the group was already standing, and Ryan hurriedly got to her feet. Everyone was talking at once, spending at least ten minutes in a flurry of goodbyes. After they left, Jim said, "I suppose I shouldn't be one of those guests you have to throw out."

"Don't be silly," Catherine said. "Let's all go into the living room and have some brandy." She slipped her hand around his arm and led him out of the room, as Jamie gave her partner a puzzled shrug.

"Jamie's been telling me about this big project you're working on, Ryan. Is it something a political science major can understand?" Jim asked.

Ryan took a sip of her brandy, a spirit she'd decided she rather liked. "Uhm…the science of it is pretty far out there, but you might be interested in the results."

"Hit me. I'm willing to show my ignorance."

"I get this one, Dad. It's a snap."

"Even better."

"Like I said," Ryan began, "the science is pretty difficult, but what I'm trying to do is use a formula to predict the stock market."

"Hasn't that been done before?" Jim asked. "A thousand times?"

"Yeah, sure. But this theory is based on physics and math and—"

"Don't tell me," he said, "Biology?"

"No." She laughed. "Computer science."

He snapped his fingers. "I should have guessed that one."

"The point was to show I knew enough physics and math to work out the formulas. It's almost incidental whether or not it works, but I sure as heck thought it was going to."

"And it hasn't?" Catherine asked.

"Not as accurately as it should. If my work was correct, the market would have started to tank about two months ago."

"Things have slowed down a little," Jim said. "And Alan Greenspan has been urging caution for what…two years?"

"I don't know. The stock market isn't my thing…at least until I started working on this. Now it's holding my interest."

"It's like gambling," Jamie said, gazing fondly at her partner. "Ryan loves to gamble."

"Me too," Jim said. "We'll have to go to Las Vegas some time."

"I don't have enough money to throw away. Let me get a job first."

"Don't you share…?"

"Sore subject," Jamie interrupted. "Ryan refuses to think of my money as her own."

"That's because it's *not* my own." Ryan gave her a sweet smile. "I'm sorry I can't blow through your money, but I'm really bad at being a spendthrift."

Jim's interest had clearly been whetted and he directed the conversation back to the stock market. "I know Greenspan has been bearish, but I talk to a lot of economists. Many of them think there might be no limit to how high the market can go. They think the equilibrium of the past might really be over."

"Because of technology?" Ryan asked.

"Yes. Technological innovations might have created a whole new ballgame."

"I could buy that if this boom was based on manufacturing or services, but it seems more like the tulip frenzy in Amsterdam."

"I knew the Dutch loved tulips, but I hadn't realized it was a frenzy," Jim said.

"Oh, not now. This was in the seventeen hundreds. In the space of a month, the price of a single tulip bulb went from a relatively consistent price to an astronomical one. Like from one dollar to two hundred."

"For one bulb?" Catherine asked in disbelief.

"Yep. And there was nothing special about the bulbs. These were the same old tulips they'd always had."

"Why the rise?" Catherine asked.

"No one knows, but it lasted a long time. It was the beginning of the Dutch bulb trade, and that lasts to this day. So this bubble started a new trade, kinda like internet stocks might be doing now."

"You do agree that internet stocks have potential, don't you?" Jim asked. "It's not possible that they're a total bust."

She chuckled. "Well, it is possible, but I think the bubble will settle down and people will start investing in things that can make money. Before this craze started, that used to matter to people."

"It still does," Jim said. "But people are betting on the potential of these companies."

"I understand that. But there aren't many predictors that show these companies are doing much to actually make money. They're using venture capital that people are literally handing over without much investigation."

"But, as you said, there was a legitimate tulip market that was created after that speculation."

"Right. But tulips never reached those crazy prices again. They call that kind of speculation 'the greater fool' theory. You're not crazy to buy a tulip for $1,000 if there's a greater fool who's willing to pay $1,010."

"It seems foolish not to be in that market," Jamie said.

"True," Ryan said. "People were making money hand over fist. And people from all over Europe heard about this and went to Amsterdam to get in on the action, increasing the pool of fools."

"So, what happened?"

"One day—and no one knows why—a guy stood up in a tavern and offered a rare bulb for…let's say two hundred dollars. No takers. He dropped the price and kept dropping it. Everybody was frozen…like they'd all just realized they were thinking of buying a bulb for a ridiculous amount of money."

"Did he get a buyer?" Jamie asked.

"I don't know. But within two days, you couldn't give a tulip bulb away. People lost fortunes, true fortunes. And some of these people had gone from nothing to the equivalent of millions and back down to nothing in a couple of years."

The room was quiet for a couple of minutes, then Catherine said, "If you were in the market, what would you do?"

"I'd get out of tech stocks completely. That's what I did in my play portfolio."

"Completely?"

"Yeah, I would. I'd look at what I'd earned so far as a very nice profit, and then take my money and hide."

"But if tech stocks crash, so will the whole market," Jim said.

"Yeah," Ryan said, scratching her head. "I guess I'd get out of the whole market and invest in bonds. Then stick my head out in a while and see if the bottom has hit."

"You're alone in that prediction. I know you're a very bright woman, but economics isn't your forte."

"All true. I'm not saying I'm right, just that my theory says the market's past its zenith."

"It makes sense to me," Catherine said. "I've made a ridiculous amount of money in the market in the last few years. Maybe it's time to be a little more cautious."

Jamie looked at her mother. "What do your brokers say?"

"Buy, buy, buy. I've had to fight them to let me be more conservative than they want me to be."

"I've been pretty conservative too," Jim said. "I try to invest in companies that are going to make something or sell a service that I think people will want. Things like Webvan, and other companies that have a lot of capital behind them. I've made a thirty-seven percent return this past year, and I'm not going to walk away from that kind of money."

Ryan nodded. "I'm certainly not saying I'm smarter than economists who've been doing this for thirty years. I guess I have a vested interest in the market crashing. So maybe I'm making a bigger deal out of small signs. But I've seen enough hints—like the Palm/3Com spin-off—to make me think it's time to hide. I might lose some profit—but I won't lose what I've made so far."

Jim looked at her for a moment, his eyes slightly closed in thought. "You've obviously spent a lot of time on this, but for the economy's sake—I hope you're wrong. I'm willing to bet you are."

"I did work hard, but I kinda hope I'm wrong too. San Francisco has sure benefited from all of the money people are throwing at local technology companies and start-ups." Everyone was quiet for a minute, the topic clearly exhausted.

"It's late, baby," Jamie said, scratching Ryan's back. "You must be tired."

Ryan stood and stretched. "Yeah, sitting on the bench is more tiring than it looks."

Jamie bent and kissed her father, then her mother. "See you in the morning, Mom. And I'll see you the next time you're in town, Dad."

Jim stood and shook Ryan's hand. "I had a very nice time talking with you tonight. I can see why Jamie says she's never bored."

"Well," Ryan said, smiling at her partner, "we don't really talk about the stock market very often—"

Jamie put her hand over Ryan's mouth. "Too much information." She giggled. "Let's go before you say something I'll regret."

Jim watched the young women walk upstairs. "They're a pair, aren't they?"

"They are."

"How could I have thought she was happy with Jack? They had no spark at all."

"I was fairly sure she wasn't happy, but I didn't step in. I still feel criminally negligent about that." She stood up and started for the door.

Jim followed her and leaned against the wall, putting his hands in his pockets. "It's a good thing she knows herself better than we did."

"And it's a good thing she didn't let us…especially you," she added, smiling impishly, "stop her from doing what she felt was right."

"Let's not revisit that, shall we? Being an idiot was bad, thinking about it is worse." He smiled at her, looking very relaxed and comfortable. "Are you really thinking of following Ryan's advice?"

"I am. And not just because of her theory. I've been skittish for a while now, and my brokers get more aggressive every time I try to back off. I don't like that."

"Mmm…I see what you mean, but I don't think we're at the peak. I'd hate to lose ten or fifteen percent on the basis of Ryan's school project."

"It sounds silly when you say it like that," Catherine admitted, "but she's worked awfully hard on this and her advisors agree that it's very well done."

"I hate to undersell Ryan, but I'm gonna go with the economists in Washington." He grinned. "It's a close call, I know, but I've gotta believe the guys whose entire careers are riding on these things—not just an incomplete."

"I won't tell her," Catherine said, tilting her head and gazing at him through half-closed eyes. "If you make millions in the next few months, I might have to ask for alimony, though."

"I'd give you everything I have, Cat." He gazed into her eyes so deeply that her heart started to race.

She reached out and opened the door, allowing the fresh air that flowed in help her get back on track. "I'm sure you would. It's been nice seeing you, Jim. Next time you're in town, we'll have to make it over to the city to see my new place."

He made a face. "Right. I got involved with a few things and the time flew by."

"Next time." She hugged him, pulling away while he was still holding on tight. "Good night."

Chapter Nineteen

Jamie opened her eyes on Sunday morning, slowly smiling at her lover, who was sitting on the window seat looking at a large photo album. "Is your cute little bare ass on my mother's imported silk fabric?"

"Morning," Ryan said, returning her smile. She stood up and flung the T-shirt she'd been sitting on at Jamie. "I'm not a wild animal." She jumped onto the bed, acting exactly like the beast she claimed she was not.

"Stop it! My mother's gonna come in here and you'll be embarrassed!" Jamie was giggling so hard she could hardly form words.

"She wouldn't dare. She knows I'm wild and untamed." She attached herself to Jamie's neck, sucking and licking and nibbling in a frenzy.

Her flanks were exposed, so Jamie gave her a wallop right on the butt.

"Yow!" Ryan yelped, covering her ass with her hands. "You're vicious!"

Batting her eyes, Jamie said, "Was that too hard, honey?"

"Yeah, but I liked it. You know I love stimulation of any kind." She slid off the bed and did some jumping jacks, making Jamie ogle her bouncing body parts. "Let's do something fun."

"I was dreaming about going to Pebble Beach. Don't know why." She shrugged. "We could take a couple of days off from school…"

Ryan sat down on the window seat, then jumped up, grabbed the T-shirt and placed it carefully on the fabric before sitting again. "Damn, why do you have such great ideas when we can't act on 'em?"

"We can't?"

"No," Ryan grumbled. "We've gotta go home. Mia's leaving today and I wanna take her to the airport."

Jamie gritted her teeth. "How could I forget that? My mind's not working right." She slid out of bed and took Ryan's hand. "Let's have breakfast with Mom and then hit the road. Maybe we can go to Pebble Beach next month."

"If not, we can go in June. If you want to celebrate our anniversary there, that is. I sure do."

"I do, too," Jamie said, taking Ryan's hand and leading her into the shower.

Later that morning, Jim Evans stood at the first tee of Olympic Country Club, feeling content and at home. His old friends and golfing partners, John Chase and Gary Swibel had been playing with Adam Christopher and Jim for nearly ten years, and the men quickly fell into their usual routine of teasing and taunting each other. Jim was pleased and relieved that none of them treated him any differently than they had when they were all local lawyers.

After the round they had lunch in the grill, and when Gary left the table to take a phone call, John commented, "It's nice to see that you're doing so well, Jim. Your divorce had to have been a blow, but it's best to get on with your life. Are you seeing anyone yet?"

"Yes, I am. I don't think it'll last, but it's fun for a while."

"That's great," John said. "It was nice to see Catherine at the big fundraiser for the opera a couple of weeks ago. She looked great."

"Ahh…that's one of her favorite events," Jim mused fondly. Then he made a face and said, "I hope she doesn't find it too awkward to go alone."

His friend looked at him with surprise, but didn't add a word.

"What?" Jim asked immediately. "Did she take one of her stunningly gay friends with her?" Catherine had always been a magnet for gay men, and he assumed she'd recruit some of them to escort her until she was ready to start dating.

"I uhm…I suppose the guy she was with might have been gay, but if he was, he sure wasn't obvious. He looked like he could have been an actor or a model though," he said thoughtfully. "He was in great shape, I'll give him that."

Jim's gaze sharpened and he demanded, "Describe him to me."

"Uhm…I…I didn't spend a lot of time looking at him, but Marcy kept staring at him, wondering who he was."

"Should I call Marcy?" Jim asked, tired of waiting for his friend to get to the point.

"No, I think I remember. He was big…very big…dark hair…very good looking…a real rugged kinda guy…looked like he spends most of his day in the gym."

"Black hair? Blue eyes?"

"Yeah. As a matter of fact, Marcy made a big deal about how beautiful his eyes were. Hey…" He gave Jim a thoughtful look. "He looked like your daughter's…uhm…"

"Partner," Jim said tersely. "He's her brother. And he doesn't look like it, but that guy is the queerest of the queer. A real flamer."

"Really? He seemed so macho."

The senator gave his friend an evil smile and assured him, "It's all an act. I had dinner with him just last night and he had to leave to go to a gay dance club." He shrugged. "I think the whole family's gay. It must be genetics."

Mia got up on Sunday afternoon and wandered into the kitchen, finding Ryan making lunch for Jamie. "Any coffee?" she asked, dropping into a chair. Her eyes were barely open and her hair was going in every direction at once.

"Tough night?"

"A little. I was over-served."

"Where'd you go?" Jamie asked.

Mia let her head drop back, exposing her neck. "Everywhere. We hit every spot in the city."

"Did the boys stay with you?"

"They left about one. I'm not sure, but I think I saw a girl with them. I'm not sure which one of them she was with, though."

"I'm glad at least one of them went home happy," Ryan said.

"They had fun. We all did. After they left we went to some righteous drag bar full of fantastic-looking black men…or women." She waved her hand. "I assume they were all men, but it was sure easy to be confused."

Ryan poured Mia a cup of coffee. "Hungry?"

"Not much. We went out for a snack after the bar closed, then we found an after-hours club, then we had another snack." She made a face. "Biscuits and gravy at five a.m. Yum."

"Someone must have been smoking pot," Jamie said. "Sounds like munchie time to me."

"Yeah, I had a little."

Ryan opened her mouth and Mia held up a hand. "I can smoke once in a while. I just have to stay away from Ecstasy and acid and things like that."

"I was gonna ask if you wanted some orange juice. I don't care if you smoke a kilo of pot." She shook her head. "I *do* care, but I certainly wouldn't give you a hard time about it."

"Sorry," Mia said, looking up contritely. "But I know you don't like it and you don't want Jamie to do it."

"Jamie can do it if she wants to. But I don't have to like it."

"I'm the one who decided I didn't want to smoke pot anymore," Jamie said. "It's not fun unless I'm doing it with other people, and Ryan's never gonna do it."

"Got that right," she said, smiling. "I have enough addictions."

"You don't have addictions," Mia said.

Jamie looked at her. "She does. Trust me. They're just not the usual ones. She's addicted to thrills and risk and danger, and she's obsessive about finishing something she's started and—"

"Mia's heard enough," Ryan said, clamping a hand over Jamie's mouth.

"I've got all day." She put her elbows on the table and rested her chin in her hands.

"No you don't," Ryan said. "When's your flight?"

"Oh, fuck!" She dropped her head to the table. "I forgot I have to go back."

"Don't you wanna get home to Jordan?"

"No," she pouted. "I want Jordan to come here." She stuck her tongue out at Jamie. "She could, too, if Jamie would build a new Olympic Training Center."

Ryan looked from one woman to the other. "Huh?"

"Never mind, honey. Mia had an idea that seemed logical from her slightly unique perspective."

"Well, if you're gonna build one, let me know. I'd try out for a dozen sports if I could train near home."

"Super," Jamie said, rolling her eyes.

Mia was just finishing her oatmeal when someone knocked on the front door. "I'll get it," Jamie said. "If it's someone trying to convert us,

Ryan always invites them in and listens to their whole spiel."

"I admire people who spend their time trying to promote something that's important to them. Even though they're never very good at answering my questions." She looked thoughtful. "Why would you believe in a faith that you hadn't investigated thoroughly?"

"Are you talking to me?" Mia asked, blinking when she looked up.

Laughing, Ryan said, "You're the only one here."

"Oh. Sometimes it sounds like you're talking to yourself, kinda like you're wondering out loud."

"No, no, I'm talking to you."

"Huh. Then why do you talk about things I'm not interested in?"

Ryan bent over and kissed her on the head. "There's only so much to say about sex, hip hop, and drinking."

A voice from the doorway said, "Who's kissing my woman?"

"Jordan!" Mia jumped up so quickly that she almost knocked Ryan over.

Ryan was right behind her, grabbing the small portion of Jordan's body that Mia wasn't attached to. "What in the hell are you doing here?"

"Our coaches gave us three days off. Three whole days! I could have gone home and slept, but I miss you guys."

Mia was kissing every bit of her face, but she let Jordan use her mouth to talk. "I missed you," she said, coming up for air.

Jordan looked down at her, her face creasing into a love-filled smile. "I missed you, too." She dipped her head and they started to kiss. Ryan squeezed Jordan's shoulder and went into the living room with Jamie, giving the couple time to say hello.

It took quite a while for Mia to finish welcoming Jordan home. When they finally emerged from the kitchen, their lips were deep pink and Jordan's hair was almost as disordered as Mia's. "It's good to be home," Jordan said, grinning serenely. "I haven't felt this relaxed in months."

"Sit down," Ryan said, "unless Mia's dragging you to bed."

Jordan took a seat and Mia climbed onto her lap. "I think we'll stay up. If I'd wanted to just stay in bed, I would have gone back to Colorado. I need some buddy time."

"We're really happy to see you," Jamie said. "One of the best surprises we've had in ages."

"What have you been doing?" Jordan asked Mia. "Getting into

trouble?"

"Nope. I've been sucking up to all of the people who are taking notes for me. I took all of 'em except Hannan out to lunch or dinner, and I made good copies of some of the notes I couldn't read very well."

"Why didn't Hannan get a meal?"

"'Cause she's getting a salary. Only the volunteers get benefits."

"Tell us about Russia!" Jamie said. "Did you get to do anything fun?"

Jordan shrugged. "I guess it would have been more fun if we hadn't gotten beaten so bad. We did salvage a match with Russia, which was cool, but Japan beat us like a drum. It was awful." She made a face. "We couldn't do anything right. I haven't felt that outclassed in a very long time."

"Would it have been better if I'd been there?" Mia placed a soft kiss on Jordan's forehead.

After looking at her for a minute, Jordan frowned and shook her head. "No. It was better to be able to focus...and bitch."

"Did you hang out with your teammates?"

"Yeah. We talked volleyball every minute." She gave Mia a robust hug. "I'd always rather be with you, but you would have had an awful time. I was able to put all of my energies into my game, and that's the only smart thing for me to do."

"I know." She relaxed against Jordan and said, "We'll have plenty of time to play once you're finished competing."

"She might not be on another team," Ryan said, "but she'll always be competing."

Jordan met her eyes and nodded, smiling. "Don't scare Mia off. She thinks I'm gonna be a normal person when this is over."

Mia and Jamie grew tired of volleyball talk, so they went upstairs to cancel Mia's flight. Ryan stood up and said, "Let's sit in the backyard. It's a nice day."

Jordan got up and followed her outside. They sat on the bench, both of them sticking their long legs out in front of them. "How has Mia been?" Jordan asked.

"Fine. Well, she missed you, but she seemed like her old self." Ryan gazed at her friend for a minute, then said, "You don't. Is everything okay?"

Jordan twitched her head, sending her long hair flying over her shoulder.

"Sure. Sure. Everything's fine."

"Not buyin' it, but you don't have to talk if you don't wanna."

"I'm cool with talking, I just don't have much to say. I guess I could be kinda preoccupied about the team…but that's it."

"It sucks when you aren't jelling, doesn't it?"

"Yeah. Especially when I know that we'd be doing better if we got rid of all of the extra players."

"Because they take up too much playing time?"

"Not really. It's more of a psychological thing. We all know there's a team in the group, but we're not sure who's on it. It makes us kinda tentative…know what I mean? A lot of people are trying not to screw up, rather than trying to be as good as they can be."

"Mmm…yeah, that makes sense."

"I'd rather they made the cuts now and got it over with, but they're not gonna change the schedule."

"I wish you could get some peace of mind. It must really suck. I'm glad you have Mia around to talk things over with."

Jordan didn't reply. She was staring at the fence, looking preoccupied.

Ryan bumped her with her shoulder. "Hey. Don't you like having Mia with you?"

Jerking in surprise, Jordan said, "Oh, yeah, of course I do."

"But?" Ryan bumped her again. "Something's not right."

Looking over her shoulder, Jordan's eyes scanned the windows. "Can they hear us?"

"No. Not unless you yell."

Chuckling, Jordan said, "I'm not that frustrated."

"But you *are* frustrated. I can see it on your face."

"Okay, okay. I *am* frustrated, and it pisses me off."

"What pisses you off? Mia?"

"No, Mia doesn't piss me off…most of the time. We've had a couple of tough days, but circumstances are getting to us more than anything."

"Like the team roster?"

"No, that gets to me, not Mia. She knows I'll make it." She grinned and added, "She thinks I'm the best volleyball player in the world."

"You *are* good," Ryan said, smiling.

"And we both know there are about thirty women playing right now who are much better, Boomer."

"Thirty seems high, but I know what you mean."

"The things that bother me the most are big things…like Mia not being happy with where we live or with our roommates."

"She didn't mention either item. It must not be on her mind."

"She's been a trooper, Boom, really. Being in Colorado has been hard for her. The problem is that the last thing I need is to worry about her." She leaned over and rested her chin on her hand. "It didn't occur to me that having her with me would make my life harder." She closed her eyes and shivered. "I hate to say it, but I'd rather she moved back here."

"Wow." Ryan didn't say anything for a few moments. "It's that bad?"

Clearly frustrated, Jordan shook her head. "No, it's not bad. It's just… not good. She's not happy unless I'm home, and that's only a few hours a day. She doesn't have any friends or any interests, and we don't have enough money for her to go shopping." When she looked up and met Ryan's eyes, she laughed briefly.

Ryan lowered her voice just in case Jamie's hearing had grown substantially better in the last few minutes. "I wouldn't like being around Jamie if she couldn't go shopping."

"It's little things like that. Nothing huge. And I hate to be so self-involved, but I *have* to be right now."

"Of course you do. Doesn't Mia get that?"

"Yeah, she does. But it's one thing to understand and another thing to be the one who's self-involved. She's not as me-involved as I am." She smiled wryly.

"Can you tell her that you'd rather she moved back?"

Jordan's wry grin grew bigger. "Yeah, that'd go over great. I might not know much about being in a relationship, but I know not to tell a woman who had a major fight with her family over me to pack up and get out."

"I thought you could be a little more subtle. I'm not sure how, but…"

"Right. There's no way. We spent days arguing about whether she was gonna go to Russia with me. I just can't spend that much time and energy on stuff like that. I know that makes me sound like a jerk, but…"

Ryan put her arm around Jordan's shoulders and hugged her roughly. "No it doesn't. I understand, bud. I get just as focused as you do, and if I were trying to make the cut for something that meant as much to me as this does to you, I'd want to live in a cave. I couldn't even stand roommates, much less a girlfriend."

"Yeah." Jordan nodded thoughtfully. "That's it. This doesn't have hardly anything to do with Mia. It's my need to focus. The little things she wants would hardly register if I was back at school."

"But you're not. You're at a critical point in a quest you've had for fifteen years. You might have to gut it up and tell her that you'd rather she leave."

Jordan was already shaking her head. "I can't do that, Boom. Volleyball means an awful lot, but Mia's more important. I can't risk hurting her—and our relationship. I don't know if she'd ever get over the rejection."

After thinking for a few minutes, Ryan nodded. "I don't think Jamie would either, if we were in your position. That sucks."

"Yep. It sure does."

"Wanna go find 'em?"

"Yep. I miss her already."

They stayed up late; talking and catching up on all of the small details of their lives. Eventually, they wound up in Mia's room, with Jamie and Ryan sitting on the end of the bed, still chattering away. Ryan finally looked at her watch. "I've gotta get to bed or I'll be dragging tomorrow." She and Jamie got up and started to walk to their room. Ryan paused at the door and turned to look at their friends. "Now that the children are home, everything seems right with the world."

Even though Ryan had said she was tired, she looked wide awake as she flopped onto the bed on her back. "Can we keep them? I love having them here."

Jamie lay down next to her and started to play with her hair. Running her fingertips across Ryan's scalp made her partner's eyes close. "I wish we could. I miss them so much. It seems so…normal to have them sitting at the dinner table."

"Yeah," Ryan said, her voice soft and low. "That's when I miss them the most. Eating dinner together was such a nice way to connect and keep up with everyone's day."

"Did you have a nice time talking with Jordan this afternoon? I tried to give you two some time alone."

Ryan's eyes blinked open. "Did you really?"

"Yeah. I know you both talk more when you're alone."

Grinning, Ryan asked, "If we're alone, how do you know we're talking?"

"'Cause you often have a new perspective or information after you spend time with Jordan. I think she opens up with you."

"Yeah, I guess that's true."

"So…?"

Ryan turned and smiled placidly. "So…what?"

"What did Jordan have to say? How does she think things are going?"

"Not good." She shook her head. "The team isn't playing well and she's afraid she's not gonna get the chance to show her stuff if they don't sync up soon."

Jamie slapped at her shoulder playfully. "I mean her real life. Not the team."

Blinking ingenuously, Ryan asked, "What's a real life?"

"Fine. You don't have to tell me." Jamie rolled onto her side and slid off the bed. "Mia and I have secrets too."

Ryan grasped her arm and pulled her back onto the bed, then sprawled across her body. "That's good, babe. Mia needs you to confide in. She knows she can tell you things that won't get back to Jordan."

Biting Ryan's earlobe, Jamie said, "Don't be so superior. I wouldn't tell you anything Mia said that she didn't want me to talk about."

"I know. One more reason not to tell you anything juicy. I won't get a good return on my investment."

"I'll give you a return…" Jamie bit a little harder, making Ryan squirm under her. She started to daintily touch various parts of Ryan's ear with the tip of her tongue, not stopping until her lover was purring. "Are you too tired to make love?"

Ryan paused, then smiled when she heard a squeal coming from Mia's room. "I believe we're gonna be up anyway. Let's turn on some music though. I don't wanna have a four-some."

"I love 'em," Jamie agreed. "But not like that."

Mia woke from a deep sleep to find her partner gazing at her. Jordan was lying on her side, her head propped on her hand, her long golden hair swaying gently with the cool spring breeze from the nearby window.

Grinning happily, Mia said, "Now this is how to wake up. In our bed, with the sun shining and our buddies here or someplace close. It's nice to be home, isn't it?"

Jordan responded with a soft, moist kiss. She stayed right where she was and added another longer kiss. "I was just thinking about how good it feels to be here." She shifted and held her head up again. "I don't really have a home right now. Since I gave up my apartment I don't even have a permanent address. But being here reminds me that this feels like home—even though I've never officially lived here."

Mia gave her a beatific smile. "This is where we fell in love. What better home could we have?"

"Do you think Jamie would really like us to come back here when I… don't have to be in Colorado any more?"

Threading her fingers through Jordan's hair, Mia looked into her eyes, amazed at the feelings that always burned in her chest when she gazed into the cool, blue depths. "I know they want us to come back. I have no doubt."

"You look happy. Happier than you've been for the last couple of weeks."

"I am." Mia tightened her grip on Jordan's hair and tugged her forward. They kissed for a few moments; Jordan pressing her weight forward and resting against Mia. They were both silent for a while, their heads sharing a pillow, eyes focused on the other. "I'm happy here, Jordy. But I *need* to be with you. You make me happy no matter where I am."

"Is that true?" Jordan moved back just enough to be able to focus.

"That I love you?"

"No, baby. I know how much you love me." A smile borne of certainty settled on Jordan's lips and she lay back on the pillow. "I want to know if you're happy no matter where we are."

"Yeah, I am."

"Then why do you seem…energized in a way you haven't been?"

"Well, it was good to be with my peeps. I saw all of my friends and hung out with 'em. Now I'm filled up again and I can go back to Colorado and be with my sweetie."

"So…coming here helped you…right?"

"Yeah. I guess I'd have to say it did. It helped to see my parents, too. And my grandparents."

"So…it looks to me like being with me *isn't* enough for you. You need some time back here to make you truly happy."

Mia sat up and gave Jordan a vaguely perturbed look. "What's on your mind? I feel like I'm being questioned at police headquarters."

"No, no, nothing like that. I just want to understand."

"This is all there is to understand." Mia pushed Jordan onto her back. "I love you, Jordan Ericsson, and I want to be with you every minute of every day. But we can't always be together, and when we're not, other people help boost me up. Twenty of them helped make up for your not being here." She leaned over her partner and kissed her gently. "Barely."

"I think it's more than that."

Snuggling against Jordan's body, Mia put her hand on her belly and gave it a playful tickle. "And I bet you're gonna tell me what it is, aren't you."

"Yeah, I am. I don't want to drop this until we both understand each other. I think you need to be here once in a while. Not just that it's something to do when you can't be with me. And I think you should come here whenever I'm on an extended trip. I think it's good for you and good for your family. And...it's good for me because I know you're happy."

Still stroking her tummy, Mia moved her mouth just enough to be able to nibble and kiss around Jordan's ear, something that always gave her chills. "I want to make you happy. I'd do anything to make sure of that, Jordy. And I think you're trying to make my needs more important than yours. I know you were disappointed I didn't go to Russia with you—"

"I was at first," Jordan admitted. "But once we got there I realized that Toni and Jill were right. It's no fun to go on a trip like that unless you're playing. It'll be different at the Games because there'll be lots of things to do and lots of parties and stuff. But a regular tournament is boring as hell if you're not involved. I'm sure of that now, babe. Totally sure. And I barely had time to make sure I ate and slept. I wouldn't have been there for you—at all. And that's no way to travel together."

"No, I guess it's not."

"So, make plans now to come back here during my next trip. It'll be better for all of us."

"Jamie said the same thing. She wants me to make reservations so she doesn't have to send me a last-minute ticket."

"Even Jamie hates to throw money away." Jordan smiled at her partner, then kissed her, teasing her mouth open with her tongue.

Mia responded immediately, wrapping her arms around her lover and grinding against her. "I've missed you," she murmured. "I like you. A lot." With a wicked grin, she crawled down Jordan's body and captured a pink nipple in her mouth. Gently suckling, she relished the feel of the supple skin in her mouth. Lifting her head, she purred, "I've missed these. They're nice." Her hand slid under a breast and jiggled it. "They're getting bigger. You're starting to put a little weight back on."

"I've gained two pounds in a week. Two pounds of muscle, I'm glad to say."

Mia dipped her head and focused on Jordan's breasts again, sucking and licking them with rapt attention.

Her eyes were half-closed, and Jordan's lazy voice asked, "How did you manage to go without sex all this time?"

"I didn't go without. I just thought about you and imagined your hand was touching me." She climbed back up and licked all around Jordan's tender ear. "But my imagination doesn't come close to the real thing."

"Sex didn't enter my mind. Not once." She spent a moment kissing Mia, building up the intensity of her desire. "But it's making a comeback. Big time."

"That's my girl." Mia returned her kisses, managing to take Jordan's breath away in a matter of seconds. "I missed you," she whispered. "So much."

"Me too." They kissed for another minute, their hearts starting to beat more rapidly. "Maybe having little breaks is good for us. God knows I can hardly keep my hands off you."

"Your hands and every other part are supposed to be on me. Bring it on, baby. I'm ready for you."

When they finally emerged from their room, Jamie and Ryan were long gone. "I want to go to the volleyball offices and see if anyone's around," Jordan said. "Wanna go with me?"

"No thanks. After she's finished with class, Jamie and I are going to a day spa."

"Ooo…sounds like fun."

Mia's smile brightened. "Come with us!"

"No, I'd rather try to find some of my old teammates. I know where they hang out on campus. Then off to softball practice. Heather will be there and Ryan says Ashley's usually there too."

"That's cool. If we're finished we'll go to practice too."

"Sounds good. Are you ready?"

"No way. I've gotta have breakfast, then I'll make some calls. I can't be rushed in the morning."

Ostentatiously looking at the clock, Jordan said, "You're back in your Berkeley mode. It's twelve thirty, honey."

Mia grinned happily. "It's morning to me."

Jamie and Mia lay side-by-side on massage tables, both of them covered from head to toe in warm towels. Their faces were partially exposed, with each wearing warm packs on their eyes, adding to their relaxation.

"I love a clay body wrap as much as a girl can love dirt," Mia murmured.

"I like this pink clay a lot. It doesn't seem as dirty as regular clay."

"Such a prude."

"I'm not a prude, I'm clean. There's a big difference."

"I guess so. Our hour isn't up yet, is it?"

"We might be close. But we've still got other things in store for us."

"We do?" Mia's voice rose in pitch. "What?"

"We're gonna have a citrus body scrub after massages."

"Ooo…" Mia sounded like she was on the verge of orgasm, making Jamie giggle.

"You're easy to please, girlfriend. Just put you on a table and pamper you and you're as happy as can be."

"That's the key, James. Pampering is highly underrated."

"You didn't even seem to mind having your legs waxed."

"I don't mind it. I'm not crazy about the bikini line, but I'd never subject Jordy to stubble. That's inhumane."

"I believe stubble is mentioned in the Geneva Convention."

"Do you think Ryan will notice you've been plucked like a chicken?"

"I have no idea. But if she doesn't ask, I'm not gonna tell. She doesn't have to know *everything* about me. A girl's gotta have some secrets."

After softball, Jamie and Mia stopped at the market and bought dinner. Jamie didn't want to spend their last night together cooking, so she bought cold cuts and various kinds of cheese along with two kinds of bread. She and Mia had everything arranged on platters by the time Ryan and Jordan got home. "What took you guys so long?" Mia asked.

Jordan went to her and kissed her quickly. "We were talking to Heather and Ashley. Time got away from us."

"Go wash your dirty little mitts," Jamie instructed her partner. "Dinner's ready."

Ryan playfully dangled her filthy hands in front of Jamie's nose.

"Eww! They smell like dirty leather."

"There's no clean leather involved in softball. Be right back."

When she returned, Ryan had not only washed her face and hands, she'd changed into a polo shirt and jeans. Jamie didn't comment, but she gave her a knowing glance and a wink, silently thanking her for continuing to eschew sweats at the dinner table.

Mia and Jordan each took a platter to carry into the dining room. Jamie started to follow them, but caught a quick look at her partner. There was something wrong, but she had no idea what could have happened in the last few seconds to cause Ryan to look so sad.

Ryan went into the refrigerator to take a beer and when she passed, Jamie snagged her belt loop. "What's wrong, Tiger?"

Replying with an anemic smile, Ryan shook her head. "Nuthin'."

"You look sad."

Shrugging, Ryan looked away. "They're leaving tomorrow."

"Ooo." Jamie slipped her arm around Ryan and hugged her. "That makes you sad, huh?"

Another shrug. "A little."

"Hey." Reaching up, Jamie tugged on her chin, forcing eye contact. "A really smart woman once told me that she tried to live her life in the moment. She said she wanted to enjoy each day because she knew the next day wasn't guaranteed."

A smirk slowly formed on Ryan's face. "Sounds like psychobabble."

"No way." Hugging her even tighter, Jamie rocked her lover back and forth. "I believe everything this wise woman told me. I think you should try it. Enjoy dinner, baby. Let's have fun with our friends. Don't miss them before they leave."

Bending, Ryan placed a gentle kiss on Jamie's lips. "Good advice. I'll give it a try." She rubbed her nose against her partner's. "Thanks."

"Any time, slugger. Any time at all."

The next afternoon, Ryan was in her room going over her French homework when she heard the front door close quietly. "Jamie?"

"Guess again," Jordan called up.

"Cool! Come up here and save me from going nuts."

Long legs and a quick stride had Jordan standing by the desk in seconds. She ruffled Ryan's hair and sat on the bed. Kicking off her shoes she twisted around and lay on her stomach. "What's going on?"

Ryan turned in her chair. "I don't understand why I have to be able to read a foreign language to be able to study math or science in grad school.

Who's the idiot who came up with this stupid idea?"

"You shoulda taken a language when you were in high school, Boom. That's what the smart kids did."

"Funny. You went to a French school. You and Jodie Foster."

"She was there waaaay before me. Want help with your homework?"

"No, I just have to study. No shortcuts."

"French didn't seem hard when I was fourteen. It just…" She waved her hand. "Came to me. I barely noticed I was learning a language."

Ryan took a large rubber band from the desk and hit her friend squarely in the ass. "Good shot!" Jordan declared. "You must have been doing that when the other kids were taking language class."

"You're quite a smart-ass today. Feelin' good?"

"Yep, but I'd sure like to stay longer."

"I'd like to hold you both hostage. But somebody from the team would probably track you down."

"That wouldn't be too hard. I had to tell them where I was going, how long I was staying, what flight I'd be on going back, etcetera. They're worse than parents."

"But you don't mind going back, do you?"

Jordan smiled, and Ryan noted once again that her friend's smile changed her face more than anyone she knew. Jordan looked open and playful and younger than her age. The change from her often cool, aloof, overly-mature image still managed to catch Ryan by surprise despite their close friendship.

"I'm ready to get back to work. It doesn't take long to get out of a groove."

"Are you happy?" Ryan asked, gazing at her intently.

She nodded decisively. "I've got everything I've ever wanted. And I think Mia and I have figured out how to make things easier for her. She's agreed to come here whenever I have to go on a long trip. I think that'll work better for both of us."

"Both of you guys are welcome here. Any time. You don't even have to tell us you're coming. Just come in and make yourselves at home."

Jordan's smile lit up her entire face. "That means a lot to me, Boom. I couldn't do that with either of my parents, so…" She shrugged, looking embarrassed. "It means a lot."

Ryan rolled her desk chair across the floor. When she reached the bed she patted Jordan firmly on the back, then propped her bare feet up on the bed. "You're part of our family. That's permanent."

Nodding, Jordan said, "I know you don't say things like that unless you mean 'em."

Ryan met her eyes, but didn't comment. She knew she didn't have to with Jordan.

"How's your…head?" Jordan asked. "I mean your—"

"Emotional stability?" Ryan asked, crossing her eyes and sticking out her tongue.

"Yeah," Jordan said, laughing. "You seem back to your old self."

"I guess I am most of the time. Things are a lot better."

"Is everything okay with you and Jamie?"

It sounded like a tossed-off comment, but Ryan took it more seriously than that. Her tone turned a little sharp. "Yeah. Why? Did Mia say something?"

Jordan visibly recoiled. "No! Damn, why would Mia say anything? *Is* everything all right?"

"Yeah, yeah," Ryan muttered. "I just…we've been having a little trouble. Nothing too big, but I thought Jamie might have said something to Mia."

"If she did, Mia didn't say anything to me. What's going on?"

Ryan crossed her arms over her chest, debating with herself about what to say. "Uhm…let me ask you a question."

"Oh-oh. I hate these kinds of questions."

Nudging her not-so-gently with her foot, Ryan said, "You don't know what I'm gonna ask."

"No, but if I answer one way I'm on your side and if I answer the other way I'm on Jamie's."

"No sides," Ryan said. "Honest. I just wanted to know if you and Mia ever talk about your pasts."

Jordan half-closed one eye and tilted her head. "Our pasts?"

"Yeah. Things you did before you got together."

"Like sex? Relationships?"

"Yeah."

"No." Jordan didn't elaborate, giving Ryan a blank look.

"No? Just no?"

"Yep. Just no. I don't really have a past and if Mia wants to tell me something, she will. I never ask. Never have. Never will."

"'Cause you're…worried about what she might say?"

"Not really. I don't much care what Mia did before we were together. I mean, I'm interested in anything she shares with me, but I don't hunt for info. That's not my style."

Ryan's head dropped back and she threaded her fingers through her hair, freeing it of tangles. "I wish it wasn't Jamie's style."

"Mmm…Jamie's not like me. She's much more…what would you call it…?"

"That depends on the day," Ryan said, chuckling evilly. "Usually she just wants to understand me better and she does that by trying to learn about everything that shaped me. All of the experiences that made me who I am."

"You can't know people by knowing things about them," Jordan said rather flippantly. "You know what they show you. That's what matters to me. If you used to be a self-involved jerk who didn't care about her friends, that wouldn't make you any less of a friend to me. And knowing you used to be that way would only make me look for signs of jerkiness."

"Exactly!" Ryan said, slapping the bed with her open palm. "Jamie knows about some things I did that she thinks are wrong. She claims she doesn't judge me, but I know she does. It's in the back of her mind and she brings it up every time she gets a little insecure."

"You didn't kill a prior lover in her sleep, did you?"

"No, nothing that dramatic. But you heard I was a player before we'd ever met. Jamie knows too much, and I'm pissed with myself for telling her a lot of things. I should have just told her that her past was hers and mine was mine."

"I don't know how I knew to keep my nose out of Mia's past, but I knew. I can't imagine anything I'd learn that would make our lives better."

"Wish I would've asked you for some advice before I started flapping my trap."

Jordan rolled onto her side and looked at her friend for a few moments. "You're just an open person, Boom. Jamie wants to know stuff and you like to be honest." She giggled, her nose wrinkling up. "Bad combo."

Chapter Twenty

That evening, Ryan pulled the BMW into the driveway and cast an appraising glance at Jamie, who'd barely spoken on the trip back from the airport. The silence unbroken, they went into the house, where Ryan headed for the refrigerator, her stomach rumbling.

She munched on a piece of cold pizza as she walked into the living room. Jamie was going through the mail, throwing items into the categories that she used to organize the hefty volume. Ryan picked up a catalogue from a lingerie store. "Mmm...nice. What pile is this?"

"That's the 'things Ryan might want to look at' pile."

"Really? You're the lingerie queen. Why isn't it in your pile?"

"There's the bills to pay pile, the things one of us ordered or will definitely want to see pile and the 'perhaps' pile for each of us. The things I think you might want to see go into your perhaps pile."

"Again," Ryan said, rolling up the catalogue and looking through it like a telescope, "why isn't it in *your* perhaps pile?"

Jamie gave her a puzzled look. "That lingerie is trashy. I don't wear things that make me look cheap."

With a half-grin, Ryan said, "But you think I like to look at women in trashy lingerie?" Jamie didn't answer. She just raised an eyebrow and nodded when Ryan put the catalogue in her own "definite" pile. "You don't have to look so smug."

"I'm not being smug. I just know you."

"Wanna bite?" Ryan asked, putting the pitifully small bit of pizza that remained in front of her.

"No, thanks." She glanced at the assorted stacks of mail. "I'm done; I guess I'll go upstairs and read."

Her voice held so little enthusiasm that Ryan put her hand on her shoulder and turned her around. "What's wrong, sweetums?"

Laughing soundlessly, Jamie said, "Sweetums is a little down. My team's playing in the PAC-10 championships, and I really was looking forward to that. I think we could have done pretty well."

Ryan lifted Jamie's arm and kissed her hand, which had finally begun to look normal. "Of course you could have. If you were playing, you probably would have won the whole thing."

"I'm not saying that, but I wanted to play."

"Anything else?"

"Yeah. I miss Mia…and Jordan."

"Me too. But I think Mia might be coming home more often." When Jamie gave her a quizzical look, she added, "Jordan said you convinced Mia that it's better for their relationship if she's happy, and that coming home when Jordan travels makes her happy."

Jamie smiled up at her. "That makes me feel a little better."

"And even though you want to play, you'd be all alone up in Eugene." She took Jamie by the hand and led her to the sofa. Ryan sat down and pulled Jamie onto her lap, where she settled in comfortably. "It's no fun to be all alone, is it?"

"No. It's not," she said wistfully.

"Isn't it more fun to be together?"

"Yes. You know it is." She rested her head on Ryan's shoulder. Patting Ryan's belly, she said, "Okay, you've cheered me up. I can get to work now."

Ryan locked her arms around Jamie's waist. "Do you have to?"

"Uhm…" Tentatively smiling, Jamie asked, "Why?"

"I was just thinking of some things we could do, things we couldn't do if you were in Eugene."

"Ooo…were you now?" Relaxing against her, Jamie asked, "What kinda things were you thinking of?"

Ryan looked down, letting her gaze run up and down Jamie's body. "I don't know." She trailed her hand over Jamie's torso, letting it settle on her breast. "I like some of these curvy parts." Cupping Jamie's flesh, she weighed it in her hand. "I'm sure I could think of something fun to do with this."

"You do have a good track record."

"If you really wanted to," Ryan murmured, "you could find some parts on me that you like to play with. No obligation, of course."

"Know what I'd like?"

"No." Ryan nuzzled against Jamie's neck until she could feel the goosebumps start, then she pressed her lips against her ear and hummed, "Tell me."

"I'll do better than that, I'll show you." Draping her good arm around Ryan's neck, she pulled her close and kissed her gently. Pulling away just an inch or two, she stared at the full, pink lips and whispered, "I just want to kiss you. There's nothing better than kissing you."

"Mmm…great idea." Ryan lifted her knees enough to cause Jamie to press against her more firmly, then she kissed her—slowly and gently and lovingly.

Minutes passed with only the soft sounds of their breathing and the sweet press of lips merging and separating breaking the silence of the house. "So nice," Jamie breathed. "No rush. No goals."

"None," Ryan said, sighing. She dropped a gentle kiss on Jamie's forehead. "Check that. One goal. To show you how much I love you."

"Mission accomplished."

Jamie pulled back and smiled at her, and Ryan took her in, noting the gentle tilt of her head, eyelids slightly closed, lips pink and moist. "You're such a beautiful woman." She ran her hand over Jamie's face, then traced her lips with her thumb. "You're too pretty for words."

"I never feel prettier than I do when you look at me just like you are now. It…makes my heart race."

Ryan's hand moved to her lover's chest, covering her heart. "Mmm…it is a little fast. Let's slow it down." She tightened her hold and snuggled Jamie into her body, rubbing their faces together until Jamie began to giggle.

"That tickles."

Purring almost imperceptibly, Ryan shifted and started to kiss her again, keeping up a slow, aimless exploration of her mouth. They traded back and forth and back and forth…one leading, the other following… for a very long time.

Jamie was astonished that Ryan didn't try to press for more. It was so nice to have her partner really listen to her needs and back off from what had clearly been an invitation to have sex. But after kissing those sexy lips, she was ready to move along. Knowing that a little signal went a long way, she took Ryan's hand and placed it on her breast, pressing the strong hand into her flesh.

Amazingly, Ryan didn't take the bait. She kept kissing at the same leisurely pace, seemingly perfectly content to go no further.

Not to be dissuaded, Jamie covered Ryan's hand and firmly pressed it into her flesh, urging her to take the hint. She could feel Ryan start to smile, and knew her lover had been playing with her.

"Have an itch?" Ryan asked.

"Yes," she whispered, keeping her lips so close to Ryan's that she spoke into her mouth. "Help me scratch it, will you?"

Ryan cupped her breast and gave it a gentle squeeze, making Jamie press her thighs together in response. She made a gurgling sound and pressed against Ryan's hand, asking for more.

Holding the breast in her hand, Ryan moved it around in a circle, all the while probing Jamie's mouth with her tongue.

"Harder," Jamie murmured.

"Still itchy?"

Pale blue eyes blinked slowly and Jamie wrapped an arm around her neck. "Don't play with me, O'Flaherty."

"Play? I'm not playing. You said you wanted to kiss. If you want something else…"

Tilting her head, Jamie looked into her eyes. "You want specifics?"

"I suppose so. I'm not catching on."

Ryan was the picture of innocence, and Jamie imagined how remarkably easy it must have been for her to get away with murder when she was young. "Okay. Here's what I'd like. I want you to take off your shirt—that's a nice one, by the way—then your bra, then your shoes, then your socks, then your slacks. You look good in those khakis, too." She reached down and traced along Ryan's thigh. "And your underwear."

"You want me to do all that?" Ryan's eyebrows lifted.

"Uh-huh. Then I want you to take every stitch of clothing off me. Let me know when you're finished and I'll give you the rest of your instructions."

Grinning lasciviously, Ryan followed her instructions to the letter. A few minutes later, they were standing, facing each other, stark naked. Jamie took her hand and led her into the library, then pushed her until Ryan sat on the leather sofa. "Now I'm going to have you. Any complaints?"

"None." Ryan smiled up at her, and held out her arms. "Anything you want is exactly what I want."

"This splint is a little problem, so I might have to direct you a bit. Is that cool?"

"The coolest. Top me."

"I'd be happy to, if you hadn't engineered this entire evening," Jamie said, tweaking Ryan's nose. "I thought the top was supposed to be in charge."

"Nah. The bottom's always in charge, the top just thinks she is."

After surveying her very receptive lover and the sofa, Jamie sat down. "Will you lie on top of me with those stupendous breasts very near my mouth?"

In a flash, Ryan scooted down to the end of the sofa, giving Jamie plenty of room to lie down. As soon as she was settled, Ryan rested her weight on her arms and offered her breasts to Jamie, who immediately filled her mouth with the luxuriantly soft skin. Her appetite for Ryan was voracious, and she suckled and nipped and mouthed her breasts for so long that Ryan's nipples were swollen and nearly mauve when she paused for breath. "Good God," Jamie breathed. "I can't get enough of you."

Ryan's face was flushed, her skin dewy and pink. "Could you," she panted, "please lift your leg? I've gotta…" Her eyes closed when Jamie immediately responded, and Ryan pressed hard against her thigh. With her breast being firmly suckled, Ryan started to pump her hips, moving up and down Jamie's thigh—her moisture coating the skin lavishly. Her eyes were tightly closed, and Jamie could see her lips moving—but not a sound came out.

The harder Jamie sucked, the faster and harder Ryan pumped. Light-headed with lust, Jamie grasped her ass with her hand and pulled Ryan's entire breast into her mouth, then started to bring her teeth together. With a whoosh of air, Ryan grabbed her lover's shoulders and thrust hard, moaning loudly. She eventually began to slow her pace and her power until she was barely moving her hips, just a slight tilting of her vulva pressing against Jamie's; her body wet, hot, slippery and very heavy.

Jamie ran her hand through Ryan's hair, whispering to her while she recovered. It took longer than usual, but Ryan finally lifted her head. "You almost killed me," she said, her speech slightly slurred.

"If you weren't so heavy, I'd have my hand between my thighs right now," Jamie purred. "I'll come if you so much as brush against me."

Ryan pushed herself up, then maneuvered so that she was sitting on the floor. Tugging at Jamie's legs, she slung them over her shoulders and opened her with her fingers. Mesmerized by the glistening flesh, she delicately began to taste, stunned when Jamie grabbed the back of her head and panted out a quiet, quick orgasm. Not moving her head, Ryan stroked her thighs, waiting until her flesh stopped pulsing to tentatively start to nuzzle against her again.

"Wait," Jamie moaned. "Give me a minute..."

But Ryan didn't obey this time. She slipped her index fingers inside and played with her, stretching and probing until Jamie's body grew relaxed and limp. "Go on," she finally purred. "This is good."

Ryan dipped her head again and started to lap lazily, once again surprised when Jamie groaned, "Oh! I'm coming...ahh...yeah...yeah," while pushing her vulva against Ryan's mouth.

Waiting patiently, Ryan finally looked up and said, "How about a little more?"

"Give me a few minutes. Come up here and hold me." She scooted over onto her side, giving Ryan room to cuddle.

"I meant me," Ryan said, grinning shyly.

Jamie's eyes opened wide. "Really? Do you think you can?"

Lips pursed, she said, "I'm still really turned on. And I've been reading about orgasms. I haven't found any research that says there's a physiological reason for my not being able to have more than one orgasm in a day."

"You've had two a couple of times."

"Not often, and you know I hate to miss an opportunity to be a glutton." She chuckled. "And I *am* really turned on."

Jamie turned and kissed her. "Where do you want me?"

"Would you mind if I kinda...got on top of you? I'm dying to feel your mouth on me."

"Let's go, Tiger. I'd love to be able to play with you all night long."

Ryan made a few adjustments, getting Jamie at just the right angle. Then she slowly lowered herself to her lover's mouth, moaning in relief when the warm, wet tongue touched her throbbing skin. "Oh, Jesus, that feels fantastic."

Jamie looked up to see her lover pinching and pulling on her own nipples, her eyes closed and her mouth open just enough to show the tip of her tongue. Without thought, she reached around Ryan and started to play with her own clit, gently touching herself just enough to keep her high going.

Moving her hips in a stunningly sexy fashion, Ryan sought more and more pressure from Jamie, finally pressing so hard she whimpered in pain. "Fuck," she growled, lifting her hips and sliding off. Standing on rubbery legs she said, "This isn't gonna work, but I'm desperate to come." Her look of frustration turned to delight when she saw where Jamie's hand was. "May I?"

Jamie pulled her hand away. "Not right now. I'm just keeping it warm. What can we do for you?"

Ryan thought for a moment, then said, "Do you mind a little help?"

"Not as long as it's not another woman."

"Ha! Who'd want that?" She started for the door. "Don't go away."

"Where would I go?" Jamie asked, looking down at her wet, slippery body.

In a few minutes Ryan was back, carrying the small bag of sex toys she'd brought from home. "I was wondering if we'd ever use any of that stuff," Jamie said, sitting up to look over Ryan's shoulder.

"I haven't had the need," Ryan mumbled. "Ahh…this should work." She pulled out a good-sized vibrator and handed it to Jamie. "Do you want to…or should I?"

"You do it," Jamie said, eyes sparkling. "I'll just watch."

Ryan's eyebrows waggled and she scampered to plug in the device. Sitting down, she said, "This is a little…clinical. I mean, it doesn't have the same feel that our lovemaking—"

"I get it. I just wanna watch you come again. No biggie. I don't think the things in your bag are a substitute for making love. They're…like sprinkles on a sundae."

"Good one!" Ryan put her arm around her. "My arousal has taken a nose-dive. Having to get up and rummage around in a closet isn't really erotic."

"May I?"

"Please."

Jamie put her arm around Ryan and kissed her softly. Moving away, she stuck out her lower lip in a slight pout. "Making love to you was so incredibly hot that I'm still throbbing. Feel me," she whispered, taking Ryan's hand and pressing it between her lips. "You made me that wet." She kissed Ryan hard, then pulled back and licked all around her lips. "You had me so hot, so fast…" She grasped the back of Ryan's head and held her still while she kissed her so thoroughly that she wound up with her knee between Ryan's legs. When she released her grip, Ryan's head fell back onto the sofa.

Lifting her head, she gave Jamie a totally blank look, then turned on the vibrator and started running the blunt, bullet-like end of it against herself. Her eyes closed and her head fell back again as she kept the device on the outside of her vulva.

This surprised Jamie, but the pleasured half-smile on Ryan's face showed that it was working. Jamie leaned over and started to kiss her again, getting hotter as their kisses got harder and needier. She moaned and Ryan opened her mouth and sucked her tongue in, pulling on it hungrily. Jamie put her hand down to feel the vibrations, amazed at how strong they were. Then she felt Ryan's hand move and she shifted so she could watch her.

Ryan held the vibrator in one hand and pressed it hard against herself, using her other hand to apply even more pressure. Jamie was amazed at how rough she was being, given that Ryan begged for nothing but a gentle touch when she was on the verge of orgasm. Even though she wasn't touching her clitoris, the vibrator was thrumming against her relentlessly, and Jamie couldn't even imagine what her lover was feeling. Giving in to her curiosity, she slipped her fingers into Ryan, watching as her eyes closed and she grimaced for a few seconds before she grunted loudly and began to shake, her flesh gripping and releasing around Jamie's fingers. A long, lingering climax rolled through her body, and when Ryan dropped the still humming vibrator to the floor, she looked completely exhausted.

Jamie pulled the vibrator up by its cord and turned it off, then slid her arm around Ryan and cradled her to her body, peppering her face with kisses.

Ryan eventually opened her eyes. "I'm gonna regret that tomorrow," she said, grinning crookedly.

"Really?" Jamie kissed her temple. "Why don't you use it on me so I can empathize?"

Ryan's eyes shifted and she shook her head, chuckling, "Gotta see for yourself, huh?"

"Yeah." Her eyes were sparkling with interest. "You almost sprained my fingers when you came. I want some of that."

"Oh, all right," Ryan said, feigning exasperation. "But I'm not gonna use the big gun on you. You won't need it."

"Why?" Jamie hefted it in her hand. "I want the big one."

"Let's start with something more…delicate. Then we can move up if you want."

Ryan took out a small, lipstick sized blue vibrator and put a pair of watch batteries into it. "I feel a little like a gynecologist," she said, grinning. "This is even more clinical."

"Just *do* me," Jamie growled, giving her a scowl which turned into a giggle.

Ryan kissed her quickly and knelt down. "Ready?"

"No foreplay?"

Ryan's voice dropped. "You won't need it. Trust me."

She turned on the vibrator and spread Jamie's lips apart. Very delicately, she slid the little blue toy along Jamie's inner lips, smiling when her partner gasped, "Wow!"

"Uh-huh." Ryan lifted it then slid it around again, barely touching her skin.

Jamie purred with delight, making some of the sexiest moans Ryan had ever heard. Then she put her hand on top of Ryan's and pressed the vibrator against her clit, growling and thrusting her hips as she came once again.

Ryan started to pull it away, but Jamie opened her eyes and said, "More."

"Such a greedy girl." Ryan kissed her and started touching her again, letting the little toy bring her partner to one orgasm after another. After six climaxes in just a few minutes, Jamie pushed Ryan's hand away and collapsed, hardly able to breathe.

Ryan held her and pressed her ear to her heart, listening to it go from a galloping rhythm to a much more normal beat.

"Throw those things away," Jamie weakly ordered.

"You don't like my toys? Those rapid-fire orgasms belie your protests."

"You're cute when you talk like that. You sound like an eighty-year-old English teacher." She kissed Ryan gently. "And yes, I like your toys. I like them too much. You don't have to throw 'em out, but don't make them too available. They're like crack cocaine."

"Okay, baby. We'll stick to nature."

Jamie opened an eye. "Maybe once in a while…"

Ryan kissed her gently. "Can I take you to bed?"

"I'm begging you," she said dramatically, "truly *begging* you to."

Ryan got up the next morning and got into the shower, waiting for Jamie to join her. She grinned at her partner when she entered the steaming shower. "How do you feel?"

"Great! You?"

"Itchy. And not good itchy."

"Really?" Jamie frowned and patted Ryan gently between her legs. "Here?"

"Yep. I'll itch all day."

"Why? Do you know?"

"Not really. All I know is that when I force myself to have a second orgasm I always feel kinda swollen and irritated the next day."

Jamie let the water wash over her face, then sputtered some of it at Ryan. "Then why do it?"

Ryan kissed her. "'Cause you make me hot, goofy. I get turned on and want more sex. But my body doesn't think it's a good idea."

"That's a damned shame. 'Cause I could get the vibrator out and peel off another dozen." She giggled, showing Ryan her teeth.

"Yes, I'm jealous. You know, some of the studies I read say that multiple orgasms can give you a kind of high. Did you feel that?"

"Hmm…kinda. If we'd kept going I could have gotten into a zone I think."

Ryan started to wash Jamie's hair, since Jamie still couldn't bend her left arm. "Every time you come, you release endorphins. If you don't rest between them, they build up and don't dissipate. So you can literally fuck yourself into a stupor." She laughed and blew a raspberry against Jamie's bare back. "Who would have thought a stupor could sound good, huh?"

"I'm trying to think of what I'm not gonna get done today," Jamie teased. "My stupor calls."

Ryan sat in Ellen's office on Thursday morning, tapping her feet and moving her shoulders a little to a beat only she could hear. "You know, Ryan," Ellen said, "I would hardly believe you were the same person who first showed up for group therapy. Are you feeling as good as you look?"

For a few moments Ryan was perfectly still, then she nodded slowly. "I…guess I am." She smiled and shifted her gaze from Barb to Ellen. "I'm not sure when I started feeling better, but I really do feel good."

"You seem much more comfortable talking about the things that upset you," Barb said. "You don't look like you're being tortured any more."

"It doesn't feel like torture. You know, the first few times, I felt like I had lead in my pockets when I left here, but now I feel energized most days. Talking in here lets me live my life without stuffing all of my fears down." She met both of their gazes. "Being here has really helped me, and having it be just the three of us has made me feel safer."

"That's very good to hear," Ellen said. "How's your travel schedule? I know you were having trouble when you had to be away from home."

"It was more when Jamie had to leave, but I didn't like to go, either. I've got to go to Seattle this afternoon, and then to Los Angeles on Friday, and I'm actually looking forward to it. Of course, Jamie's going with me, thanks to her broken elbow. I never would have thought that her being injured could be such a good thing, but it really has made my life better." She grinned impishly. "I'm not going to tell her this in so many words, but her break has helped me heal."

Jamie woke up on Friday morning, reached out, and patted an empty space next to her on the bed. "Where's my teddy bear?"

Ryan got up from the chair and walked over to the bed. Sitting down, she wrapped Jamie in a warm hug. "Right here. I was going over some conjugations. Now that my project is mostly finished, I've gotta start breathing French."

"I'll speak French at home if that would help. Speaking of home, why aren't we in our bed?"

"'Cause we're in Seattle. And it might help if you speak French at home. But you have to talk as if you're talking to a small, dull-witted child."

"That's how I think of you." Jamie smiled sweetly and winced when Ryan pinched her.

"I've got to go to breakfast soon. Want me to bring you something?"

"Nah. I saw some decent looking places when we came in last night. I'm gonna poke around Seattle and then come to your game."

"Baby, you don't have to come. You've seen enough softball for three lifetimes. Why not go shopping or do something fun?"

"Hmm…I've never been to Pike's Place Market. I'd like to see them throw fish."

"Then do that. Go there and hang out and check out Puget Sound. It's really beautiful."

"I'll see. If I miss you, I'll come to the game; if not, I'll wander around."

"Cool. Just be at the softball field at the end of the game to catch the bus."

"If I wander, I'll just take a cab to the airport. I don't wanna have to rush."

"Okay. The flight's at four fifteen. Alaska Airlines."

"I won't miss it. And don't worry about me, okay? I have years of experience getting to airports on time."

Ryan kissed her, lingering for a few moments. "Have fun. That's your job today."

"Yes, ma'am. And your job is to have fun and play well."

"If I play."

"I always assume your coach will figure out a way to use extra players. He's smart."

Fifteen minutes before their flight was scheduled to depart, Ryan was standing at the gate, scanning the crowd. She let out an audible sigh of relief when Jamie came rounding a corner, her cheeks flushed and a charming grin on her face.

"Told you I'd make it," she panted.

"Barely! What took you so long?"

"I've been shopping. You know I lose track of time." Jamie held up the shopping bags that filled her hands. "I bought you stuff!"

"Oh, boy!" Ryan said, her lack of enthusiasm apparent. "New clothes?"

"Yep. If you're dressing up to please me, I might as well choose your stuff."

Ryan took her hand to board the plane. "There's a certain logic to your actions. It eludes me, but I know it's there."

They arrived at their hotel at seven thirty. Jamie got their room key while the rest of the team was standing in the lobby waiting for the student manager to get everything sorted out. They slid away from the group and got on the elevator before anyone saw them.

"I hate to admit how nice it is to be able to just check in and get out of that crowd," Ryan said. "I don't even mind having to pay for a separate room…which is remarkable in itself."

Jamie put an arm around her and hugged her. "You're so cute."

Giving her the hesitant smile she always showed when she wanted Jamie to elaborate on a compliment, Ryan said, "Cute? Why?"

"I was just looking at you downstairs. Everybody else had on warm-ups or sweats or jeans and T-shirts. You, however," she snuck her fingers into the placket of Ryan's neatly ironed pink and white checked shirt, "look like you thought about what you put on today. You look put together."

"I want to look like I belong with you." She auspiciously eyed her partner. "You look fantastic. Heck, you've even managed to wear clothes that don't show you've got a broken arm! I don't know how you do that."

They reached their floor and made the short walk to their room. "Ooo… right by the ice maker," Ryan said, chuckling. "They must have saved a special room just for us."

"Wanna move? Just say the word."

"No, I don't care about that. I don't hear anything when I sleep with you. It's just when I'm alone that I hear every cockroach."

"Eww! Did you have to say that? Now I'm gonna be itching."

Ryan dropped her bag and wrapped Jamie in an enthusiastic, unexpected hug. "I'll scratch you. Anyplace you want."

Jamie stood on her tiptoes and kissed her. "I'll consider your offer. Hungry?"

"Yep. And if we hurry, we can make our reservation."

Smiling with delight, Jamie looked up at her. "Reservation? What kinda reservation?"

"A restaurant reservation. What else?"

Jamie gaped at her lover. "You know how to make restaurant reservations?"

"Ha. Ha. Wash your hands, put on your lip gloss, and get your bag. We're going out."

"Is it my birthday?" Jamie asked, tapping her chin with her finger.

"No, but it's gonna be the day we go to bed without dinner if you don't shake a leg."

Ryan knew the absolute best way to make dinner reservations: she'd called Catherine and asked her where Jamie might like to go. Always happy to lend a hand, Catherine had called a friend in LA to ask what was new and notable. She'd made the reservations, dropping her friend's name to make sure a good table would await the girls.

Jamie was amazed when their cab dropped them in West Hollywood at a lovely, obviously wildly popular restaurant. She'd never heard of it, but it seemed that everyone in Los Angeles had—and they'd all decided to eat there that very night.

With the nearly regal bearing that Ryan could summon when she needed to, she led the way through the crowd milling about on the sidewalk. Jamie smiled up at her as Ryan confidently approached the host. "O'Flaherty. Party of two. Eight o'clock."

He gave her a quick glance to see if she was anyone, then looked at his book. There were two red stars by her name, indicating she should be seated quickly and well. He was a bit surprised, because she didn't dress like a well-connected Angelino, but the reservations staff only gave a guest two stars if they were. "It may take a moment, but I'll have your table ready as soon as possible," he said, giving her a generous smile. "May I get you a drink while you wait?"

"Not for me. Jamie?"

Stunned at the treatment her lover was receiving, Jamie managed to shake her head. "I'll wait until we're seated."

"Very good," the man said, his nod confirming that she'd just made the perfect decision.

Their table was ready in just a few minutes, and, rather than handing them off to one of his lovely young assistants, the host escorted them himself.

He pulled a chair out for Jamie, then did the same for Ryan. "Your server will be with you in a moment. Please enjoy yourselves, and let me know if there's anything I can do for you."

"I will," Ryan said, acting like she was catered to at every meal she ate.

Before Jamie had time to ask what magic she'd used to make the host grovel, a young woman arrived, bearing two glasses of champagne on a tray. "Hi, I'm Geneva, your server. I've brought you a little starter. Do you like champagne?"

"We do," Ryan said, and Jamie nodded her assent.

"Great." She set down the glasses and handed them menus. "I'll let you study the menu for a minute, then I'll come back and confuse you by describing all of the specials we have." She leaned over and said conspiratorially, "If you like beef, don't bother looking at the menu. I have a special you'll kill for."

Ryan closed the menu and smiled up at the woman. "I trust you," she said, showing her even teeth.

"I'll be back."

Jamie picked up her glass and held it aloft. Ryan mimicked her as the rims of their glasses touched. "Here's to you, Ms. O'Flaherty. I don't know what you did to have these people treat you like a super-model, but I'm lovin' it."

Sharing bites of her peeky-toe crab appetizer with Ryan, Jamie said, "Remember the last time we were in LA?"

"Wish I didn't, but, yes, I do. Why? Do you want another broken chair to add to your collection?" Ryan smiled wryly, and Jamie could tell she didn't mind talking about the trip—the one that ended with Ryan having a meltdown in their hotel room.

"No, I think one is enough. But I was just thinking…" She put her fork to Ryan's lips, watching her pull the bite in with the tip of her tongue. "It's only been about a month, but you seem so much better. It amazes me."

"Thanks. I feel better. I was just telling Ellen that yesterday."

Jamie sipped the delicate white Bordeaux that the sommelier had recommended. "Fabulous wine. Sip?"

"Sure." Ryan let Jamie bring the glass to her lips, angling her head to avoid spilling. "That is good. But I don't wanna trade."

"That's a good cabernet. I thought you'd like it." She took another bite of her appetizer and chewed thoughtfully. "Why do you think you've made so much progress so quickly?"

"Quickly? It's almost May! You call this quick?"

"Yes I do, given that just a month ago you were so down."

Ryan sipped at her wine, letting the cherry-tinged liquid slide down her throat and warm her from within. "I'm not sure why I feel better, but I sure do. It's kinda like I finally stopped fighting and cut myself a break." She looked at Jamie, clearly puzzled. "I have no idea why that helped, but it did."

"It's hard to feel better when you're angry with yourself. If you're not on your side, who is?"

"Yeah, I guess that's true. I stopped being so harsh with myself. It was all kind of unconscious, though. I didn't do much work." She held up her hands, looking rather amazed.

"Sometimes that's the best thing to do. Stop trying so hard."

"That makes no sense," Ryan said, smiling. "Hard work is always the answer."

"That's where you're wrong, sweet cheeks. Sometimes the best thing is to slow down and let yourself heal. Just stay out of the way." She held up her arm. "I wouldn't be healing well if I took off my splint and made myself use my arm as usual."

"No, I don't think that experiment would last very long. Maybe…two minutes."

"Right. It'd never work. I think some emotional wounds are like that. You can't rush them. They heal at their own pace, and being angry at yourself for not healing fast enough doesn't do a thing for you. It just makes you depressed."

"Been there. Didn't like it."

"I didn't like it either. But sometimes you have to go through those periods. There's not a heck of a lot you can do to get through them, either. You just have to ride them out."

Ryan made a face that had Jamie laughing. "But I don't like to wait," she said, sounding like a child. "I have no patience."

"Yes, you do. And I think it's being patient that has helped you feel better."

"Maybe," Ryan said, taking another sip of her wine. "Let's make a deal that we won't have any more big traumatic events, then we won't have to test your hypothesis."

"It's a deal, buddy." Jamie raised her glass and Ryan touched the rim with her own.

"To boring, routine lives."

"Life with you will never be boring, stretch. But no matter what happens to us, we can get through it together. That's the important part."

"To togetherness," Ryan said, smiling broadly. "The important part."

The End

By Susan X Meagher

Novels

Arbor Vitae
All That Matters
Cherry Grove
Girl Meets Girl
The Lies That Bind
The Legacy
Doublecrossed
Smooth Sailing
How To Wrangle a Woman
Almost Heaven
The Crush
The Reunion

Serial Novel

I Found My Heart In San Francisco

Awakenings
Beginnings
Coalescence
Disclosures
Entwined
Fidelity
Getaway
Honesty
Intentions
Journeys
Karma
Lifeline
Monogamy
Nurture
Osmosis

Anthologies

Undercover Tales
Outsiders

To purchase these books and eBooks visit
www.briskpress.com

To find out more, visit Susan's website at
www.susanxmeagher.com

You'll find information about all of her books, events she'll be attending and links to groups she participates in.

All of Susan's books are available in paperback and various e-book formats at www.briskpress.com

Follow Susan on Facebook.
www.facebook.com/susamxmeagher